OTHER WORKS
BY SUZY MCKEE CHARNAS

NOVELS

The Vampire Tapestry (1980)
Dorothea Dreams (1986)
The Kingdom of Kevin Malone (1993)

PLAYS

Vampire Dreams (2001)

NONFICTION

My Father's Ghost: The Return of My Old Man and Other Second Chances (2002)
Strange Seas (2001)

HOLDFAST CHRONICLES

Walk to the End of the World (1974)
Motherlines (1978)
The Furies (1994)
The Conqueror's Child (1999)

THE SORCERY HALL TRILOGY

The Bronze King (1985)
The Silver Glove (1988)
The Golden Thread (1989)

AS REBECCA BRAND

The Ruby Tear (1997)

STAGESTRUCK VAMPIRES
& Other Phantasms

STAGESTRUCK VAMPIRES
& Other Phantasms

Suzy McKee Charnas

TACHYON

Tachyon Publications
San Francisco, California

STAGESTRUCK VAMPIRES
& OTHER PHANTASMS

Book design by Ann Monn

Tachyon Publications
1459 18th Street #139
San Francisco, CA 94107
(415) 285-5615

www.tachyonpublications.com

Edited by Jacob Weisman

ISBN: 1-892391-21-X

Printed in the United States of America
by Phoenix Color Corporation

First Edition: 2004

0 9 8 7 6 5 4 3 2 1

TABLE OF CONTENTS

DEDICATION

To all the great practitioners (both antique and modern) of the more subtle, dark, and thoughtful side of literary fantasy, whose skill at providing such delicious and mind-blowing thrills led me to try my own hand at it. The shoulders of such giants afford magnificent views to those who make the climb, whetting the appetite of ambition.

ACKNOWLEDGEMENTS

I am grateful to all those story-mavens (either editors or writers acting as editors) who have bought these tales from me: George R. R. Martin, Robert McCammon, Ellen Datlow, Marta Randall, Melinda Snodgrass, Charlie Grant, Pam Keesey, Cecilia Tan, Martin Greenberg, Kris Rusch, Gardner Dozois, several foreign editors, and anybody I've lost track of over time or space. Because of help, recognition, and encouragement from of each of you, I was forced to stop thinking of myself as a novelist who didn't—who just couldn't—write the shorter forms of fiction. Thank you all.

THE CHARNAS TAPESTRY
OR
LISTENING TO SUZY

By Paul Di Filippo

As of this writing, I have not had the pleasure of meeting Suzy McKee Charnas face to face. She lives in the sunny desert paradise of Albuquerque (or, as Homer Simpson once charmingly and perhaps fittingly referred to it, "I'll be quirky"), while I inhabit the benighted non-Euclidean warrens of Providence. I suspect that one day sooner or later we *will* meet, given the melting-pot allure of the science-fiction and fantasy convention circuit, and I fully expect that encounter to be a pleasant one, with its share of mutual surprises and confirmations. But right now, despite a lack of non-virtual time together, I still feel I can describe Ms. Charnas to you well enough that you'll be able to recognize her, should you chance to bump into her.

Suzy McKee Charnas is a human-sized sentient female lizard named Walter Drake who boasts a human lover.

She is a lonely tarot-card expert named Edie, charged with shepherding a child messiah through peril.

She is a nervous housewife named Fran who is obsessed with a strange circle of mushrooms on her lawn.

She is a young girl nicknamed "Boobs" Bornstein who finds herself transformed into a vengeful supernatural entity.

She is a misshapen recluse living beneath the Paris Opéra house with an abducted child bride.

She is a middle-aged psychiatrist named Floria who finds herself forming a fatal identification with a patient named Dr. Weyland, a man who believes he is a vampire.

And perhaps most vividly, she is Dr. Weyland himself, immortal, anguished, jaded, violent, a curse to humanity and his own peace of mind.

But wait, I hear you protest: these are only Charnas's characters, not her true self. Charnas is the historically locatable woman who debuted in the SF world some thirty years ago, with her excellent post-apocalypse novel *Walk to the End of the World* (later followed by three sequels). She's the writer who's won a Hugo and a Nebula and a Mythopoeic Award, the one who has had successes in the theater. That's the gal we need you, as introducer, to describe.

Well, I reply, if your interest is *that* shallow, I imagine you can find pictures of Charnas easily enough, on her various dustjackets or with the help of Google. But those photos won't help you identify what's really unique and important, the inner essence of Charnas, the soul-glow that will allow you to spot her amidst a mob much more readily than by knowing mere tilt of head or jut of jaw, curve of lip or wrinkle of brow. No, those inner qualities are only apprehendable by diving into her stories and getting acquainted with her characters. For what is an author if not the composite of those she chooses to write about?

And what fine, intriguing, well-crafted stories and characters they are! Charnas has never been one of those ultra-prolific genre writers, deluging the world with a book or three per year. And, in these stories at least, she does tend to focus on a certain deliberately restricted set of themes and settings and personages, rather than going in for gallivanting about the universe with a bunch of casual acquaintances. But the limits of her fiction are the limits of, say, a Virginia Woolf, and her relative sparsity is belied by the richness of what she chooses to gift us with.

Charnas obviously has a certain reputation as a feminist writer, and one would naturally expect her to "do women well." This is borne out by the touching portraits of Fran in her suburban disintegration ("Evil Thoughts"); of "Boobs" Bornstein in her exultant transcendence ("Boobs"); of Floria in her gray-haired sensual blossoming ("Unicorn Tapestry"); and of Christine in her unwilling marriage to a monster ("Beauty and the Opéra or the Phantom Beast"). But Charnas is much more than a blindered journalist focused on a single gender. Her imaginative and empathetic depiction of Michael Flynn, one of the few human survivors in a world of lizards ("Listening to Brahms") and her multiplex rendering across three stories ("A Musical Interlude," "Unicorn Tapestry," and "Advocates") of the vampire Weyland proves that she can tap into the universal currents that animate both men and women. And children as well, given her intimate portrayal of Holluth and Serchio, juvenile seekers from another world ("Peregrines").

Charnas embeds these characters in worlds where art matters, where an esthetic discipline or spiritual practice can provide both the setting for a story and the key to its resolution. Whether it's theater or opéra, tarot-card reading or psychiatry, classical music or law, she delivers the message that while suffering cannot be kept completely from one's doorstep by such practices, these templates that humans have invented down the millennia serve to blunt the hurt and point us toward what endures. And occasionally, Charnas revels in pure physicality as an antidote to the vices and illnesses of civilization, most notably in the glorious carnal transmogrification of "Boobs" Bornstein.

On the surface, Charnas is a serious and even grim writer. Her stories could rightly be called tragedies for the most part. But poke a little deeper, and I think you'll see a strain of comedy, of black humor, that clears her fiction of any charges of imbalance, and lends perspective to her moral universe. If you don't think that the account by "Boobs" of her first taste of human flesh is delightfully Grand Guignol, then you're not opened up enough to the irony Charnas intends. Likewise with some of Weyland's more tart comments to his psychiatrist. The laugh with the bubble of blood at the corner of the lips is what we have here.

Charnas seems to me to bear an affinity with several fine predecessors and contemporaries. Sometimes her work recalls the similar stylings and concerns of Elizabeth Hand or Kathe Koja. A piece like "Advocates" (co-written with Chelsea Quinn Yarbro) summons up comparisons to Harlan Ellison's "The Prowler in the City at the Edge of the World." Jack Williamson's magnificent *Darker than You Think* (1948) can surely lay claim to being grandfather to "Boobs." And surely Charnas's fascination with and use of the theater is the most pronounced in the genre since the heyday of Fritz Leiber. This reverence for ancestors is a vital part of any honest and self-respecting fantasist's makeup.

But surely you're tired of me weaving my Charnas tapestry by now, however intriguing the figures are against their mysteriously variegated background. It's time for you to listen to Suzy.

I'm sure you won't have any trouble picking her out of the crowd.

BEAUTY AND THE OPÉRA
OR
THE PHANTOM BEAST

For the first few months it was very hard to take my meals with him. I kept my gaze schooled to my own plate while he hummed phrases of music and dribbled crumbs down his waistcoat. His mouth, permanently twisted and swollen on one side, held food poorly. Unused to dining company, he barely noticed.

But to write of such things I must first set the stage. No more need be known, I think, than anyone might learn from M. Gaston Leroux's novel *The Phantom of the Opéra*, which that gentleman wrote using certain details he had from me in the winter of 1907 (he was a very persuasive and convivial man, and I spoke far too freely to him); or even from this "moving picture" they have made now from his book.

M. Leroux tells (as best he can in mere words) of a homicidal music genius who wears a mask to hide the congenital deformity of his face. This monstrous prodigy lives secretly under the Paris Opéra, tyrannizing the staff as the mysterious "Phantom" of the title. He falls in love with a foolish young soprano whose voice he trains and whose career he advances by fair means and foul.

She, thinking him the ghost of her dead father or else an angel of celestial inspiration, is dominated by him until *she* falls in love—with a rich young aristocrat, the Vicomte Raoul de Chagny (the name I shall use here also). The jealous Phantom courts her for himself, with small hope of success however, since he sleeps in a coffin and has cold, bony hands that "smell of death."

Our soprano, although pliant and credulous, is not a complete dolt: not surprisingly, she chooses the Vicomte. Enraged, the

Phantom kidnaps her—

It was the night of my debut as Marguerite in *Faust*. The Opéra's Prima Donna was indisposed, due perhaps to the terrible accident that had interrupted the previous evening's performance: one of the counterweights of the great chandelier had unaccountably fallen, killing a member of the audience.

Superstitious people (which in a theatre means everyone) whispered that this catastrophe was the doing of the legendary Phantom of the Opéra, whom someone must have displeased. If so, that someone, I knew, was me. Raoul de Charny and I had just become secretly engaged. My eccentric and mysterious teacher, whom I was certain was the person known as the Phantom, surely had other plans for me than marriage to a young man of Society.

Nervously, I anticipated confronting my tutor over the matter of the fatal counterweight when next he appeared in my dressing room to give me a singing lesson. I was sure that he would come when the evening's performance was over, as was his habit.

But just as I finished my first number in Act Three, darkness flooded the theatre. Gripped in mid-breath by powerful arms, I dropped, a prisoner, through a trap in the stage.

I was mortified at being snatched away with my performance barely begun, but knowing that I had not sung well I also felt rather relieved. It is possible, too, that some drug was used to calm me. At any rate I did not scream, struggle, or swoon as my abductor carried me down the cellar passages at an odd, crabwise run that was nonetheless very quick. I knew it was the Phantom, for I had felt the cool smoothness of his mask against my cheek.

No word passed between us until I found myself sitting in a little boat lit by a lantern at the bow. Opposite me sat my mentor, rowing us with practiced ease across the lake that lies in the fifth cellar down, beneath the opera house.

"I am sorry if I frightened you, Christine," he said, his voice echoing hollowly in that watery vault, "but 'Il était un Roi de Thule' was a disgrace, wobbling all over the place, and you ended a full quarter tone flat! You see the result of your distracting flirtation with a shallow boy of dubious quality, titled though he may be. I could not bear to hear what you would have made of the Jewel Song, let alone the duet!"

"My voice was not sufficiently warmed up," I murmured, for indeed Marguerite does not truly begin to sing until the third act. "I might have improved, had I been given time."

"No excuses!" he snapped. "You were not concentrating."

I ought to have challenged him about the lethal counterweight, to which my concentration had in fact fallen victim; but alone with him on that black, subterranean water, I did not dare.

"It was nerves," I said, cravenly. "I never meant to disappoint you, Maestro."

We completed the crossing in silence. In some way that I could not quite see he made the far wall open and admit us to his secret home, which I later learned was hidden between the thick barriers retaining the waters of the lake.

In an ordinary draped and carpeted drawing room, amid a profusion of fresh-cut flowers and myriad gleaming brass candlesticks and lamps, my teacher swore that he loved me and would love me always (despite the inadequate performance I had just attempted in *Faust*). He knelt before me and asked me to live with him in the city above as his wife.

Now I was but a girl, and even down on his knee he was an imposing figure. He always wore formal dress, which flatters any tall man; carried himself with studied grace and dignity; and had (till tonight) behaved impeccably toward me. I imagined the features behind the white, half-face mask he always wore as being sad and noble, concealed for a vow of love or honor, or both.

But he had always seemed much older than I was and, acting as the Opéra's demonic spirit, must live at best a highly irregular life. I had simply never imagined him as a suitor.

In fact I had named him from the first my "Angel of Music," not because I thought he was some sort of Heavenly visitor—I was a singer, not a convent-school girl—but to both state and remind him of a standard of conduct that I wished him to uphold in his dealings with me (it had not escaped my notice that he asked no payment for my lessons).

Taken aback by his proposal—and with Raoul's ring hanging hidden on a chain round my neck!—I temporized: "I am flattered, Monsieur. As my father is dead, you must speak with my guardian. But, forgive me, I do not even know your name, or who you are."

The side of his mouth that I could see curved in a smile. "Your guardian is both deaf and senile; it is no use talking to him. As for me, I am the Opéra Ghost, as you surmise. My name is Erik." He paused, breathed deeply, and added, "There, I have told you who I am; now I shall show you!"

With a sudden, extravagant gesture, he swept off his mask and with it all of his thick, dark hair—a wig! I gasped, hardly believing my eyes as he displayed to me the full measure, the positively baroque detail and extraordinary extent, of his phenomenal ugliness.

Large and broad, with bruise-colored patches staining the pallid skin, his head resembled nothing so much as an overripe melon. The fully-revealed face was a nightmare. One eye was sunk in a crooked socket, the nose was half-formed and cavernous, and his cheek resembled a welter of ornamental plaster work, all lumps and hollows and odd tags of skin. His mouth spread and twisted on that same side into a shocking blur of pink flesh, moist and shining. Only his ears were fine, curled tightly to the sides of his freckled crown with its scanty dusting of pale, lank hair. In short, he was a stomach-turning sight.

Abject and defiant at once this monster gazed up at me, dearly apprehending how I recoiled but bearing it in silence while he awaited my answer.

In that blood-freezing instant all my childish fancies and conceits—that with his teaching I would become a great singer, that he and my dear Raoul would gladly join forces to that end—were swept away. Words from the interrupted third act of *Faust* came unbidden to my mind: "Oh, let me, let me, gaze upon your face!" I nearly burst into shrieks of hysterical laughter.

I managed to say, "I think you must be mad, Monsieur, to ask me to accept you!"

"Mad? Certainly not!" He sprang to his feet and glared down at me. "But I am every bit as dangerous as Opéra gossip makes me out to be. Do you remember the stagehand Joseph Buquet, who supposedly hanged himself last Christmas? He died at my hands to stop his chattering about me. You may look to me also in the death caused by the fallen counterweight. I was ***very*** displeased with your behavior on the roof of my theatre the other evening with the importunate young man whose ring you wear secretly even now; and I made my protest.

"Also that crash, with certain communications from me, is what persuaded Madame Carlotta to step aside tonight and give you your chance to sing Marguerite, of which you made so little. I tell you these things so that you will believe me when I say that your Vicomte's life depends upon your answer, and other lives also."

My heart dropped. "You haven't hurt Raoul! Where is he?"

"Why, he is here, unharmed. Only his fine feathers are somewhat ruffled." He drew a heavy curtain, revealing a window into an adjoining room.

There sat the Vicomte de Chagny, struggling wildly in a chair to which he was lashed by a crisscrossing of thin, bright chains. His clothes were all awry from his wrenchings to get loose, his opera cape was rucked up on the floor at his feet, and his top hat lay on its side in a corner.

Seeing me, Raoul began shouting mightily, his face so reddened that I feared apoplexy. The Phantom touched some switch in the wall and Raoul's voice became audible, bawling out my name: "Christine! Christine, has he touched you, has he insulted you? Charlatan! Scoundrel! Let me go! You ugly devil, I will break you in pieces, I will—"

The curtain fell again. Raoul's yells subsided into frustrated grunting as he renewed his attempts to free himself.

I was horrified. I loved Raoul for his (normally) ebullient and affectionate nature and I dreaded to see him hurt. Of course he was as artistically sensitive as a large veal calf, but we cannot all serve the Muses; nor is it a capital offense to be a Philistine.

I sank onto a velvet-seated chair, trying to collect myself. The Opéra Ghost stepped close and said darkly, "His life is in your hands, Christine."

Now I understood his meaning, and I was aghast; yet my heart rose up in exhilaration at the grant of such power. That love of justice found mainly in children burned in my breast. Feeling at fault for the death of the counterweight victim at least, I longed to do right. The Phantom's words seemed to mean that right lay within my grasp—if I had the courage to seize it.

Gripping the arms of my chair, I looked up into his awful face with I hoped would seem a fearless gaze. "Monsieur Erik, I see in you a man of violence and cruelty. You wish to hurt Raoul because he loves me, and from what you say you plan some wider gesture of destruction as well if I refuse to be your wife."

A vindictive gleam in his eyes confirmed this. I trembled for myself, and for Raoul who groaned and struggled in the next room. Clearly he could not rescue me; I must rescue *him*, and, with him, apparently, others unknown to me but equally at risk.

In fact this great goblin in evening dress who called himself Erik, whom I had rashly taken for a friend and mentor, offered me a role grander than any I had yet sung on stage (this was the spring of 1881; *Tosca* had not yet been written), a challenge of breathtaking proportions. Still costumed as honest Marguerite and bursting with her unsung music, I determined to meet the test. I was very young.

"Here is my answer," I said. "If you let Raoul go and swear, moreover, to commit no further violence so long as you live, I will stay with you—for five years."

One does not survive in the arts without learning to bargain.

"Five years!" exclaimed the Ghost. "Why, I have lived with *her* for ten, and there have been no complaints!" He indicated with a wave the major oddity of his décor, a fashion mannequin seated at the piano wearing my costume as Susanna in *The Marriage of Figaro*.

"Monsieur Erik," I replied, "I mean what I say: I offer my talent, such as it is, for you to shape and train as you choose, as well as my acceptance of your love—" my throat nearly closed on these words, and I was afraid I might vomit "—on the terms I have stated, for five years."

I chose the number out of the air; five years was the length of time I had been at the Paris Opéra.

How well prepared I was for that moment I understood only upon later reflection. A French music professor had seen my father and me performing in our native Sweden, and, thinking my father a rustic genius on the violin, had brought us both to France. But my father—more at ease, perhaps, as an exhibitor of my talents than as someone else's prize exhibit—had gone into a steep decline.

Extremity makes a monster of any dying man to those who must answer his incessant, heart-wringing, and ultimately vain demands for help and comfort. I did not begrudge the duty I had owed, and paid; but I had learned in those long months the price of yielding to another person unbounded power over my days and nights. In life as in art, limitation is all.

The Phantom frowned, plainly perplexed by a response he had not foreseen. I added hurriedly, "And we must live here below, not out in the everyday world. The strain of pretending to be just like other people would be more than I could bear. That is my offer. Will you take it?"

He showed wolfish teeth. "Remember where you are. I can take what I want and keep what I like, for as long as I wish."

"But, my dear Angel," I quavered, "you may not like to have me with you even as long as five years. You are accustomed to your own ways, untrammeled by considerations of the wants of a living companion." I glanced aside at the undemanding mannequin to make my meaning dear. "And we will not be honing my talents for public performance but only for our own satisfaction, which may lessen the pleasure of my constant company."

What do you mean?" he demanded. "I have promised from the

first to make a famous diva of you!"

"Maestro," I said, "please understand: you have allowed your passions to drive you too far. I doubt that the Opéra managers would accept your direction of my career now on any terms. You have just said that you killed a stagehand and loosed the counterweight on the head of a helpless old woman. In the world above, you are not a great music-master but a callous murderer."

"In the world above—" he repeated intently. "But not here below? Then you forgive me?"

"I do not presume to forgive crimes committed against others," said I, with the lofty severity of youth. "But neither can anything you or I might do bring back your victims alive and well, so what use is blame and condemnation? You have treated me—for the most part—with consideration and respect, and I mean to respond in kind. But I can accept no more advancement of my career by your efforts. I must reject a success made for me by the heartless criminality of the Opéra Ghost."

He wrung his hands, a poignant gesture when coupled with his ghastly head and threatening demeanor. "But what have I to offer you, except my knowledge of music and my influence here at the Opéra?"

"That we must discover," I replied more gently, for his question had touched me. As the answer was "nothing," I dared to hope that I might induce him to acknowledge the futility of his plans and release Raoul and me. "But making a career for me is out of the question now. Please put that possibility from your mind."

Drawing a square of cambric from his pocket and patting his lips dry with it, he stared gloomily at the floor. No apology, no instant grant of liberty was forthcoming. I saw that he would not reconsider, and it was too late for me to do so.

"So" I finished dejectedly, "my choice is to join you in exile and obscurity, not fame and glory. All crimes have their costs, it seems, with or without forgiveness."

"Then you won't sing in my opera, when it is staged?" he said, sounding near to tears himself. "But I composed it for you!" He had previously told me that he had been working on this opus for twenty years and that it was too advanced for me in any case; but I judged his emotion honest enough.

"And I will sing it for you if you wish," I said quickly, "here in your home. Won't that suffice? Can it be, my angel and teacher, that you do not want *me* at all, just my voice for your opera? Is it only my talent, put to use for your own recognition, that you love?

I am sorry, but you must give that up. Guiltless as I am of your crimes, if I let you raise me up with hands tainted by murder I shall be as bloodstained as you are yourself."

He blinked at me in pained bafflement. "How is it, Christine, that I love you to the depths of my soul, but I do not understand you at all? You are scarcely more than a child, yet you speak like a jurist! What do you want of me? What must I do?"

Taking a deep breath of the warm, flower-scented air I repeated my terms: "You must release the Vicomte, unharmed. You must swear to do no more violence to him or to anyone. And five years from now you must let me go, too."

He flung away from me and began to pace the carpeted floor, raising puffs of dust with every step (for he had no servants, and, like many artistic people, he was an indifferent housekeeper). Freed from his oppressive hovering, I arose from my chair and surreptitiously breathed in the calming way that he himself had taught me.

"I have said that I love you," he said sulkily over his shoulder, "And I mean love that lasts and informs a lifetime—not the trifling fancy of an Opéra dandy whose true loves are the gaming tables and the racetrack!"

This jeer, spoken with deliberate loudness, provoked renewed sounds of struggle in the next room, which I resolutely ignored.

"I am young yet, Maestro," I said meekly. "Five years is a very long time to me." He sighed, crossed his arms on his breast, and bowed his dreadful head. "But I can school myself to spend that time with you so long as I know there is an end to it; and if you will promise to sing for me, often, in your splendid voice that I have never heard equaled."

"With songs or without them, I can keep you here forever if I choose," he muttered.

"As a prisoner filled with hatred for you, yes," I dared to reply, for I sensed that he was losing heart. "But prisoners are the chains of their jailers, and they often pine and die. If I were to perish here, my poor dead body would stink and rot like any other. You would be worse off than you are now with your poupette, there, that you have dressed in my costume. I offer more than that, dear Angel; for five years, no less and no more."

I think that no one had argued with Erik, face-to-face, for a very long time. He certainly had not expected reasoned opposition from me. I was sure that he was on the verge of giving way.

Raoul chose this moment to issue a challenge at the top of his lungs from next door: "Fight me like a man, if you *are* a man, you filthy freak! Choose your weapons and fight for her!"

The Phantom's head came sharply up and he rounded on me so fiercely that I could not keep from flinching.

"Liar!" he shouted. "It's a trick! You maneuver to save your little Vicomte, that is all! Do you think he would wait for you? Do you think he would *want* you, after I have had you by me for even your paltry five years? You would be sadly disappointed, Ma'amselle. Or do you mean to coax and befool me, and then escape in a month or two when my back is turned and run to your Raoul? I will kill him first. You lying vixen, I will kill you both!"

"I am not a liar!" I cried, my eyes brimming over at last.

"Prove it!" he screamed, in a very ecstasy of grief and rage. "Liar! Little liar! Prove it!"

I stepped forward, caught him round the neck, and kissed him. I shut my eyes, I could not help that, but I pressed my mouth full on his bloated, glistening lips and leant my breast on his. My trembling hands fitted themselves to the back of his nearly naked head, holding his face tight to mine; and he was not cold and toad-like to the touch as I had anticipated, but vigorous and warm.

How can I describe that kiss? It was like putting my mouth to an open wound, as intimate an act as if I had somehow slipped my hand in among his entrails.

After a blind and breathless moment, I stepped away again, much shaken. He had not moved but had gone utterly rigid from head to foot in my embrace. We looked one another in the eyes in shocked silence.

"So be it." he said at last in a hoarse voice. "The boy goes free, and I will submit my hatreds to your authority." His eyes narrowed. "But you must marry me, Christine. I will have no shadow cast upon your name or character on my account; and there must be no misunderstanding between us as to the duties owed whilst you live with me."

"I accept," I whispered, though I quailed inwardly at the mention of those "duties."

He left me. There came some muffled, unsettling sounds from the next room, during which I had time to wonder wretchedly how my Raoul had fallen into the hands of this monster.

But according to Opéra gossip the Phantom was supremely clever, while I had reluctantly noticed in Raoul flashes (if that is the word) of the obdurate, uncomprehending stupidity of the privileged. I was familiar with this quality from my childhood days of entertaining, with my father, the wealthy farmers and burghers who hired us to make music for them. Apparently the addition of noble blood only exacerbated the condition.

In a few moments, Erik reappeared holding his rival's limp body in his arms like that of a sleeping child. Raoul had recently begun growing a beard, and he looked very downy and dear. The sight of him all but undid me.

"He is not hurt," said the Phantom gruffly. "Bid him good-bye, Christine. You shall not see him again in my domain."

I longed to press a parting kiss to Raoul's flushed and slack-jawed face for he looked like Heaven itself to me. But my kisses were pledged now, every one. I must wait, in an agony of mingled terror and queasy anticipation, for their claimed redemption—not by Raoul, but by the Opéra Ghost.

I slipped off the chain with Raoul's ring on it, wound it round his hand, and stood back helplessly as Erik bore him away.

Left alone, I rushed about the underground house like a bird trapped in a mine shaft. Fear drove me this way and that and would not let me rest. I was locked in, for Erik quite correctly mistrusted me; had I found a way out, I would have taken it.

The rooms of his house, modest and snug, were warm, with lamps and candles burning everywhere. The furniture, apart from a pair of pretty Empire chairs in the drawing room, consisted of heavy, dark, provincial pieces. A few murky landscape paintings hung on the walls. There were shelves of books and of ornamental oddments—a little glass shoe full of centime pieces, some carved jade scent bottles, a display of delicate porcelain flowers—which I dared not touch lest I doom myself forever, like Persephone eating the pomegranate seeds in Hades.

In my distraction I intruded into my captor's bedroom, which was hung with tapestries of hunting scenes and pale green bed-curtains dappled in gold, like a vision from the life of the young Siegfried. The sylvan effect was diminished by the presence of a number of gilded, elaborate clocks showing not only the hour but whether it was day or night. I did not own a clock, being unable to afford one; clearly I was not in the home of a poor man.

There was no mirror in which to see my frightened face (nor even a windowpane, for behind the drapes lay blank walls). The only sound was the ticking of the clocks.

At last, I sank onto a divan in the drawing room and gave way to sobs of misery and bitter self-reproach. I could scarcely believe myself caught in such a desperate coil. Yet here I was, a foreigner, a poor orphan with no family but my fellow workers at the Opéra. I had made friends among the ballet rats, but no one listens to an alarm raised by a clutch of fifteen-year-old girls. The professor, my guardian, was only intermittently aware of my existence these days. Who would miss me, who would search?

Raoul was my one hope. I had met him years before, during a summer I had spent with my father at Chagny. Grown to be a handsome, lively man of fashion, the young Vicomte had turned up lately in Paris as the proud new owner of a box at the Opéra. I had been flattered that he even remembered me.

His proposal of marriage was typical of his impetuous and optimistic nature. In my more realistic moments I had not really believed that his family would ever permit such a joining. Now I had not even his ring to remember him by.

But he would save me, surely! I told myself that Raoul loved me, that he would lead an attack on the underground house and never give up until he had me back again.

How he might overcome the obstacle of my having spent—however long it was to be—unchaperoned in the home of another man, I could not imagine. Raoul's people were not Bohemians. His brother the Comte had already expressed displeasure over the warm relations between Raoul and me, and that was without a kidnapping.

Still, my cheerful and enthusiastic Vicomte would not allow me to languish in captivity (I tried to blot out the image of him, red-faced, roaring, and chained to a chair). I had only to stand fast and keep my head and he would rescue me.

Erik, returning at long last, showed me to a very pretty little bedroom with my meager selection of clothing already hanging in the wardrobe and my toiletries laid out on the table.

He behaved from this point as a gracious host, always polite, faultlessly turned out, and considerately masked. This surface normality was all that enabled me to keep my own composure. At night I slept undisturbed (when I did sleep), although there was no lock on my door. Daytimes the Phantom spent absorbed in composition, humming pitches and runs under his breath, pausing to play a phrase on the piano or to stab his pen into a brass inkwell in the shape of a spaniel's head.

I continued my own work as best I could. Each morning he listened to me vocalize, but he made no comment. When I ventured to ask him for a lesson, trying to restore our relationship to some semblance of its old footing, he said, "No, Christine. You must see how you get along without the aid of your Angel of Music."

So I saw that my initial rejection still rankled, and that he was inclined to hold a grudge.

The third morning after *Faust*, I burst into tears over breakfast: "You said you would free Raoul! He would come back for me if he were alive! You monster, you have killed him!"

Erik tapped his fingers impatiently upon the smooth white cheek of his mask. "Why should I do such a thing? He is an absurd young popinjay with no understanding of music, but I do not hate him; after all, you are here with me, not run off with him."

I flung down my napkin, knocking over my water glass. "You murdered poor Joseph Buquet for gossiping about you. I daresay you did not ***hate*** him, but you killed him all the same!"

Erik moved his knee to avoid the dripping water. "Oh, Buquet! One deals differently with aristocrats. I assure you, the boy is alive and well. His brother has taken him home to Chagny. Now eat your omelette Christine. Cold eggs are bad for the throat."

That evening he brought a ledger from the Opéra offices and set before me a page showing that the Vicomte de Chagny had given up his box two days after the night of *Faust*. Raoul had signed personally for the refund of the remainder of the season's fee. There was no doubt; I recognized his writing.

So in his own way Erik *had* chosen his weapons, had fought for me—and won. At least no blood had been shed. I ceased accusing him and resigned myself to making the best of my situation.

I spent two weeks as his guest, solicitously and formally attended by him in my daily wants. He even took me on a tour of the lake in the little boat, and showed me the subterranean passage from the Opéra cellars to the Rue Scribe through which he obtained provisions from the outside world.

Then, during the wedding procession in a performance of *Lohengrin*, the Opéra Ghost and I exchanged vows beneath the stage. He placed upon my finger a ring that had been his mother's, or so he supposed since he had found it in a bureau of hers (most of his furniture he had inherited from his mother, he told me; and that was all the mention he ever made of her).

He solemnly wrote out and presented to me a very handsome and official-looking civil certificate, and he said that having had his first kiss already he would not trouble me for another yet, since he was so ugly and must be gotten used to.

Thus began my marriage to the Phantom of the Opéra.

In M. Leroux's story the Phantom's heart is melted by the

compassion of the young singer. He releases the lovers and dies soon after, presumably of a morbid enlargement of the organ of renunciation. The soprano and her Vicomte take a train northward and are never heard of again.

But that is not what happened.

When he said "first kiss," Erik may have spoken literally. Like any man in funds he could buy sexual favors, and had certainly done so in the past. But with what wincing, perfunctory haste those services must have been rendered! And he was proud and in his own way gallant, or at any rate he wished to be both proud and gallant. I thought then and think still that although more than twice my age at least, he was very inexperienced with women.

For my part, I was virginal but not completely naive. Traveling with my father I had observed much of life in its cruder aspects, in particular that ubiquitous army of worn-out, perpetually gravid country girls through whose lives we had briefly passed. My own mother, whom I scarcely recalled, had died bearing a stillborn son when I was two years old.

I regarded sexual matters as I did the stinks and wallowings of the pigsty. Before Raoul's reappearance I had determined to remain celibate, reserving all my energies for my art. Even my dalliance with him had been chaste, barring a kiss or two. In any case, I had no idea what to expect from a monster.

No expectation could have prepared me for what followed.

For two nights Erik came and sat silently in a chair by my bed. I sensed him listening in the dark to my breathing and to the small rustlings I made as I shifted and turned, unable to sleep. I felt observed by some nocturnal beast of prey that might claw me to pieces at any moment.

On the third night he brought a candle. I saw that he was masked and wore a long red silken robe. His feet, which like his hands were strong and well-shaped, gleamed palely on the dark Turkish carpet.

He set the candle on the little table by my bed and said in a hushed tone, "Christine, you are my wife. Take off your gown."

In those days decent women did not show their nakedness to anyone, not even their own husbands. But I had stepped beyond the pale; no convention or nicety protected me in Grendel's lair.

He turned away, and when I had done as he said and lain down again in a trembling sweat of fear, he leaned over me and folded back the sheet, exposing the length of my body to the warm air of the room. Then he sat in his chair and looked at me. I stared at the ceiling, tears of shame and terror running from the corners of my eyes into my hair, until I fell into an exhausted sleep.

Next morning I lay a long time in bed wondering how much more I could bear of his stifled desire. I thought he meant to be considerate, gentling me to his presence as a rider gentles an unbroken horse, little by little.

Instead, he was crushing me slowly to death.

The following night he came again and set the candle down. "Christine, take off your gown."

I answered, "Erik, you are my husband. Take off your mask."

A moment passed during which I dared not breathe. Then he snatched off the mask, in his agitation dropping it on the floor. He managed not to grab after it but stood immobile under my scrutiny, his face turned away only a little.

When I could gaze on that grotesque visage without my gorge rising, I knew I was as ready as I could ever be. I shrugged out of my nightdress, and taking his hand I drew him toward me. With a sharp intake of breath he reached quickly to pinch out the candle.

"No," I said, "let it burn," and I turned down the sheet.

After that he always came to my bed unmasked. He would lie so that I looked straight into his terrible face while his hands touched me, rousing and warming the places where his mouth would soon follow, that hideous mouth that devoured without destruction all the juices, heats, and swellings of passion.

He proved a barely banked fire, scorched and scorching with a lifetime of need. And I—I went up like summer grass, I flamed like pitch, clasped to his straining breast. As beginners, everything that we did was unbearably disgusting to us both, and so frantically exciting that we could not stop nor hold back anything. My God, how we burned!

Knowing himself to be only a poor, rough sketch of a man, he had few expectations and never thought to blame me for his own shortcomings (or, for that matter, for mine). He was at first too swift for my satisfaction, but he set himself to master the gratifications of lust as he might a demanding musical score. Some very rare books appeared on his shelves.

He studied languor, lightness of touch, and the uses of raw energy. I learned to lure him from his work, to meet his advances with revulsion and open arms at once, and to invite to my shrinking cheek his crooked kisses that came all intermixed with moans and whisperings and that seemed to liquefy my heart.

I learned to twine my legs round his, guiding him home to that secret part of myself, the odorous, the blood-seeping, the unsightly, puckered mouth of my sex. To whom else could I have exposed that humid breach in my body's defenses, all sleek with avidity? With what other person could I have shared my sweat, my spit, my rising deliriums of need and release filled with animal cries and groans?

Initially I suffered the utmost, soul-wringing terror and shame. But then came an intoxication that I can only compare to the trance of song, and this was the lyric of that song: my monster adored the monstrous in me.

Oh, he enjoyed my pretty face, my good figure, and my long, thick hair, all the simple, human handsomeness denied him in his own right. But what he craved was the gorgon under my skirts. His deepest pleasure depended on the glaring difference between my comely outward looks and the seeming deformity of my hidden female part. He loved to love me with his twisted mouth, monster to monster, gross and shapeless flesh to its like, slippery heat to slippery heat, and cry to convulsion.

We awoke new voices in one another. To the slow coiling of our entangled limbs we crooned like doves. His climax wrung from him half-strangled, exultant cries like those of a soul tearing free from its earthly roots. In turn, I sang for him the throaty songs of a body drowning rapturously in its own depths.

I commanded, praised, begged, and reviled him, calling him my loathsome demon, my leprous ape, my ruined, rutting angel, never stooping to the pretense that he was other than awful to look at. I felt that if I treated his appearance as normal, he would be grateful; but in time he would come to hate and despise me for accepting what he hated and despised in himself. A man who feels this way beats the woman who shares his life, whether he is a handsome man or an ugly one.

Erik did strike me once.

It was quite early in our life together. We were studying Antonia's trio with her mother and Dr. Miracle from The *Tales of Hoffmann*, which Erik had heard at its Opéra Comique premiere some three months earlier. From memory, he played Dr. Miracle's music on the piano; and he sang the dead mother's part, transposed downward, with an otherworldly tenderness and nobility that greatly moved and distracted me.

I struggled vainly with Antonia's music (which he had written out for me), until Erik's largely unsolicited advice spurred me to observe rather tartly that he was very arrogant in his opinions, for an ugly man who lived in a cellar singing songs and writing music that no one would ever hear.

He leaped to his feet and sharp as a whip he slapped me. I stood my ground, my cheek hot and stinging, and said, "Erik, stop! By the terms of our bargain, you are not to be that sort of monster."

"Am I not?" he snapped, glaring hatefully at me. "You go tripping out onstage in your finery and you open your mouth and everyone throws flowers and shouts the house down. I have twice the voice of any singer in Paris, but as you so kindly remind me, no audience will ever hear me and beg me for an encore! If you write a little song that is not too terrible, they will say what a clever creature you are to be able to sing songs and make them too. But they will never be brought to tears by my music. So what sort of monster will *you* allow *me* to be, Christine?"

"I am sorry for what I said," I replied. I could not help but see how his lips gleamed with the saliva sprayed out during this tirade; repelled, I thrust my handkerchief toward him.

He snatched it from me and blotted his mouth, snarling, "Oh, spare me your so-called apologies! Why should you care for the feelings of a miserable freak?"

"I have said I am sorry for my words," I said, more angrily than I had meant to. "I have not heard you say that you are you sorry for your action. Do you understand that the next time you strike me, whatever the provocation, I will leave you and I will never, ever come back? You will have to kill me to stop me; and then I will be revenged in the pain it will cost you if I die in your house, at your hands, that are beautiful and strong and that wish only to love me."

He stared down at the handkerchief clenched in his fingers, and I knew by the droop of his shoulders that the perilous moment was past. Still I forged recklessly onward, for my heart was in a turmoil of confused and painful emotion. "If you must hit something go and beat the poupette which you have dressed in my old costume, until your rage is spent. But never raise your hand to me again!"

In low tones he began, "Christine, I—"

"It is all your fault!" I burst out. "You should not have sung her music, the dead mother's music!"

"Ah," he said. "The dead mother's music."

I stiffened, dreading that I had exposed a weakness to him that he would surely exploit. But he only raised his head and sang once more, unaccompanied and more gloriously than before, that same lofty music of the ghostly mother urging her daughter to sing.

"Now," he said afterward, "if you are moved to say cutting things to me, say them. I will endure it quietly."

My eyes stung, for the music had again affected me deeply. So had the realization that he of all men knew why it did so, for surely his own mother had been dead to him from the day she first saw his terrible face. In his way, he was offering a very handsome apology indeed.

I shook my head, not trusting my voice.

He nodded gravely. "Very good, your restraint is commendable. After all, Christine, it is our task to master the music, not to let the music master us. Now, let us begin again."

We began again.

Other crises arose, of course. His habitual cruelty and malice inclined him toward outrageous gestures of annoyance, as when I found him one afternoon preparing to burn alive a chorus girl's little poodle that he had lured away for the purpose. The animal's backstage yapping had disturbed an otherwise unusually good *Abduction from the Seraglio*.

I seized the matches from his unresisting hands. With the shawl from the costumed mannequin I blotted as much lamp oil as I could from the dog's coat. Then I carried the terrified creature to the appropriate dressing area and left it there, its muzzle still tied shut with Erik's handkerchief (the dog was not seen, or heard, at the Opéra again).

Returning, I found Erik in an agony of penitence, offering to drink lamp oil himself or to wear a tightly tied gag for as long as I chose, to redeem his transgression. He showed no remorse for the agonies he had meant to inflict on the dog and its owner, but he was deeply agitated at having nearly failed his promise again, and in such a spectacular fashion.

I approved the gag as a fitting punishment. That night the Opéra Ghost cried like a cat into the layered thicknesses of cloth crushing his lips, while on my knees I ignited our own sweet-burning immolation.

Don't misunderstand: in music he was my master and would be my master still if he stood here now. His talent and learning were broad, discriminating, and seemingly inexhaustible. It was he who led me to the study that became my absorbing delight, of the sorts of chromatic and key shifts that irresistibly evoke certain powerful emotions in the hearer.

But his violence was mine to rule, so long as I had the strength and the wit to command it, by the submission I had won from him with that first kiss.

Between us we sustained a steep pitch of passion despite the muting effects of familiarity, I think because of the time limit I had set. Never repeat even the prettiest melody more than thrice at a go, my father used to say. Knowing it must end enhances its beauty and prevents boredom in its hearers.

Domestic chores gave Erik's life a sense of normality; he yielded them only reluctantly to me. Nor did I wish to become his drudge. However, his standards of housekeeping and cooking (two areas in which he had no talents whatsoever) were far below mine; and I did not expect him to wait on me as he had when I was his guest. I had chosen a life (albeit a truncated one), not an escapade.

We wrangled cautiously over household duties and came to a rough arrangement, with many exceptions and renegotiations as circumstances required. When his compositional impulse flagged, if he could not relieve his frustration by prowling the opera house I did not hesitate to assign him extra chores. More than once I sent him out of the house with a dusty carpet, a heater, and instructions to vigorously apply the latter to the former.

Having had none of the normal social experience that matures ordinary people, he could behave very childishly. This lent him an air of perennial youthfulness at once attractive and extremely trying. His emotions, when tapped, poured from him like lava, and he had great difficulty mastering the molten flow once it began. Physical work, like the demands of operatic singing, helped to bleed off at least some of his ungovernable energy.

In our leisure time I asked about his past. I had thought him an aristocrat, but his arrogance was that of talent, not of blood. He was the son of a master mason in Rouen. When he was still a child his parents had either given or sold him (he did not know which) to a traveling fair.

As a young man he had ranged far and wide, living by his wits and his abilities as an artificer of ingenious structures and devices. He regaled me with tales of his exotic travels before he had settled in Paris, where, commanding some Turkish laborers (whose language he spoke) at work on Garnier's great opera house, he had secretly constructed his home in its bowels. He had always worn a kerchief over his nose and mouth "for the dust," but his workmen had been less interested in his face than in the extra wages he paid for their clandestine labor.

Given my knowledge of his character I guessed that he omitted much repellent detail from these lively narratives. Though troubled, I never pressed him, reasoning that such matters lay between him, the souls of those he had harmed, and God.

In my turn I read aloud to him from the biographies and travel books that he favored, or repeated anecdotes of cafe life and gossip (no matter how stale) about composers and performers whose names he knew. I taught him some Swedish, a language of interest to him because of its strong tonal element, and he enjoyed hearing songs and legends of the northern lands, which he had never visited. As a child, I had absorbed many tales from folk tradition and from books, which now stood me in good stead. People raised in countries with long winters treasure stories and tell them well.

Outside of music, Erik was not so widely read as I had supposed. Many of his books had only a few of their pages cut. He hungered for books but was impatient with their contents once he had them. In the first place he was sure that he knew more about everything than anyone else did because he was a prodigy and well-traveled in the world.

And then, he spent far more time roaming "his" opera house and working on the various small, mechanical contrivances he was always inventing and refining than he did reading. Indeed, he was in a continual ferment of activity of one kind or another, from the orbit of which I sometimes had to withdraw simply to rest myself.

I came to regard him as a flood of notes and markings falling in a tempestuous jumble upon the blank page of his life. He had instinctively tried to create order in himself through composing, with limited success: a well-orchestrated life is not typified by ferocious obsessions and quixotic crimes. I believe he submitted to my scoring, as it were, in order to experience his own melody, in place of a ceaseless chaos of all but random noise.

Weeks and months passed, bringing our scheduled parting closer by increments almost too small to notice, and never spoken of. Even inadvertent allusions to my future departure sent Erik storming off to work on the darkest of his music, with its plunging, wheeling figures of mockery and despair.

It hurt me, that music. I think it hurt him. I never tried to sing any of it, nor, despite his previously stated intentions, did he ask me to.

In his opera, *Don Juan Triumphant*, Don Juan seduces an Archangel who helps him to master the Devil in Hell. From this position of power, the Don decrees a regime of true justice on Earth that wins over Heaven also to his side; whereupon God, dethroned, pulls down Creation in a mighty cataclysm in which all are swallowed up. A moral tale, then (as operas tend to be), the music and lyrics of which combined wild extremes of fury, yearning, and savage satire.

Of its quality, I will say this: Erik's music was magnificent but too radical to have been accepted, let alone admired, in its time (as he often said himself). Some days, his raw, raging chords drove me out to walk beside the lake in blessed quiet. Some days I sat weak with weeping for the extraordinary beauty and poignance of what I heard. His music offered nothing familiar, comforting, or merely pretty. Parisian audiences would not have stood it.

Nonetheless, he spent hours planning the premiere of his opera, which he projected for the turn of the century. All the great men of the world would be invited, and all would come (or else). The experience would change their lives. The course of history itself would be altered for the better by Erik's music.

My lessons resumed soon after the night of *Lohengrin*. Erik taught me the rudiments of composition, which I spent many hours refining in practice. In particular he had me sing and play my own alternate versions of musical figures from the works of the masters, by comparison with which I learned the measure of true genius (as well as the best directions of my own modest talents). This, he said, was how he had taught himself.

He was critical of men like Bizet, Wagner, Verdi, and Gounod, and fiercely jealous of their fame. Yet he worked long and hard with me on their music, for he did not deny greatness when he heard it. At leisure, he would play Bach on the piano with a stiff but sure touch; and then his eyes often glittered with tears—of gratitude, I think, for the sublime *order* of that music.

It was a terror and a joy to sing for him. I have never known anyone to whom music was so all-absorbing, so demanding, and so painfully essential.

His vocal instruction was founded on carefully designed drill and on breathing techniques that he had learned in the Orient. Freed from constriction, my voice began to show its natural qualities. I saw that I might move from the bright but relatively empty soubrette repertoire to the lower-lying, richer, lyric roles.

"Your voice will darken as it ages," he said, "but you have the vocal capacity for some of the great lyric roles already, I can hear it. And the emotional capacity, too; you are not the child you were, Christine. Your Marguerite is much improved, and you will soon be ready to attempt Violetta."

Under his tutelage my range expanded downward with minimal loss of agility above, and I gained a certain sumptuosity of tone overall. I would hear myself produce a beautifully floated pianissimo and wonder how on earth I had done it.

Of course, the next day it was unattainable—these achievements torment singers by their evanescence. Erik would not permit me to overwork my voice, striving to retake such heights. "Wait," he said. "Rest. It will come." About such things he was almost always right.

I bitterly missed performing in public with my improved skills. But in my heart I knew this sacrifice to be well-suited to my collusion (however innocent) in Erik's most recent crimes.

There was much that I was incapable of learning from him, for he was gifted with a degree of musicality that I simply did not possess. I came to prefer hearing him sing for me (as he did often, true to his promise) to producing the finest singing of which I myself was capable. One's most glorious tones are inevitably distorted out of true inside one's own head

Also, I came to realize that I had a very good voice but not a great one. He said otherwise; but he was in love. And I think he was well content—knowingly or unknowingly—to train up a good voice that was still not quite as fine as his own.

For he sang like a god, with a beauty that cannot be imagined by those who never heard him. He had a tenor voice of remarkable power, flexibility, and range, which because of his superb musicianship was never merely, monotonously, perfect. I was reminded of descriptions I had read of the singing of the great castrati of the previous century.

Without apparent effort, Erik produced long, flowing lines of a thrilling richness, like molten gold pouring improbably from the mouth of a stony basilisk. Joyous, meditative, amorous, wild or sad, his singing enraptured me; I could not hear enough of it. As we worked together, he increased the bolder, rougher, more dramatic capabilities of his own voice, producing song expressive enough to pierce a heart of steel.

Or to calm a heart in panic. I had been prey to night terrors from an early age; when I cried out in my sleep Erik would come with a candle to remind me that I lived with a veritable walking nightmare of flesh, so how could I allow mere dreams to trouble me? Then he would sit by my bed and sing. Often he chose "Cielo e Mar," from *Gioconda*, which he rendered with a soothing sweetness that soon sent me drifting off again.

How his moisture-spraying travesty of a mouth could produce song of such precision, versatility, and lustre I never understood. He ought not even to have sung tenor; tall men are almost always baritones. But he was anomalous in so many respects that I gave up trying to account for him. Every time I heard him sing I reminded myself that from the first I had named him an angel.

Sometimes he talked of traveling together like gypsies, singing for our supper as each of us had in youth. He was fascinated by the resemblances in our respective upbringings, I as a child-performer accompanying my peripatetic father, he as a circus freak astonishing audiences with feats of legerdemain and song, and of course with his shocking appearance.

But I saw the differences, which were stark.

My father was a country fiddler with no education, a hard drinker and a fanatical gambler. He had not hesitated to exploit my pretty face and voice at the fairs, fine homes, and festivals where we performed. He played, I sang. Ours was not a sentimental relationship. Yet while he lived I never went hungry or found myself thrown naked upon the spiny mercies of the world.

Erik, expelled from his home like a leper, had ranged the earth in the isolation to which his repulsive face condemned him. Leaving the circus, he had worked for despots who half the time would have murdered him instead of paying him, had he not outwitted them like some branded Odysseus. He had taken the name "Erik," he said, because he liked its bold, Viking sound.

Occasionally, wondering how I had come to this strange new life, I fantasized that he and I were magical siblings, the ugly one and the pretty one, the "bad" one and the "good" one, joined at the soul by music. Parted early through mischance, we were now drawn close again—voluptuously, unlawfully close—by that indissoluble bond.

I did not share such fancies with Erik. He was stubbornly conventional about some things, family among them. But I was mated to a monster: what better occasion for my most perverse imaginings?

Erik's own imaginings were far more dangerous.

One day when I called him to our noon meal, he sprang up from his writing desk and made me come sit down in his place.

Pressing a pen into my hand and closing my fingers hard upon it, he tried to force me to shape letters on the blank page before me.

"Write," he said tightly in my ear. "Surely there is some message you wish to send? Write to Raoul, at Chagny. You let him kiss you that night on the roof. Don't you think about those expert kisses of his? Of course you do—you think of them when my clumsy mouth kisses you. Write and tell him, make him glad!"

The wildness of his accusations, the painful grip of his fingers on mine, and the palpable heat of jealous rage pouring off him all combined to scare me half out of my wits.

"Let me go!" I cried. I managed to lift my hand a little and fling the pen away. My arm knocked down the inkwell, which fortunately was nearly empty and which did not break.

Erik stooped to retrieve it, muttering furiously, "Now see what you have done!"

"See what *you* have done," I answered. "You have raised your hand."

"Coward!" he spat. "I barely touched you!"

"Your words are blows, just as you intend them to be," I said. "I have told you what I will do if you abuse me."

"Go or stay, it is all the same!" he shouted. "Your promise is a sham! Do you think me such a fool? You lie in my arms and dream of your pretty Vicomte, and in your heart you mock me!"

His face was dark with hatred—hatred of *me*, for my power to cause him pain. It meant nothing that I intended him no ill and in truth had no such power, save what he himself assigned to me. I saw that I was lost, for his fury was fed not by any actions of mine but by his own inner demons, which only he could master.

Terror closed my throat. Injustice drove me to speak.

"Now you have clenched your fist," I choked out. "Very well. Hit hard, Erik, punish the fraud you wrongly say I am. But strike to kill, for living or dead I shall be lost to you for good."

In his rage he may not have heard my words; but he heard their music (for it welled from the same dark sources as his own) and he could not help but stop and listen.

"Why do you prevent me?" He struck his fist hard upon his thigh. "It is the pretext you long for, the blow that will free you! Why do you thwart me? Why?"

Even as he spoke I saw the obvious answer dawn upon him (as it dawned upon me at the same moment): that I did not wish to be freed, but to live out my commitment to the end.

The frenzied glare died from his face, leaving him pale and

haggard. "Oh, Christine," he said. "Sometimes I imagine horrible things, and now have nearly made them come true."

"Do you think you have not?" I said, savage in my turn. "I warned you!"

I did not truly mean to leave him, now that his fury was in retreat. But I did mean to hurt him, and I succeeded. He stared at me with a stricken look.

Then he cast himself down before me, stretched prone upon the floor in a posture of such limitless submission that in the West it is only ever displayed before God. At one stroke he transformed himself from a cultured, willful man of my own world (albeit outcast in it) into a faceless beggar groveling before some barbarian overlord or the lawless caprice of Fate.

It was a vertiginous moment, appalling, piteous, and thrilling. I longed to stoop at once, all merciful forgiveness, and lift him up again; or else to grind my heel into the nape of his neck until he writhed, gasping, at my feet. Paralyzed, I stared down at him, scarcely breathing.

In a hollow voice he begged my pardon. I stammered that I would pardon him when I could, for he had wronged me very deeply. He accepted this, rising without a word.

He would not look me in the face or touch even the sleeve of my dress afterward. Two dismal days passed. Then I bade him to my bed, where we fell desperately upon one another as if deprived for two years, not two nights.

Resting beside him while our hearts' tumult slowed again, I said, "You were thinking of someone just now, Erik; who?"

"I thought of you," he whispered. "There is no other."

With the lightest touch I cupped my hand to his twisted cheek, encompassing as much as I could of what his mask normally concealed. "It is just the same for me. If you can believe me when I say so, then you are forgiven."

He groaned and pressed his face blindly into my palm, wetting my fingers with his tears.

Raoul's name was never spoken between us again.

Otherwise (and apart from his run-of-the-mill sulks and fits of spleen) Erik continued to show me the most constant and ardent regard. This was not as pleasant as it sounds. Worship from afar is flattering, but to be loved with consuming intensity by a person who lives cheek by jowl with all one's frailties and failings is not only exhilarating but tremendously exhausting.

For my part, I continually reminded him what a triumph of

character it was (his character as well as mine, since he managed for the most part to fulfill his side of our agreement) for me to keep my word and stay with him. Even when his deformity had acquired a strange beauty of its own in my eyes, I still called upon him (while we fervidly plundered each other's bodies) as my disgusting incubus, my foul and greedy gargoyle, my lecherous ogre.

I must have been a wise child. I knew that love worthy of the name gives not what the beloved needs, but what the beloved wants.

What Erik needed was recognition of his full humanity, in spite of his repulsive looks and criminal behavior, from another human being who addressed him as an equal. What he ***wanted*** was to worship a woman exalted by both quality and attainment who could be repeatedly persuaded to descend to the level of his own base and hideous physicality, thus demonstrating again and again her exceptional love for him.

As for me, I exulted in each leap from my pedestal. What lesser achievement could be worth such a plunge into the bestial, ecstatic depths?

Well, we were opera folk. Only extremes would do.

So I continued to merit his devotion and my own self-respect, despite and because of the fact that I lived for that shudder of delicious horror when he laid his hand on me, and the exquisite creeping of my skin into tiny peaks at the touch of his wet, misshapen lips. In my eager body he took his revenge many times over on all the well-made men in the world. I suppose I had my vengeance too, although I do not know upon whom.

Perhaps I harp on this "distasteful" subject. Perhaps I should refer more circumspectly to the craving of my ghastly Caliban for the delight of the flesh. Or is Caliban's craving acceptable but not his gratification? And what of ***my*** desires and delights? I can guess what Raoul de Chagny would have said had I begged of him those kisses thought in his world to be proper only between men and their whores.

Between the Opéra Ghost and myself, nothing was "proper" or "improper." "Morality" meant my dictum that he must not express his critical judgment by murdering people who annoyed him.

For the rest, we consumed each other with willful abandon, two starvelings at a feast.

AFTER AN EARLY PHASE of keeping me close (I had expected this and endured it patiently), he began to open his world to me. He showed me the trap doors and passages he used to get quietly about the Opéra. The Phantom patrolled "his" theatre often, restless, watchful, and intensely critical of all that occurred there. He seemed pleased that I found my own uses for his private pathways.

He routinely helped himself to fresh clothes from the costume racks, altering garments to fit and returning them to be cleaned with the rest (the wardrobe mistress, grown weary of constantly undoing his tailoring, now left a selection of clothing at the very back of the racks to be worn only by the Opéra Ghost).

Taking a leaf from his book, I filched the more tattered costumes of the chorus and ballet rats, mended them in my leisure time (for I had been taught that idleness is both wasteful and a sin), and stealthily returned them again.

The Opéra girls, struggling along in their difficult and demanding world, took to leaving chocolates for their "good fairy" as well as the occasional pretty ribbon or fresh-cut bloom. If they guessed my secret, they kept it. I pitied their passions and their pains. They had no potent Angel of Music to inspire and encourage them. There was only one of those, and he devoted himself to me alone.

In time, Erik ventured outside with me. I always wore a veil and he went masked and covered in cloak and wide-brimmed hat. Some evenings he would hire a carriage and take me driving in the Bois de Boulogne to listen to gypsy music played in the restaurants there. Or we would take a night train out of town for a country walk. An eager amateur astronomer, he taught me to recognize not only the constellations but many stars by name.

In the city, we spent fine evenings strolling the grandes boulevardes. We even attended, anonymous in costume, the lavish masquerade balls given at the Opéra itself, although for us these were not precisely ***social*** occasions.

We always came late, and left early to avoid the midnight supper after the gala. As we danced (he was a correct but uninspired dancer) or looked on from some quieter vantage point, Erik would murmur in my ear a stream of comments on the flirtations, machinations, and vendettas that he claimed to observe transpiring around us. These vitriolic, often scurrilous remarks always made me laugh, despite my resolve not to encourage the exercise of his more malevolent humor.

On our first anniversary he gave me my own key to the iron gate of the passage to the Rue Scribe. I made frequent use of it, for living as we did we needed time out of each other's company. Most of the daily marketing he did himself, being very pleased with his skill at passing unremarked (as he imagined) among ordinary folk. Closely muffled even in warm weather, he was not, I am sure, so inconspicuous as he thought. But he was both proud and jealous of his self-sufficiency, and I took care not to intrude upon it. He often bought gifts for me—a book of poetry, a pair of gloves, a pretty bit of Meissen, or fresh flowers.

For my part, I brought back reports of the day and what occurred in it, and perhaps a colorful poster to replace one of the dreary pictures on his walls, a book for him from the stalls along the Seine, or a box of the little sweet meringues that he loved.

I took upon myself the task of posting the mail. I wrote to no one, but Erik was an enthusiastic, if menacing, correspondent to whomever caught his attention in the world of music. We attended most Opéra performances, seated in a sort of blind he had built in the shelter of a large, carved nymph on the wall (I always noticed with a pang the strangers seated in Raoul's old box). Afterward, Erik often addressed pages of venomous criticism to the managers, the newspapers, and to composers and artists as well.

Many of these missives I intercepted. But sometimes he mailed a letter himself while he was out, for there were occasional replies to be picked up addressed to "Erik Rouen," Poste Restante. He did not share their contents with me.

We were always buying candles and lamp oil; it took great quantities of fuel to heat and light Erik's home. He could well afford it: we lived on the spoils of years of extortion from the Opéra managers. In fact, by means of threats enforced by ingenious acts of sabotage, Erik had accumulated a small fortune.

He exhibited a lordly carelessness about money, mislaying sizable sums with evident unconcern; but in the normal course of things he spent modestly on books, wine, and other minor luxuries. It was apparent that he had extracted large payments from the Opéra managers primarily to demonstrate his power over them. I was always free to draw what cash needed for my errands abroad.

Herbs and medicines were staples on my shopping list. Erik was prey to fevers, and to other ailments stemming perhaps from distortion of his internal organs. He had learned, of necessity, to doctor himself.

A deformity of the pelvic bones affected his carriage and his gait. His sinewy body was prodigiously strong, but the strain of holding himself straight and moving with a fluidity not natural to him caused him severe muscular tension and cramping; for the easing of which I brought home one day an almond-scented rubbing oil.

But I had hardly begun gliding my oiled palms down the long muscles on either side of his spine when he began to tremble, then to shake with dreadful, racking sobs. I was bewildered that I could have hurt him so. My touch was light, and in any case he was normally stoical, being accustomed to chronic aches and pains.

Now he gasped, "No, don't!" and twisted violently away. He sat rocking and crying, his clasped hands wedged tight between his knees as if to prevent even his own touch on his body.

This was not pain. It was grief.

I saw that while in my bed sheer lust carried him triumphant on its tide, the everyday intimacy of casual contact was more than he could bear. Even as an infant he must have been rarely *touched* by anyone, let alone touched kindly. The undemanding pressure of my hands had wakened in him the vast, deep-rooted anguish of that irremediable loss.

I could no more withstand this upwelling of sorrow—a child's sorrow ravaging a man's body—than he could. All childhoods leave scars. Old hurts of my own throbbed in bitter sympathy with his. I fled to walk by the lake, filled with impotent rage against the common cruelty and indifference of humankind. And I cursed my own deficiency in that same cruelty and indifference; placed as I was, how much pity could *I* afford?

But I could not let the matter rest. The next day, with great difficulty, I persuaded him to let me try again on the understanding that he must stop me when his emotions threatened to overpower him. He did so, saying in a strained whisper, "Thank you, Christine!" Persevering in this fashion we extended his endurance to well over an hour at a time. Rubbing him down became a routine for which I searched out fine oils and salves on my forays above ground.

It was strange, how the slow, wordless process of kneading the knots and torsions out of his muscles wove a spell of peace over us both. In those placid hours of mute, almost animal tranquility nothing was to be heard but our breathing, mine effortful and deliberate, his marked by the occasional painful gasp or deep, surrendering sigh.

I had no great experience at massage, and, as I discovered, no healing gift. I could soothe and sweeten, but I could not mend. Yet he came to openly look forward to these sessions, which he clearly valued and benefited by.

So did I. In the attentive handling of his gnarled and canted body I could express my tenderer feelings without putting myself at his mercy, which quality I knew to be in short supply and that unreliable at best.

For his more intractable pains I bought laudanum, which he hated because it clouded his mind but accepted from me when all else failed.

Abroad alone in the noisy streets, I looked at the tradesmen bustling about their business, the ladies with their parasols or their muffs, the swaggering gentlemen swinging their canes, the very sparrows pecking the pavements; and I considered escape. Once or twice I thought I saw Raoul, but this was only fancy. Nor did I need his help, nor anyone's.

At any time I might have betrayed Erik to the authorities. Or I might have silently slipped away with enough of his money to buy my passage back to Sweden, or to anywhere.

But what could it mean, to wander freely in the wide, inhospitable world, when the dark angel whose life I shared owned all Paris at night? How could social chatter or the giggling gossip of friends rival the joy of spinning melody out of empty air, with Erik standing rapt like some lightning-struck Titan or else raising his awful head to embrace my song and lift it with his own supple and ravishing voice?

Whenever I seriously contemplated flight, I had only to remind myself that beyond the Rue Scribe gate I was just another woman going about her domestic business. In the house under the Opéra, I was someone potent enough to raise fallen Lucifer into the splendor of Heaven, again and again. Underground, we soared.

And I had given my word.

I cannot pretend to know all that he felt. My absences seemed to increase his attachment to me. Perhaps the risk brought him to the sharpened edge of life, reminding him of his younger, more adventuresome years. I do know that he dreaded that one day I would fly for good, lured by some stranger's wholesome beauty. It need not be Raoul. Any man was handsomer than Erik.

Often he followed me clandestinely through the streets. I made no objection. I had observed how the lovers of pretty singers imagined treachery where there was none. So long as Erik could see for himself how I comported myself when I was abroad "alone," he would be better able to hold his fear and suspicion in check.

I always knew he had been tracking me when he questioned me upon my return: whom had I seen or spoken to, by what route had I gone to the stationer's? At my answers (which he knew by his own furtive observation to be true) he exuded such a vibrancy of relief and joy that my own heart was invariably lightened.

But I wondered sometimes whether it was right and good to make him happy, for by any sane standard he was a wicked man.

I could not deny that it pleased me to dissolve his rages, griefs, and anxieties into something approaching, and sometimes far exceeding, contentment. Doing so made life with him pleasanter, of course; but beyond that, such ease as I could grant him seemed all the sweeter in the giving for being completely gratuitous.

Was I, then, wicked too? I went into a church one damp afternoon and prayed for guidance on this point. As usual in my experience none was forthcoming, so I used the time to assess my spiritual situation, and, insofar as it was perceptible to me, his.

All that I had been taught told me that in due course God must condemn Erik to the torments of Hell. To pardon him would be outrageous: what of Joseph Buquet, whose murder cried out to Heaven? Or the woman crushed beneath the counterweight, which Erik had thrown down in a fit of pique? "Thou shalt not kill"; having made that law, God must surely punish a murderer.

Not being God, however, I could do otherwise, like disobedient Eve. I already had: I had comforted the wicked, and gladly.

As I saw it, I could repent of my error and henceforth grudgingly yield up only the bare minimum of my promise. Or I could willfully continue to offer to Erik, for whom life in this world was already Hell and always had been, such solace as I had power to confer.

This latter course, for good or ill, was the one I chose. How could I not? It might be all the mercy there is.

That evening he sat behind me brushing my hair as I read aloud from the *Revue Musicale* about a new production of *Tristan and Isolde*. He interrupted to remark how my long tresses glowed in the lamplight. Had I taken off my hat and veil to let the sun shine on my hair, chancing recognition and exposure?

"It was raining," I said. "I spent much of the day sheltering in a church, and of course I kept my hat on. But the softened air is doubtless healthy for the hair even so."

With a sigh he pressed his naked face to the back of my neck. My blood leaped. He stroked my skin, following with his fingertips the beat of that thick pulse which shook me softly from root to crown. "How can you give up the freedom of the day and come back to this dim grave where neither sunlight nor rain ever falls?"

What could I answer that he did not already know? Wordless, I leaned my throat into his hand, the warm, muscular, bloodstained hand of the Minotaur of the Opéra labyrinth.

"But I forget," he added in low and husky tones, "you are a northern girl and used to darkness from your childhood. Turn and kiss your darkness, Christine; he loves and misses you."

The sun's finest glories—its corona and its great, flaring prominences—only show when the moon eclipses it completely; he had told me that. I meant to remind him of it as he bent close over me, shrouding my face in his shadow. But I had already given up my mouth and my breath, and later, I forgot.

Another time, having been delayed an hour past when I had said I would be back, I found unlocked the door to the gunpowder room (which he had planned to blow up, obliterating himself along with the Opéra and everyone in it, if I had refused him). While I was gone he must have paced among the neatly stacked little barrels of death, goading the sleeping demon of his fury to make sure it was still alive and purposeful in case I failed to reappear.

I did not become pregnant. God cannot admire brainlessness in his creatures, to whom he has gone to the trouble to give very good brains indeed. In all likelihood Erik was sterile, like most sports of Nature. Still, I regularly used certain preparations to subdue my fertility as best I might. Erik agreed wholeheartedly with this practice. He said he had no wish to perpetuate the horrors of his own childhood (nor, I believe, to share my attention with a helpless and demanding infant).

We did quarrel sometimes, as couples do. The newspapers were a constant provocation, for Erik's political views were barbaric.

I maintained that the world would benefit from rather more kindness and mutual care than from less, as he himself had reason to know. He espoused brutal notions of social order, supporting his position with bloodcurdling accounts of punishments and tortures he had seen in his travels. As men are both wicked and foolish, he said, they must have priests to keep them penitent and kings to keep them obedient, and the harsher the better.

Sometimes he mocked my "naivete" and "tenderheartedness" so pitilessly that I left the room in tears. It always ended in his kissing my hands and begging a penance for having upset me; but his Draconian ideas never changed.

He deplored the new freedom of the press from government censorship but devoured news of sensational crimes, which excited his most wrathful responses: "Listen to this, Christine! A water carrier in Montmartre has beaten his infant daughter to death, having first burnt her in the kitchen fire. He threw her body into a bucket of slops and went to sleep in his bed. The French working man is the only brute beast in the world with the vote!"

Looking up from my sewing I replied as steadily as I could, "Then what a good thing that now, by law, his surviving children must go to school, where they can learn to be less brutal than their father and to use their votes intelligently."

"You cannot teach an ass to sing," he said scathingly, casting the newspaper down at his feet. "Republicanism is no more than government by brutes representing brutes."

I could not resist answering. "Yet some say that poor people are better off now, and that your 'brutes' do no worse than all the monarchs and dictators France has had in this century."

"Precisely the problem!" he said triumphantly. "There has been no political stability since the Terror, and there never will be so long as the mob is encouraged in rebellion. Without public order no nation can prosper, but your common man hates nothing so much as the rule of law."

I said, "Can *you* speak of the 'rule of law'?"

Bending upon me a very knowing and ironic glance he said, "Why, I think I know a little about it."

I saw that he referred to the rule of ***my*** law that he had accepted over his own conduct; and I had no ready answer.

He nodded approvingly. "Good, you had best not argue further. You are a fine student of music, but careless and ill-informed when it comes to other matters."

"I do the best I can," I retorted, "having little education myself except in music."

"Weak," he said, "a very weak answer, Christine. But you are of the weaker sex, so I suppose I must allow it; which is how your weakness weakens me." He held up his hand to check my objection. "This is implicit in our bargain, by which you secured the right to wind me round your little finger. I make no complaint. But do not imagine your authority to be absolute, however compliantly I may bend to your will; I am a ugly man, not a stupid one."

"Erik," I said, "the last word I would ever apply to you is 'stupid.' Will you tell me plainly what you mean?"

"No more than I have said," he replied, and with that he got up and returned, humming to himself, to a project that he had recently begun behind locked doors.

A few days after this exchange, he invited me to accompany

him to the public execution of a convicted murderer outside La Roquette Prison. I accepted. I had never witnessed such a degrading spectacle but felt that I was sworn to share Erik's life as fully as I might. And I did not like him saying that I was weak.

As we joined the crowd of spectators (which was dismayingly large for such a happening, and on such a cold dawn), a man hissed sharply, "Look, Death Mask is here!" They drew aside before us. Erik strode the path thus made for him with princely hauteur, and I saw people reach furtively to touch his cloak as he passed. We ended much nearer to the guillotine than I wished to be.

Of what followed, the less said the better. The curious can still see such things for themselves.

My companion offered no comfort. Erik's scorn for the doomed criminal, the presiding officials and the watching crowd was boundless, his approval of the execution itself unclouded by any hint of empathy or horror. He dearly did not imagine himself pinned beneath the roaring blade, for all that he was guilty of extortion, two murders at least, and, I was sure, much else.

On the way home, profoundly disturbed by what we had witnessed, I said accusingly that the people had seemed to know him there, as if by his repeated presence.

"Yes, the habitués see me often," he replied, his mask gleaming pale as a skull in the dimness of our carriage. "But they do not know me. No one knows me but you, Christine."

"Yet I do *not* know," I said, "why you join the mob you profess to despise in this depraved and disgusting diversion!"

"To see done such justice as is to be had in this world," he said, "and to remind myself what death is. Also I like to think that my presence lends some distinction to the proceedings. They miss me when I am absent, and sometimes call upon the executioners to wait a little in case I am only delayed."

I never discovered whether he was joking about this. He was fully capable of it.

After that, I always went with him to La Roquette. I never grew used to it. Yet I went. The satisfaction he took in these gruesome displays forced me to acknowledge that subjection of his crueler impulses to my ban was not the same thing as change in his own character. It is very tempting to overestimate one's influence upon another.

It must also be said that, disdaining everyone equally, Erik did not share the common prejudices of the time. He did not hate the English or the Germans more than other nations, and he taught me to recognize the ingrained anti-Semitism and xenophobia of the French (which I had taken for granted) for the spiteful, willful ignorance that it was and is.

But he was no champion of the downtrodden; his sympathies were reserved entirely for himself. He frequently worked up a fine passion of resentment over the availability to others of advantages that he had never enjoyed. There was nothing to do but wait out these moods of bitter self-pity.

Nor could I persuade him away from the vengefulness his life had taught him. Given the nature of that life, it was perhaps arrogant of me to have tried.

As for the secret project conducted behind locked doors, it proved to be his gift to me that Christmas. I gave him a dressing gown sewn of velvet patches I had cut from discarded costumes. He gave me a replica in miniature of the Taj Mahal that he had carved and painted in wood. He had once visited that monument to tragic love to examine and memorize every detail, an adventure in itself that he recounted zestfully to me over our holiday meal.

Indeed, a whole lifetime of hitherto unshared incident was lavished upon me during my years with him, like fine wine poured eagerly for my delectation and delight.

Had I been older and more experienced, I might have tried to reply in kind. This would have been an error. He did not need a *past* from me, having a rather over-rich one of his own. It was my *present* that he desired, all the immediate hours and days that I had promised him. And these I gave with open hands.

No doubt some would rather hear that we fought incessantly, that I tired of him or he of me, that we failed each other and parted in mutual hatred and disillusion. Had we lived in some suburb or narrow street of Paris, or worse yet on some grand boulevard, we might have come to that. Many marriages are stoven and sunk on the rocks of Parisian life.

Now and again, he reminded me that he had intended for us to vacate the Opéra cellars and lead a "normal" life like everybody else. I was always quick to point out that he was not in the least like everybody else and for that matter, on the evidence at hand, neither was I; and eventually these objections ceased.

As the end of our time together drew near, he became markedly morose and irritable. I saw that he was already grieving.

I walked through the streets and squares in chilly rain and fitful sun that last winter, chafing unbearably for my freedom now that it loomed so close. More than once I nearly flung the key to the Rue

Scribe gate into the Seine. I longed to be borne quietly away on some gliding river-barge, empty-handed and friendless perhaps but bound by no pledge or promise.

At the same time I struggled to find some way to extend my time with Erik. I could not imagine a life without him. Restless and distraught, I thought of every possibility a hundred times over and rejected them all as many times.

It seemed to me that any meddling with the deadline I had set would undercut and cheapen all that we had achieved together, making a liar of me and a fool of him. Sooner or later our hard-won mastery of ourselves must surely decline into a wretched and debasing struggle for mastery of each other. I had first pledged myself to him in ignorance; now I knew the enormity of the task, and the thoughtless self-confidence of my youth was gone. How much longer could I trust myself to be bold enough, quick enough, steady enough, my instincts true enough, for both of us?

Whole lifetimes spun out in my mind as I searched for a different conclusion. But I could find nothing acceptable other than to keep to the terms of our bargain. It is when Faust tries to fix the transient moment beyond its natural term, saying "Stay, thou art fair!" that he is lost.

I wandered miserably through Erik's rooms, touching papers and furniture and books when what I ached to do was to touch him, to press him close with feverish possessiveness. I often felt his gaze upon me, scalding with similar, unspoken agony.

He now suffered odd spells of lassitude, sitting for long periods with the newspaper yet scarcely turning a page, his face white as marble and his forehead moistly gleaming. My questions about the nature of this unwonted fatigue were met with withering rebuffs. But when I came upon him mixing up a dose of laudanum for himself, I demanded an explanation. He admitted that for some time he had been experiencing severe pains in his teeth.

The condition must have begun years before. Still, I blamed myself. If I had not got in the habit of bringing down the dainties left me by the dancers and chorus girls, he might not have indulged so immoderately his taste for sweets.

Now abscesses had developed, this much I could determine; and I was very worried. But Erik flatly refused to go to a dentist, who must of necessity see his face. So these sieges of toothache came and went, borne by him with his customary fortitude.

We continued our studies, although I was in poor voice, being easily brought to tears by emotional music (and there is no other kind in opera). The last piece that he sang through for me was "Why do you wake me," from *Werther* (we had been discussing the French insistence upon verbal articulation at the expense of beauty of tone).

At the end, he rose from the piano and sharply shut its lid. The spell of Werther's plaint was broken as if Erik had snapped the neck of a living thing between his hands.

"When you know that I am dead," he said, "—and I will make sure you learn of it, Christine—I beg you to come back here to bury me. I hope you will continue to wear my ring until that time, when I ask that you be good enough to return it to me with your prayers before you cover me over."

He meant his mother's ring, a wreath of tiny flowers in pale gold that I had worn since the night of *Lohengrin*. I turned the ring on my finger, trying to take comfort from the fact that he spoke as if he meant to go on living in my absence. But living in what manner? I could no longer avoid that question, which had been burning in my thoughts:

"When I have gone, will you keep to your promise to be good?"

"Why should I?" he growled, shooting me an evil look. Then he quoted the monster of Mary Shelley's *Frankenstein* (a book he had read, many times over by the look of its pages), "'Misery made me a fiend. Make me happy and I shall again be virtuous.'"

My heart pounded. Suddenly we stood at the edge of a precipice. "Erik, you gave your word!"

"I am not some titled nobleman," he sneered. "I have no honor to preserve."

I said, "You wrong yourself to say so. You have held to our agreement as only an honorable man would."

He turned away without replying, dabbing at his mouth with his handkerchief, and fell to moodily rearranging the porcelain flowers on their shelf. I heard every tiny tick and brush of sound of these small actions, for I was listening harder than I ever had in my life. In my mind a cowardly voice said, *Fool, have you forgotten that he is a monster? Look at him! He will never let you go! You should have fled when you had the chance!*

"So you think I have behaved honorably?" he said at last. "Well, if I have I am sorry for it."

Stung out of my fearful reverie I answered with some heat, "You have no right to be! You have been happier these past years than most men are in a lifetime. Deny it if you can!"

"I do not deny it!" He turned to me with inflamed eyes, his hands clenched at his sides. "For pity's sake, Christine, must I beg? *Don't leave.* I love you. I need you. Stay with me!"

I had been braced for sarcasm and threats; this naked entreaty pierced me through. I shook my head, unable to speak.

"Set new terms, make any rules you like," he urged. "I will keep to them, you know I can!"

"*No,*" I said, "no, Erik. It is time for you to see how you get along without your Angel of Conscience. I want my freedom, which I have won fairly."

He stared at me with those burning eyes. The walls of his house pressed in upon me like dungeon walls, and I felt a fierce passion for my liberty, sparked by the dread of losing it again before ever regaining it. In my fear, I hated him.

He said, "What if I say you must return to live with me for six months of every year? It is a nice, classical solution."

I answered angrily, "It is no solution at all!"

"I don't care." His voice rose toward the loss of control that I—and perhaps he, too—dreaded. "I want *more*!"

"Erik," I said, my mouth as dry as ashes, "you are above all a musician, and musicians know better than anyone that at some point there is no ***more***—no more beats to the measure, no more notes to the phrase, no more loudness or softness or purity or vibrato—or else music becomes mere noise: incoherent, formless and ugly. You know this to be true."

Of course he knew it. On this principle was based all his instruction and all our achievement together. I wished that he had been wearing his mask, for it was torture to watch his face.

At length he said bitterly, "You have had too good a teacher." He shielded his eyes with his hand, as he did when he wished to listen closely to my singing without visual distraction. "Have you been happy here, Christine?"

"I have been happy," I said. "I am not happy at this moment, but I ***have*** been happy."

"Good," he said; and that was all.

We spent those last nights stroking and kissing one another between fitful sleeps, pressed together to the point of pain and past it. He stayed till morning in my bed. I would have held him back had he tried to go, but once he slept I quickly put the candle out. I dared not look long at his face, open and unguarded in sleep (his utmost, cleverest plea and offering), for fear that my resolve would crumble to nothing.

He was a wise child too, but I was wiser. I knew how to defend us from each other and protect us from ourselves.

A week before I was to leave, I came in from a long, troubled walk and saw him slumped at his writing desk. When I spoke to him, he answered faintly in a language that I did not know. Alarmed, I hurried to him and caught hold of his arm to bring him to himself again. My hand flew back: his whole body quaked with massive, deep-seated shudders. At my touch he collapsed, seized by such violent chills that I thought he was having convulsions.

I held him tightly to keep him from injuring himself and to warm him as best I could; and because I had to do something and could think of nothing else. When the shaking subsided, I helped him to his bed. I saw that the infection in his jaws had attacked again with terrifying virulence: his face was swollen, his skin was searingly hot, and it was evident that he did not know me.

In his first lucid moment I implored him to let me bring a doctor. He was adamant against it, made me swear to bring no one, and would not be persuaded otherwise by anything I said.

He had committed no crimes since my taking up residence with him, of that I am certain; but he still had old deaths to answer for, and he was absolutely unwilling to risk exposure to the claims of the law. Perhaps now he could imagine his own goblin head under the blade at La Roquette before the greedy eyes of the crowd.

I imagined it; and I could not bear the thought.

So I nursed him as best I could, with drugs, folk remedies, and treatments that I found described in the medical texts on his shelves. It was not enough.

He had no pain, the nerves in his teeth being destroyed by then, but fever devoured him before my eyes. He ate nothing and kept down little of the medicines I prepared for him. At last he sank into a heavy sleep from which he rarely roused.

Late one afternoon he said, "I am so thirsty, Christine; the Devil is coming for me, and his fires are very hot!"

"No," I said, "God is coming to apologize to you for your afflictions. It is His burning remorse that you feel."

"What angel shall I send to comfort and befriend you when I am gone?" he asked. "The Angel of Death?"

"Don't talk, it only tires you." I poured him some water, spilling more than went into the cup.

"Never mind," he muttered when he had taken a few dribbling sips, "that angry angel has not done my bidding for some time now.

But I should curse you somehow before I die."

"*Curse* me?" I cried. "Oh, Erik, why?"

His febrile gaze fastened hungrily upon my face. "Because you will be alive and abroad in the world, and I will be dead, down here. Your hair will glow like polished chestnuts in the sunlight when you throw off your hat and veil. If I had had such hair, I would have ventured onto the stage despite everything. With really good makeup, would it have been so bad?"

"I hate my hair!" I said. "I'll cut it off."

"It will grow back," he answered dreamily. "As many times as you cut it, it will grow back more beautiful than ever, for the delight of other men."

"Well, go on and curse me, then!" I said fiercely, but other words echoed in my thoughts: *I will not let thee go, unless thou bless me.* Fresh, amazing tears flooded my eyes; I had thought myself drained dry as the Gobi by then.

"Oh, don't cry," Erik said with feeble exasperation. "What have you to cry about? Now I cannot fail my promise. Look, I will make you another: should this 'honor' you have required of me win me a few hours' respite from Hell, I will spend them singing for you. Listen sometimes and you may hear me." Then he exclaimed, "My opera! Where is my *Don Juan*?"

He struggled to sit up, gazing around the candlelit room with that huge-pupiled stare that I remembered from my father's deathbed. It is an unmistakable look, and seeing it again all but drove the heart right out of me.

"Your work is safe," I said. "I will get it published—"

"No, no," he broke in, with some force. "Leave it. I have told you, that music is not for this epoch. You will not let them come picking and clucking over my miserable carcass, will you? Be as kind toward my music. Bury it with me; bury it all."

He caught my hand and pressed it to his malformed cheek, and only when I agreed to do as he asked did he release me. Then he sank back, white-faced and panting, on his pillows. I saw that his time was near, and that he knew it.

"Let me at least fetch you a priest," I said, for I knew he had been born into a Catholic household.

He said, "What for? I would only frighten him to death, adding to my burden of sins. You be my priest, Christine."

So I lay down in his bed and he breathed horrific details of his past into my ear. I told him that if he truly repented of the evil he had done he must be forgiven. He said, "Just *listen*, Christine." So I did; though I dozed through much of this grim catalog, being very tired by then.

The chiming fugue of his clocks all striking woke me. It was eight at night. I opened my eyes to find him quietly watching me, his face—that freakish face that was now better known to me than my own—just inches from mine. His lips were crusted from the fever and his poisoned breath fouled the air between us.

"Good, you are awake in time to see a wonder," he whispered. "This ugly monster, the Phantom of the Opera, will make himself vanish before your very eyes; and before the eyes of everyone else there will appear, as if out of nowhere, a beautiful young woman of passion, talent, and valiant character."

I said something, "Oh, don't," or "Please." It makes no difference what I said.

His eyelids drooped and the shallow rasping of his breathing grew more regular. Unable to keep my own aching eyes open, I slept. At some later point, I heard him remark in a surprised and drowsy tone, "Do you hear birds singing, Christine? Imagine, songbirds, in a cellar! Open a door, let them out."

That night he died.

Left alone with the cooling remains of the singular creature with whom I had spent a lifetime's passion in a handful of incandescent years, I thought I would die myself. I wished that I might, stretched out beside his corpse in that damp and fetid bed with its curtains of fresh forest green.

In a while I rose, and found that I could scarcely bear to look at him. Absent the faintest animation, his face was a repulsive parody of a human face in a state of ruin and decay. I closed his eyes and set his mask in place to hide the worst.

I said no prayers then; I was too angry and too weary and could barely drive myself to do what needed doing. I washed him and dressed him in the formal attire that he had always favored and put the ring of little flowers on his finger.

My choice would have been to turn him adrift on the lake in his boat, a hundred candles flaming on the thwarts; or to build him a pyre on the bank, like Shelley's pyre. But by then I was exhausted from tending him, from grief, and from the not inconsiderable labor of preparing his lifeless body for its last rest.

So, with strength drawn from I know not where, I disposed him decently on my own clean bed, with his musical manuscripts piled round him as he had wished. I covered him with his opera cloak and used the patchwork robe that I had given him to cushion his head. Against his lunar skin the velvet folds glowed rich and deep, like a sumptuous setting for some pale, exotic jewel.

Seeing his face so remote and stony on that makeshift pillow, I understood that we touched no longer, he and I. We sped on invisible, divergent trajectories, driven farther apart by every passing instant. Nothing remained to keep me there.

In a trance of exhaustion I packed a few belongings and keepsakes, left the house, and tripped the concealed triggers he had shown me. A long, deep thundering sound followed, and I tasted stone-dust in the air.

Panic seized me: how like him it would be, to contrive beforehand to bring the whole Paris Opéra crashing down in ruins upon his grave!

But all was as he had told me, according to his design: stone blocks placed within the walls rumbled into their chiseled beds, sealing off every entrance and air shaft of the Phantom's home. Erik slept in a tomb more secure than Pharaoh's pyramid.

I paced beside the underground lake, spent and weeping. Now I prayed. I was afraid for him. Apart from everything else, if he had somehow willed himself to die then that was the sin of suicide, which grows from the sin of despair.

Yet this possibility is part of every strong union. Someone departs first, and the one left behind decides whether to die, or to stay on awhile, chewing the dusty flavor of words like "desolate" and "bereft."

In the end, fearing that somebody might have heard the noise or felt the reverberations and might come to investigate, I roused myself to the final task of sinking the little boat in the lake. Then I let myself out by the Rue Scribe gate for the last time, five years and eleven days from the night of my debut in *Faust*.

Rain had fallen overnight; puddles gleamed. A draggled white cat sheltering in a doorway watched me go.

Of my life since there is little to tell. My aged guardian having died, I was able to make arrangements to live quietly in Paris under my own name. Hardly anyone remembered the Phantom of the Opéra and the deeds attributed to him, for great cities thrive on novelty and their citizens' memories are short (that is why M. Leroux felt free to publish his nonsense later on).

I tried to avoid knowledgeable or inquisitive people. To those who knew me I said that I had been driven away by the family of a noble admirer and had been singing since in opera houses in distant lands (Raoul, I learned, had emigrated to America in the spring of 1881, shortly after my own disappearance).

While reestablishing myself, I found I could live well enough. During my years underground I had published some vocal pieces using my father's name. I continued to sell my compositions, and drew investment income as well from the remains of Erik's fortune.

But singing on the stage again disappointed me. My own voice seemed dull, and audiences—no matter how they applauded—even duller. Without an edge of fear and a need for approval, no singer can bring an audience, or a performance, to life. Having resumed my career with some success, I retired early and advertised for students. I found that I loved teaching and did it well.

Rejoicing daily in my freedom, I was nevertheless lonelier than I could bear all by myself. I took comfort where I could; there are good men from that time of whom I still think fondly. But none ever came to me trailing the clouds of sinister and turbulent glory in which the Opéra Ghost had enfolded me.

During the Great War I volunteered as a nurse. Not surprisingly, I dealt calmly with the most frightful facial wounds. Erik's awful countenance would not have been out of place on those wards, just as his music would suit perfectly the emerging character of the new century. Perhaps he was a true phantom after all, as well as a brilliant, cruel, afflicted man: a phantom of this brilliant, cruel, afflicted future.

My hospital work brought me to the admiring attention of a doctor several years my junior, and I married late in life for the first time, or so it seemed. The marriage was good, being founded in the shared trials and mutual respect of wartime service.

To the day he died, René never knew the truth of my life before. If God holds that deception against me, I stand ready to answer for it along with everything else.

Nowadays I coach voice at the Opéra, although my own instrument has of course decayed with time. A gratifying number of well-known singers have trained with me over the years. My students are like my children and I help them as I can, awarding to the needier ones small stipends out of Erik's money. He would not approve.

Does it seem incredible, to have gone from such a bizarre, outlaw existence to a placid one indistinguishable from millions of others? Yet many people walk through the world hiding shocking memories. I glance sometimes at a man or a woman in a shop or cafe, at a friend or a student sitting over a coffee with me, and I wonder what towering joys and howling depths lie concealed behind the mask of ordinary life that each one wears.

Even extraordinary lives are not entirely as they seem. Recently I discovered that the base of Erik's spaniel inkwell (into which I have just now dipped my pen) contains a secret drawer. Inside I found a sheaf of receipts all dated early in April, 1881, made out to "Erik Rouen" for large cash payments from him to various men, in settlement of the formidable debts of a third party: Raoul de Chagny.

Underneath lay a pile of bank drafts running from that time until June1885, four or five of them per year, for considerable amounts of money. Each had been signed by Erik in Paris, and cashed by Raoul de Chagny in the city of New Orleans.

Finally, my shaking fingers drew out an envelope, posted from New Orleans and addressed to Erik. It contained a yellowed news clipping in English, dated July 17, 1885, announcing the marriage of Raoul de Chagny, a rising young dealer in cotton, and Juliet Ravenal, daughter of a prominent local broker and businessman. With this notice was enclosed a final bank draft (for yet another of those large sums that Erik had been in the inexplicable habit of mislaying) returned to him uncashed. There was no letter.

The message was clear enough: Raoul did not come back for me because Erik paid him not to. My Vicomte had gone to America as a Remittance Man! At least he had had the decency (or pride or whatever it was) to refuse further bribes from his rival once established in his new country.

I wept over those papers and all that they implied. But I smiled, too, at the resourcefulness, the cunning, and the sheer determination of my incomparable monster, who had thus firmly secured his victory without breaking his promise to me.

Age robs me of easy sleep, and many nights I lie awake remembering the little glass shoe full of centimes; and the shivering poodle stinking of lamp-oil; and the brush being drawn through my heavy hair by a man who sits behind me, where I cannot see his face until I turn. In the dark, I listen for some echo of the radiant voice of my teacher, my brother, my lover and accomplished master of my body's joys, that dire, disfigured angel with whom I wrestled for over a thousand days and nights in all the youthful vigor of my hunger and my pride.

My hair is short now, in the modern style. It has turned quite white.

The Comte de Chagny (Raoul's title since his elder brother's death) arrived this month from America to see to his French holdings. He came to the Opéra asking after me. I avoided him, and he has gone away again.

Awaiting my own exit, I live my days in this brash and cynical present as other people do. But I nourish my soul on the sweet pangs of looking back, more than forty years now, to the time when the Opéra Ghost and I lived together underground, in a candlelit world of passion and music.

I have thought of writing an opera about it, but time seems short and I know my limitations. Someone else will write it, someday. They will get the story wrong, of course; but perhaps, all the same, the music will be right.

UNICORN TAPESTRY

HOLD ON," FLORIA SAID. "I know what you're going to say: I agreed not to take any new clients for a while. But wait till I tell you—you're not going to believe this—first phone call, setting up an initial appointment, he comes out with what his problem is: 'I seem to have fallen victim to a delusion of being—a vampire.'"

"Christ H. God!" cried Lucille delightedly. "Just like that, over the telephone?"

"When I recovered my aplomb, so to speak, I told him that I prefer to wait with the details until our first meeting, which is tomorrow."

They were sitting on the tiny terrace outside the staff room of the clinic, a converted town house on the upper West Side. Floria spent three days a week here and the remaining two in her office on Central Park South where she saw private clients like this new one. Lucille, always gratifyingly responsive, was Floria's most valued professional friend. Clearly enchanted with Floria's news, she sat eagerly forward in her chair, eyes wide behind Coke-bottle lenses.

She said, "Do you suppose he thinks he's a revivified corpse?"

Below, down at the end of the street, Floria could see two kids skidding their skateboards near a man who wore a woolen cap and a heavy coat despite the May warmth. He was leaning against a wall. He had been there when Floria had arrived at the clinic this morning. If corpses walked, some, not nearly revivified enough, stood in plain view in New York.

"I'll have to think of a delicate way to ask," she said.

"How did he come to you, this 'vampire'?"

"He was working in an upstate college, teaching and doing research, and all of a sudden he just disappeared—vanished, literally, without a trace. A month later he turned up here in the city. The faculty dean at the school knows me and sent him to see me."

Lucille gave her a sly look. "So you thought, ahah, do a little favor for a friend, this looks classic and easy to transfer if need be: repressed intellectual blows stack and runs off with spacey chick, something like that."

"You know me too well," Floria said with a rueful smile.

"Huh," grunted Lucille. She sipped ginger ale from a chipped white mug. "I don't take panicky middle-aged men anymore, they're too depressing. And you shouldn't be taking this one, intriguing as he sounds."

Here comes the lecture, Floria told herself.

Lucille got up. She was short, heavy, prone to wearing loose garments that swung about her like ceremonial robes. As she paced, her hem brushed at the flowers starting up in the planter boxes that rimmed the little terrace. "You know damn well this is just more overwork you're loading on. Don't take this guy; refer him."

Floria sighed. "I know, I know. I promised everybody I'd slow down. But you said it yourself just a minute ago—it looked like a simple favor. So what do I get? Count Dracula, for God's sake! Would you give that up?"

Fishing around in one capacious pocket, Lucille brought out a dented package of cigarettes and lit up, scowling. "You know, when you give me advice I try to take it seriously. Joking aside, Floria, what am I supposed to say? I've listened to you moaning for months now, and I thought we'd figured out that what you need is to shed some pressure, to start saying no—and here you are insisting on a new case. You know what I think: you're hiding in other people's problems from a lot of your own stuff that you should be working on.

"Okay, okay, don't glare at me. Be pigheaded. Have you gotten rid of Chubs, at least?" This was Floria's code name for a troublesome client named Kenny whom she'd been trying to unload for some time.

Floria shook her head.

"What gives with you? It's weeks since you swore you'd dump him! Trying to do everything for everybody is wearing you out. I bet you're still dropping weight. Judging by the very unbecoming circles under your eyes, sleeping isn't going too well, either. Still no dreams you can remember?"

"Lucille, don't nag. I don't want to talk about my health."

"Well, what about his health—Dracula's? Did you suggest that he have a physical before seeing you? There might be something physiological—"

"You're not going to be able to whisk him off to an M.D. and out of my hands," Floria said wryly. "He told me on the phone that he wouldn't consider either medication or hospitalization."

Involuntarily she glanced down at the end of the street. The woolen-capped man had curled up on the sidewalk at the foot of the building, sleeping or passed out or dead. The city was tottering with sickness. Compared with that wreck down there and others like him, how sick could this "vampire" be, with his cultured baritone voice, his self-possessed approach?

"And you won't consider handing him off to somebody else," Lucille said.

"Well, not until I know a little more. Come on, Luce—wouldn't you want at least to know what he looks like?"

Lucille stubbed out her cigarette against the low parapet. Down below a policeman strolled along the street ticketing parked cars. He didn't even look at the man lying at the corner of the building. They watched his progress without comment. Finally Lucille said, "Well, if you won't drop Dracula, keep me posted on him, will you?"

He entered the office on the dot of the hour, a gaunt but graceful figure. He was impressive. Wiry gray hair, worn short, emphasized the massiveness of his face with its long jaw, high cheekbones, and granite cheeks grooved as if by winters of hard weather. His name, typed in caps on the initial information sheet that Floria proceeded to fill out with him, was Edward Lewis Weyland.

Crisply he told her about the background of the vampire incident, describing in caustic terms his life at Cayslin College: the pressures of collegial competition, interdepartmental squabbles, student indifference, administrative bungling. History has limited use, she knew, since memory distorts; still, if he felt most comfortable establishing the setting for his illness, that was as good a way to start off as any.

At length his energy faltered. His angular body sank into a slump, his voice became flat and tired as he haltingly worked up to the crucial event: night work at the sleep lab, fantasies of blood-drinking as he watched the youthful subjects of his dream research slumbering, finally an attempt to act out the fantasy with a staff member at the college. He had been repulsed; then panic had assailed him. Word would get out, he'd be fired, blacklisted forever. He'd bolted. A nightmare period followed—he offered no details. When he had come to his senses he'd seen that just what he feared, the ruin of his career, would come from his running away. So he'd phoned the dean, and now here he was.

Throughout this recital she watched him diminish from the dignified academic who had entered her office to a shamed and frightened man hunched in his chair, his hands pulling fitfully at each other.

"What are your hands doing?" she said gently. He looked blank. She repeated the question.

He looked down at his hands. "Struggling," he said.

"With what?"

"The worst," he muttered. "I haven't told you the worst." She had never grown hardened to this sort of transformation. His long fingers busied themselves fiddling with a button on his jacket while he explained painfully that the object of his "attack" at Cayslin had been a woman. Not young but handsome and vital, she had first caught his attention earlier in the year during a *festschrift*—an honorary seminar—for a retiring professor.

A picture emerged of an awkward Weyland, lifelong bachelor, seeking this woman's warmth and suffering her refusal. Floria knew she should bring him out of his past and into his here-and-now, but he was doing so beautifully on his own that she was loath to interrupt.

"Did I tell you there was a rapist active on the campus at this time?" he said bitterly. "I borrowed a leaf from his book: I tried to take from this woman, since she wouldn't give. I tried to take some of her blood." He stared at the floor. "What does that mean—to take someone's blood?"

"What do you think it means?"

The button, pulled and twisted by his fretful fingers, came off. He put it into his pocket, the impulse, she guessed, of a fastidious nature. "Her energy," he murmured, "stolen to warm the aging scholar, the walking corpse, the vampire—myself."

His silence, his downcast eyes, his bent shoulders, all signaled a man brought to bay by a life crisis. Perhaps he was going to be the kind of client therapists dream of and she needed so badly these days: a client intelligent and sensitive enough, given the companionship of a professional listener, to swiftly unravel his own mental tangles. Exhilarated by his promising start, Floria restrained herself from trying to build on it too soon. She made herself tolerate the silence, which lasted until he said suddenly, "I notice that you make no notes as we speak. Do you record these sessions on tape?"

A hint of paranoia, she thought; not unusual. "Not without your knowledge and consent, just as I won't send for your personnel file from Cayslin without your knowledge and consent. I do, however, write notes after each session as a guide to myself and in order to have a record in case of any confusion about anything we do or say here. I can promise you that I won't show my notes or speak of you by name to anyone—except Sharpe at Cayslin, of course, and even then only as much as is strictly necessary—without your written permission. Does that satisfy you?"

"I apologize for my question," he said. "The ...incident left me ...very nervous; a condition that I hope to get over with your help."

The time was up. When he had gone, she stepped outside to check with Hilda, the receptionist she shared with four therapists here at the Central Park South office. Hilda always sized up new clients in the waiting room.

Of this one she said, "Are you sure there's anything wrong with that guy? I think I'm in love."

WAITING AT THE OFFICE for a group of clients to assemble Wednesday evening, Floria dashed off some notes on the "vampire."

> Client described incident, background. No history of mental illness, no previous experience of therapy. Personal history so ordinary you almost don't notice how bare it is: only child of German immigrants, schooling normal, field work in anthropology, academic posts leading to Cayslin College professorship. Health good, finances adequate, occupation satisfactory, housing pleasant (though presently installed in a N.Y. hotel); never married, no kids, no family, no religion, social life strictly job-related; leisure—says he likes to drive. Reaction to question about drinking, but no signs of alcohol problems. Physically very smooth-

> moving for his age (over fifty) and height; catlike, alert. Some apparent stiffness in the midsection—slight protective stoop—tightening up of middle age? Paranoic defensiveness? Voice pleasant, faint accent (German-speaking childhood at home). Entering therapy condition of consideration for return to job.

What a relief: his situation looked workable with a minimum of strain on herself. Now she could defend to Lucille her decision to do therapy with the "vampire."

After all, Lucille was right. Floria did have problems of her own that needed attention, primarily her anxiety and exhaustion since her mother's death more than a year before. The breakup of Floria's marriage had caused misery, but not this sort of endless depression. Intellectually the problem was clear: with both her parents dead she was left exposed. No one stood any longer between herself and the inevitability of her own death. Knowing the source of her feelings didn't help: she couldn't seem to mobilize the nerve to work on them.

The Wednesday group went badly again. Lisa lived once more her experiences in the European death camps and everyone cried. Floria wanted to stop Lisa, turn her, extinguish the droning horror of her voice in illumination and release, but she couldn't see how to do it. She found nothing in herself to offer except some clever ploy out of the professional bag of tricks—dance your anger, have a dialog with yourself of those days—useful techniques when they flowed organically as part of a living process in which the therapist participated. But thinking out responses that should have been intuitive wouldn't work. The group and its collective pain paralyzed her. She was a dancer without a choreographer, knowing all the moves but unable to match them to the music these people made.

Rather than act with mechanical clumsiness she held back, did nothing, and suffered guilt. Oh God, the smart, experienced people in the group must know how useless she was here.

Going home on the bus she thought about calling up one of the therapists who shared the downtown office. He had expressed an interest in doing co-therapy with her under student observation. The Wednesday group might respond well to that. Suggest it to them next time? Having a partner might take pressure off Floria and revitalize the group, and if she felt she must withdraw he would be available to take over. Of course he might take over anyway and walk off with some of her clients.

Oh boy, terrific, who's paranoid now? Wonderful way to think about a good colleague. God, she hadn't even known she was considering chucking the group.

Had the new client, running from his "vampirism," exposed her own impulse to retreat? This wouldn't be the first time that Floria had obtained help from a client while attempting to give help. Her old supervisor, Rigby, said that such mutual aid was the only true therapy—the rest was fraud. What a perfectionist, old Rigby, and what a bunch of young idealists he'd turned out, all eager to save the world.

Eager, but not necessarily able. Jane Fennerman had once lived in the world, and Floria had been incompetent to save her. Jane, an absent member of tonight's group, was back in the safety of a locked ward, hazily gliding on whatever tranquilizers they used there.

Why still mull over Jane? she asked herself severely, bracing against the bus's lurching halt. Any client was entitled to drop out of therapy and commit herself. Nor was this the first time that sort of thing had happened in the course of Floria's career. Only this time she couldn't seem to shake free of the resulting depression and guilt.

But how could she have helped Jane more? How could you offer reassurance that life was not as dreadful as Jane felt it to be, that her fears were insubstantial, that each day was not a pit of pain and danger?

She was taking time during a client's canceled hour to work on notes for the new book. The writing, an analysis of the vicissitudes of salaried versus private practice, balked at every turn. She longed for an interruption to distract her circling mind.

Hilda put through a call from Cayslin College. It was Doug Sharpe, who had sent Dr. Weyland to her.

"Now that he's in your capable hands, I can tell people plainly that he's on what we call 'compassionate leave' and make them swallow it." Doug's voice seemed thinned by the long-distance connection. "Can you give me a preliminary opinion?"

"I need time to get a feel for the situation."

He said, "Try not to take too long. At the moment I'm holding off pressure to appoint someone in his place. His enemies up here—and a sharp-tongued bastard like him acquires plenty of those—are trying to get a search committee authorized to find someone else for the directorship of the Cayslin Center for the Study of Man."

"Of People," she corrected automatically, as she always did. "What do you mean, 'bastard'? I thought you liked him, Doug. 'Do you want me to have to throw a smart, courtly, old-school gent to Finney or MacGill?' Those were your very words." Finney was a Freudian with a mouth like a pursed-up little asshole and a mind to match, and MacGill was a primal yowler in a padded gym of an office.

She heard Doug tapping at his teeth with a pen or pencil. "Well," he said, "I have a lot of respect for him, and sometimes I could cheer him for mowing down some pompous moron up here. I can't deny, though, that he's earned a reputation for being an accomplished son-of-a-bitch and tough to work with. Too damn cold and self-sufficient, you know?"

"Mmm," she said. "I haven't seen that yet."

He said, "You will. How about yourself? How's the rest of your life?"

"Well, offhand, what would you say if I told you I was thinking of going back to art school?"

"What would I say? I'd say bullshit, that's what I'd say. You've had fifteen years of doing something you're good at, and now you want to throw all that out and start over in an area you haven't touched since Studio 101 in college? If God had meant you to be a painter, She'd have sent you to art school in the first place."

"I did think about art school at the time."

"The point is that you're good at what you do. I've been at the receiving end of your work and I know what I'm talking about. By the way, did you see that piece in the paper about Annie Barnes, from the group I was in? That's an important appointment. I always knew she'd wind up in Washington. What I'm trying to make clear to you is that your 'graduates' do too well for you to be talking about quitting. What's Morton say about that idea, by the way?"

Mort, a pathologist, was Floria's lover. She hadn't discussed this with him, and she told Doug so.

"You're not on the outs with Morton, are you?"

"Come on, Douglas, cut it out. There's nothing wrong with my sex life, believe me. It's everyplace else that's giving me trouble."

"Just sticking my nose into your business," he replied. "What are friends for?"

They turned to lighter matters, but when she hung up Floria felt glum. If her friends were moved to this sort of probing and kindly advice-giving, she must be inviting help more openly and more urgently than she'd realized.

The work on the book went no better. It was as if, afraid to expose her thoughts, she must disarm criticism by meeting all possible objections beforehand. The book was well and truly stalled—like everything else. She sat sweating over it, wondering what the devil was wrong with her that she was writing mush. She had two good books to her name already. What was this bottleneck with the third?

"BUT WHAT DO YOU THINK?" Kenny insisted anxiously. "Does it sound like my kind of job?"

"How do you feel about it?"

"I'm all confused, I told you."

"Try speaking for me. Give me the advice I would give you."

He glowered. "That's a real cop-out, you know? One part of me talks like you, and then I have a dialog with myself like a TV show about a split personality. It's all me that way; you just sit there while I do all the work. I want something from *you*."

She looked for the twentieth time at the clock on the file cabinet. This time it freed her. "Kenny, the hour's over."

Kenny heaved his plump, sulky body up out of his chair. "You don't care. Oh, you pretend to, but you don't really —"

"Next time, Kenny."

He stumped out of the office. She imagined him towing in his wake the raft of decisions he was trying to inveigle her into making for him. Sighing, she went to the window and looked out over the park, filling her eyes and her mind with the full, fresh green of late spring. Yet she felt dismal. In two years of treatment the situation with Kenny had remained a stalemate. He wouldn't go to someone else who might be able to help him, and she couldn't bring herself to kick him out, though she knew she must eventually. His puny tyranny couldn't conceal how soft and vulnerable he was.

Dr. Weyland had the next appointment. Floria found herself pleased to see him. She could hardly have asked for a greater contrast to Kenny: tall, lean, that august head that made her want to draw him, good clothes, nice big hands—altogether, a distinguished-looking man. Though he was informally dressed in slacks, light jacket, and tieless shirt, the impression he conveyed was one of impeccable leisure and reserve. He took not the padded chair preferred by most clients but the wooden one with the cane seat.

"Good afternoon, Dr. Landauer," he said gravely. "May I ask your judgment of my case?"

"I don't regard myself as a judge," she said. She decided to try to shift their discussion onto a first-name basis if possible. Calling this old-fashioned man by his first name so soon might seem artificial, but how could they get familiar enough to do therapy while addressing each other as "Dr. Landauer" and "Dr. Weyland" like two characters out of a vaudeville sketch?

"This is what I think, Edward," she continued. "We need to find out about this vampire incident—how it tied into your feelings about yourself, good and bad, at the time; what it did for you that led you to try to 'be' a vampire even though that was bound to complicate your life terrifically. The more we know, the closer we can come to figuring out how to insure that this vampire construct won't be necessary to you again."

"Does this mean that you accept me formally as a client?" he said.

Comes right out and says what's on his mind, she noted; no problem there. "Yes."

"Good. I too have a treatment goal in mind. I will need at some point a testimonial from you that my mental health is sound enough for me to resume work at Cayslin."

Floria shook her head. "I can't guarantee that. I can commit myself to work toward it, of course, since your improved mental health is the aim of what we do here together."

"I suppose that answers the purpose for the time being," he said. "We can discuss it again later on. Frankly, I find myself eager to continue our work today. I've been feeling very much better since I spoke with you, and I thought last night about what I might tell you today."

She had the distinct feeling of being steered by him; how important was it to him, she wondered, to feel in control? She said, "Edward, my own feeling is that we started out with a good deal of very useful verbal work, and that now is a time to try something a little different."

He said nothing. He watched her. When she asked whether he remembered his dreams he shook his head, no.

She said, "I'd like you to try to do a dream for me now, a waking dream. Can you close your eyes and daydream, and tell me about it?"

He closed his eyes. Strangely, he now struck her as less vulnerable rather than more, as if strengthened by increased vigilance.

"How do you feel now?" she said.

"Uneasy." His eyelids fluttered. "I dislike closing my eyes. What I don't see can hurt me."

"Who wants to hurt you?"

"A vampire's enemies, of course—mobs of screaming peasants with torches."

Translating into what, she wondered—young Ph.D.s pouring out of the graduate schools panting for the jobs of older men like Weyland? "Peasants, these days?"

"Whatever their daily work, there is still a majority of the stupid, the violent, and the credulous, putting their feather-brained faith in astrology, in this cult or that, in various branches of psychology."

His sneer at her was unmistakable. Considering her refusal to let him fill the hour his own way, this desire to take a swipe at her was healthy. But it required immediate and straightforward handling.

"Edward, open your eyes and tell me what you see."

He obeyed. "I see a woman in her early forties," he said, "clever-looking face, dark hair showing gray; flesh too thin for her bones, indicating either vanity or illness; wearing slacks and a rather creased batik blouse—describable, I think, by the term 'peasant style'—with a food stain on the left side."

Damn! Don't blush. "Does anything besides my blouse suggest a peasant to you?"

"Nothing concrete, but with regard to me, my vampire self, a peasant with a torch is what you could easily become."

"I hear you saying that my task is to help you get rid of your delusion, though this process may be painful and frightening for you."

Something flashed in his expression—surprise, perhaps alarm, something she wanted to get in touch with before it could sink away out of reach again. Quickly she said, "How do you experience your face at this moment?"

He frowned. "As being on the front of my head. Why?"

With a rush of anger at herself she saw that she had chosen the wrong technique for reaching that hidden feeling: she had provoked hostility instead. She said, "Your face looked to me just now like a mask for concealing what you feel rather than an instrument of expression."

He moved restlessly in the chair, his whole physical attitude tense and guarded. "I don't know what you mean."

"Will you let me touch you?" she said, rising.

His hands tightened on the arms of his chair, which protested in a sharp creak. He snapped, "I thought this was a talking cure."

Strong resistance to body work—ease up. "If you won't let me massage some of the tension out of your facial muscles, will you try to do it yourself?"

"I don't enjoy being made ridiculous," he said, standing and heading for the door, which clapped smartly to behind him.

She sagged back in her seat; she had mishandled him. Clearly her initial estimation of this as a relatively easy job had been wrong and had led her to move far too quickly with him. Certainly it was much too early to try body work. She should have developed a firmer level of trust first by letting him do more of what he did so easily and so well—talk.

The door opened. Weyland came back in and shut it quietly. He did not sit again but paced about the room, coming to rest at the window.

"Please excuse my rather childish behavior just now," he said. "Playing these games of yours brought it on."

"It's frustrating, playing games that are unfamiliar and that you can't control," she said. As he made no reply, she went on in a conciliatory tone, "I'm not trying to belittle you, Edward. I just need to get us off whatever track you were taking us down so briskly. My feeling is that you're trying hard to regain your old stability.

"But that's the goal, not the starting point. The only way to reach your goal is through the process, and you don't drive the therapy process like a train. You can only help the process happen, as though you were helping a tree grow."

"These games are part of the process?"

"Yes."

"And neither you nor I control the games?"

"That's right."

He considered. "Suppose I agree to try this process of yours; what would you want of me?"

Observing him carefully, she no longer saw the anxious scholar bravely struggling back from madness. Here was a different sort of man—armored, calculating. She didn't know just what the change signaled, but she felt her own excitement stirring, and that meant she was on the track of—something.

"I have a hunch," she said slowly, "that this vampirism extends further back into your past than you've told me and possibly right up into the present as well. I think it's still with you. My style of therapy stresses dealing with the now at least as much as the then; if the vampirism is part of the present, dealing with it on that basis is crucial."

Silence.

"Can you talk about being a vampire: being one now?"

"You won't like knowing," he said.

"Edward, try."

He said, "I hunt."

"Where? How? What sort of—of victims?"

He folded his arms and leaned his back against the window frame. "Very well, since you insist. There are a number of possibilities here in the city in summer. Those too poor to own air-conditioners sleep out on rooftops and fire escapes. But often, I've found, their blood is sour with drugs or liquor. The same is true of prostitutes. Bars are full of accessible people but also full of smoke and noise, and there too the blood is fouled. I must choose my hunting grounds carefully. Often I go to openings of galleries or evening museum shows or department stores on their late nights—places where women may be approached."

And take pleasure in it, she thought, if they're out hunting also—for acceptable male companionship. Yet he said he's never married. Explore where this is going. "Only women?"

He gave her a sardonic glance, as if she were a slightly brighter student than he had at first assumed.

"Hunting women is liable to be time-consuming and expensive. The best hunting is in the part of Central Park they call the Ramble, where homosexual men seek encounters with others of their kind. I walk there too at night."

Floria caught a faint sound of conversation and laughter from the waiting room; her next client had probably arrived, she realized, looking reluctantly at the clock. "I'm sorry, Edward, but our time seems to be—"

"Only a moment more," he said coldly. "You asked; permit me to finish my answer. In the Ramble I find someone who doesn't reek of alcohol or drugs, who seems healthy, and who is not insistent on 'hooking up' right there among the bushes. I invite such a man to my hotel. He judges me safe, at least: older, weaker than he is, unlikely to turn out to be a dangerous maniac. So he comes to my room. I feed on his blood."

"Now, I think, our time is up."

He walked out.

She sat torn between rejoicing at his admission of the delusion's persistence and dismay that his condition was so much worse than she had first thought. Her hope of having an easy time with him vanished. His initial presentation had been just that—a performance, an act. Forced to abandon it, he had dumped on her this lump of material, too much—and too strange—to take in all at once.

Her next client liked the padded chair, not the wooden one that Weyland had sat in during the first part of the hour. Floria started to move the wooden one back. The armrests came away in her hands.

She remembered him starting up in protest against her proposal of touching him. The grip of his fingers had fractured the joints, and the shafts now lay in splinters on the floor.

Floria wandered into Lucille's room at the clinic after the staff meeting. Lucille was lying on the couch with a wet cloth over her eyes.

"I thought you looked green around the gills today," Floria said. "What's wrong?"

"Big bash last night," said Lucille in sepulchral tones. "I think I feel about the way you do after a session with Chubs. You haven't gotten rid of him yet, have you?"

"No. I had him lined up to see Marty instead of me last week, but damned if he didn't show up at my door at his usual time. It's a lost cause. What I wanted to talk to you about was Dracula."

"What about him?"

"He's smarter, tougher, and sicker than I thought, and maybe I'm even less competent than I thought, too. He's already walked out on me once—I almost lost him. I never took a course in treating monsters."

Lucille groaned. "Some days they're all monsters." This from Lucille, who worked longer hours than anyone else at the clinic, to the despair of her husband. She lifted the cloth, refolded it, and placed it carefully across her forehead. "And if I had ten dollars for every client who's walked out on me … Tell you what: I'll trade you Madame X for him, how's that? Remember Madame X, with the jangling bracelets and the parakeet eye makeup and the phobia about dogs? Now she's phobic about things dropping on her out of the sky. Just wait—it'll turn out that one day when she was three a dog trotted by and pissed on her leg just as an over-passing pigeon shat on her head. What are we doing in this business?"

"God knows." Floria laughed. "But am I in this business these days—I mean, in the sense of practicing my so-called skills? Blocked with my group work, beating my brains out on a book that won't go, and doing something—I'm not sure it's therapy—with a vampire ... You know, once I had this sort of natural choreographer inside myself that hardly let me put a foot wrong and always knew how to correct a mistake if I did. Now that's gone. I feel as if I'm just going through a lot of mechanical motions. Whatever I had once that made me useful as a therapist, I've lost it."

Ugh, she thought, hearing the descent of her voice into a tone of gloomy self-pity.

"Well, don't complain about Dracula," Lucille said. "You were the one who insisted on taking him on. At least he's got you concentrating on his problem instead of just wringing your hands. As long as you've started, stay with it—illumination may come. And now I'd better change the ribbon in my typewriter and get back to reviewing Silverman's latest best-seller on self-shrinking while I'm feeling mean enough to do it justice." She got up gingerly. "Stick around in case I faint and fall into the wastebasket."

"Luce, this case is what I'd like to try to write about."

"Dracula?" Lucille pawed through a desk drawer full of paper clips, pens, rubber bands and old lipsticks.

"Dracula. A monograph."

"Oh, I know that game: you scribble down everything you can and then read what you wrote to find out what's going on with the client, and with luck you end up publishing. Great! But if you are going to publish, don't piddle this away on a dinky paper. Do a book. Here's your subject, instead of those depressing statistics you've been killing yourself over. This one is really exciting—a case study to put on the shelf next to Freud's own wolf-man, have you thought of that?"

Floria liked it. "What a book that could be—fame if not fortune. Notoriety, most likely. How in the world could I convince our colleagues that it's legit? There's a lot of vampire stuff around right now—plays on Broadway and TV, books all over the place, movies. They'll say I'm just trying to ride the coattails of a fad."

"No, no, what you do is show how this guy's delusion is related to the fad. Fascinating." Lucille, having found a ribbon, prodded doubtfully at the exposed innards of her typewriter.

"Suppose I fictionalize it," Floria said, "under a pseudonym. Why not ride the popular wave and be free in what I can say?"

"Listen, you've never written a word of fiction in your life, have you?" Lucille fixed her with a bloodshot gaze. "There's no evidence that you could turn out a best-selling novel. On the other hand, by this time you have a trained memory for accurately reporting therapeutic transactions. That's a strength you'd be foolish to waste. A solid professional book would be terrific—and a feather in the cap of every woman in the field. Just make sure you get good legal advice on disguising your Dracula's identity well enough to avoid libel."

THE CANE-SEATED CHAIR wasn't worth repairing, so she got its twin out of the bedroom to put in the office in its place. Puzzling: by his history Weyland was fifty-two, and by his appearance no muscle man. She should have asked Doug—but how, exactly? "By the way, Doug, was Weyland ever a circus strong man or a blacksmith? Does he secretly pump iron?" Ask the client himself—but not yet.

She invited some of the younger staff from the clinic over for a small party with a few of her outside friends. It was a good evening; they were not a heavy-drinking crowd, which meant the conversation stayed intelligent. The guests drifted about the long living room or stood in twos and threes at the windows looking down on West End Avenue as they talked.

Mort came, warming the room. Fresh from a session with some amateur chamber-music friends, he still glowed with the pleasure of making his cello sing. His own voice was unexpectedly light for so large a man. Sometimes Floria thought that the deep throb of the cello was his true voice.

He stood beside her talking with some others. There was no need to lean against his comfortable bulk or to have him put his arm around her waist. Their intimacy was long-standing, an effortless pleasure in each other that required neither demonstration nor concealment.

He was easily diverted from music to his next favorite topic, the strengths and skills of athletes.

"Here's a question for a paper I'm thinking of writing," Floria said. "Could a tall, lean man be exceptionally strong?"

Mort rambled on in his thoughtful way. His answer seemed to be no.

"But what about chimpanzees?" put in a young clinician. "I went with a guy once who was an animal handler for TV, and he said a three-month-old chimp could demolish a strong man."

"It's all physical conditioning," somebody else said. "Modern people are soft."

Mort nodded. "Human beings in general are weakly made compared to other animals. It's a question of muscle insertions—the angles of how the muscles are attached to the bones. Some angles give better leverage than others. That's how a leopard can bring down a much bigger animal than itself. It has a muscular structure that gives it tremendous strength for its streamlined build."

Floria said, "If a man were built with muscle insertions like a leopard's, he'd look pretty odd, wouldn't he?"

"Not to an untrained eye," Mort said, sounding bemused by an inner vision. "And my God, what an athlete he'd make—can you imagine a guy in the decathlon who's as strong as a leopard?"

When everyone else had gone Mort stayed, as he often did. Jokes about insertions, muscular and otherwise, soon led to sounds more expressive and more animal, but afterward Floria didn't feel like resting snuggled together with Mort and talking. When her body stopped racing, her mind turned to her new client. She didn't want to discuss him with Mort, so she ushered Mort out as gently as she could and sat down by herself at the kitchen table with a glass of orange juice.

How to approach the reintegration of Weyland the eminent gray-haired academic with the rebellious vampire-self that had smashed his life out of shape?

She thought of the broken chair, of Weyland's big hands crushing the wood. Old wood and dried-out glue, of course, or he never could have done that. He was a man, after all, not leopard.

The day before the third session Weyland phoned and left a message with Hilda: he would not be coming to the office tomorrow for his appointment, but if Dr. Landauer were agreeable she would find him at their usual hour at the Central Park Zoo.

Am I going to let him move me around from here to there? she thought. I shouldn't—but why fight it? Give him some leeway, see what opens up in a different setting. Besides, it was beautiful day, probably the last of the sweet May weather before the summer stickiness descended. She gladly cut Kenny short so that she would have time to walk over to the zoo.

There was a fair crowd there for a weekday. Well-groomed young matrons pushed clean, floppy babies in strollers. Weyland she spotted at once.

He was leaning against the railing that enclosed the seals' shelter and their murky green pool. His jacket, slung over his shoulder, draped elegantly down his long back. Floria thought him rather dashing and faintly foreign-looking. Women who passed him, she noticed, tended to glance back. He looked at everyone.

She had the impression that he knew quite well that she was walking up behind him.

"Outdoors makes a nice change from the office, Edward," she said, coming to the rail beside him. "But there must be more to this than a longing for fresh air." A fat seal lay in sculptural grace on the concrete, eyes blissfully shut, fur drying in the sun to a translucent water-color umber.

Weyland straightened from the rail. They walked. He did not look at the animals; his gaze moved continually over the crowd. He said, "Someone has been watching for me at your office building."

"Who?"

"There are several possibilities. Pah, what a stench—though humans caged in similar circumstances smell as bad." He sidestepped a couple of shrieking children who were fighting over a balloon and headed out of the zoo under the musical clock.

They walked the uphill path northward through the park. By extending her own stride a little Floria found that she could comfortably keep pace with him.

"Is it peasants with torches?" she said. "Following you?"

He said, "What a childish idea."

All right, try another tack, then: "You were telling me last time about hunting in the Ramble. Can we return to that?"

"If you wish." He sounded bored—a defense? Surely—she was certain this must be the right reading—surely his problem was a transmutation into "vampire" fantasy of an unacceptable aspect of himself. For men of his generation the confrontation with homosexual drives could be devastating.

"When you pick up someone in the Ramble, is it a paid encounter?"

"Usually."

"How do you feel about having to pay?" She expected resentment.

He gave a faint shrug. "Why not? Others work to earn their

bread. I work, too, very hard, in fact. Why shouldn't I use my earnings to pay for my sustenance?"

Why did he never play the expected card? Baffled, she paused to drink from a fountain. They walked on.

"Once you've got your quarry, how do you . . ." She fumbled for a word.

"Attack?" he supplied, unperturbed. "There's a place on the neck, here, where pressure can interrupt the blood flow to the brain and cause unconsciousness. Getting close enough to apply that pressure isn't difficult."

"You do this before or after any sexual activity?"

"Before, if possible," he said aridly, "and instead of." He turned aside to stalk up a slope to a granite outcrop that overlooked the path they had been following. There he settled on his haunches, looking back the way they had come. Floria, glad she'd worn slacks today, sat down near him.

He didn't seem devastated—anything but. Press him, don't let him get by on cool. "Do you often prey on men in preference to women?"

"Certainly. I take what is easiest. Men have always been more accessible because women have been walled away like prizes or so physically impoverished by repeated childbearing as to be unhealthy prey for me. All this has begun to change recently, but gay men are still the simplest quarry." While she was recovering from her surprise at his unforeseen and weirdly skewed awareness of female history, he added suavely, "How carefully you control your expression, Dr. Landauer—no trace of disapproval."

She did disapprove, she realized. She would prefer him not to be committed sexually to men. Oh, hell.

He went on, "Yet no doubt you see me as one who victimizes the already victimized. This is the world's way. A wolf brings down the stragglers at the edges of the herd. Gay men are denied the full protection of the human herd and are at the same time emboldened to make themselves known and available.

"On the other hand, unlike the wolf I can feed without killing, and these particular victims pose no threat to me that would cause me to kill. Outcasts themselves, even if they comprehend my true purpose among them they cannot effectively accuse me."

God, how neatly, completely, and ruthlessly he distanced the homosexual community from himself! "And how do you feel, Edward, about their purposes—their sexual expectations of you?"

"The same way I feel about the sexual expectations of women

whom I choose to pursue: they don't interest me. Besides, once my hunger is active, sexual arousal is impossible. My physical unresponsiveness seems to surprise no one. Apparently impotence is expected in a gray-haired man, which suits my intention."

Some kids carrying radios swung past below, trailing a jumble of amplified thump, wail, and jabber. Floria gazed after them unseeingly, thinking, astonished again, that she had never heard a man speak of his own impotence with such cool indifference. She had induced him to talk about his problem all right. He was speaking as freely as he had in the first session, only this time it was no act. He was drowning her in more than she had ever expected or for that matter wanted to know about vampirism. What the hell: she was listening, she thought she understood—what was it all good for? Time for some cold reality, she thought; see how far he can carry all this incredible detail. Give the whole structure a shove.

She said, "You realize, I'm sure, that people of either sex who make themselves so easily available are also liable to be carriers of disease. When was your last medical checkup?"

"My dear Dr. Landauer, my first medical checkup will be my last. Fortunately, I have no great need of one. Most serious illnesses—hepatitis, for example—reveal themselves to me by a quality in the odor of the victim's skin. Warned, I abstain. When I do fall ill, as occasionally happens, I withdraw to some place where I can heal undisturbed. A doctor's attentions would be more dangerous to me than any disease."

Eyes on the path below, he continued calmly, "You can see by looking at me that there are no obvious clues to my unique nature. But believe me, an examination of any depth by even a half-sleeping medical practitioner would reveal some alarming deviations from the norm. I take pains to stay healthy, and I seem to be gifted with an exceptionally hardy constitution."

Fantasies of being unique and physically superior; take him to the other pole. "I'd like you to try something now. Will you put yourself into the mind of a man you contact in the Ramble and describe your encounter with him from his point of view?"

He turned toward her and for some moments regarded her without expression. Then he resumed his surveillance of the path. "I will not. Though I do have enough empathy with my quarry to enable me to hunt efficiently, I must draw the line at erasing the necessary distance that keeps prey and predator distinct.

"And now I think our ways part for today." He stood up,

descended the hillside, and walked beneath some low-canopied trees, his tall back stooped, toward the Seventy-second Street entrance of the park.

Floria arose more slowly, aware suddenly of her shallow breathing and the sweat on her face. Back to reality or what remained of it. She looked at her watch. She was late for her next client.

Floria couldn't sleep that night. Barefoot in her bathrobe she paced the living room by lamplight. They had sat together on that hill as isolated as in her office—more so, because there was no Hilda and no phone. He was, she knew, very strong, and he had sat close enough to her to reach out for that paralyzing touch to the neck—

Just suppose for a minute that Weyland had been brazenly telling the truth all along, counting on her to treat it as a delusion because on the face of it the truth was inconceivable.

Jesus, she thought, if I'm thinking that way about him, this therapy is more out of control than I thought. What kind of therapist becomes an accomplice to the client's fantasy? A crazy therapist, that's what kind.

Frustrated and confused by the turmoil in her mind, she wandered into the workroom. By morning the floor was covered with sheets of newsprint, each broadly marked by her felt-tipped pen. Floria sat in the midst of them, gritty-eyed and hungry.

She often approached problems this way, harking back to art training: turn off the thinking, put hand to paper and see what the deeper, less verbally sophisticated parts of the mind have to offer. Now that her dreams had deserted her, this was her only access to those levels.

The newsprint sheets were covered with rough representations of Weyland's face and form. Across several of them were scrawled words: *"Dear Doug, your vampire is fine, it's your ex-therapist who's off the rails. Warning: Therapy can be dangerous to your health. Especially if you are the therapist. Beautiful vampire, awaken to me. Am I really ready to take on a legendary monster? Give up—refer this one out. Do your job—work is a good doctor."*

That last one sounded pretty good, except that doing her job was precisely what she was feeling so shaky about these days.

Here was another message: "*How come this attraction to someone so scary?*" Oh ho, she thought, is that a real feeling or an aimless reaction out of the body's early-morning hormone peak? You don't want to confuse honest libido with mere biological clockwork.

Deborah called. Babies cried in the background over the Scotch Symphony. Nick, Deb's husband, was a musicologist with fervent opinions on music and nothing else.

"We'll be in town a little later in the summer," Deborah said, "just for a few days at the end of July. Nicky has this seminar-convention thing. Of course, it won't be easy with the babies …I wondered if you might sort of coordinate your vacation so you could spend a little time with them?"

Baby-sit, that meant. Damn. Cute as they were and all that, damn! Floria gritted her teeth. Visits from Deb were always difficult. Floria had been so proud of her bright, hard-driving daughter, and then suddenly Deborah had dropped her studies and rushed to embrace all the dangers that Floria had warned her against: a romantic, too-young marriage, instant breeding, no preparation for self-support, the works. Well, to each her own, but it was so wearing to have Deb around playing the empty-headed hausfrau.

"Let me think, Deb. I'd love to see all of you, but I've been considering spending a couple of weeks in Maine with your Aunt Nonnie." God knows I need a real vacation, she thought, though the peace and quiet up there is hard for a city kid like me to take for long. Still, Nonnie, Floria's younger sister, was good company. "Maybe you could bring the kids up there for a couple of days. There's room in that great barn of a place, and of course Nonnie'd be happy to have you."

"Oh, no, Mom, it's so dead up there, it drives Nick crazy—don't tell Nonnie I said that. Maybe Nonnie could come down to the city instead. You could cancel a date or two and we could all go to Coney Island together, things like that."

Kid things, which would drive Nonnie crazy and Floria too before long. "I doubt she could manage," Floria said, "but I'll ask. Look, hon, if I do go up there, you and Nick and the kids could stay here at the apartment and save some money."

"We have to be at the hotel for the seminar," Deb said shortly. No doubt she was feeling just as impatient as Floria was by now. "And the kids haven't seen you for a long time—it would be really nice if you could stay in the city just for a few days."

"We'll try to work something out." Always working something

out. Concord never comes naturally—first we have to butt heads and get pissed off. Each time you call I hope it'll be different, Floria thought.

Somebody shrieked for "oly," jelly that would be, in the background—Floria felt a sudden rush of warmth for them, her grandkids for God's sake. Having been a young mother herself, she was still young enough to really enjoy them (and to fight with Deb about how to bring them up).

Deb was starting an awkward goodbye. Floria replied, put the phone down, and sat with her head back against the flowered kitchen wallpaper, thinking, Why do I feel so rotten now? Deb and I aren't close, no comfort, seldom friends, though we were once. Have I said everything wrong, made her think I don't want to see her and don't care about her family? What does she want from me that I can't seem to give her? Approval? Maybe she thinks I still hold her marriage against her. Well, I do, sort of. What right have I to be critical, me with my divorce? What terrible things would she say to me, would I say to her, that we take such care not to say anything important at all?

"I think today we might go into sex," she said.

Weyland responded dryly, "Might we indeed. Does it titillate you to wring confessions of solitary vice from men of mature years?"

Oh no you don't, she thought. You can't sidestep so easily. "Under what circumstances do you find yourself sexually aroused?"

"Most usually upon waking from sleep," he said indifferently.

"What do you do about it?"

"The same as others do. I am not a cripple, I have hands."

"Do you have fantasies at these times?"

"No. Women, and men for that matter, appeal to me very little, either in fantasy or reality."

"Ah—what about female vampires?" she said, trying not to sound arch.

"I know of none."

Of course: the neatest out in the book. "They're not needed for reproduction, I suppose, because people who die of vampire bites become vampires themselves."

He said testily, "Nonsense. I am not a communicable disease."

So he had left an enormous hole in his construct. She headed straight for it: "Then how does your kind reproduce?"

"I have no kind, so far as I am aware," he said, "and I do not reproduce. Why should I, when I may live for centuries still, perhaps indefinitely? My sexual equipment is clearly only detailed biological mimicry, a form of protective coloration." How beautiful, how simple a solution, she thought, full of admiration in spite of herself. "Do I occasionally detect a note of prurient interest in your questions, Dr. Landauer? Something akin to stopping at the cage to watch the tigers mate at the zoo?"

"Probably," she said, feeling her face heat. He had a great backhand return shot there. "How do you feel about that?"

He shrugged.

"To return to the point," she said. "Do I hear you saying that you have no urge whatever to engage in sexual intercourse with anyone?"

"Would you mate with your livestock?"

His matter-of-fact arrogance took her breath away. She said weakly, "Men have reportedly done so."

"Driven men. I am not driven in that way. My sex urge is of low frequency and is easily dealt with unaided—although I occasionally engage in copulation out of the necessity to keep up appearances. I am capable, but not—like humans—obsessed."

Was he sinking into lunacy before her eyes? "I think I hear you saying," she said, striving to keep her voice neutral, "that you're not just a man with a unique way of life. I think I hear you saying that you're not human at all."

"I thought that this was already clear."

"And that there are no others like you."

"None that I know of."

"Then—you see yourself as what? Some sort of mutation?"

"Perhaps. Or perhaps your kind are the mutation."

She saw disdain in the curl of his lip. "How does your mouth feel now?"

"The corners are drawn down. The feeling is contempt."

"Can you let the contempt speak?"

He got up and went to stand at the window, positioning himself slightly to one side as if to stay hidden from the street below.

"Edward," she said.

He looked back at her. "Humans are my food. I draw the life out of their veins. Sometimes I kill them. I am greater than they are. Yet I must spend my time thinking about their habits and their drives, scheming to avoid the dangers they pose—I hate them."

She felt the hatred like a dry heat radiating from him. God, he really lived all this! She had tapped into a furnace of feeling. And now? The sensation of triumph wavered, and she grabbed at a next move: hit him with reality now, while he's burning.

"What about blood banks?" she said. "Your food is commercially available, so why all the complication and danger of the hunt?"

"You mean I might turn my efforts to piling up a fortune and buying blood by the case? That would certainly make for an easier, less risky life in the short run. I could fit quite comfortably into modern society if I became just another consumer.

"However, I prefer to keep the mechanics of my survival firmly in my own hands. After all, I can't afford to lose my hunting skills. In two hundred years there may be no blood banks, but I will still need my food."

Jesus, you set him a hurdle and he just flies over it. Are there no weaknesses in all this, has he no blind spots? Look at his tension—go back to that. Floria said, "What do you feel now in your body?"

"Tightness." He pressed his spread fingers to his abdomen.

"What are you doing with your hands?"

"I put my hands to my stomach."

"Can you speak for your stomach?"

"'Feed me or die,'" he snarled.

Elated again, she closed in: "And for yourself, in answer?"

"'Will you never be satisfied?'" He glared at her. "You shouldn't seduce me into quarreling with the terms of my own existence!"

"Your stomach is your existence," she paraphrased.

"The gut determines," he said harshly. "That first, everything else after."

"Say, 'I resent . . .'"

He held to a tense silence.

"'I resent the power of my gut over my life,'" she said for him.

He stood with an abrupt motion and glanced at his watch, an elegant flash of slim silver on his wrist. "Enough," he said.

THAT NIGHT AT HOME she began a set of notes that would never enter his file at the office, notes toward the proposed book.

Couldn't do it, couldn't get properly into the sex

thing with him. Everything shoots off in all directions. His vampire concept so thoroughly worked out, find myself half believing sometimes—my own childish fantasy-response to his powerful death-avoidance, contact-avoidance fantasy. Lose professional distance every time—is that what scares me about him? Don't really want to shatter his delusion (my life a mess, what right to tear down others' patterns?)—so see it as real? Wonder how much of "vampirism" he acts out, how far, how often. Something attractive in his purely selfish, predatory stance—the lure of the great outlaw.

Told me today quite coolly about a man he killed recently—inadvertently—by drinking too much from him. *Is* it fantasy? Of course—the victim, he thinks, was college student. Breathes there a professor who hasn't dreamed of murdering some representative youth, retaliation for years of classroom frustration? Speaks of teaching with acerbic humor—amuses him to work at cultivating the minds of those he regards strictly as bodies, containers of his sustenance. He shows the alienness of full-blown psychopathology, poor bastard, plus clean-cut logic. Suggested he find another job (assuming his delusion at least in part related to pressures at Cayslin); his fantasy-persona, the vampire, more realistic than I about job-switching:

"For a man of my apparent age it's not so easy to make such a change in these tight times. I might have to take a position lower on the ladder of 'success' as you people assess it." Status is important to him? "Certainly. An eccentric professor is one thing; an eccentric pipe-fitter, another. And I like good cars, which are expensive to own and run." Then, thoughtful addition, "Although there are advantages to a simpler, less visible life." He refuses to discuss other "jobs" from former "lives." We are deep into the fantasy—where the hell going? Damn right I don't control the "games"—preplanned therapeutic strategies get whirled away as soon as we begin. Nerve-wracking.

Tried again to have him take the part of his enemy-victim, peasant with torch. Asked if he felt himself rejecting that point of view? Frosty reply: "Naturally. The peasant's point of view is in no way my own. I've been reading in your field, Dr. Landauer. You work from the Gestalt orientation—" Originally yes, I corrected; eclectic now. "But you do proceed from the theory that I am projecting some aspect of my own feelings outward onto others, whom I then treat as my victims. Your purpose then must be to maneuver me into accepting as my own the projected 'victim' aspect of myself. This integration is supposed to effect the freeing of energy previously locked into maintaining the projection. All this is an interesting insight into the nature of ordinary human confusion, but I am not an ordinary human, and I am not confused. I cannot afford confusion." Felt sympathy for him—telling me he's afraid of having own internal confusions exposed in therapy, too threatening. Keep chipping away at delusion, though with what prospect? It's so complex, deep-seated.

Returned to his phrase "my apparent age." He asserts he has lived many human lifetimes, all details forgotten, however, during periods of suspended animation between lives. Perhaps sensing my skepticism at such handy amnesia, grew cool and distant, claimed to know little about the hibernation process itself: "The essence of this state is that I sleep through it—hardly an ideal condition for making scientific observations."

Edward thinks his body synthesizes vitamins, minerals (as all our bodies synthesize vitamin D), even proteins. Describes unique design he deduces in himself: special intestinal microfauna plus super-efficient body chemistry extracts enough energy to live on from blood. Damn good mileage per calorie, too. (Recall observable tension, first interview, at question about drinking—my note on possible alcohol problem!)

Speak for blood: "'Lacking me, you have no life. I flow to the heart's soft drumbeat through lightless prisons of flesh. I am rich, I am nourishing, I am difficult to attain.'" Stunned to find him positively lyrical on subject of his "food." Drew attention to whispering voice of blood. "'Yes. I am secret, hidden beneath the surface, patient, silent, steady. I work unnoticed, an unseen thread of vitality running from age to age—beautiful, efficient, self-renewing, self-cleansing, warm, filling—' " Could *see* him getting worked up. Finally he stood: "My appetite is pressing. I must leave you." And he did.

Sat and trembled for five minutes after.

New development (or new perception?): he sometimes comes across very unsophisticated about own feelings—lets me pursue subjects of extreme intensity and delicacy to him.

Asked him to daydream—a hunt. (Hands—mine—shaking now as I write. God. What a session.) He told of picking up a woman at poetry reading, 92nd Street Y—has N.Y.C. all worked out, circulates to avoid too much notice any one spot. Spoke easily, eyes shut without observable strain: chooses from audience a redhead in glasses, dress with drooping neckline (ease of access), no perfume (strong smells bother him). Approaches during intermission, encouraged to see her fanning away smoke of others' cigarettes—meaning she doesn't smoke, health sign. Agreed in not enjoying the reading, they adjourn together to coffee shop.

"She asks whether I'm a teacher," he says, eyes shut, mouth amused. "My clothes, glasses, manner all suggest this, and I emphasize the impression—it reassures. She's a copy editor for a publishing house. We talk about books. The waiter brings her a gummy-looking pastry. As a non-eater, I pay little attention to the quality of restaurants, so I must apologize to her. She waves this away—is engrossed, or pretending to be engrossed, in talk." A longish dialog between interested woman and Edward doing shy-lonesome-scholar act—dead wife, competitive young colleagues who don't understand him, quarrels in professional journals with big shots in his field—a version of what he first told me. She's attracted (of course—lanky, rough-cut elegance plus hints of vulnerability all very alluring, as intended). He offers to take her home.

Tension in his body at this point in narrative—spine clear of chair back, hands braced on thighs. "She settles beside me in the back of the cab, talking about problems of her own career—illegible manuscripts of Biblical length, mulish editors, suicidal authors—and I make comforting comments, I lean nearer and put my arm along the back of the seat, behind her shoulders. Traffic is heavy, we move slowly. There is time to make my meal here in the taxi and avoid a tedious extension of the situation into her apartment—if I move soon."

How do you feel?

"Eager," he says, voice husky. "My hunger is so roused I can scarcely restrain myself. A powerful hunger, not like yours—mine compels. I embrace her shoulders lightly, make kindly-uncle remarks, treading that fine line between the game of seduction she perceives and the game of friendly interest I pretend to affect. My real purpose underlies all: what I say, how I look, every gesture is part of the stalk. There is an added excitement, and fear, because I'm doing my hunting in the presence of a third person—behind the cabbie's head."

Could scarcely breathe. Studied him—intent face, masklike with closed eyes, nostrils slightly flared; legs tensed, hands clenched on knees. Whispering: "I press the place on her neck. She starts, sighs faintly, silently drops against me. In the stale stench of the cab's interior, with the ticking of the meter in my ears and the mutter of the radio—I take hold here, at the tenderest part of her throat. Sound subsides into the background—I feel the sweet blood beating under her skin, I taste salt at the moment before I—strike. My saliva thins her blood so that it flows out, I draw the blood into my mouth swiftly, swiftly, before she can wake, before we can arrive . . ."

Trailed off, sat back loosely in chair—saw him swallow. "Ah. I feed." Heard him sigh. Managed to ask about physical sensation. His low murmur, "Warm. Heavy, here—" touches his belly—"in a pleasant way. The good taste of blood, tart and rich, in my mouth . . ."

And then? A flicker of movement beneath his closed eyelids: "In time I am aware that the cabbie has glanced back once and has taken our—embrace for just that. I can feel the cab slowing, hear him move to turn off the meter. I withdraw, I quickly wipe my mouth on my handkerchief. I take her by the shoulders and shake her gently; does she often have these attacks, I inquire, the soul of concern. She comes around, bewildered, weak, thinks she has fainted. I give the driver extra money and ask him to wait. He looks intrigued—'What was that all about,' I can see the question in his face—but as a true New Yorker he won't expose his own ignorance by asking.

"I escort the woman to her front door, supporting her as she staggers. Any suspicion of me that she may entertain, however formless and hazy, is allayed by my stern charging of the doorman to see that she reaches her apartment safely. She grows embarrassed, thinks perhaps that if not put off by her 'illness' I would spend the night with her, which moves her to press upon me, unasked, her telephone number. I bid her a solicitous good night and take the cab back to my hotel, where I sleep."

No sex? No sex.

How did he feel about the victim as a person? "She was food."

This was his "hunting" of last night, he admits afterward, not a made-up dream. No boasting in it, just telling. Telling me! Think: I can go talk to Lucille, Mort, Doug, others about most of what matters to me. Edward has only me to talk to and that for a fee—what isolation! No wonder the stone, monumental face—only those long, strong lips (his point of contact, verbal and physical-in-fantasy, with world and with "food") are truly expressive. An exciting narration; uncomfortable to find I felt not only empathy but enjoyment. Suppose he picked up and victimized—even in fantasy—Deb or Hilda, how would I feel then?

Later: truth—I also found this recital sexually stirring. Keep visualizing how he looked finishing this "dream"—he sat very still, head up, look of thoughtful pleasure on his face. Like handsome intellectual listening to music.

KENNY SHOWED UP unexpectedly at Floria's office on Monday,

bursting with malevolent energy. She happened to be free, so she took him—something was definitely up. He sat on the edge of his chair.

"I know why you're trying to unload me," he accused. "It's that new one, the tall guy with the snooty look—what is he, an old actor or something? Anybody could see he's got you itching for him."

"Kenny, when was it that I first spoke to you about terminating our work together?" she said patiently.

"Don't change the subject. Let me tell you, in case you don't know it: that guy isn't really interested, Doctor, because he's a fruit. A faggot. You want to know how I know?"

Oh Lord, she thought wearily, he's regressed to age ten. She could see that she was going to hear the rest whether she wanted to or not. What in God's name was the world like for Kenny, if he clung so fanatically to her despite her failure to help him?

"Listen, I knew right away there was something flaky about him, so I followed him from here to that hotel where he lives. I followed him the other afternoon too. He walked around like he does a lot, and then he went into one of those ritzy movie houses on Third that open early and show risqué foreign movies—you know, Japs cutting each other's things off and glop like that. This one was French, though.

"Well, there was a guy came in, a Madison Avenue type carrying his attache case, taking a work break or something. Your man moved over and sat down behind him and reached out and sort of stroked the guy's neck, and the guy leaned back, and your man leaned forward and started nuzzling at him, you know—kissing him.

"I saw it. They had their heads together and they stayed like that a while. It was disgusting: complete strangers, without even 'hello.' The Madison Avenue guy just sat there with his head back looking zonked, you know, just swept away, and what he was doing with his hands under his raincoat in his lap I couldn't see, but I bet you can guess.

"And then your fruity friend got up and walked out. I did too, and I hung around a little outside. After a while the Madison Avenue guy came out looking all sleepy and loose, like after you-know-what, and he wandered off on his own someplace.

"What do you think now?" he ended, on a high, triumphant note.

Her impulse was to slap his face the way she would have

slapped Deb-as-a-child for tattling. But this was a client, not kid. God give me strength, she thought.

"Kenny, you're fired."

"You can't!" he squealed. "You can't! What will I—who can I—"

She stood up, feeling weak but hardening her voice. "I'm sorry. I absolutely cannot have a client who makes it his business to spy on other clients. You already have a list of replacement therapists from me."

He gaped at her in slack-jawed dismay, his eyes swimmy with tears.

"I'm sorry, Kenny. Call this a dose of reality therapy and try to learn from it. There are some things you simply will not be allowed to do." She felt better: it was done at last.

"I hate you!" He surged out of his chair, knocking it back against the wall. Threateningly he glared at the fish tank, but, contenting himself with a couple of kicks at the nearest table leg, he stamped out.

Floria buzzed Hilda: "No more appointments for Kenny, Hilda. You can close his file."

"Whoopee," Hilda said.

Poor, horrid Kenny. Impossible to tell what would happen to him, better not to speculate or she might relent, call him back. She had encouraged him, really, by listening instead of shutting him up and throwing him out before any damage was done.

Was it damaging, to know the truth? In her mind's eye she saw a cream-faced young man out of a Black Thumb Vodka ad wander from a movie theater into daylight, yawning and rubbing absently at an irritation on his neck …

She didn't even look at the telephone on the table or think about whom to call, now that she believed. No; she was going to keep quiet about Dr. Edward Lewis Weyland, her vampire.

Hardly alive at staff meeting, clinic, yesterday—people asking what's the matter, fobbed them off. Settled down today. Had to, to face him.

Asked him what he felt were his strengths. He said speed, cunning, ruthlessness. Animal strengths, I said. What about imagination, or is that strictly human? He defended at once: not human only. Lion, waiting at water hole where no zebra yet drinks, thinks "Zebra—eat," therefore performs feat of imagining event yet-to-come. Self experienced as animal? Yes—reminded me that humans are also animals. Pushed for his early memories; he objected: "Gestalt is here-and-now, not history-taking." I insist, citing anomalous nature of his situation, my own refusal to be bound by any one theoretical framework. He defends tensely: "Suppose I became lost there in memory, distracted from dangers of the present, left unguarded from those dangers."

Speak for memory. He resists, but at length attempts it: "'I am heavy with the multitudes of the past.'" Fingertips to forehead, propping up all that weight of lives. "'So heavy, filling worlds of time laid down eon by eon, I accumulate, I persist, I demand recognition. I am as real as the life around you—more real, weightier, richer.'" His voice sinking, shoulders bowed, head in hands—I begin to feel pressure at the back of my own skull. "'Let me in.'" Only a rough whisper now. "'I offer beauty as well as terror. Let me in.'" Whispering also, I suggest he reply to his memory.

"Memory, you want to crush me," he groans. "You would overwhelm me with the cries of animals, the odor and jostle of bodies, old betrayals, dead joys, filth and anger from other times—I must concentrate on the danger now. Let me be." All I can take of this crazy conflict, I gabble us off onto something else. He looks up—relief?—follows my lead—where? Rest of session a blank.

No wonder sometimes no empathy at all—a species boundary! He has to be utterly self-centered just to keep balance—self-centeredness of an animal. Thought just now of our beginning, me trying to push him to produce material, trying to control him, manipulate—no way, no way; so here we are, someplace else—I feel dazed, in shock, but stick with it—it's real. Therapy with a dinosaur, a Martian.

"You call me 'Weyland' now, not 'Edward.'" I said first name couldn't mean much to one with no memory of being called by that name as a child, silly to pretend it signifies intimacy where it can't. I think he knows now that I believe him. Without prompting, told me truth of disappearance from Cayslin. No romance; he tried to drink from a woman who worked there, she shot him, stomach and chest. Luckily for him, small-caliber pistol, and he was wearing a lined coat over three-piece suit. Even so, badly hurt. (Midsection stiffness I noted when he first came—he was still in some pain at that time.) He didn't "vanish"—fled, hid, was found by questionable types who caught on to what he was, sold him "like a chattel" to someone here in the city. He was imprisoned, fed, put on exhibition—very privately—for gain. Got away. "Do you believe any of this?" Never asked anything like that before, seems of concern to him now. I said my belief or lack of same was immaterial; remarked on hearing a lot of bitterness.

He steepled his fingers, looked brooding at me over tips: "I nearly died there. No doubt my purchaser and his diabolist friend still search for me. Mind you, I had some reason at first to be glad of the attentions of the people who kept me prisoner. I was in no condition to fend for myself. They brought me food and kept me hidden and sheltered, whatever their motives. There are always advantages . . ."

Silence today started a short session. Hunting poor last night, Weyland still hungry. Much restless movement, watching goldfish darting in tank, scanning bookshelves. Asked him to be books. "'I am old and full of knowledge, well made to last long. You see only the title, the substance is hidden. I am a book that stays closed.'" Malicious twist of the mouth, not quite a smile: "This is a good game." Is he feeling threatened, too—already "opened" too much to me? Too strung out with him to dig when he's skimming surfaces that should be probed. Don't know how to *do* therapy with Weyland—just have to let things happen, hope it's good. But what's "good"? Aristotle? Rousseau? Ask Weyland what's good, he'll say "Blood."

Everything in a spin—these notes too confused, too fragmentary—worthless for a book, just a mess, like me, my life. Tried to call Deb last night, cancel visit. Nobody home, thank God. Can't tell her to stay away—but damn it—do not need complications now!

Floria went down to Broadway with Lucille to get more juice, cheese and crackers for the clinic fridge. This week it was their turn to do the provisions, a chore that rotated among the staff. Their talk about grant proposals for the support of the clinic trailed off.

"Let's sit a minute," Floria said. They crossed to a traffic island in the middle of the avenue. It was a sunny afternoon, close enough to lunchtime so that the brigade of old people who normally occupied the benches had thinned out. Floria sat down and kicked a crumpled beer can and some greasy fast-food wrappings back under the bench.

"You look like hell but wide awake at least," Lucille commented.

"Things are still rough," Floria said. "I keep hoping to get my life under control so I'll have some energy left for Deb and Nick and the kids when they arrive, but I can't seem to do it. Group was awful last night—a member accused me afterward of having abandoned them all. I think I have, too. The professional messes and the personal are all related somehow, they run into each other. I should be keeping them apart so I can deal with them separately, but I can't. I can't concentrate, my mind is all over the place. Except with Dracula, who keeps me riveted with astonishment when he's in the office and bemused the rest of the time."

A bus roared by, shaking the pavement and the benches. Lucille waited until the noise faded. "Relax about the group. The others would have defended you if you'd been attacked during the session. They all understand, even if you don't seem to: it's the summer doldrums, people don't want to work, they expect you to do it all for them. But don't push so hard. You're not a shaman who can magic your clients back into health."

Floria tore two cans of juice out of a six-pack and handed one to her. On a street corner opposite, a violent argument broke out in typewriter-fast Spanish between two women. Floria sipped tinny juice and watched. She'd seen a guy last winter straddle another on that same corner and try to smash his brains out on the icy sidewalk. The old question again: What's crazy, what's healthy?

"It's a good thing you dumped Chubs, anyhow," Lucille said "I don't know what finally brought that on, but it's definitely a move in the right direction. What about Count Dracula? You don't talk about him much anymore. I thought I diagnosed a yen for his venerable body."

Floria shifted uncomfortably on the bench and didn't answer. If only she could deflect Lucille's sharp-eyed curiosity.

"Oh," Lucille said. "I see. You really are hot—or at least warm. Has he noticed?"

"I don't think so. He's not on the lookout for that kind of response from me. He says sex with other people doesn't interest him, and I think he's telling the truth."

"Weird," Lucille said. "What about *Vampire on My Couch*? Shaping up all right?"

"It's shaky, like everything else. I'm worried that I don't know how things are going to come out. I mean, Freud's wolf-man case was a success, as therapy goes. Will my vampire case turn out successfully?"

She glanced at Lucille's puzzled face, made up her mind, and plunged ahead. "Luce, think of it this way: suppose, just suppose, that my Dracula is for real, an honest-to-God vampire—"

"Oh *shit!*" Lucille erupted in anguished exasperation. "Damn it, Floria, enough is enough—will you stop futzing around and get some help? Coming to pieces yourself and trying to treat this poor nut with a vampire fixation—how can you do him any good? No wonder you're worried about his therapy!"

"Please, just listen, help me think this out. My purpose can't be to cure him of what he is. Suppose vampirism isn't a defense he has to learn to drop? Suppose it's the core of his identity? Then what do I do?"

Lucille rose abruptly and marched away from her through a gap between the rolling waves of cabs and trucks. Floria caught up with her on the next block.

"Listen, will you? Luce, you see the problem? I don't need to help him see who and what he is, he knows that perfectly well, and he's not crazy, far from it—"

"Maybe not," Lucille said grimly, "but you are. Don't dump this junk on me outside of office hours, Floria. I don't spend my time listening to nut-talk unless I'm getting paid."

"Just tell me if this makes psychological sense to you: he's healthier than most of us because he's always true to his identity, even when he's engaged in deceiving others. A fairly narrow, rigorous set of requirements necessary to his survival—that *is* his identity, and it commands him completely. Anything extraneous could destroy him. To go on living, he has to act solely out of his own undistorted necessity, and if that isn't authenticity, what is? So he's healthy, isn't he?" She paused, feeling a sudden lightness in herself. "And that's the best sense I've been able to make of this whole business so far."

They were in the middle of the block. Lucille, who could not on her short legs outwalk Floria, turned on her suddenly. "What the hell do you think you're doing, calling yourself a therapist? For God's sake, Floria, don't try to rope me into this kind of professional irresponsibility. You're just dipping into your client's fantasies instead of helping him to handle them. That's not therapy, it's collusion. Have some sense! Admit you're over your head in troubles of your own, retreat to firmer ground—go get treatment for yourself!"

Floria angrily shook her head. When Lucille turned away and hurried on up the block toward the clinic, Floria let her go without trying to detain her.

THOUGHT ABOUT LUCILLE'S ADVICE. After my divorce going back into therapy for a while did help, but now? Retreat again to being a client, like old days in training—so young, inadequate, defenseless then. Awful prospect. And I'd have to hand over W. to somebody else—who? I'm not up to handling him, can't cope, too anxious, yet with all that we do good therapy together somehow. I can't control, can only offer; he's free to take, refuse, use as suits, as far as he's willing to go. I serve as resource while he does own therapy—isn't that therapeutic ideal, free of "shoulds," "shouldn'ts"?

Saw ballet with Mort, lovely evening—time out from W.—talking, singing, pirouetting all the way home, feeling safe as anything in the shadow of Mort-mountain; rolled later with that humming (off-key), sun-warm body. Today W. says he saw me at Lincoln Center last night, avoided me because of Mort. W. is ballet fan! Started attending to pick up victims, now also because dance puzzles and pleases.

"When a group dances well, the meaning is easy—the dancers make a visual complement to the music, all their moves necessary, coherent, flowing. When a gifted soloist performs, the pleasure of making the moves is echoed in my own body. The soloist's absorption is total, much like my own in the actions of the hunt. But when a man and a woman dance together, something else happens. Sometimes one is hunter, one is prey, or they shift these roles between them. Yet some other level of significance exists—I suppose to do with sex—and I feel it—a tugging sensation, here—" touched his solar plexus—"but I do not understand it."

Worked with his reactions to ballet. The response he feels to pas de deux is a kind of pull, "like hunger but not hunger." Of course he's baffled—Balanchine writes that the pas de deux is always a love story between man and woman. W. isn't man, isn't woman, yet the drama connects. His hands hovering as he spoke, fingers spread toward each other. Pointed this out. Body work comes easier to him now: joined his hands, interlaced fingers, spoke for hands without prompting: "'We are similar, we want the comfort of like closing to like.'" How would that be for him, to find—likeness, another of his kind? "Female?" Starts impatiently explaining how unlikely this is—No, forget sex and pas de deux for now; just to find your like, another vampire.

He springs up, agitated now. There are none, he insists; adds at once, "But what would it be like? What would happen? I fear it!" Sits again, hands clenched. "I long for it."

Silence. He watches goldfish, I watch him. I withhold fatuous attempt to pin down this insight, if that's what it is—what can I know about his insight? Suddenly he turns, studies me intently till I lose my nerve, react, cravenly suggest that if I make him uncomfortable he might wish to switch to another therapist—

"Certainly not." More follows, all gold: "There is value to me in what we do here, Dr. Landauer, much against my earlier expectations. Although people talk appreciatively of honest speech they generally avoid it, and I myself have found scarcely any use for it at all. Your straightforwardness with me—and the straightforwardness you require in return—this is healthy in a life so dependent on deception as mine."

Sat there, wordless, much moved, thinking of what I don't show him—my upset life, seat-of-pants course with him and attendant strain, attraction to him—I'm holding out on him while he appreciates my honesty.

Hesitation, then lower-voiced, "Also, there are limits on my methods of self-discovery, short of turning myself over to a laboratory for vivisection. I have no others like myself to look at and learn from. Any tools that may help are worth much to me, and these games of yours are—potent." Other stuff besides, not important. Important: he moves me and he draws me and he keeps on coming back. Hang in if he does.

Bad night—Kenny's aunt called: no bill from me this month, so if he's not seeing me who's keeping an eye on him, where's he hanging out? Much implied blame for what *might* happen. Absurd, but shook me up: I did fail Kenny. Called off group this week also; too much.

No, it was a good night—first dream in months I can recall, contact again with own depths—but disturbing. Dreamed myself in cab with W. in place of the woman from the Y. He put his hand not on my neck but breast—I felt intense sensual response in the dream, also anger and fear so strong they woke me.

Thinking about this: anyone leans toward him sexually, to him a sign his hunting technique has maneuvered prospective victim into range, maybe arouses his appetite for blood. *I don't want that.* "She was food." I am not food, I am a person. No thrill at languishing away in his arms in a taxi while he drinks my blood—that's disfigured sex, masochism. My sex response in dream signaled to me I would be his victim—I rejected that, woke up.

Mention of *Dracula* (novel). W. dislikes: meandering, inaccurate, those absurd fangs. Says he himself has a sort of needle under his tongue, used to pierce skin. No offer to demonstrate, and no request from me. I brightly brought up historical Vlad Dracul—celebrated instance of Turkish envoys who, upon refusing to uncover to Vlad to show respect, were killed by spiking their hats to their skulls. "Nonsense," snorts W. "A clever ruler would use very small thumbtacks and dismiss the envoys to moan about the streets of Varna holding their tacked heads." First spontaneous play he's shown—took head in hands and uttered plaintive groans, "Ow, oh, ooh." I cracked up. W. reverted at once to usual dignified manner: "You can see that this would serve the ruler much more effectively as an object lesson against rash pride."

Later, same light vein: "I know why I'm a vampire; why are you a therapist?" Off balance as usual, said things about helping, mental health, etc. He shook his head: "And people think of a vampire as arrogant! You want to perform cures in a world which exhibits very little health of any kind—and it's the same arrogance with all of you. This one wants to be President or Class Monitor or Department Chairman or Union Boss, another must be first to fly to the stars or to transplant the human brain, and on and on. As for me, I wish only to satisfy my appetite in peace."

And those of us whose appetite is for competence, for effectiveness? Thought of Green, treated eight years ago, went on to be indicted for running a hellish "home" for aged. I had helped him stay functional so he could destroy the helpless for profit.

W. not my first predator, only most honest and direct. Scared; not of attack by W., but of process we're going through. I'm beginning to be up to it (?), but still—utterly unpredictable, impossible to handle or manage. Occasional stirrings of inward choreographer that used to shape my work so surely. Have I been afraid of that, holding it down in myself, choosing mechanical manipulation instead? Not a choice with W.—thinking no good, strategy no good, nothing left but instinct, clear and uncluttered responses if I can find them. Have to be my own authority with him, as he is always his own authority with a world in which he's unique. So work with W. not just exhausting—exhilarating too, along with strain, fear.

Am I growing braver? Not much choice.

Park again today (air-conditioning out at office).

Avoiding Lucille's phone calls from clinic (very reassuring that she calls despite quarrel, but don't want to take all this up with her again). Also meeting W. in open feels saner somehow—wild creatures belong outdoors? Sailboat pond N. of 72nd, lots of kids, garbage, one beautiful tall boat drifting. We walked.

W. maintains he remembers no childhood, no parents. I told him my astonishment, confronted by someone who never had a life of the previous generation (even adopted parent) shielding him from death—how naked we stand when the last shield falls. Got caught in remembering a death dream of mine, dream it now and then—couldn't concentrate, got scared, spoke of it—a dog tumbled under a passing truck, ejected to side of the road where it lay unable to move except to lift head and shriek; couldn't help. Shaking nearly to tears—remembered Mother got into dream somehow—had blocked that at first. Didn't say it now. Tried to rescue situation, show W. how to work with a dream (sitting in vine arbor near band shell, some privacy).

He focused on my obvious shakiness: "The air vibrates constantly with the death cries of countless animals large and small. What is the death of one dog?" Leaned close, speaking quietly, instructing. "Many creatures are dying in ways too dreadful to imagine. I am part of the world; I listen to the pain. You people claim to be above all that. You deafen yourselves with your own noise and pretend there's nothing else to hear. Then these screams enter your dreams, and you have to seek therapy because you have lost the nerve to listen."

Remembered myself, said, Be a dying animal. He refused: "You are the one who dreams this." I had a horrible flash, felt I was the dog—helpless, doomed, hurting—burst into tears. The great therapist, bringing her own hangups into session with client! Enraged with self, which did not help stop bawling.

W. disconcerted, I think; didn't speak. People walked past, glanced over, ignored us. W. said finally, "What is this?" Nothing, just the fear of death. "Oh, the fear of death. That's with me all the time. One must simply get used to it." Tears into laughter. Goddamn wisdom of the ages. He got up to go, paused: "And tell that stupid little man who used to precede me at your office to stop following me around. He puts himself in danger that way."

Kenny, damn it! Aunt doesn't know where he is, no answer on his phone. Idiot!

Sketching all night—useless. W. beautiful beyond the scope of line—the beauty of singularity, cohesion, rooted in absolute devotion to demands of his specialized body. In feeding (woman in taxi), utter absorption one wants from a man in sex—no score-keeping, no fantasies, just hot urgency of appetite, of senses, the moment by itself.

His sleeves worn rolled back today to the elbows—strong, sculptural forearms, the long bones curved in slightly, suggest torque, leverage. How old?

Endurance: huge, rich cloak of time flows back from his shoulders like wings of a dark angel. All springs from, elaborates, the single, stark, primary condition: he is a predator who subsists on human blood. Harmony, strength, clarity, magnificence—all from that basic animal integrity. Of course I long for all that, here in the higgledy-piggledy hodgepodge of my life! Of course he draws me!

Wore no perfume today, deference to his keen, easily insulted sense of smell. He noticed at once, said curt thanks. Saw something bothering him, opened my mouth seeking desperately for right thing to say—up rose my inward choreographer, wide awake, and spoke plain from my heart: thinking on my floundering in some of our sessions—I am aware that you see this confusion of mine. I know you see by your occasional impatient look, sudden disengagement—yet you continue to reveal yourself to me (even shift our course yourself if it needs shifting and I don't do it). I think I know why. Because there's no place for you in world as you truly are. Because beneath your various facades your true self suffers; like all true selves, it wants, needs to be honored as real and valuable through acceptance by another. I try to be that other, but often you are beyond me.

He rose, paced to window, looked back, burning at me. "If I seem sometimes restless or impatient, Dr. Landauer, it's not because of any professional shortcomings of yours. On the contrary—you are all too effective. The seductiveness, the distraction of our—human contact worries me. I fear for the ruthlessness that keeps me alive."

Speak for ruthlessness. He shook his head. Saw tightness in shoulders, feet braced hard against floor. Felt reflected tension in my own muscles.

Prompted him: "'I resent . . .'"

"I resent your pretension to teach me about myself! What will this work that you do here make of me? A predator paralyzed by an unwanted empathy with his prey? A creature fit only for a cage and keeper?" He was breathing hard, jaw set. I saw suddenly the truth of his fear: his integrity is not human, but my work is specifically human, designed to make humans more human—what if it does that to him? Should have seen it before, should have seen it. No place left to go: had to ask him, in small voice, Speak for my pretension.

"No!" Eyes shut, head turned away.

Had to do it: Speak for me.

W. whispered, "As to the unicorn, out of your own legends—'Unicorn, come lay your head in my lap while the hunters close in. You are a wonder, and for love of wonder I will tame you. You are pursued, but forget your pursuers, rest under my hand till they come and destroy you.'" Looked at me like steel: "Do you see? The more you involve yourself in what I am, the more you become the peasant with the torch!"

Two days later Doug came into town and had lunch with Floria.

He was a man of no outstanding beauty who was nevertheless attractive: he didn't have much chin and his ears were too big, but you didn't notice because of his air of confidence. His stability had been earned the hard way—as a gay man facing the straight world.

Some of his strength had been attained with effort and pain in a group that Floria had run years earlier. A lasting affection had grown between herself and Doug. She was intensely glad to see him.

They ate near the clinic. "You look a little frayed around the edges," Doug said. "I heard about Jane Fennerman's relapse—too bad."

"I've only been able to bring myself to visit her once since."

"Feeling guilty?"

She hesitated, gnawing on a stale breadstick. The truth was, she hadn't thought of Jane Fennerman in weeks. Finally she said, "I guess I must be."

Sitting back with his hands in his pockets, Doug chided her gently. "It's got to be Jane's fourth or fifth time into the nuthatch, and the others happened when she was in the care of other therapists. Who are you to imagine—to demand—that her cure lay in your hands? God may be a woman, Floria, but She is not you. I thought the whole point was some recognition of individual responsibility—you for yourself, the client for himself or herself."

"That's what we're always saying," Floria agreed. She felt curiously divorced from this conversation. It had an old-fashioned flavor: Before Weyland. She smiled a little.

The waiter ambled over. She ordered bluefish. The serving would be too big for her depressed appetite, but Doug wouldn't be satisfied with his customary order of salad (he never was) and could be persuaded to help out.

He worked his way around to Topic A. "When I called to set up this lunch, Hilda told me she's got a crush on Weyland. How are you and he getting along?"

"My God, Doug, now you're going to tell me this whole thing was to fix me up with an eligible suitor!" She winced at her own rather strained laughter. "How soon are you planning to ask Weyland to work at Cayslin again?"

"I don't know, but probably sooner than I thought a couple of months ago. We hear that he's been exploring an attachment to an anthropology department at a western school, some niche where I guess he feels he can have less responsibility, less visibility, and a chance to collect himself. Naturally, this news is making people at Cayslin suddenly eager to nail him down for us. Have you a recommendation?"

"Yes," she said. "Wait."

He gave her an inquiring look. "What for?"

"Until he works more fully through certain stresses in the

situation at Cayslin. Then I'll be ready to commit myself about him." The bluefish came. She pretended distraction: "Good God, that's too much fish for me. Doug, come on and help me out here."

HILDA WAS CROUCHED over Floria's file drawer. She straightened up, looking grim. "Somebody's been in the office!"

What was this, had someone attacked her? The world took on a cockeyed, dangerous tilt. "Are you okay?"

"Yes, sure, I mean there are records that have been gone through. I can tell. I've started checking and so far it looks as if none of the files themselves are missing. But if any papers were taken out of them, that would be pretty hard to spot without reading through every folder in the place. Your files, Floria. I don't think anybody else's were touched."

Mere burglary; weak with relief, Floria sat down on one of the waiting-room chairs. But only her files? "Just my stuff, you're sure?"

Hilda nodded. "The clinic got hit, too. I called. They see some new-looking scratches on the lock of your file drawer over there. Listen, you want me to call the cops?"

"First check as much as you can, see if anything obvious is missing."

There was no sign of upset in her office. She found a phone message on her table: Weyland had canceled his next appointment. She knew who had broken into her files.

She buzzed Hilda's desk. "Hilda, let's leave the police out of it for the moment. Keep checking." She stood in the middle of the office, looking at the chair replacing the one he had broken, looking at the window where he had so often watched.

Relax, she told herself. There was nothing for him to find here or at the clinic.

She signaled that she was ready for the first client of the afternoon.

THAT EVENING she came back to the office after having dinner with friends. She was supposed to be helping set up a workshop for next month, and she'd been putting off even thinking about it, let alone doing any real work. She set herself to compiling a suggested bibliography for her section.

The phone light blinked.

It was Kenny, sounding muffled and teary. "I'm sorry," he moaned. "The medicine just started to wear off. I've been trying to call you everyplace. God, I'm so scared—he was waiting in the alley."

"Who was?" she said, dry-mouthed. She knew.

"Him. The tall one, the faggot—only he goes with women too, I've seen him. He grabbed me. He hurt me. I was lying there a long time. I couldn't do anything. I felt so funny—like floating away. Some kids found me. Their mother called the cops. I was so cold, so scared—"

"Kenny, where are you?"

He told her which hospital. "Listen, I think he's really crazy, you know? And I'm scared he might …you live alone …I don't know—I didn't mean to make trouble for you. I'm so scared."

God damn you, you meant exactly to make trouble for me, and now you've bloody well made it. She got him to ring for a nurse. By calling Kenny her patient and using "Dr." in front of her own name without qualifying the title she got some information: two broken ribs, multiple contusions, a badly wrenched shoulder, and a deep cut on the scalp which Dr. Wells thought accounted for the blood loss the patient had sustained. Picked up early today, the patient wouldn't say who had attacked him. You can check with Dr. Wells tomorrow, Dr.—?

Can Weyland think I've somehow sicced Kenny on him? No, he surely knows me better than that. Kenny must have brought this on himself.

She tried Weyland's number and then the desk at his hotel. He had closed his account and gone, providing no forwarding information other than the address of a university in New Mexico.

Then she remembered: this was the night Deb and Nick and the kids were arriving. Oh, God. Next phone call. The Americana was the hotel Deb had mentioned. Yes, Mr. and Mrs. Nicholas Redpath were registered in room whatnot. Ring, please.

Deb's voice came shakily on the line. "I've been trying to call you." Like Kenny.

"You sound upset," Floria said, steadying herself for whatever calamity had descended: illness, accident, assault in the streets of the dark, degenerate city.

Silence, then a raggedy sob. "Nick's not here. I didn't phone you earlier because I thought he still might come, but I don't think he's coming, Mom." Bitter weeping.

"Oh, Debbie. Debbie, listen, you just sit tight, I'll be right down there."

The cab ride took only a few minutes. Debbie was still crying when Floria stepped into the room.

"I don't know, I don't know," Deb wailed, shaking her head. "What did I do wrong? He went away a week ago, to do some research, he said, and I didn't hear from him, and half the bank money is gone—just half, he left me half. I kept hoping...they say most runaways come back in a few days or call up, they get lonely ...I haven't told anybody—I thought since we were supposed to be here at this convention thing together, I'd better come, maybe he'd show up. But nobody's seen him, and there are no messages, not a word, nothing."

"All right, all right, poor Deb," Floria said, hugging her.

"Oh God, I'm going to wake the kids with all this howling." Deb pulled away, making a frantic gesture toward the door of the adjoining room. "It was so hard to get them to sleep—they were expecting Daddy to be here, I kept telling them he'd be here." She rushed out into the hotel hallway. Floria followed, propping the door open with one of her shoes since she didn't know whether Deb had a key with her or not. They stood out there together, ignoring passersby, huddling over Deb's weeping.

"What's been going on between you and Nick?" Floria said. "Have you two been sleeping together lately?"

Deb let out a squawk of agonized embarrassment, "Mo-*ther!*" and pulled away from her. Oh, hell, wrong approach.

"Come on, I'll help you pack. We'll leave word you're at my place. Let Nick come looking for you." Floria firmly squashed down the miserable inner cry, How am I going to stand this?

"Oh, no, I can't move till morning now that I've got the kids settled down. Besides, there's one night's deposit on the rooms. Oh, Mom, what did I do?"

"You didn't do anything, hon," Floria said, patting her shoulder and thinking in some part of her mind, Oh boy, that's great, is that the best you can come up with in a crisis with all your training and experience? Your vaunted professional skills are not so hot lately, but this bad? Another part answered, Shut up, stupid, only an idiot does therapy on her own family. Deb's come to her mother, not to a shrink, so go ahead and be Mommy. If only Mommy had less pressure on her right now—but that was always the way: everything at once or nothing at all.

"Look, Deb, suppose I stay the night here with you."

Deb shook the pale, damp-streaked hair out of her eyes with a determined, grown-up gesture. "No, thanks, Mom. I'm so tired I'm just going to fall out now. You'll be getting a bellyful of all this when we move in on you tomorrow anyway. I can manage tonight, and besides—"

And besides, just in case Nick showed up, Deb didn't want Floria around complicating things; of course. Or in case the tooth fairy dropped by.

Floria restrained an impulse to insist on staying; an impulse, she recognized, that came from her own need not to be alone tonight. That was not something to load on Deb's already burdened shoulders.

"Okay," Floria said. "But look, Deb, I'll expect you to call me up first thing in the morning, whatever happens." And if I'm still alive, I'll answer the phone.

All the way home in the cab she knew with growing certainty that Weyland would be waiting for her there. He can't just walk away, she thought; he has to finish things with me. So let's get it over.

In the tiled hallway she hesitated, keys in hand. What about calling the cops to go inside with her? Absurd. You don't set the cops on a unicorn.

She unlocked and opened the door to the apartment and called inside, "Weyland! Where are you?"

Nothing. Of course not—the door was still open, and he would want to be sure she was by herself. She stepped inside, shut the door, and snapped on a lamp as she walked into the living room.

He was sitting quietly on a radiator cover by the street window, his hands on his thighs. His appearance here in a new setting, her setting, this faintly lit room in her home place, was startlingly intimate. She was sharply aware of the whisper of movement—his clothing, his shoe soles against the carpet underfoot—as he shifted his posture.

"What would you have done if I'd brought somebody with me?" she said unsteadily. "Changed yourself into a bat and flown away?"

"Two things I must have from you," he said. "One is the bill of health that we spoke of when we began, though not, after all, for Cayslin College. I've made other plans. The story of my disappearance has of course filtered out along the academic grapevine so that even two thousand miles from here people will want evidence of my mental soundness. Your evidence. I would type it myself and forge your signature, but I want your authentic tone and language. Please prepare a letter to the desired effect, addressed to these people."

He drew something white from an inside pocket and held it out. She advanced and took the envelope from his extended hand. It was from the western anthropology department that Doug had mentioned at lunch.

"Why not Cayslin?" she said. "They want you there."

"Have you forgotten your own suggestion that I find another job? That was a good idea after all. Your reference will serve me best out there—with a copy for my personnel file at Cayslin, naturally."

She put her purse down on the seat of a chair and crossed her arms. She felt reckless—the effect of stress and weariness, she thought, but it was an exciting feeling.

"The receptionist at the office does this sort of thing for me," she said.

He pointed. "I've been in your study. You have a typewriter there, you have stationery with your letterhead, you have carbon paper."

"What was the second thing you wanted?"

"Your notes on my case."

"Also at the—"

"You know that I've already searched both your work places, and the very circumspect jottings in your file on me are not what I mean. Others must exist: more detailed."

"What makes you think that?"

"How could you resist?" He mocked her. "You have encountered nothing like me in your entire professional life, and never shall again. Perhaps you hope to produce an article someday, even a book—a memoir of something impossible that happened to you one summer. You're an ambitious woman, Dr. Landauer."

Floria squeezed her crossed arms tighter against herself to quell her shivering. "This is all just supposition," she said.

He took folded papers from his pocket: some of her thrown-aside notes on him, salvaged from the wastebasket. "I found these. I think there must be more. Whatever there is, give it to me, please."

"And if I refuse, what will you do? Beat me up the way you beat up Kenny?"

Weyland said calmly, "I told you he should stop following me. This is serious now. There are pursuers who intend me ill—my former captors, of whom I told you. Whom do you think I keep watch for? No records concerning me must fall into their hands. Don't bother protesting to me your devotion to confidentiality. There is a man named Alan Reese who would take what he wants and be damned to your professional ethics. So I must destroy all evidence you have about me before I leave the city."

Floria turned away and sat down by the coffee table, trying to think beyond her fear. She breathed deeply against the fright trembling in her chest.

"I see," he said dryly, "that you won't give me the notes; you don't trust me to take them and go. You see some danger."

"All right, a bargain," she said. "I'll give you whatever I have on your case if in return you promise to go straight out to your new job and keep away from Kenny and my offices and anybody connected with me—"

He was smiling slightly as he rose from the seat and stepped soft-footed toward her over the rug. "Bargains, promises negotiations—all foolish, Dr. Landauer. I want what I came for."

She looked up at him. "But then how can I trust you at all? As soon as I give you what you want—"

"What is it that makes you afraid—that you can't render me harmless to you? What a curious concern you show suddenly for your own life and the lives of those around you! You are the one who led me to take chances in our work together—to explore the frightful risks of self-revelation. Didn't you see in the air between us the brilliant shimmer of those hazards? I thought your business was not smoothing the world over but adventuring into it, discovering its true nature, and closing valiantly with everything jagged, cruel, and deadly."

In the midst of her terror the inner choreographer awoke and stretched. Floria rose to face the vampire.

"All right, Weyland, no bargains. I'll give you freely what you want." Of course she couldn't make herself safe from him—or make Kenny or Lucille or Deb or Doug safe—any more than she could protect Jane Fennerman from the common dangers of life. Like Weyland, some dangers were too strong to bind or banish. "My notes are in the workroom—come on, I'll show you. As for the letter you need, I'll type it right now and you can take it away with you."

She sat at the typewriter arranging paper, carbon sheets, and white-out, and feeling the force of his presence. Only a few feet away, just at the margin of the light from the gooseneck lamp by which she worked, he leaned against the edge of the long table that was twin to the table in her office. Open in his large hands was the notebook she had given him from the table drawer. When he moved his head over the notebook's pages, his glasses glinted.

She typed the heading and the date. How surprising, she thought, to find that she had regained her nerve here, and now. When you dance as the inner choreographer directs, you act without thinking, not in command of events but in harmony with them. You yield control, accepting the chance that a mistake might be part of the design. The inner choreographer is always right but often dangerous: giving up control means accepting the possibility of death. What I feared I have pursued right here to this moment in this room.

A sheet of paper fell out of the notebook. Weyland stooped and caught it up, glanced at it. "You had training in art?" Must be a sketch.

"I thought once I might be an artist," she said.

"What you chose to do instead is better," he said. "This making of pictures, plays, all art, is pathetic. The world teems with creation, most of it unnoticed by your kind just as most of the deaths are unnoticed. What can be the point of adding yet another tiny gesture? Even you, these notes—for what, a moment's celebrity?"

"You tried it yourself," Floria said. "The book you edited, *Notes on a Vanished People.*" She typed: "… temporary dislocation resulting from a severe personal shock …"

"That was professional necessity, not creation," he said in the tone of a lecturer irritated by a question from the audience. With disdain he tossed the drawing on the table. "Remember, I don't share your impulse toward artistic gesture—your absurd frills—"

She looked up sharply. "The ballet, Weyland. Don't lie." She typed: "… exhibits a powerful drive toward inner balance and wholeness in a difficult life situation. The steadying influence of an extraordinary basic integrity …"

He set the notebook aside. "My feeling for ballet is clearly some sort of aberration. Do you sigh to hear a cow calling in a pasture?"

"There are those who have wept to hear whales singing in the ocean."

He was silent, his eyes averted.

"This is finished," she said. "Do you want to read it?"

He took the letter. "Good," he said at length. "Sign it, please. And type an envelope for it." He stood closer, but out of arm's reach, while she complied. "You seem less frightened."

"I'm terrified but not paralyzed," she said and laughed, but the laugh came out a gasp.

"Fear is useful. It has kept you at your best throughout our association. Have you a stamp?"

Then there was nothing to do but take a deep breath, turn off the gooseneck lamp, and follow him back into the living room. "What now, Weyland?" she said softly. "A carefully arranged suicide so that I have no chance to retract what's in that letter or to reconstruct my notes?"

At the window again, always on watch at the window, he said, "Your doorman was sleeping in the lobby. He didn't see me enter the building. Once inside, I used the stairs, of course. The suicide rate among therapists is notoriously high. I looked it up."

"You have everything all planned?"

The window was open. He reached out and touched the metal that guarded it. One end of the grille swung creaking outward into the night air, like a gate opening. She visualized him sitting there waiting for her to come home, his powerful fingers patiently working the bolts at that side of the grille loose from the brick-and-mortar window frame. The hair lifted on the back of her neck.

He turned toward her again. She could see the end of the letter she had given him sticking palely out of his jacket pocket.

"Floria," he said meditatively. "An unusual name—is it after the heroine of Sardou's *Tosca*? At the end, doesn't she throw herself to her death from a high castle wall? People are careless about the names they give their children. I will not drink from you—I hunted today, and I fed. Still, to leave you living ... is too dangerous."

A fire engine tore past below, siren screaming. When it had gone Floria said, "Listen, Weyland, you said it yourself: I can't make myself safe from you—I'm not strong enough to shove you out the window instead of being shoved out myself. Must you make yourself safe from me? Let me say this to you, without promises, demands, or pleadings: I will not go back on what I wrote in that letter. I will not try to recreate my notes. I mean it. Be content with that."

"You tempt me to it," he murmured after a moment, "to go from here with you still alive behind me for the remainder of your little life—to leave woven into Dr. Landauer's quick mind those threads of my own life that I pulled for her ... I want to be able sometimes to think of you thinking of me. But the risk is very great."

"Sometimes it's right to let the dangers live, to give them their place," she urged. "Didn't you tell me yourself a little while ago how risk makes us more heroic?"

He looked amused. "Are you instructing me in the virtues of danger? You are brave enough to know something, perhaps, about that, but I have studied danger all my life."

"A long, long life with more to come," she said, desperate to make him understand and believe her. "Not mine to jeopardize. There's no torch-brandishing peasant here; we left that behind long ago. Remember when you spoke for me? You said, 'For love of wonder.' That was true."

He leaned to turn off the lamp near the window. She thought that he had made up his mind, and that when he straightened it would be to spring.

But instead of terror locking her limbs, from the inward choreographer came a rush of warmth and energy into her muscles and an impulse to turn toward him. Out of a harmony of desires she said swiftly, "Weyland, come to bed with me."

She saw his shoulders stiffen against the dim square of the window, his head lift in scorn. "You know I can't be bribed that way," he said contemptuously. "What are you up to? Are you one of those who come into heat at the sight of an upraised fist?"

"My life hasn't twisted me that badly, thank God," she retorted. "And if you've known all along how scared I've been, you must have sensed my attraction to you too, so you know it goes back to—very early in our work. But we're not at work now and I've given up being 'up to' anything. My feeling is real—not a bribe, or a ploy, or a kink. No 'love me now, kill me later,' nothing like that. Understand me, Weyland: if death is your answer, then let's get right to it—come ahead and try."

Her mouth was dry as paper. He said nothing and made no move; she pressed on. "But if you can let me go, if we can simply part company here, then this is how I would like to mark the ending of our time together. This is the completion I want. Surely you feel something, too—curiosity at least?"

"Granted, your emphasis on the expressiveness of the body has instructed me," he admitted, and then he added lightly, "Isn't it extremely unprofessional to proposition a client?"

"Extremely, and I never do; but this, now, feels right. For you to indulge in courtship that doesn't end in a meal would be unprofessional, too, but how would it feel to indulge anyway—this once? Since we started, you've pushed me light-years beyond my profession. Now I want to travel all the way with you, Weyland. Let's be unprofessional together."

She turned and went into the bedroom, leaving the lights off. There was a reflected light, cool and diffuse, from the glowing night air of the great city. She sat down on the bed and kicked off her shoes. When she looked up, he was in the doorway.

Hesitantly, he halted a few feet from her in the dimness, then came and sat beside her. He would have lain down in his clothes, but she said quietly, "You can undress. The front door's locked and there isn't anyone here but us. You won't have to leap up and flee for your life."

He stood again and began to take off his clothes, which he draped neatly over a chair. He said, "Suppose I am fertile with you; could you conceive?"

By her own choice any such possibility had been closed off after Deb. She said, "No," and that seemed to satisfy him.

She tossed her own clothes onto the dresser.

He sat down next to her again, his body silvery in the reflected light and smooth, lean as a whippet and as roped with muscle. His cool thigh pressed against her own fuller, warmer one as he leaned across her and carefully deposited his glasses on the bedtable. Then he turned toward her, and she could just make out two puckerings of tissue on his skin: bullet scars, she thought, shivering.

He said, "But why do I wish to do this?"

"Do you?" She had to hold herself back from touching him.

"Yes." He stared at her. "How did you grow so real? The more I spoke to you of myself, the more real you became."

"No more speaking, Weyland," she said gently. "This is body work."

He lay back on the bed.

She wasn't afraid to take the lead. At the very least she could do for him as well as he did for himself, and at the most, much better. Her own skin was darker than his, a shadowy contrast where she browsed over his body with her hands. Along the contours of his ribs she felt knotted places, hollows—old healings, the tracks of time. The tension of his muscles under her touch and the sharp sound of his breathing stirred her. She lived the fantasy of sex with an utter stranger; there was no one in the world so much a stranger as he. Yet there was no one who knew him as well as she did, either. If he was unique, so was she, and so was their confluence here.

The vividness of the moment inflamed her. His body responded. His penis stirred, warmed, and thickened in her hand. He turned on his hip so that they lay facing each other, he on his right side, she on her left. When she moved to kiss him he swiftly averted his face: of course—to him, the mouth was for feeding. She touched her fingers to his lips, signifying her comprehension.

He offered no caresses but closed his arms around her, his hands cradling the back of her head and neck. His shadowed face, deep-hollowed under brow and cheekbone, was very close to hers. From between the parted lips that she must not kiss his quick breath came, roughened by groans of pleasure. At length he pressed his head against hers, inhaling deeply; taking her scent, she thought, from her hair and skin.

He entered her, hesitant at first, probing slowly and tentatively. She found this searching motion intensely sensuous, and clinging to him all along his sinewy length she rocked with him through two long, swelling waves of sweetness. Still half submerged, she felt him strain tight against her, she heard him gasp through his clenched teeth.

Panting, they subsided and lay loosely interlocked. His head was tilted back; his eyes were closed. She had no desire to stroke him or to speak with him, only to rest spent against his body and absorb the sounds of his breathing, her breathing.

He did not lie long to hold or be held. Without a word he disengaged his body from hers and got up. He moved quietly about the bedroom, gathering his clothing, his shoes, the drawings, the notes from the workroom. He dressed without lights. She listened in silence from the center of a deep repose.

There was no leavetaking. His tall figure passed and repassed the dark rectangle of the doorway, and then he was gone. The latch on the front door clicked shut.

Floria thought of getting up to secure the deadbolt. Instead she turned on her stomach and slept.

SHE WOKE AS she remembered coming out of sleep as a youngster—peppy and clearheaded.

"Hilda, let's give the police a call about that break-in. If anything ever does come of it, I want to be on record as having reported it. You can tell them we don't have any idea who did it or why. And please make a photocopy of this letter carbon to send to Doug Sharpe up at Cayslin. Then you can put the carbon into Weyland's file and close it."

Hilda sighed. "Well, he was too old anyway."

He wasn't, my dear, but never mind.

In her office Floria picked up the morning's mail from her table. Her glance strayed to the window where Weyland had so often stood. God, she was going to miss him; and God, how good it was to be restored to plain working days.

Only not yet. Don't let the phone ring, don't let the world push in here now. She needed to sit alone for a little and let her mind sort through the images left from ...from the pas de deux with Weyland. It's the notorious morning after, old dear, she told herself; just where have I been dancing, anyway?

In a clearing in the enchanted forest with the unicorn, of course, but not the way the old legends have it. According to them, hunters set a virgin to attract the unicorn by her chastity so they can catch and kill him. My unicorn was the chaste one, come to think of it, and this lady meant no treachery. No, Weyland and I met hidden from the hunt, to celebrate a private mystery of our own ...

Your mind grappled with my mind, my dark leg over your silver one, unlike closing with unlike across whatever likeness may be found: your memory pressing on my thoughts, my words drawing out your words in which you may recognize your life, my smooth palm gliding down your smooth flank . . .

Why, this will make me cry, she thought, blinking. And for what? Does an afternoon with the unicorn have any meaning for the ordinary days that come later? What has this passage with Weyland left me? Have I anything in my hands now besides the morning's mail?

What I have in my hands is my own strength, because I had to reach deep to find the strength to match him.

She put down the letters, noticing how on the backs of her hands the veins stood, blue shadows, under the thin skin. How can these hands be strong? Time was beginning to wear them thin and bring up the fragile inner structure in clear relief. That was the meaning of the last parent's death: that the child's remaining time has a limit of its own.

But not for Weyland. No graveyards of family dead lay behind him, no obvious and implacable ending of his own span threatened him. Time has to be different for a creature of an enchanted forest, as morality has to be different. He was predator and a killer formed for a life of centuries, not decades; of secret singularity, not the busy hum of the herd. Yet his strength, suited to that nonhuman life, had revived her own strength. Her hands were slim, no longer youthful, but she saw now that they were strong enough.

For what? She flexed her fingers, watching the tendons slide under the skin. Strong hands don't have to clutch. They can simply open and let go.

She dialed Lucille's extension at the clinic.

"Luce? Sorry to have missed your calls lately. Listen, I want to start making arrangements to transfer my practice for a while. You were right, I do need a break, just as all my friends have been telling me. Will you pass the word for me to the staff over there today? Good, thanks. Also, there's the workshop coming up next month … Yes. Are you kidding? They'd love to have you in my place. You're not the only one who's noticed that I've been falling apart, you know. It's awfully soon—can you manage, do you think? Luce, you are a brick and a lifesaver and all that stuff that means I'm very, very grateful."

Not so terrible, she thought, but only a start. Everything else remained to be dealt with. The glow of euphoria couldn't carry her for long. Already, looking down, she noticed jelly on her blouse, just like old times, and she didn't even remember having breakfast. If you want to keep the strength you've found in all this, you're going to have to get plenty of practice being strong. Try a tough one now.

She phoned Deb. "Of course you slept late, so what? I did, too, so I'm glad you didn't call and wake me up. Whenever you're ready—if you need help moving uptown from the hotel, I can cancel here and come down … Well, call if you change your mind. I've left a house key for you with my doorman.

"And listen, hon, I've been thinking—how about all of us going up together to Nonnie's over the weekend? Then when you feel like it maybe you'd like to talk about what you'll do next. Yes, I've already started setting up some free time for myself. Think about it, love. Talk to you later."

Kenny's turn. "Kenny, I'll come by during visiting hours this afternoon."

"Are you okay?" he squeaked.

"I'm okay. But I'm not your mommy, Ken, and I'm not going to start trying to hold the big bad world off you again. I'll expect you to be ready to settle down seriously and choose a new therapist for yourself. We're going to get that done today once and for all.

Have you got that?"

After a short silence he answered in a desolate voice, "All right."

"Kenny, nobody grown up has a mommy around to take care of things for them and keep them safe—not even me. You just have to be tough enough and brave enough yourself. See you this afternoon."

How about Jane Fennerman? No, leave it for now, we are not Wonder Woman, we can't handle that stress today as well.

TOO RESTLESS to settle down to paperwork before the day's round of appointments began, she got up and fed the goldfish, then drifted to the window and looked out over the city. Same jammed-up traffic down there, same dusty summer park stretching away uptown—yet not the same city, because Weyland no longer hunted there. Nothing like him moved now in those deep, grumbling streets. She would never come upon anyone there as alien as he—and just as well. Let last night stand as the end, unique and inimitable, of their affair. She was glutted with strangeness and looked forward frankly to sharing again in Mort's ordinary human appetite.

And Weyland—how would he do in that new and distant hunting ground he had found for himself? Her own balance had been changed. Suppose his once perfect, solitary equilibrium had been altered too? Perhaps he had spoiled it by involving himself too intimately with another being—herself. And then he had left her alive—a terrible risk. Was this a sign of his corruption at her hands?

"Oh, no," she whispered fiercely, focusing her vision on the reflection in the smudged window glass. Oh, no, I am not the temptress. I am not the deadly female out of legends whose touch defiles the hitherto unblemished being, her victim. If Weyland found some human likeness in himself, that had to be in him to begin with. Who said he was defiled anyway? Newly discovered capacities can be either strengths or weaknesses depending on how you use them.

Very pretty and reassuring, she thought grimly; but it's pure cant. Am I going to retreat now into mechanical analysis to make myself feel better?

She heaved open the window and admitted the sticky summer

breath of the city into the office. There's your enchanted forest, my dear, all nitty-gritty and not one flake of fairy dust. You've survived here, which means you can see straight when you have to. Well, you have to now. Has he been damaged? No telling yet, and you can't stop living while you wait for the answers to come in. I don't know all that was done between us, but I do know who did it: I did it, and he did it, and neither of us withdrew until it was done. We were joined in a rich complicity—he in the wakening of some flicker of humanity in himself, I in keeping and, yes, enjoying the secret—his implacable blood hunger. What that complicity means for each of us can only be discovered by getting on with living and watching for clues from moment to moment. His business is to continue from here, and mine is to do the same, without guilt and without resentment. Doug was right: the aim is individual responsibility. From that effort, not even the lady and the unicorn are exempt.

Shaken by a fresh upwelling of tears, she thought bitterly, Moving on is easy enough for Weyland; he's used to it, he's had more practice. What about me? Yes, be selfish, woman—if you haven't learned that, you've learned damn little.

The Japanese say that in middle age you should leave the claims of family, friends, and work, and go ponder the meaning of the universe while you still have the chance. Maybe I'll try just existing for a while, and letting grow in its own time my understanding of a universe that includes Weyland—and myself—among its possibilities.

Is that looking out for myself? Or am I simply no longer fit for living with family, friends, and work? Have I been damaged by him—by my marvelous, murderous monster?

Damn, she thought, I wish he were here, I wish we could talk about it. The light on her phone caught her eye; it was blinking the quick flashes that meant Hilda was signaling the imminent arrival of—not Weyland—the day's first client.

We're each on our own now, she thought, shutting the window and turning on the air-conditioner.

But think of me sometimes, Weyland, thinking of you.

BOOBS

THE THING IS, IT'S LIKE YOUR BRAIN wants to go on thinking about the miserable history mid-term you have to take tomorrow, but your body takes over. And what a body! You can see in the dark and run like the wind and leap parked cars in a single bound.

Of course you pay for it the next morning (but it's worth it). I always wake up stiff and sore, with dirty hands and feet and face, and I have to jump in the shower fast so Hilda won't see me like that.

Not that she would know what it was about, but why take chances? So I pretend it's the other thing that's bothering me. So she goes, "Come on, sweetie, everybody gets cramps, that's no reason to go around moaning and groaning. What are you doing, trying to get out of going to school just because you've got your period?"

If I didn't like Hilda, which I do even though she is only a stepmother instead of my real mother, I would show her something that would keep me out of school forever, and it's not fake, either.

But there are plenty of people I'd rather show that to.

I already showed that dork Billy Linden.

"Hey, Boobs!" he goes, in the hall right outside homeroom. A lot of kids laughed, naturally, though Rita Frye called him an asshole.

Billy is the one that started it, sort of, because he always started everything, him with his big mouth. At the beginning of term, he came barreling down on me hollering, "Hey, look at Bornstein, something musta happened to her over the summer!

What happened to Bornstein? Hey, everybody, look at Boobs Bornstein!"

He made a grab at my chest, and I socked him in the shoulder, and he punched me in the face, which made me dizzy and shocked and made me cry, too, in front of everybody.

I mean, I always used to wrestle and fight with the boys, being that I was strong for a girl. All of a sudden it was different. He hit me hard, to really hurt, and the shock sort of got me in the pit of my stomach and made me feel nauseous, too, as well as mad and embarrassed to death.

I had to go home with a bloody nose and lie with my head back and ice wrapped in a towel on my face and dripping down into my hair.

Hilda sat on the couch next to me and patted my arm. She goes, "I'm sorry about this, honey, but really, you have to learn it sometime. You're all growing up and the boys are getting stronger than you'll ever be. If you fight with boys, you're bound to get hurt. You have to find other ways to handle them."

To make things worse, the next morning I started to bleed down there, which Hilda had explained carefully to me a couple of times, so at least I knew what was going on. Hilda really tried hard without being icky about it, but I hated when she talked about how it was all part of these exciting changes in my body that are so important and how terrific it is to "become a young woman."

Sure. The whole thing was so messy and disgusting, worse than she had said, worse than I could imagine, with these black clots of gunk coming out in a smear of pink blood—I thought I would throw up. That's just the lining of your uterus, Hilda said. Big deal. It was still gross.

And plus, the smell.

Hilda tried to make me feel better, she really did. She said we should "mark the occasion" like primitive people do so it's something special, not just a nasty thing that just sort of falls on you.

So we decided to put poor old Pinkie away, my stuffed dog that I've slept with since I was three. Pinkie is bald and sort of hard and lumpy since he got put in the washing machine by mistake, and you would never know he was all soft plush when he was new, or even that he was pink.

Last time my friend Gerry-Anne came over, before the summer, she saw Pinkie laying on my pillow and though she didn't say anything, I could tell she was thinking that was kind of babyish.

So I'd been thinking about not keeping Pinkie around any more.

Hilda and I made him this nice box lined with pretty scraps from her quilting class, and I thanked him out loud for being my friend for so many years, and we put him up in the closet, on the top shelf.

I felt bad about it, but if Gerry-Anne decided I was too babyish to be friends with any more, I could end up with no friends at all. When you have never been popular since the time you were skinny and fast and everybody wanted you on their team, you have that kind of thing on your mind.

Hilda and Dad made me go to school the next morning so nobody would think I was scared of Billy Linden (which I was) or that he could keep me away just by being such a dork.

Everybody kept sneaking funny looks at me and whispering, and I was sure it was because I couldn't help walking funny with the pad between my legs and they could smell what was happening, which as far as I knew hadn't happened to anybody else in Eight A yet. Just like nobody else in the whole grade had anything real in their stupid training bras except me, thanks a lot!

Anyway I stayed away from everybody as much as I could and wouldn't talk to Gerry-Anne, even, because I was scared she would ask me why I walked funny and smelled bad.

Billy Linden avoided me just like everybody else, except one of his stupid buddies purposely bumped into me so I stumbled into Billy on the lunch-line. Billy turns around and goes, real loud, "Hey, Boobs, when did you start wearing black-and-blue makeup?"

I didn't give him the satisfaction of knowing that he had actually broken my nose, which the doctor said. Good thing they don't have to bandage you up for that. Billy would have been hollering up a storm about how I had my nose in a sling as well as my boobs.

That night I got up after I was supposed to be asleep and took off my underpants and T-shirt that I sleep in and stood looking at myself in the mirror. I didn't need to turn a light on. The moon was full and it was shining right into my bedroom through the big dormer window.

I crossed my arms and pinched myself hard to sort of punish my body for what it was doing to me.

As if that could make it stop.

No wonder Edie Siler starved herself to death in the tenth grade! I understood her perfectly. She was trying to keep her body down, keep it normal-looking, thin and strong, like I was too, back when I looked like a person, not a cartoon that somebody would call "Boobs."

And then something warm trickled in a little line down the inside of my leg, and I knew it was blood and I couldn't stand it any more. I pressed my thighs together and shut my eyes hard, and I did something.

I mean I felt it happening. I felt myself shrink down to a hard core of sort of cold fire inside my bones, and all the flesh part, the muscles and the squishy insides and the skin, went sort of glowing and free-floating, all shining with moonlight, and I felt a sort of shifting and balance-changing going on.

I thought I was fainting on account of my stupid period. So I turned around and threw myself on my bed, only by the time I hit it, I knew something was seriously wrong.

For one thing, my nose and my head were crammed with these crazy, rich sensations that it took me a second to even figure out were smells, they were so much stronger than any smells I'd ever smelled. And they were—I don't know—*interesting* instead of just stinky, even the rotten ones.

I opened my mouth to get the smells a little better, and heard myself panting in a funny way as if I'd been running, which I hadn't, and then there was this long part of my face sticking out and something moving there—my tongue.

I was licking my chops.

Well, there was this moment of complete and utter panic. I tore around the room whining and panting and hearing my toenails clicking on the floorboards, and then I huddled down and crouched in the corner because I was scared Dad and Hilda would hear me and come to find out what was making all this racket.

Because I could hear them. I could hear their bed creak when one of them turned over, and Dad's breath whistling a little in an almost-snore, and I could smell them too, each one with a perfectly clear bunch of smells, kind of like those desserts of mixed ice cream flavors they call a medley.

My body was twitching and jumping with fear and energy, and my room—it's a converted attic-space, wide but with a ceiling that's low in places—my room felt like a jail. And plus, I was terrified of catching a glimpse of myself in the mirror. I had a pretty good idea of what I would see, and I didn't want to see it.

Besides, I had to pee, and I couldn't face trying to deal with the toilet in the state I was in.

So I eased the bedroom door open with my shoulder and

nearly fell down the stairs trying to work them with four legs and thinking about it, instead of letting my body just do it. I put my hands on the front door to open it, but my hands weren't hands, they were paws with long knobby toes covered in fur, and the toes had thick black claws sticking out of the ends of them.

The pit of my stomach sort of exploded with horror, and I yelled. It came out this wavery "woooo" noise that echoed eerily in my skullbones.

Upstairs, Hilda goes, "Jack, what was that?" I bolted for the basement as I heard Dad hit the floor of their bedroom.

The basement door slips its latch all the time, so I just shoved it open and down I went, doing better on the stairs this time because I was too scared to think. I spent the rest of the night down there, moaning to myself (which meant whining through my nose, really) and trotting around rubbing against the walls trying to rub off this crazy shape I had, or just moving around because I couldn't sit still. The place was thick with stinks and these slow-swirling currents of hot and cold air. I couldn't handle all the input.

As for having to pee, in the end I managed to sort of hike my butt up over the edge of the slop-sink by Dad's workbench and let go in there. The only problem was that I couldn't turn the taps on to rinse out the smell because of my paws.

Then about three a.m. I woke up from a doze curled up on a bare place on the floor where the spiders weren't so likely to walk, and I couldn't see a thing or smell anything much either, so I knew I was okay again even before I checked and found fingers on my hands again instead of claws.

I zipped upstairs and stood under the shower so long that Hilda yelled at me for using up the hot water when she had a load of wash to do. I was only trying to steam the stiffness out of my muscles, but I couldn't tell her that.

It was really weird to just dress and go to school after a night like that. One good thing, I had stopped bleeding after only one day, which Hilda said wasn't so strange for the first time. So it had to be the huge greenish bruise on my face from Billy's punch that everybody kept staring at.

That and the usual thing, of course. Well, why not? They didn't know I'd spent the night as a wolf.

So Fat Joey grabbed my book bag in the hallway outside the Science lab and tossed it to some kid from Eight B. I had to run after them to get it back, which of course was set up so the boys could cheer the jouncing of my boobs under my shirt.

I was so mad I almost caught Fat Joey, except I was afraid if I grabbed him, maybe he would sock me like Billy had.

Dad had told me, Don't let it get you, kid, all boys are jerks at that age.

Hilda had been saying all summer, Look, it doesn't do any good to walk around all hunched up with your arms crossed, you should throw your shoulders back and walk like a proud person who's pleased that she's growing up. You're just a little early, that's all, and I bet the other girls are secretly envious of you, with their cute little training bras, for Chrissake, as if there was something that needed to be *trained*.

It's okay for her, she's not in school, she doesn't remember what it's like.

So I quit running and walked after Joey until the bell rang, and then I got my book bag back from the bushes outside where he threw it. I was crying a little, and I ducked into the girls' room.

Stacey Buhl was in there doing her lipstick like usual and wouldn't talk to me like usual, but Rita came bustling in and said somebody should off that dumb dork Joey, except of course it was really Billy that put him up to it. Like usual.

Rita is okay except she's an outsider herself, being that her kid brother has AIDS, and lots of kids' parents don't think she should even be in the school. So I don't hang around with her a lot. I've got enough trouble, and anyway I was late for Math.

I had to talk to somebody, though. After school I told Gerry-Anne, who's been my best friend on and off since Fourth Grade. She was off at the moment, but I found her in the library and told her I'd had a weird dream about being a wolf. She wants to be a psychiatrist like her mother, so of course she listened.

She told me I was nuts. That was a big help.

That night I made sure the back door wasn't exactly closed, and then I got in bed with no clothes on—imagine turning into a wolf in your underpants and T-shirt!—and just shivered, waiting for something to happen.

The moon came up and shone in my window, and I changed again, just like before, which is not one bit like how it is in the movies—all struggling and screaming and bones snapping with horrible cracking and tearing noises, just the way I guess you would imagine it to be, if you knew it had to be done by building special machines to do that for the camera and make it look real: if you were a special-effects man, instead of a werewolf.

For me, it didn't have to look real, it *was* real. It was this melting and drifting thing, which I got sort of excited by it this time. I mean it felt—interesting. Like something I was doing, instead of just another dumb body-mess happening to me because some brainless hormones said so.

I must have made a noise. Hilda came upstairs to the door of my bedroom, but luckily she didn't come in. She's tall, and my ceiling is low for her, so she often talks to me from the landing.

Anyway I'd heard her coming, so I was in my bed with my whole head shoved under my pillows, praying frantically that nothing showed.

I could smell her, it was the wildest thing—her own smell, sort of sweaty but sweet, and then on top of it her perfume, like an ice-pick stuck up my nose. I didn't actually hear a word she said, I was too scared, and also I had this ripply shaking feeling inside me, a high that was only partly terror.

See, I realized all of a sudden, with this big blossom of surprise, that I didn't have to be scared of Hilda or anybody. I was strong, my wolf-body was strong, and anyhow one clear look at me and she would drop dead.

What a relief, though, when she went away. I was dying to get out from under the weight of the covers, and besides I had to sneeze. Also I recognized that part of the energy roaring around inside me was hunger.

They went to bed—I heard their voices even in their bedroom, though not exactly what they said, which was fine. The words weren't important any more, I could tell more from the tone of what they were saying.

Like I knew they were going to do it, and I was right. I could hear them messing around right through the walls, which was also something new, and I have never been so embarrassed in my life. I couldn't even put my hands over my ears, because my hands were paws.

So while I was waiting for them to go to sleep, I looked myself over in the big mirror on my closet door.

There was this big wolf head with a long slim muzzle and a thick ruff around my neck. The ruff stood up as I growled and backed up a little.

Which was silly of course, there was no wolf in the bedroom with me. But I was all strung out, I guess, and one wolf, me in my wolf-body, was as much as I could handle the idea of, let alone two wolves, me and my reflection.

After that first shock, it was great. I kept turning one way and another for different views.

I was thin, with these long, slender legs, but strong, you could see the muscles, and feet a little bigger than I would have picked. But I'll take four big feet over two big boobs any day.

My face was terrific, with jaggedy white ripsaw teeth and eyes that were small and clear and gleaming in the moonlight. The tail was a little bizarre, but I got used to it, and actually it had a nice plumey shape. My shoulders were big and covered with long, glossy-looking fur, and I had this neat coloring, dark on the back and a sort of melting silver on my front and underparts.

The thing was, though, *my tongue*, hanging out. I had a lot of trouble with that, it looked gross and silly at the same time. I mean, that was *my* tongue, about a foot long and neatly draped over the points of my bottom canines. That was when I realized that I didn't have a whole lot of expressions to use, not with that face, which was more like a mask.

But it was alive, it was my face, those were my own long black lips that my tongue licked.

No doubt about it, this was me. I was a werewolf, like in the movies they show over Halloween weekend. But it wasn't anything like your ugly movie werewolf that's just some guy loaded up with pounds and pounds of makeup. I was *gorgeous*.

I didn't want to just hang around admiring myself in the mirror, though. I couldn't stand being cooped up in that stuffy, smell-crowded room.

When everything else settled down and I could hear Dad and Hilda breathing the way people do when they're asleep, I snuck out.

The dark wasn't very dark to me, and the cold felt sharp like vinegar, but not in a hurting way. Everyplace I went, there were these currents like waves in the air, and I could draw them through my long wolf nose and roll the smell of them over the back of my tongue. It was like a whole different world, with bright sounds everywhere and rich, strong smells.

And I could run.

I started running because a car came by while I was sniffing at the garbage bags on the curb, and I was really scared of being seen in the headlights. So I took off down the dirt alley between our house and the Morrisons' next door, and holy cow, I could tear along with hardly a sound, I could jump their picket fence without even thinking about it. My back legs were like steel springs and I came down solid and square on four legs with almost no shock at all, let alone worrying about losing my balance or turning an ankle.

Man, I could run through that chilly air all thick and moisty with smells, I could almost fly. It was like last year, when I didn't have boobs bouncing and yanking in front even when I'm only walking fast.

Just two rows of neat little bumps down the curve of my belly. I sat down and looked.

I tore open garbage bags to find out about the smells in them, but I didn't eat anything from them. I wasn't about to chow down on other people's stale hotdog-ends and pizza crusts and fat and bones scraped off their plates and all mixed in with mashed potatoes and stuff.

When I found places where dogs had stopped and made their mark, I squatted down and pissed there too, right on top, I just wiped them out.

I bounded across that enormous lawn around the Wanscombe place, where nobody but the Asian gardener ever sets foot, and walked up the back and over the top of their BMW, leaving big fat pawprints all over it. Nobody saw me, nobody heard me, I was a shadow.

Well, except for the dogs, of course.

There was a lot of barking when I went by, real hysterics which at first made me really scared. But then I popped out of an alley up on Ridge Road, right in front of about six dogs that run together. Their owners let them out all night and don't care if they get hit by a car.

They'd been trotting along with the wind behind them, checking the garbage set out for pickup the next morning. When they saw me, one of them let out a yelp of surprise, and they all skidded to a stop.

Six of them. I was scared. I growled.

The dogs turned fast, banging into each other in their hurry, and trotted away.

I don't know what they would have done if they met a real wolf, but I was something special, I guess.

I followed them.

They scattered and ran.

I ran too, and this was a different kind of running. I mean, I stretched, and I raced, and there was this joy. I chased one of them.

Zig, zag, this little terrier-kind of dog tried to cut left and dive under the gate of somebody's front walk, all without a sound—he was running too hard to yell, and I was happy running quiet.

Just before he could ooze under the gate, I caught up with him and without thinking I grabbed the back of his neck and pulled him off his feet and gave him a shake as hard as I could, from side to side.

I felt his neck crack, the sound vibrated through all the bones of my face.

I picked him up in my mouth, and it was like he hardly weighed a thing. I trotted away holding him up off the ground, and under a bush in Baker's Park I held him down with my paws and bit into his belly, that was still warm and quivering.

Like I said, I was hungry.

The blood gave me this rush like you wouldn't believe. I stood there a minute looking around and licking my lips, just sort of panting and tasting the taste because I was stunned by it, it was like eating honey or the best chocolate malted you ever had.

So I put my head down and chomped that little dog like shoving your face into a pizza and inhaling it. God, I was *starved*, so I didn't mind that the meat was tough and rank-tasting after that first wonderful bite. I even licked blood off the ground after, never mind the grit mixed in.

I ate two more dogs that night, one that was tied up on a clothesline in a cruddy yard full of rusted-out car parts down on the South side, and one fat old yellow dog out snuffling around on his own and way too slow. He tasted pretty bad and by then I was feeling full, so I left a lot.

I strolled around the park, shoving the swings with my big black wolf nose, and I found the bench where Mr. Granby sits and feeds the pigeons every day, never mind that nobody else wants the dirty birds around crapping on their cars. I took a dump there, right where he sits.

Then I gave the setting moon a goodnight, which came out quavery and wild, "Loo-loo-loo!" And I loped toward home, springing off the thick pads of my paws and letting my tongue loll out and feeling generally super.

I slipped inside and trotted upstairs, and in my room I stopped to look at myself in the mirror.

As gorgeous as before, and only a few dabs of blood on me, which I took time to lick off. I did get a little worried—I mean, suppose that was it, suppose having killed and eaten what I'd killed in my wolf shape, I was stuck in this shape forever? Like, if you wander into a fairy castle and eat or drink anything, that's it, you can't ever leave. Suppose when the morning came I didn't change back?

Well, there wasn't much I could do about that one way or the other, and to tell the truth, I felt like I wouldn't mind; it had been worth it.

When I was nice and clean, including licking off my own bottom which seemed like a perfectly normal and nice thing to do at the time, I jumped up on the bed, curled up, and corked right off. When I woke up with the sun in my eyes, there I was, my own self again.

It was very strange, grabbing breakfast and wearing my old sweatshirt that wallowed all over me so I didn't stick out so much, while Hilda yawned and shuffled around in her robe and slippers and acted like her and Dad hadn't been doing it last night, which I knew different.

And plus, it was perfectly clear that she didn't have a clue about what I had been doing, which gave me a strange feeling.

One of the things about growing up which they're careful not to tell you is, you start having more things you don't talk to your parents about. And I had a doozie.

Hilda goes, "What's the matter, are you off Sugar Pops now? Honestly, Kelsey, I can't keep up with you! And why can't you wear something nicer than that old shirt to school? Oh, I get it; disguise, right?"

She sighed and looked at me kind of sad but smiling, her hands on her hips. "Kelsey, Kelsey," she goes, "if only I'd had half of what you've got when I was a girl—I was as flat as an ironing board, and it made me so miserable, I can't tell you."

She's real thin and neat-looking, so what does she know about it? But she meant well, and anyhow I was feeling so good I didn't argue.

I didn't change my shirt, though.

That night I didn't turn into a wolf. I laid there waiting, but though the moon came up, nothing happened no matter how hard I tried, and after a while I went and looked out the window and realized that the moon wasn't really full any more, it was getting smaller.

I wasn't so much relieved as sorry. I bought a calendar at the school book sale two weeks later, and I checked the full moon nights coming up and waited anxiously to see what happened.

Meantime, things rolled along as usual. I got a rash of zits on my chin. I would look in the mirror and think about my wolf-face, that had beautiful sleek fur instead of zits.

Zits and all I went to Angela Durkin's party, and the next day Billy Linden told everybody that I went in one of the bedrooms at Angela's and made out with him, which I did not. But since no grown-ups were home and Fat Joey brought grass to the party, most of the kids were stoned and didn't know who did what or where anyhow.

As a matter of fact, Billy once actually did get a girl in Seven B high one time out in his parents' garage and him and two of his friends did it to her while she was zonked out of her mind, or anyway they said they did, and she was too embarrassed to say anything one way or another, and a little while later she changed schools.

How I know about it as the same way everybody else does, which is because Billy was the biggest boaster in the whole school, and you could never tell if he was lying or not.

So I guess it wasn't so surprising that some people believed what Billy said about me. Gerry-Anne quit talking to me after that. Meantime, Hilda got pregnant.

This turned into a huge discussion about how Hilda had been worried about her biological clock so she and Dad had decided to have a kid, and I shouldn't mind, it would be fun for me and good preparation for being a mother myself later on, when I found some nice guy and got married.

Sure. Great preparation. Like Mary O'Hare in my class, who gets to change her baby sister's diapers all the time, yick. She jokes about it, but you can tell she really hates it. Now it looked like it was my turn coming up, as usual.

The only thing that made life bearable was my secret.

"You're laid back today," Devon Brown said to me in the lunchroom one day after Billy had been specially obnoxious, trying to flick rolled up bits of bread from his table so they would land on my chest. Devon was sitting with me because he was bad at French, my only good subject, and I was helping him out with some verbs. I guess he wanted to know why I wasn't upset because of Billy picking on me. He goes, "How come?"

"That's a secret," I said, thinking about what Devon would say if he knew a werewolf was helping him with his French: *loup, manger.*

He goes, "What secret?" Devon has freckles and is actually kind of cute-looking.

"A secret," I go, "so I can't tell you, dummy."

He looks real superior and he goes, "Well, it can't be much of a secret, because girls can't keep secrets, everybody knows that."

Sure, like that kid Sara in Eight B who it turned out her own father had been molesting her for years, but she never told anybody until some psychologist caught on from some tests we all had to take in seventh grade. Up 'til then, Sara kept her secret fine.

And I kept mine, marking off the days on the calendar. The only part I didn't look forward to was having a period again, which last time came right before the change.

When the time came, I got crampy and more zits popped out on my face, but I didn't have a period.

I changed, though.

The next morning they were talking in school about a couple of prize miniature schnauzers at the Wanscombes that had been hauled out of their yard by somebody and killed, and almost nothing left of them.

Well, my stomach turned a little when I heard some kids describing what Mr. Wanscombe had found over in Baker's Park, "the remains," as people said. I felt a little guilty, too, because Mrs. Wanscombe really loved those little dogs, which somehow I didn't think about at all when I was a wolf the night before, trotting around hungry in the moonlight.

I knew those schnauzers personally, so I was sorry, even if they were irritating little mutts that made a lot of noise.

But heck, the Wanscombes shouldn't have left them out all night in the cold. Anyhow, they were rich, they could buy new ones if they wanted.

Still and all, though. I mean, dogs are just dumb animals. If they're mean, it's because they're wired that way or somebody made them mean, they can't help it. They can't just decide to be nice, like a person can. And plus, they don't taste so great, I think because they put so much junk in commercial dog-foods—anti-worm medicine and ashes and ground up fish, stuff like that. Ick.

In fact after the second schnauzer I had felt sort of sick and I didn't sleep real well that night. So I was not in a great mood to start with; and that was the day that my new brassiere disappeared while I was in gym. Later on I got passed a note telling me where to find it: stapled to the bulletin board outside the Principal's office, where everybody could see that I was trying a bra with an underwire.

Naturally, it had to be Stacey Buhl that grabbed my bra while I was changing for gym and my back was turned, since she was now hanging out with Billy and his friends.

Billy went around all day making bets at the top of his lungs on how soon I would be wearing a D-cup.

Stacey didn't matter, she was just a jerk. Billy mattered.

He had wrecked me in that school forever, with his nasty mind and his big, fat mouth. I was past crying or fighting and getting punched out. I was boiling, I had had enough crap from him, and I had an idea.

I followed Billy home and waited on his porch until his mom came home and she made him come down and talk to me. He stood in the doorway and talked through the screen door, eating a banana and lounging around like he didn't have a care in the world.

So he goes, "Watcha want, Boobs?"

I stammered a lot, being I was so nervous about telling such big lies, but that probably made me sound more believable.

I told him that I would make a deal with him: I would meet him that night in Baker's Park, late, and take off my shirt and bra and let him do whatever he wanted with my boobs if that would satisfy his curiosity and he would find somebody else to pick on and leave me alone.

"What?" he said, staring at my chest with his mouth open. His voice squeaked and he was practically drooling on the floor. He couldn't believe his good luck.

I said the same thing over again.

He almost came out onto the porch to try it right then and there. "Well, shit," he goes, lowering his voice a lot, "why didn't you say something before? You really mean it?"

I go, "Sure," though I couldn't look at him.

After a minute he goes, "Okay, it's a deal. Listen, Kelsey, if you like it, can we, uh, do it again, you know?"

I go, "Sure. But Billy, one thing: this is a secret, between just you and me. If you tell anybody, if there's just one other person hanging around out there tonight—"

"Oh, no," he goes, real fast, "I won't say a thing to anybody, honest. Not a word, I promise!"

Not until afterward, of course, was what he meant, which if there was one thing Billy Linden couldn't do, it was to keep quiet if he knew something bad about another person.

"You're gonna like it, I know you are," he goes, speaking strictly for himself as usual. "Jeez, I can't believe this!"

But he did, the dork.

I couldn't eat much for dinner that night, I was too excited, and

I went upstairs early—to do homework, I told Dad and Hilda.

Then I waited for the moon, and when it came, I changed.

Billy was in the park. I caught a whiff of him, very sweaty and excited, but I stayed cool. I snuck around for a while, as quiet as I could—which was real quiet—making sure none of his stupid friends were lurking around. I mean, I wouldn't have trusted his promise for a million dollars.

I passed up half a hamburger lying in the gutter where somebody had parked for lunch next to Baker's Park. My mouth watered, but I didn't want to spoil my appetite. I was hungry and happy, sort of singing inside my own head, "Shoo, fly, pie, and an apple-pan-dowdie ..."

Without any sound, of course.

Billy had been sitting on a bench, his hands in his pockets, twisting around to look this way and that way, watching for me—my human self—to come join him. He had a jacket on, being it was very chilly out.

Which he didn't stop to think that maybe a sane person wouldn't be crazy enough to sit out there and take off her top leaving her naked skin bare to the breeze. But that was Billy all right, totally fixed on his own greedy self without a single thought for somebody else. I bet all he could think about was what a great scam this was, to feel up old Boobs in the park and then crow about it all over school.

Now he was walking around the park, kicking at the sprinkler-heads and glancing up every once in a while, frowning and looking sulky.

I could see he was starting to think that I might stand him up. Maybe he even suspected that old Boobs was lurking around watching him and laughing to herself because he had fallen for a trick. Maybe old Boobs had even brought some kids from school with her to see what a jerk he was.

Actually that would have been pretty good, except Billy probably would have broken my nose for me again, or worse, if I'd tried it.

"Kelsey?" he goes, sounding mad.

I didn't want him stomping off home in a huff. I moved up closer, and I let the bushes swish a little around my shoulders.

He goes, "Hey, Kelse, it's late, where've you been?"

I listened to the words, but mostly I listened to the little thread of worry flickering in his voice, low and high, high and low, as he tried to figure out what was going on.

I let out the whisper of a growl.

He stood real still, staring at the bushes, and he goes, "That you, Kelse? Answer me."

I was wild inside. I couldn't wait another second. I tore through the bushes and leaped for him, flying.

He stumbled backward with a squawk—"What!"—jerking his hands up in front of his face, and he was just sucking in a big breath to yell with when I hit him like a demo-derby truck.

I jammed my nose past his feeble claws and chomped down hard on his face.

No sound came out of him except this wet, thick gurgle, which I could more taste than hear because the sound came right into my mouth with the gush of his blood and the hot mess of meat and skin that I tore away and swallowed.

He thrashed around, hitting at me, but I hardly felt anything through my fur. I mean, he wasn't so big and strong laying there on the ground with me straddling him all lean and wiry with wolf-muscle. And plus, he was in shock. I got a strong whiff from below as he let go of everything right into his pants.

Dogs were barking, but so many people around Baker's Park have dogs to scare away burglars, and the dogs make such a racket all the time, that nobody pays any attention. I wasn't worried. Anyway, I was too busy to care.

I nosed in under what was left of Billy's jaw and I bit his throat out.

Now let him go around telling lies about people.

His clothes were a lot of trouble and I really missed having hands. I managed to drag his shirt out of his belt with my teeth, though, and it was easy to tear his belly open. Pretty messy, but once I got in there, it was better than Thanksgiving dinner. Who would think that somebody as horrible as Billy Linden could taste so *good?*

He was barely moving by then, and I quit thinking about him as Billy Linden any more. I quit thinking at all, I just pushed my muzzle in and pulled out delicious, steaming chunks and ate until I was picking at tidbits, and everything was getting cold.

On the way home I saw a police car cruising the neighborhood the way they do sometimes. I hid in the shadows and of course they never saw me.

There was a lot of washing up to do that night, and when Hilda saw my sheets in the morning she shook her head. She goes, "You should be more careful about keeping track of your period so as not to get caught by surprise like this."

Everybody in school knew something had happened to Billy Linden, but it wasn't until the day after that they got the word. Kids stood around in little huddles trading rumors about how some wild animal had chewed Billy up. I would walk up and listen in and add a really gross remark or two, part of the game of thrilling each other green and nauseous with made-up details to see who would upchuck first.

Not me, though it was a near thing. I mean, when somebody went on about how Billy's whole head was gnawed down to the skull and they didn't even know who he was except from the bus pass in his wallet, I got a little urpy. It's amazing the things people will dream up.

But when I thought about what I had actually done to Billy, I had to smile. And it felt totally wonderful to walk through the halls without having anybody yelling, "Hey, Boobs!"

There are people who just plain do not deserve to live. And the same goes for Fat Joey, if he doesn't quit crowding me in science lab, trying to get a feel.

One funny thing, though, I don't get periods at all any more. I get a little crampy, and my breasts get sore, and I break out more than usual—and then instead of bleeding, I change.

Which is fine with me, though I take a lot more care now about how I hunt on my wolf nights. I stay away from Baker's Park. The suburbs go on for miles and miles, and there are lots of places I can hunt and still get home by morning. A running wolf can cover a lot of ground.

And I make sure I make my kills where I can eat in private, so no cop car can catch me unawares, which could easily have happened that night when I killed Billy, I was so deep into the eating thing that first time. I look around a lot more now when I'm on a kill, I keep watch.

Good thing it's only once a month this happens, and only a couple of nights. "The Full Moon Killer" has the whole state up in arms and terrified as it is. Eventually I guess I'll have to go somewhere else, which I'm not looking forward to it at all. If I can just last until I can have a car of my own, life will get a lot easier.

Meantime, some wolf nights I don't even feel like hunting. Mostly I'm not as hungry as I was those first times. I think I must have been storing up my appetite for a long time. Sometimes now I just prowl around, and I run, boy do I run. If I am hungry, sometimes I eat from the garbage instead of killing somebody. It's no fun, but you do get a taste for it. I don't mind garbage as long as once in a while I can have the real thing fresh-killed, nice and wet. People can be awfully nasty, but they sure taste sweet.

I do pick and choose, though. I look for people sneaking around in the middle of the night, like Billy waiting in the park that time. I figure they've got to be out looking for trouble at that hour, so whose fault is it if they find it? I have done a lot more for the burglary problem around Baker's Park than a hundred dumb "watchdogs," believe me.

Gerry-Anne is not only talking to me again, she has invited me to go on a double-date with her. Some guy she met at a party invited her, and he has a friend. They're both from Fawcett Junior High across town, which will be a nice change. I was nervous, but finally I said yes. We're going to the movies next weekend. My first real date! I am still pretty nervous, to tell the truth.

For New Years, I have made two solemn vows.

One is that on this date I will not worry about my chest, I will not be self-conscious, even if the guy stares.

The other is, I'll never eat another dog.

EVIL THOUGHTS

THE CRAZY LADY'S GODDAMN DOGS were barking again. Fran shunted the breakfast dishes into the dishwasher (what had won her to the new house was that dishwasher) and swore under her breath.

"What's the matter?" said Jeffrey, as he went on carefully layering books and notepads into his backpack.

Dear Jeffrey. He so charmingly lived in his youthful mind and was so tolerant even when you pointed out to him the things that should be driving him nuts the way they drove you nuts, even though you weren't an old married couple, only live-togethers, slightly mismatched. By age, anyway.

"I said I wish somebody would run over those damn dogs of hers," Fran growled. "Save me, Lord, from little dogs! Everybody knows little dogs are crazy, from being so much smaller than everybody else that they're scared all the time. And in this case their owner is crazy too."

"Who, Whatsername next door?" Jeffrey said. "I thought she was a nurse. Do they let crazy people be nurses?"

"No, dummy, not that one. I mean Whatsername up our street two or three houses, toward the park," Fran said, glaring at the window over the sink; it was stuck again and would have to be worked on by somebody (not Jeffrey, who was not handy). "That's where the dogs are. God, Jeff, don't you hear them?"

"Sure," he said equably, "but heck, they're probably the only company she's got if she's as nutty as you think. I can't find my torts text."

"Nuttier." Fran rooted under the sink for the dishwashing fluid.

"She really is nuts, no kidding. Did I tell you? She yelled at me for walking past her place, in the back. Around twilight yesterday, while the oven was heating up to make dinner, I took a stroll in the lane behind the houses, up to the park. As I passed her place, all of a sudden these dogs started yapping and a floodlight came on, if you can believe that, at the corner of the house; and she started screaming at me from inside. Waving her arms at me through the kitchen window. It was the damnedest thing."

Jeffrey patiently lifted up the piles of old newspapers, mail, bills, catalogs, and so on, looking for his book. He would be late for class again, but did he get nervous or rushed? Not him. It was one of the things she loved about him, one of the things that had made the move bearable. When she wasn't feeling completely jangled herself, and resenting his calm.

"Screaming what?" he said. "What did she say?"

"I don't know, exactly. I could only catch a few words. It was all so violent and wild—something about burglars. Do I look like a burglar to you? I was just an ordinary, undangerous woman walking along a public thoroughfare in broad daylight, and you'd have thought it was the hordes of Ghengis Khan, come to rape and pillage or something."

"Thought you said 'twilight'," he observed mildly, pausing to read something from the heap of junk mail.

"All right, twilight, but good grief, Jeff, it was ridiculous! What did she think I was going to do? I could hear her shrieking, and those damn little dogs of hers yipping, all the way to the end of the lane."

"Maybe she's been burgled a lot," Jeffrey said, putting the paper down, "or pestered to death by commercial solicitations. What was I looking for?"

"Torts."

He was probably right. Their own house had been equipped at some recent point with a fancy burglar alarm (much too complex, a nuisance to use), which indicated something about the neighborhood, she supposed. Hell, give the crazy lady in 408 the benefit of the doubt. At least the damned dogs had quit yelping at last.

Jeffrey rolled his bike outside, carrying his book-stuffed pack slung on his back. "Hey, Fran?" he called.

"Um?" she said, reading the directions on the inside of the dishwasher cover again.

"How often are you watering the grass? Look: there's a bunch of mushrooms sprouting on the lawn."

Fran tied her bathrobe belt more tightly around her waist and padded outside to stand barefoot on the cement front step and look where he was pointing. She saw a clutch of pale, striated bubbles clustered on a little rise in the grass. The raised place was a writhe of half-buried root that had reached far from the thick-trunked mountain cottonwood that leaned toward the house. Roots showed like gnarled dolphins surfacing all over the lawn.

"I've been watering three times a week, just as you said to," she said, "because it's been so hot, for September."

"But sometimes it drizzles at night," Jeffrey replied. "Too much moisture could be bad for the grass. Let's try cutting down a little."

"Sure," she said. She went to the curb on the concrete path and hugged him, and he almost fell over, bike and all. They giggled and made a minor spectacle of themselves, and then he pedaled away up the quiet suburban street toward the university.

Take that, neighbors, Fran thought, palming her hair back from her face. She almost regretted her youthful looks, which kept it from being obvious (at any distance, anyway) that she was older than Jeffrey. "Older Woman Kisses Law School Lover Goodbye." Yum.

Never mind, she would show any watching neighbors that she was a worthy householder no matter what. She would tend to her lawn.

The smooth slope of grass from the front wall of the house down to the sidewalk really was a source of pleasure, roots and all. The sprinkler system was a thrill—all that control, at the mere turn of a handle! All that grass, under the high, dappled canopy of the one large tree. It was a far cry from the little apartment with the tiny brick patio where they had started living together.

She picked her way across the wet grass (alert for deposits left by wandering neighborhood dogs) and inspected the little stand of mushrooms.

They must have popped up overnight; they certainly hadn't been there yesterday. How nice if they should prove to be edible: sauteed mushrooms, fresh picked, some rare type stuffed with healthful and exotic vitamins, no doubt.

But they didn't look edible. Seen up close, each mushroom was about as big as a knuckle of her hand, round, and of a particularly unattractive greasy pallor that made her wrinkle her nose. They looked—well, *fungoid*, anything but fresh and wholesome; alien, actually. Alien to the dinner table, anyway, unless it was some French dinner table regularly graced with sauced animal glands and such.

Well, sunlight would no doubt kill the pallid little knobs. People grew mushrooms in cellars, didn't they? Her newly acquired southwestern lawn was hardly a dark cellar. She was no gardener, but this much she could figure out.

She typed medical transcripts from her tape machine until the dishwasher made a weird sound and vomited dirty water onto the floor. A session with an outrageously expensive plumber, plus his doltish (also expensive) apprentice, followed, and there went the rest of the morning.

At least her ancient and rusted Volks started without fuss. But when Fran delivered the transcript pages she had finished, Carmella, her supplier, informed her that two of the doctors were going on vacation (at the same time, of course). There would be less work for a while.

Fran cursed all the way home. If only Carmella had told her sooner that this was coming! If only Fran herself had remembered this seasonal problem from last year (it was exactly the same in Ohio). What could she have done about it, though? Not bought that little rug for the front hallway at the flea market, that's what.

A package had been left for her with her neighbor on the north, a plump girl who brought it over and introduced herself as Betsy. As Jeff had mentioned, she was a nurse with a late shift at a nearby hospital. To Fran she seemed awfully young and feather-headed to be taking care of sick people.

Betsy wandered around admiring the rather scanty furniture and the posters Fran had hung on the walls while she answered Fran's delicate soundings about the neighborhood around Baker's Park.

Yeah, the "convenience" store down on Rhoades Avenue was a rip-off joint, but the shoemaker next door to it was okay if the work wasn't anything complicated. And it was a good idea to keep your car doors locked even when it was parked in your driveway. They did have burglaries sometimes, which was why so many people had dogs. Not that the dogs did much good. No, Betsy didn't have dogs herself and neither did her housemates, one an elementary school teacher, one in social work, all three renting from the older couple (retired now to Florida) who owned the house.

"Anyway," she added, "those two little monsters in 408 are more than enough for the whole neighborhood!"

Fran laid aside the totally inappropriate blouse her sister had sent her for her birthday (I'm not a little old biddy yet, she thought irritably, but her sister was a decade younger and clearly still had a child's view of anyone over thirty) and offered Betsy tea. "What about that woman?" she said, sitting down across the kitchen table from her visitor. "The one with the dogs?"

"Oh, she's weird," Betsy said with cheerful enthusiasm. "Nutty as a fruitcake, if you ask me. I hear her screaming in her place all the time, just yelling like—well, like my mother used to yell at me when I was giving her a really hard time. At first I thought she had kids living in there with her, and me and my roommates seriously considered calling the cops in case the old loon was abusing a child. It always sounds so violent."

She sat back, shrugging in the oversize shirt she wore in a vain attempt to minimize her sizable bust. "But I've never seen anybody else go in or out, not in a year and a half of living here. So I guess she's just screaming at the dogs, or the TV. I bet she drinks. Female alkies are thin. They drink instead of eating."

Fran admitted that she hadn't had a good look at the crazy lady yet but had mostly just heard her.

"Oh, she looks okay, sort of," Betsy said cautiously. "But boy, is she nuts."

Fran laughed. "Then I guess it's lucky that Jeff and I didn't end up living right next to her. Poor you, being so much closer!"

"I'll say," Betsy said vehemently. "She's craziest of all about men. Watch out, Fran. If that cute guy I saw leaving this morning was your Jeff, she'll be after him in no time."

"Then she'll have a fight on her hands," Fran retorted. "Jeffrey is mine, as in significant other, life partner, whatever they call it these days."

In the evening before dinner, while the stew simmered, Fran and Jeffrey walked up the block toward the uneven triangle of green that was Baker's Park. Passing the crazy lady's house on the stroll back, Fran looked across the street and saw the bluish glimmer of a TV screen inside the big front window. The house itself was pretty from the front, with a shapely porch, and two jauntily nautical porthole-shaped windows flanking the recessed doorway.

Suddenly a report like a gunshot snapped out from the porch: the screen door, banging hard against the front wall. Two little dogs came skittering down the brick walk, barking wildly, and skidded to a dancing halt at the edge of the crazy lady's lawn.

"Jeez!" Jeffrey said, protectively grabbing Fran's arm and picking up their pace, "what did she do, sic them on us? We're not even on her side of the street!"

"I told you," Fran said. "The woman is bonkers, and everybody knows it."

"Well, at least they're not Dobermans," he said, looking back over his shoulder at the bouncing, yammering animals.

"Shhh," said Fran, "you don't want to give her any ideas."

❃

SECRETLY, SHE WAS relieved to have the little dogs come after her and Jeffrey like that, validating what she had told him about the woman and her animals. And after what Betsy had said, better the dogs than the woman herself, with Jeffrey there.

She cut the grass the next day with the old hand-mower they had found in the toolshed. The mower kept sticking on the raised roots that veined the turf, and she gave up with the job half-done (it was a lot harder than she had imagined).

But she made sure to drag the machine back and forth a couple of times over the bubbly clot of white mushrooms, like greasy blisters, which had expanded rather than drying up and blowing away as she had hoped. Under the grinding blades the mushrooms disintegrated with satisfying ease.

The tape she transcribed after lunch was from Doctor Reeves, a plastic surgeon who specialized in burn patients. His dry, dispassionate notes on two children who had been caught in a burning trailer out on the west edge of town made her feel sick.

She quit (there was no rush, with the volume of work slowed to an impoverishing trickle) and went for a walk, hands jammed in her jeans pockets.

Her new neighborhood was made up of small, sturdy houses in an unexpectedly whimsical mixture of styles, most of them several decades old by the look of them. Some showed endearing turns of fantasy, like the two with roofs of tightly layered green tiling cut like the thatched roofs of English cottages, and a small white house higher on the hill that had a miniature fairy-tale tower for a front hallway. There was nothing like the bland sameness of the city's newer developments; Fran's spirits lifted.

She found herself at the foot of her own street, and out of sheer devilment—and to see what would happen this time—instead of going in she walked up the lane again, back toward Baker's Park.

The sandy wheel-track was choked with weeds, vines, and branches hanging over from adjacent yards. The lanes, she knew, had once been used for garbage pickup. Then the city had bought a whole new fleet of garbage trucks which were only afterward discovered to be too wide for the lanes, which now served the purposes of kids, gas men who read your meter with binoculars from their truck windows, the occasional pair of discreetly parked lovers, and (to judge by the crazy lady, anyway) burglars.

As Fran swung boldly toward the head of the lane, a sharp rapping sound snapped at her from the back of the crazy lady's house. A lean figure in a flowered housecoat hovered behind the closed kitchen window: the crazy lady herself, presumably, in a beehive hairdo, banging her fist on the glass in a kind of manic aggression.

Fran smiled and waved as if returning a friendly greeting and walked on, managing not to flinch from the incredible racket of the little dogs shrilling at her back. The crazy lady must have let the dogs into the side yard just so they could rush to the back wall and bark at Fran.

Jesus, Fran thought, striding quickly around the corner and back down the street toward her own place. I shouldn't have waved at her, I should have fired a rock through her damned window! Who the hell does she think she is, the witch! The lanes are city property, I can walk in them if I like.

What if she has a gun? A paranoid like that, she probably does. Hell, I bet she could shoot me and say she thought I was a burglar and get away with it! People like that shouldn't be allowed to live on their own. The woman should be in an institution.

The mushrooms were back the next morning, but they were different. Fran couldn't help noticing them when she went out on the porch to look for the mail. They were brown and flat, growing in overlapping layers along the shaggy arm of root that seemed to be the seat of the infestation.

She went over to squat down and examine them. They were wet from the overnight showers and their frilled edges glistened a pallid pink.

"Yuck!" she said aloud. "What evil-looking mushrooms!" She prodded them gingerly with a twig dropped by the huge old cottonwood above her.

"They're your evil thoughts."

It was a hoarse voice from the sidewalk, the voice of the crazy lady (Fran knew this before she looked up; who else could it be, saying that, in that voice?). There she stood, disconcertingly thin and slight in a pastel pantsuit, a cigarette smoldering between two of her sharp-knuckled fingers. She had enough lipstick on for six mouths, and she wasn't smiling.

Fran gaped at her, at a loss for words. The woman looked like a bona fide witch out of a modern fairy tale, and what do you say to a witch who comes calling? With intense satisfaction Fran said to herself, She's older than I am. She's older, old, like an old witch is supposed to be!

The crazy lady said, "Have you seen a little dog? He's about a foot high, with black and white spots."

"No, sorry," Fran said with forced heartiness. "I've been in the back of the house, working."

"He got out this morning," the crazy lady said, looking around with a frown. Did she think the dog might pop up at any moment from under Fran's lawn?

Fran said, "If I do see him, I'll be sure and let you know."

"Thank you," the crazy lady said, as if she had never banged on the window or screamed at Fran—maybe she didn't recognize her? She walked away, holding her cigarette out from her side at an elegant angle that she must have picked up from Bette Davis or some other glamour queen from the days of black and white movies.

Fran stared at the mushrooms. "Those are your evil thoughts"? What kind of a thing was that to say to her?

The woman was a crackpot just as Betsy had said, one step short of being a bag-lady talking to herself on the street. She must be living on an inheritance or the pension left by a dead husband, so she could keep a roof over her head. A person like that couldn't possibly hold down a job.

But the mushrooms really did look evil, old and wrinkled and evil. They looked like—

Fran sat back on her heels, blushing. What an idea! They looked like an exaggerated parody of the folds of her vagina, that was what they looked like. No, not hers, some old hag's swollen and discolored sex.

She scrambled to her feet muttering, "Don't be an idiot, you idiot," and with the back of the straight rake she whacked the new crop of fungus to flying fragments.

Over pizza that night with a few of Jeffrey's friends from law school, she didn't mention the conversation with the crazy lady. She didn't feel altogether comfortable with Jeffrey's friends, except for a woman a little older than herself who had begun law school after a divorce.

On her way next day to pick up some tapes from a back-up source who sometimes gave her work, Fran saw the crazy lady's dog, or anyway it might have been the crazy lady's dog, jittering back and forth on the far side of Rhoades Avenue. It made one mad dash to cross, was honked at by an approaching car, and dodged back again to the far side where it hopped up and down furiously on its stiff little legs and barked ferociously at the traffic.

She considered driving back to tell the crazy lady, but she had lost time over the pizza and beer last night and she was in a hurry now. And when she did get back she didn't see the dog again and besides the crazy lady was occupied.

She was having an altercation with a jogger, from the safety of her porch. Fran parked and sat in the Volks and watched.

The jogger marked time at the curb, his head turned toward 408 with its two round windows flanking the open doorway. "I'm not doing anything in your yard, lady," he declared. "I didn't touch your yard."

On the porch the crazy lady stood with her hips shot to one side in an aggressive slouch and shouted furiously, "I saw you on my grass! You ran over my grass!"

"I don't run on grass," he answered. "It's slippery, and you can't see your footing." He was middle-aged and a bit flabby around the middle, but he held his ground, running in place while he argued.

"I saw you!" the crazy lady yelled. Her remaining dog shot past her ankles, barking. It made mad little dashes in the direction of the jogger, none of which carried it more than halfway across the lawn. "This is private property! You stay off it!"

"Gladly," the jogger retorted. "Lady, you're nuts, you know that?" He headed on up toward the park, shaking his head, elbows pumping, pursued by the barking of the dog. The crazy lady began screaming at the dog, which finally gave up barking and skulked back into the house, whereupon the screen door gave another mighty bang, and all grew quiet.

Oh the hell with it, Fran thought, I'm not going to say a thing about the other dog. Someone like that shouldn't even have pets, any more than she should have kids. The little beast is probably better off in the traffic.

She locked the car and walked up onto her own patch of grass, where she automatically checked the mushroom site. A new crop, and a different type again, seemed to have sprouted there overnight.

There were six of them, tallish, on spindly stalks, and they had elongated, domed caps with dark, spidery markings along their lower fringes. Like odd, tiny lampshades trimmed with black lace, or six otherworldly missiles waiting to be launched.

Evil thoughts.

Oh, bull, Fran thought, looking up the street at the crazy lady's house. What about *her* evil thoughts, where were they displayed?

She didn't touch the new crop. Let them just sit there and do whatever mushrooms did until they reached their natural term and died. She was tired of beating them to bits and then having them show up again. It was too much like losing some kind of struggle, which was ridiculous, because there was no struggle. You don't have a struggle with a bunch of mushrooms.

She blew up at Jeffrey about the records he brought home that night. She hated salsa for starters, and then there was the expense. It didn't help that they were used, of course, very cheap, from the secondhand bookstore on Rhoades.

Of course they made up, and made love. He was forgiving by nature, and she had no defense against his lanky charm. Look at the gangly length of him, the lively tumble of his auburn hair, his intent young face. How did I get so lucky? she thought. Oh, how did I get so lucky, to have this lovely boy to love me?

Fran couldn't sleep right away afterward. She lay on her back and amused herself wondering which of her evil thoughts those slender, silvery mushrooms represented.

She paid for the sleepless hours, as usual. In the morning she looked hagged-out. She always checked herself in the bathroom mirror when she woke up, searching for the dry skin and branching wrinkles that Jeffrey was bound to see someday, someday.

Not yet, though.

She crawled back into bed and stayed there while he made himself breakfast, so that he wouldn't see her without the repairs of makeup. She looked too awful, sagging and bruised around the eyes.

She was gratified to see that the overnight chill seemed to have killed some of the damned mushrooms. Four of the six had withered so that their caps hung upside-down from stalks that looked as if they had been pinched hard in the middle. The flattened caps drooped inside-out, exposing the blue-black slits of their undersides to the sky. She thought of the gills of strange fish, dead and decaying in the cool morning air, fossil remains of ancient forms from prehistoric seas.

On the other hand, several new growths had come up.

It hadn't rained for two nights. The grass looked a little dry, but she didn't turn on the sprinklers.

That afternoon Fran took a welcome break from unpacking books and organizing them on the brick-and-board shelves Jeff had made (she had to re-set everything for balance, of course) and observed the crazy lady in what seemed at last like civilized conversation with a man out in front of 408.

He was a heavy guy in gray work clothes and he stood with his head bent, listening to her. Then he would crouch down and examine something in the grass, and stand up and talk and listen some more, and they would move over a little and do it all again. For a moment Fran thought, My God, she's got mushrooms too. She felt a tilt of vertigo (more evil thoughts, out on show—hers? Or Fran's, on some kind of northward mushroom-migration? The Thoughts That Ate Baker's Park).

Then she realized that the man was examining the heads of the crazy lady's sprinkler system. You would never have guessed this from the way she minced and preened and waved her cigarette. Her voice, if not her words, carried: a high, artificial mewling tone like the voice of Betty Boop, while her red mouth twisted in a parody of a fetching smile.

She was positively grotesque. Fran watched from her own porch, fascinated and repelled, until the crazy lady sashayed back up to her front steps, trilling over her shoulder in an impossibly arch manner at the workman, and opened her screen door. Then came a flurry of screams, presumably at the little dog (it must be trying to get out), and finally the customary door-slam.

The man in gray headed for a truck parked in front of Betsy's house.

"Excuse me!" Fran waved.

He ambled over.

"You're a lawn-man, right?" she said. God, he was massive as a steer; she caught a whiff of stale tobacco and beer on his breath. This was what the crazy lady had been flirting with?

She felt a sudden stab of deep, embarrassed pity. After all, the crazy lady couldn't be all that much older than Fran was herself, and Fran only had Jeffrey by wild, undeserved and unpredictable good luck.

"Maybe you can advise me about this mess that keeps coming up over here." She showed the man the mushrooms.

He hunkered down and stared at them. "I only do sprinklers," he said. "Don't know much about grass. But it's been wet this fall, and it looks like you got a dead root running along under here. Mushrooms like to grow on old dead wood."

Today the cluster had a new addition. There was a grayish round one, a small gourd-like shape, trailing a snaky little stalk like a withered umbilical cord. She preferred the silvery ones with their inky hems, which by comparison at least had a sort of gleaming style about them, the polished perfection of bullets aimed up at her out of the crooked elbow of the exposed root.

"That's a dead root?" she said uncertainly. "I thought all these roots belonged to the big tree, there."

He shook his head and looked around. "Nope. This one's dead, and that root there looks dead too. Must have been another tree here once that got took out."

"Oh," she said. "I've never had a lawn before, I don't know a thing about this. The mushrooms aren't likely to spread, then, and crowd out the grass?"

"What, these fellers?" he said, drawing a blunt fingertip along the edge of one of the silvery ones. "Heck, no, they're real fragile. Soon as it gets a little colder you won't see no more of them."

Fran suddenly saw the similarity of the silver mushrooms to penises, polished metal phalluses with a delicate tracery of dark veins under their thin skins. The lawn man's grimy finger touching one of them made her skin prickle.

"Oh, right, sure, I noticed that myself," she stammered, straightening up quickly. "They only last a day or two, and then they they just sort of wilt and shrivel up—"

Like an old man's cock, she thought, though these words didn't get out, thank God. Worse and worse. She stood there smiling sickly and thinking, I'm as loony a spectacle as the crazy lady herself, in my own way.

As the sprinkler man drove off, Fran saw cigarette smoke curling up from the shadows under the porch of 408.

Jeffrey only had time for a short stroll that night, up to and around the park where a couple of dogs were chasing each other, no owners in sight. He remarked that people sure didn't take care of their pets around here, letting them run loose like that. Fran thought about having seen the crazy lady's other dog and not saying anything to her. She drew Jeffrey home along a parallel street two blocks away, so as not to pass the crazy lady's house.

"Too bad we can't eat those mushrooms," Jeffrey said as they walked back up toward their front door. "We've sure got a lot of them."

The uplifted caps shone like pewter in the lofty radiance of the corner street light. Fran found herself oddly relieved that Jeffrey noticed them too, that he *saw* them. What would he say if she told him he was seeing her evil thoughts?

"What are you smiling about?" he said.

"Nothing," she said. "A secret joke too dumb to say out loud." She dug her keys out of her pocket and unlocked the front door. "I hate those damned mushrooms. I think I'll see if I can buy something somewhere, some kind of poison I can use to get rid of them once and for all."

Jeffrey laughed. "You want to poison some mushrooms? That's cute. Speaking of food, by the way, my mom wants us to come for Thanksgiving."

"What, already?" Fran said, instantly deflated and anxious. They stood in the dark little hall. "It's still September, for God's sake!"

He took her hand and squeezed it softly, thumbing her knuckles with sensuous pleasure. "She just wants to make sure we don't make other plans first."

"But I want to make other plans," Fran said, shrinking from the prospect of an evening of being delicately put down by Jeff's blue-haired and protective mother for being an "older woman" instead of some fresh young thing.

"She's not going to be around forever, you know," Jeffrey said a bit plaintively, "and I've gotten to be, well, better friends with her now that we're living in the same city." He turned on the hall light, and they trailed through the house getting ready for bed and wrangling in a desultory way about Thanksgiving.

I look like shit, Fran thought, staring despondently at her reflection in the cabinet mirror as she brushed her teeth. He's getting fed up with me.

Had that vein been there before, a bluish-gray pathway under the skin of her neck? Just wait 'til his mom sees that!

Later on in bed, in a wave of guilt and self-disgust Fran pushed him away when he touched her breast. They slept with their backs to each other.

Two more of the rounded, gourd-like things lay among the dangling corpses of the silver bullets next morning. Fran interrupted her work several times to go look at them, unhappily walking around and around the small, cursed spot on the lawn.

Last night she had dreamed of Jeffrey sleeping splayed on his back, a bullet-shaped metallic mushroom growing upright between his legs.

And these roundish ones, moored to their twisted scrap of vine and showing faint dark patterns under their greenish skins: were they her evil thoughts about Jeffrey's mother?

The crazy lady must see the mushrooms when she minced down the street with her one dog from time to time, smoking and throwing her hips from side to side like an old cartoon whore. No doubt she looks and tells herself, Goodness me, look at that—my new neighbor has some very evil thoughts.

"What's the matter?" Jeffrey said at dinner. "I've got cases to work on and you're pacing around like a panther. Please, Fran, I can't concentrate."

"Carmella returned some of my work today," Fran said angrily. "Too sloppy, the doc said, do it better. He should try making out all that slurred muttering he puts on there."

"Why don't you go watch TV for a little while?" Jeffrey said.

"Thanks," she snapped, "have you looked at what's on? Just because I'm not in school, that doesn't mean I'm an idiot, you know, to sit glassy-eyed in front of an endless parade of sit-coms and game shows."

"Jeez, I never said—"

He stared up at her, open-mouthed, and for a second she stared back in blazing contempt. God, what a whiny, moon-faced child he was! No wonder he clung so hard to his mother's apron-strings!

Then the hurt in his expression melted her into a shuddering confusion of fear and contrition—what in the world *was* wrong with her?—and she hugged him and apologized. They ended up in front of the TV together, murmuring and kissing on the couch, neither of them watching the screen.

"I think moving here was harder on you than you realize," he said. "You look tired, Fran. I wish I could have been around more to help you with the details of settling in, but with starting school and all ..." She wished he hadn't noticed the marks of strain in her face, the ones she noticed every morning.

Age, real age, so soon? She was only thirty-four, for Christ's sake! It had to be just strain, as he said. And he was so sweet about it, how could she resent his remark?

But she did.

It turned really cold that night for the first time, and the wind blew. Leaves covered much of the lawn in the morning, and all of the mushrooms had withered and vanished, except for one of the ovoid ones. Its sibling on the same desiccated vine had shrunk to a wrinkled brown nut, but the survivor was now the size of a tennis ball and shone livid white in the dark, rough-cut grass.

Like an egg, Fran thought uneasily, studying it. A green nest with a giant, monstrous egg in it—a bad egg (naturally). Already a dark veining of decay was visible, like crazing in old porcelain.

No other growths had appeared. Pretty soon the frost would kill this one too, and Fran's evil thoughts would be private again, invisible even to the greedy, smoky gaze of the crazy lady in 408.

Fran asked Betsy and her housemates to a Thanksgiving party, and Carmella too. Jeffrey said he didn't know what Fran was doing or why, but he meant to go across town to his mother's on Thanksgiving. Fran had a lot of evil thoughts about that, but no more mushrooms came up.

The next time she looked, the one remaining fungus was as big and white as a baseball, and marbled all over with black. There was a delicacy as of great antiquity about it now, an almost ethereal look, as if the bluish-white and shining shell glowed coldly from within, silhouetting the dark tracery.

"I've had enough of this," she muttered, and she gave the thing a sharp kick.

The pale shell disintegrated without a sound, releasing a puff of thick black dust. In the wreckage stood a sooty stub, a carbonized yoke, which yielded, moist and pulpy, when she kicked at it again, frantically, in a rush of horror and disgust.

The shrunken black knob emitted another breath of inky powder under the impact of her shoe, but clung to its twist of vine. She had to trample it for long moments before she was able to flatten the whole mess into a dark stain on the earth, through which splinters of the rotten root beneath protruded palely like shards of bone.

She gasped and realized that she had been holding her breath to keep from inhaling the spores, or whatever the black dust was that had been packed between the decayed center and the outer shell.

Who was watching, who had seen her mad dance on the front lawn under the old cottonwood?

No one. Betsy's house was quiet, the people across the street were doing whatever they did all day without a sound. The crazy lady's driveway was empty, her old gray Pontiac absent.

How ridiculous, that a person as crazy as that was allowed to drive!

No more mushrooms sprouted.

"It's too cold for them," Jeffrey said. "Don't tell me you miss the ugly things! A little while ago you wanted to poison them."

No, Fran didn't miss them. But she found herself wondering, in a nagging, anxious way, where her evil thoughts were growing now that they weren't showing up on the lawn.

After all, the thoughts didn't stop.

Like when she saw Jeffrey with Betsy one evening while he was setting out the bagged garbage on the curb. The two of them stood chatting there, and Fran saw a spark of easy warmth between them and cursed it to herself.

He said, "Maybe we should drive somewhere over the Thanksgiving break, to hell with your party and dinner at Mom's and the whole thing. This is a tough term for me, I'm all frazzled. And you're not in top shape yourself, Frannie. Look at yourself in the mirror. I'm afraid you might get sick."

She did look, and she knew it wasn't that she was getting sick. She was worrying too much. She was becoming more sensitive to noise, too, and woke up often at night. She would get up alone, careful not to disturb Jeffrey, pour herself a glass of wine in the kitchen, and go look at herself in the bathroom mirror until she'd drunk enough to stumble back to bed and fall asleep again.

Carmella said, "You better pull yourself together, Fran. I've had some complaints from the docs you type for."

The docs who mumbled, the docs who paid too little out of their immense incomes for the services they couldn't get along without, the docs who rattled along about burned kids and dying old people and all the rest as if the sufferers were sides of meat. The docs should feel the pain their patients felt.

That was an evil thought, wasn't it?

Fran ordered a turkey at the supermarket, for her Thanksgiving party. Jeffrey wasn't going to his mother's for Thanksgiving dinner after all. His mother had had a fall and was in the hospital with a broken hip. Jeffrey spent a lot of time there with her now, which Fran resented. She soothed herself with dark imaginings of death, an ending between Jeffrey and his mother once and for all.

But where were these evil thoughts? The dead roots on the lawn stayed bare, like bones worked to the surface of an old battlefield.

The turkey was ready to pick up well in advance of Thanksgiving. She hoped it would fit; she had only the freezer compartment of the mid-sized fridge that had come with the house to store it in.

On her way back from the supermarket, Fran pulled up in the

street. The crazy lady was on the steps of her porch, screeching dementedly, "Get back here, you hear me? You get back here this minute, you filthy thing!"

The one little dog she had left was down at the edge of her ragged brown lawn, alternately turning its rear to the questing nose of a brisk gray poodle, and sitting down to avoid being sniffed. The poodle pranced and wagged with delight, and darted at the smaller dog with stiffened front legs, trying to turn it, mount it, hump it there in the gutter.

"Get away, get away from her!" shrieked the crazy lady, waving her hands wildly, though apparently she was afraid to run down there and chase the poodle away. She thrust her head forward and screamed at the poodle from a rage-distended mouth, "Don't even think about it!"

Fran knew she would explode if she had to hear that raw, mad voice for another second. She leaned out of the window of the Volks and yelled, "For Christ's sake, lady, will you shut up? Let them screw if they want to screw, they're just dogs, that's what they do!"

The crazy lady stood still and lifted one bony hand to shield her eyes from the bright fall sunlight. Her other hand stayed at her hip, cocked at an angle, a butt smoking between the thin fingers.

Fran recoiled from the unseen glare of those shadowed eyes. She drove quickly on to her own driveway, where she sat afraid to move for some time. She watched in her rear view mirror until the crazy lady, trailed by the little dog once the poodle had lost interest, withdrew into 408 without another word.

Jeffrey said, "I got an "A." You've brought me luck! I love you."

They were up late, kissing and sighing and stretching against each other's warm skins. A steady breeze blew all night, hissing and seething like surf. Fran listened and drowsed, lulled by the sound, but not sleeping.

Jeff left early for class, bouncing with energy. Fran lay in bed late, luxuriating in the languor of the night's long loving and heartened by the shimmer of sunshine glowing through the drapes: not winter yet.

After a steamy shower, she stationed herself in front of the mirror to rub moisturizer into her damp skin. And stopped, staring, frozen by the hammering recognition of something that could not be.

Her skin was an unearthly pearly color, moist and shining, like the skin of a soprano dying endlessly in Act Three of consumption, like the skin of a delicate Victorian lady vampire, like the skin of a guest made up for a Halloween party. But Halloween was past.

The lines and smudges the mirror had been showing her for weeks had spread and joined each other in a flowing network of shadowy tributaries that covered her features from her throat upward and spread away past her hairline, onto her scalp. The lines were mauve and blue and gray, and when she turned her agonized face so that sunlight fell on her cheek, there was a slightly greenish tinge of iridescence to those veinings under the translucent surface of her skin.

She ran to the mirror in the bedroom, and the one in the little bathroom near the kitchen, her eyes glaring in disbelief out of smoky pits in the horrible mask. Her voice creaked and wheezed desperate protests in her throat, her hands fluttered nervelessly—her own pink-knuckled, flesh-tinted, still youthful hands that didn't dare touch the ancient, marbled pallor of her face.

This was where the evil thoughts had been growing, in their true home, their natural seat, their place of origin. Nothing lay ahead but inevitable disintegration of the outer shell, exposing the blackened, shrunken ruin of the brain still damp and clinging with feeble persistence to the quivering stem, the living body.

On the wild winds of her panic she tossed to and fro in the sunlit rooms of the house, screams dammed in her throat by her own terror of what the force of them would do to her fragile shell of a face.

Stifling, she flung open the front door and plunged outside into the cool, bright morning. She stumbled across the lawn, past the big tree with its leaves rustling in the soft breeze, and flung herself down at the dead root on which her evil thoughts had first appeared.

As soon as her forehead touched the bleached, bare wood, she felt the eggshell of her face soundlessly break and fall away. A swirl of sooty powder choked her breath as darkness broke in her and from her and bore her down into bottomless night.

PREFACE TO "ADVOCATES"

"Advocates" is a story that I co-authored with Chelsea Quinn Yarbro (author of the Saint-Germain Chronicles) as a special project. The Horror Writers of America decided to publish a shared-world anthology of stories by well-known members as a benefit and publicity boost for this relatively new organization. Quinn and I were asked if we might bring our two well-known blood-drinkers—Dr. Weyland and the Comte de Saint Germain—together for the collection, called Under the Fang.

The premise of the anthology (to the parameters of which all included stories would be tailored—that's the "shared" part of the "shared world" concept) was this: at some point in the near future, vampires have taken over the world and established their rule over the human population. Everything has become theirs—government, commerce, war, education, fashion, the ambition to reach the stars.

So, what do they make of their sovereignty, and what do we make of it as their human subjects—and their prey?

Quinn and I agreed to give it a try; but the task was formidable. Dr. Weyland, my vampire creation in The Vampire Tapestry, *is a lone hunter in a world of prey, an ancient creature that looks like a man but is generally as sympathetic to his human livestock as a lion is to a herd of zebra. Saint Germain is an immortal human with a compassionate and dignified soul trying to avoid being mangled by the bloody course of human history. The two of them are opposites—the cold-hearted, brilliant predator and the somber, cultivated gentleman.*

Why, and how, could these twain meet?

In fact, it didn't take long to come up with a story idea; that part was easy. Quinn and I were friends as well as colleagues, having often served together on midnight vampire panels at various science fiction and fantasy conventions and having visited each other's homes. We enjoyed batting around the possibilities. But our writing methods were so different!

I bang out a first draft as fast as I can type, content to hit the target at all; then I revise my story until it drives right to the bull's eye. Quinn told me that she didn't revise at all, because her work was finished as it first appeared on the manuscript page (many authors do most of the work in their minds before putting words to paper). So she said that she would not revise our story; I said that I would not turn in unpolished, first draft material. How the heck were we to meld our disparate methods to make a seamless-seeming story, and stay friends as well?

And then there were the actual mechanics of collaboration: I had never worked with another author before, and so far as I knew neither had Quinn. She lived on the West Coast. I lived in New Mexico. Taking turns writing different bits and mailing them back and forth until we had hammered them together satisfactorily was out (although many writing teams work in just this way) because neither of us felt comfortable putting words into the mouth of the other's vampire character. Our two guys had very disparate attitudes and speaking styles, and, as seems to happen with fictional vampires, each had become very close to his creator's heart (nobody knows why this happens, or why readers tend to become deeply partisan about their own favorite literary blood-suckers).

In some writing teams each author takes over a different aspect of the work (action vs. dialogue, say, or plotting vs. character development). But we didn't know where our story would go until our two vampires worked it out between them, and we already had our characters and as much plot as we could manage without writing the thing out fully—which task, of course, was our problem in the first place.

Here's what we did: we agreed by phone that instead of the five or six drafts that I would normally do of any story with my name on it we would compromise at three, changes to be made by me and then approved by Quinn (or not, in which case they would not stand). Then we picked a weekend, and I flew out and stayed with her. We sat and talked a little about the idea that we had come up with, exploiting the differences between these—men?—and how they would regard each other. Then Quinn sat down at her computer and wrote an opening paragraph, diving into the action from the first sentence.

Pretty soon she got up and I took a turn at the keyboard to take over where she had left off. We alternated, gaining confidence as we went along. If she wrote a line of dialog or reflection for Weyland, I would check it and (most often) recast it into a more authentic tone when my turn came, and vice versa, guaranteeing that we kept the voices and the minds of our respective creations true. With scenes between other characters, we wrote and rewrote each other's words freely and even playfully.

In the end, I took the printout home with me and, as agreed, worked it over and then sent it back to Quinn. She reviewed the changes with me over the phone, then sent the story on to our editor, Robert MacCammon. When the galley proofs came back I revised again, lightly, in my part of the copy-editing process. This was, in effect, the third revision that Quinn and I had agreed upon at the outset. And "Advocates" was done.

We are still friends, these many years later. I haven't done another collaboration since and I don't think she has either, although the experience of that one time felt to me like a real accomplishment. Quinn and I have both reprinted "Advocates" in collections of our own work, as each of us is entitled to do (we both "own" the story equally); so I think we're both pleased, still, with the results.

But the ending stands as it does because we could not, between us, take the story any further and still agree. I guess collaboration has its limitations after all.

ADVOCATES

IT WAS SHORTLY AFTER TEATIME when the three Watchmen found the Renegade. He crouched over a thin woman who lay sprawled on the floor. There was blood in her tangled hair, on the top of her other dress, and on his mouth.

"Christ," whispered the biggest Watchman, who had never seen a vampire feeding in daylight before.

The other two Watchmen were silent, prepared to do battle.

The Renegade stepped back over the still-living body of his undead victim, ready to bolt.

"Stop him!" shouted the youngest Watchman as the Renegade sprang for the rusty door.

"Get him!" roared the biggest, plunging after the fleeing, bloodied figure.

As the Renegade seized the door handle it tore away, metal shrieking; he staggered back, slamming into the oldest Watchman.

At once the biggest Watchman lunged, catching the Renegade about the knees. The impact carried them all to the floor, the third Watchman landed on top of the pile with everything he had.

"Shit, he's strong," said the biggest as the Renegade struggled in silent desperation to get free.

"Get the Damper," gasped the youngest Watchman. "We can't hold him much longer."

"Where're the restraints?" yelled the man on top fumbling with a small spray can.

"In the truck," said the biggest. Only when the spray can had been fired into their captive's face and the powerful body relaxed did he dare to let go of the vampire's legs.

The man on the top climbed off. "Keep him out. Give him another inhale. I'll be right back." He did not walk quite steadily, and he was breathing too fast.

As the other two rose gingerly from the supine figure, the younger Watchman stared at the Renegade, his face pale. "I didn't believe it. I didn't really believe it."

"What?" asked the other Watchman. He stood straddling the unconscious Renegade, eager to kick him in the jaw if he regained consciousness. "What didn't you believe?"

The younger man shook his head, eyes haunted. "I didn't believe about the daylight. Fuck it! Who ever saw a vampire hunting in the daylight?"

Years ago the hotel had catered to the most affluent business travelers. The pillars and the floor in the lobby were green-veined marble, the sconces were solid brass, the carpets on the stairs and in the halls were from the finest Canadian mills. But it was no longer the splendid hostelry it had been; six years ago it was pressed into service as the Magistrates' Center. Now the carpets were worn, the brass was unpolished, and the tremendous wall mirrors were gone.

In the basement of the Magistrates' Center, four large storage rooms had been converted into holding cells. They brought the Renegade to the most remote of these, left him secured to metal cleats in the wall and hurried away; no one wanted to be there when he regained consciousness.

Inspector Frederick Samson had been awake less than half an hour when the three Watchmen brought him the good news.

"We found him by accident," the oldest admitted with a quick look of apology to the other two. "We heard a sound in a deserted warehouse. We didn't anticipate—"

The biggest Watchman nodded emphatically. "He'd got her."

"What about the … remains? Do we know who she is?" asked the inspector.

"Not yet. We brought it along. It's in the morgue," said the oldest.

"The Grand Ballroom," corrected the inspector. "With the others."

"And the Renegade's down in cell number four," said the

youngest of the Watchmen, his eyes flicking nervously from the inspector to the other Watchmen. "The Damper'll wear off in about half a hour."

The inspector took a deep breath and straightened his black foulard vest. "That'll give me time to look at the victim before I talk to the Renegade. Good work. We couldn't have done it without you." He hesitated. "I don't suppose there's any chance you made a mistake?"

"Look at the victim: a remainder," said the biggest. "Same condition as all the others. Undead and comatose." He tried to suppress his shudder.

"That makes twenty-eight," said the youngest Watchman, and looked away from Frederick Samson as if the very number were a recrimination.

Half a dozen Cybertooths were waiting in the lobby, their studded black leather and chains no longer able to create the sensation they had once. The one called Demon Star strutted toward Samson as she caught sight of him, the jingle of her chains a counterpoint to the crack of her five-inch boot heels.

"They say you found the guy who did the Renegade killings." Her voice grew derisive. "Someone you found in *daylight*."

"We're investigating," said Samson, trying not to glare at the statuesque figure with the white hair standing out in four-inch spikes around her head. "And until our investigation is completed, I have nothing more to say to you."

"You Beaux are all alike," jeered Demon Star, light shining from the red glitter on her eyelids. "I want to see this monster you've got in the basement."

"If he's the Renegade, he *is* a monster," said Samson, his manner quiet and serious. "And you're not going to see him."

"I have the right. He's cutting into our territory," said Demon Star. "And don't tell me he isn't cutting into your—"

Samson stood a little straighter. "Is that all that concerns you—who's raiding your livestock?" He knew it was not wise to rise to the bait of these Cybertooths, but he could not stop himself issuing them a challenge. "Come with me," he said sharply. "I want you to see what the Renegade has done. Maybe that will give you some notion of the scope of our problem here."

Demon Star flung back her fantastical head and laughed. "Trying to shock us? Hey, drain a vein, who cares?" She signaled to the others with her to follow and began a loose-limbed saunter down the decaying elegance of the hall leading to the Grand

Ballroom.

Half a dozen orderlies worked among the gurneys, tending to the victims of the Renegade. The latest victim was nearest the door. Her body was decently covered by a sheet, but her face was visible. Nothing had been done about the bloody mess in her hair.

"So?" said Demon Star as she nudged the latest victim with the riding crop she always carried. "Like the others. You got the right guy."

"In daylight," said Inspector Samson.

"Bullshit," answered Demon Star. "It was early evening. What's this plasma-pus about daylight?" She laughed again, even more theatrically.

"Twenty-eight vampires are...vegetables, thanks to the Renegade. They're too drained to ever be anything other than in a coma, but they have not died the true death." He made a gesture of helpless frustration. "Doesn't that mean anything to you?"

"It means she's a remainder, like all the rest." She shrugged so that the elaborate pattern of studs on her shoulder glistened in the light. "What else?"

Angrily Inspector Samson pushed by her back into the hall, not caring that the Cybertooths followed after him. He would have liked the luxury of yelling at them, but had given that up after the third victim had been brought to him.

"Squeamish about a remainder?" Demon Star taunted, but for once her brittle scorn rang false.

"Aren't you?" the inspector flung over his shoulder. He was so irritated that he almost ran into the black-clad clerk who hastened up to him holding out a sheet of paper.

"Inspector Samson, Inspector Samson," the clerk insisted as he turned in pursuit of the inspector. "Just a moment."

"Your flunkey wants you," called out Demon Star.

As much as he wanted to ignore her, Inspector Samson stopped and swung around to face the clerk. "What is it?" he demanded.

The clerk quailed. "It's … it's about the prisoner."

His wrath evaporated. "What about the prisoner?"

Now the Cybertooths came nearer, silent for once.

"We have a name for him, for the Renegade. That's all." The clerk looked from Inspector Samson to Demon Star and back. "We think we know who he is."

"And who's that?" asked Demon Star with such sardonic intent that it was not until later that Inspector Samson thought it had not been wise to permit the clerk to answer.

"Weyland," said the clerk eagerly. "Edward Lewis Weyland."

"They tell me you're a professor of anthropology," said Frederick Samson as he faced the Renegade across the cement floor of the holding cell.

Weyland gave a single, determined pull at his restraints.

"They tell me your name is Edward Lewis Weyland." He waited for a response.

"Who tells you this?" the Renegade said. His eyes locked on Samson's face.

Samson looked down at his glossy calf-high boots, deliberately avoiding the penetrating stare of his prisoner. "You're accused of preying on vampires, Weyland. Do you mind if I call you Weyland? For convenience?"

"Call me what you like, I can hardly prevent you," the other said. He turned his head and looked off into a corner of the cell as if the interview were over.

"How do you propose to answer the charge?" Samson inquired.

"I propose nothing," Weyland said. "I am not in a position to propose."

"There are over twenty vampires in our … morgue. They aren't truly dead. You've left them nothing but life enough to be in Hell." He had not intended this last to be so passionate.

"They were not vampires," Weyland said, "and I suspect that it is I who am in Hell."

Samson pushed himself away from the wall, his face rigid with the effort of mastering his revulsion. "We are better than that, Renegade. We do not prey on our own kind. We leave that to human beings."

"Perfectly appropriate," Weyland snapped. "You *are* humans, all of you. That is all you ever were, or ever can be. I hunt my prey, that is all."

For an instant Samson imagined the satisfaction of severing Weyland's head from his body, watching the blood run out of him. Then he looked down and fingered his lapels. "You will answer for what you did, Weyland. You will answer for what you *are*."

"I have already answered far too much," Weyland said. "You will get no more from me." He slumped against the wall and shut his eyes.

Samson accepted the impasse; he needed to consider what he would recommend to the Magistrates. Yet he permitted himself a parting shot. "I wouldn't wager on that."

The roll-up door of the loading dock was stiff and noisy with disuse.

"Keep it quiet!" hissed Demon Star, flicking her crop at the Cybertooth who had been foolish enough to let the door groan as it was opened halfway. "We don't want any Beaux finding us in here."

"I can't help it," said Dog, his tongue bright pink against his black-painted lips. "The thing's old."

She struck him again, harder. "That's for talking back," she said, then ducked down to slip inside the cellars of the Magistrates' Center. She took a moment to orient herself, the memorized cellar plans coming slowly to her mind. She cursed; it was getting late and she was growing lethargic. Dawn was only an hour away.

"Where to?" Dog whispered, motioning the other eight to come nearer.

"Left at the corner," she said. "There's a patrol due around in ten minutes. We have seven minutes to get to the Renegade's cell." She grabbed Dog's shoulder. "You stay here. I don't want anyone cutting off our way out."

"No one," Dog promised, kneeling to lick her hand.

There were few lights in the corridors—most had burned out long ago and there was no reason for vampires to replace them—and the cameras mounted to reveal intruders had not been modified to register those of their blood. "This way," Demon Star said, pointing toward the side-hallway where the holding cells were. "They post their human guards at dawn."

Slicker giggled. "We could grab one for a snack."

"We won't have room," Demon Star said. "Will we?"

They moved through the shadows making no particular effort to go undetected, for they had been told that at the slack end of the night these basement corridors were poorly guarded.

"That's the cell," said Sweet Blue, her cherub's face leering in anticipation.

Slicker had the crowbars for the locks, and between him and Long Poison the door was open in less than a minute.

"Don't bother to unhook him," said Demon Star as she shoved

through the others into the cell. "Just do him."

The figure at the wall stood in a tense crouch, feet braced as widely as his chains allowed. He uttered no sound, and for an instant his stillness held them off, like a wall formed equally of his will and their apprehension.

They had expected a cowering victim. They faced what appeared to be a desperate and resolute opponent.

"What are you waiting for?" Demon Star said with sudden force, and she caught Slicker by the arm and shoved him toward the Renegade, whipping along Sweet Blue and Hot Licks at the same time. They fell on the Renegade like a storm of leather and steel. He staggered beneath their weight. Hunched tightly against their onslaught, he lashed out with hands and feet to the extent that his restraints permitted. He caught Sweet Blue a crack in the face with his head that sent her reeling back with a yelp, both hands shielding her broken lips.

But the others bore him down in a heaving, cursing tangle, and Demon Star planted one boot against his shoulder and clawed at the side of his head, holding the curve of his throat taut and exposed for the plunging attacks of the others. He threshed and coiled under them like a python, but they clung hard, digging in with their fingers and their knees. They shoved each other and grunted in their eagerness to feed.

They were too embroiled to hear the hurried footsteps behind them, or see the beams of flashlights carried by half a dozen Watchmen.

"We'll cut you all down if we must!" shouted Inspector Samson. "Get away from him." His men crowded into the cell.

Demon Star turned toward the intruders. She bared her teeth, blood slathered over her face. "You're too late."

Samson advanced implacably. "Get away, all of you." He could barely control the distress he felt at the loss of his prisoner.

Sweet Blue broke and ran for the door, elbows up to shove the Watchmen out of the way. A sharp blow from a cudgel brought her down.

"Fuckers!" shrieked Demon Star, and her crop sliced the air toward Samson.

As he stepped back, the Cybertooths pushed past the door, Slicker scooping up Sweet Blue as he fled.

Samson issued a few terse orders, then moved forward to examine his prisoner. "Catch them if you can," he told the Watchmen, relieved that none of the Cybertooths had fallen to them. Only when they were gone did Samson kneel beside Weyland, expecting to find him as inert and drained as the undead husks in the Grand Ballroom.

To his amazement, Weyland was not sunk in unendable coma. The Renegade glared up at Samson, bloody faced, and croaked, "I told you—Hell."

Samson rose in silence, considering with rising excitement what nature of being he had confined in this basement cell.

ON HIS DESK only the formal memo from the Magistrates was out of place. Samson felt himself drawn to it again, trying to decide how to answer it.

> *We have decided that the Renegade's acts cannot go unpunished.*

Samson agreed with them, but he could not second the Magistrates' demand for a summary execution. He had to find a way to keep Weyland alive, at least until he knew more about him. He picked up the memo again, as if in rereading it he would discover that the message had changed.

When he drew his own stationery from its case, he wrote out his response in his best hand, taking pains to make the memo as elegant as the one the Magistrates had sent him.

> *While I share the desire for justice, I believe that we cannot withhold some process of justice from the prisoner. An execution, ordered out-of-hand, would serve only to compound the crimes committed. It would subvert our order here; all later attempts at justice would be derided.*
>
> *The prisoner has demonstrated certain characteristics that deserve our examination, and this will certainly not be possible if he is dispatched without recourse to a hearing to determine the most appropriate sentence.*
>
> *I believe that no one in this city, vampire or human, can offer the prisoner the defense he must have if we are to conduct a hearing that is not a travesty. I volunteer to secure an advocate for him, one who will be acceptable to you Magistrates and to the great majority of our populace regarding the final disposition of the case, and to make every*

attempt to see that impartiality is maintained throughout the proceedings.

Never before had he been presented such an opportunity, never had he been given the chance to excel in his own area of science. Or would he lose the chance he had sought for so long, and that had been denied him?

Had he been human still, his pulse would have been racing as he reached for the telephone.

Samson was Beau enough to be disappointed by the advocate's appearance—his immaculate dark suit lacked a Beau's brass buttons and his cravat was merely a conservative silken burgundy—but he did his best to conceal this as he opened the inner door of the hotel suite. "We can make arrangements for a coffin if you prefer," he said as he indicated the bed.

"That won't be necessary," said the advocate. "My manservant will attend to it." He returned to the sitting room, gesturing toward the settee. "Please."

"I've brought the information you wanted," Samson told him as he took his seat. "And I'm delighted to answer any questions you might have."

The advocate gave a quick, ironic smile. "Are you?" He opened the case he carried and took out a sheaf of papers. "Then perhaps you wouldn't mind reviewing these?"

"What are they?" Samson asked, taken aback.

"Records," said the advocate as he settled back in the high-backed chair.

"Of what?" Samson had no idea how to respond to this sally. He looked at the neat stack. "Why?"

The advocate's dark eyes clouded. "Your city isn't the only one to have had this trouble," he said quietly. "There have been others. Yours is only the most recent."

Samson was shocked. "There are others like Weyland?"

"Or Weyland travels," said the advocate. "Let us hope."

The implication of this remark struck Samson forcibly. "But he couldn't get away with it, not for any length of time. Could he?"

"Tell me what you think after you read those records," the advocate recommended. "And while you are doing that," he said, rising, "I will have a word with my … client."

Weyland dozed fitfully on the iron bed they had given him after the Cybertooths' attack. Despite frequent drafts of blood brought him from the Center's stores, he was still subject to waves of weakness that terrified him, and he spent most of his time trying to conserve his strength for those dizzying moments.

Someone was coming, crisp steps in the corridor, accompanied by none of the grumble and chatter of the day guards which invariably raised the specter of reprisal at the hands of his accustomed victims, now that he lay chained in their possession. So this would be one of the others, the humans who called themselves vampires, and who had themselves become his food.

With an effort he sat up, aware of thirst—for water only—and the ache in his throat where those phantasmagoric people had savaged him. Beneath the constant nagging apprehension, he felt the tingle of curiosity.

Though the cell was dark, the advocate had no difficulty in seeing Weyland. He came to the edge of the iron bed.

"According to the reports, you drain vampires of their blood. Do you?"

Weyland said, "It's nothing to me what they tell you. Who are you and what do you want here?"

"I've been asked to represent you before the Magistrates; it seems they want to provide you with a hearing." He did not flinch at the hard glare from Weyland.

Weyland said, "What would be the point? Here I am, and I will tell you this much frankly, here I expect to die, with a hearing—whatever that may mean—or without one."

"Then you might as well accept the hearing," said the advocate; at the back of his dark eyes was something too ancient to be understanding. He glanced toward the door. "Twenty-eight victims here—what do you call them?"

"I don't call them anything," Weyland retorted. "You people call them remainders, I believe; a usage with a certain morbid charm, to a former author of books. In this place and circumstance, I suppose I should appreciate any charm I can find."

"It might be wisest to leave esthetics until later," said the advocate. "For now, our greatest concern must be those twenty-eight …

remainders and why you attacked them." He gave a long, thoughtful look at Weyland. "Why remainders, and why other vampires? Do you have a reason?"

"Certainly," Weyland replied, moving to fold his arms across his chest but checked in this gesture by his chains. "Now explain to me precisely who you are and why you want to represent me at this so-called hearing, and I may choose to tell you my reasons, my secrets, my autobiography, my telephone number, and anything else you wish to know; or not."

The advocate did not answer at once, and when he did his voice was mild but precise. "You have been known as Edward Lewis Weyland, professor of anthropology. You have taught at Columbia and UCLA most recently. Your last known address was 153 Goethe Circle in Toronto. You have no records of spouses or long-term lovers. Most of your academic credentials are sham, and your childhood information a fiction. Your last known telephone number was 555-3881. Would you like me to continue?"

"'A hit; a very palpable hit,'" said Weyland drily, though his heart was beating hard. It was long since he had felt so exposed to unknown and dangerous factors. "But you most definitely have the advantage of me at the moment. My credentials may be largely fabricated, but at least I have them. What are yours? You seem unusually levelheaded for this place. You surely realize that I see no profit to myself in revealing any small rag of information about myself that I may still accurately call my own, if indeed such a thing exists."

"Humility doesn't become you, Professor," said his advocate lightly. "Still, I don't suppose it would hurt either of us for you to know that I am qualified to speak for you, by weight of years if nothing else. You see, little as I approve of what you have done, I do not want you or any other vampire made a scapegoat. Will that suffice?"

"No one is qualified to speak for me," Weyland said, feeling the onset of one of those dreaded waves of weakness, and with it the black hopelessness with which he had so far endured his days in this place. "Nothing will suffice, and no one who thinks I have anything in common with those who presently call themselves vampires can even begin to understand why."

"Those who presently call themselves vampires?" echoed his advocate. "That's an … interesting distinction. Are you willing to explain it?"

"To whom?" There was a rushing in Weyland's head and his chains were suddenly much heavier.

His advocate went to the door to summon help, then came back to the bedside. He stood watching Weyland for several seconds, and then, making up his mind, said, "Not that it will mean anything to you, Professor: for the present I answer to Saint-Germain."

It was nearing twelve, the busiest time of the night; Frederick Samson made a last careful adjustment of the discreet ruffles at his wrists before riding up four floors to the Magistrates' level. He carried a tooled leather case that contained all his files on Weyland as well as the additional material Saint-Germain had supplied. At the door of the Presidential Suite he stopped to permit a clerk to search his case and his jacket before being admitted to the chambers of Isodora Ruthven.

Near the window where the damask draperies were drawn open to the night was a tall stand, and on it a vase filled with white spider mums. The paneled walls glowed in the lantern light, though her desk—a high-fronted Victorian rolltop—was caught in the beam of two electric bulbs. As Samson looked around him, a door in the far wall swung wide and Isodora Ruthven stepped into the room.

Samson offered her a sociable bow before kissing her hand. "I'm—"

"Inspector Frederick Samson," said the Magistrate.

"Uh … yes." He felt the need to recover the initiative he had lost with her. "I realize you receive many petitions; this isn't one. I wouldn't have asked to see you unless I thought there was good reason to speak to you before the hearing of Professor Weyland's case begins."

She went to her desk, turning her chair around to face him before sinking into it. "Anything else would be a waste of time," she said cordially but with a clear warning in her tone.

"Exactly," said Samson, determined to gain her support. "I don't want to waste any time. That's why I thought it would be best to discuss the investigation with you." He indicated the case he carried. "There's a great deal of information in here."

"Condense it for me," said Magistrate Ruthven.

This was precisely what Samson wanted to hear. "I'll try," he said, and launched into his prepared discourse. "You know it started with these remainders. You've seen them in the Grand Ballroom. No one knows what to do about them. We've never had a vampire prey on vampires before, and we've never had to deal with the consequences."

Magistrate Ruthven toyed with the onyx inkwell on her desk. "One consequence," she observed coolly, "is a certain pruning back of our own numbers. There are some of us who feel that in the exuberance of our initial takeover, far too many human beings were carelessly added to our ranks. This Renegade has taken his prey largely from among newer vampires and older solitaries who have small tolerance even for our social system. There is something to be said for this. But it is not the sort of thing we would like to see continued; it sets a bad example. I think we will know what to do with your monster, Inspector."

"But you don't understand," said Samson, unable to control his agitation. "No other vampire has done what Weyland does."

"I'm aware of that. What's your point?" she inquired.

"We need to know why. It isn't enough just to execute him, Your Honor; we need to know why he can do what the rest of us apparently cannot." He said it in a rush, his enthusiasm undenied.

Magistrate Ruthven leaned back and looked at him, her body relaxed but her eyes snapping. "What makes you think we will find out?"

Samson was prepared to answer that. "I was a biochemist before I became a vampire. I worked for ten years on analyzing the genetic makeup of variant forms of the same species of mammals. Politics and money made it impossible for me to go on then. I was gifted; that wasn't enough. But I know what someone like Weyland represents." He set down the case and walked toward her. "I know I'm rushing too fast. You may not be able to help me. But I want you to know that we could learn a tremendous amount from Weyland if we were given the chance."

Isodora Ruthven regarded him steadily. Then in a single fluid movement she rose from her chair. "You're suggesting that Weyland might be willing to enter into some sort of bargain with us?"

"It isn't impossible," said Samson carefully.

"Why should he?" She was standing by the vase with the mums, her pale hair as pretty as the flowers.

"Because he doesn't want to die," said Samson.

"Are you sure of that?" She lifted her head. "Why consult him at all? Why not make the terms of his condemnation be that he is placed in the hands of those prepared to do research?" Her smile was sensual and attractive so long as you did not look at her eyes. "There is no reason to negotiate with him."

Although this was what Samson wanted most, he could not conceal his shock. "How can you do that?"

She pulled a single mum from the vase. "Because I'm a Magistrate, Inspector, and the law is what I say it is."

At Saint-Germain's insistence a table had been brought into the cell. Like Weyland's iron bed, it was bolted to the floor, and the two chairs with it were lightweight molded plastic, unable to inflict much damage if hefted or thrown.

"Here's the report on the remainders," he said, handing the pages to Weyland. "They'll be asking you about each of them. It might be helpful if you take the time to learn a few of the names, at least. The Magistrates are prepared to listen to your side if you don't fly in their faces."

Weyland spread the papers on the bed and scanned them. He glanced up at Saint-Germain. "Of course you realize that in the eyes of these people—your own kind, I assume—I have no justifiable 'side' to present."

"That might be our strategy," Saint-Germain said, his manner cool. As he shifted in the uncomfortable plastic chair he went on, "You may have contempt for those of us who were born as human as the rest of them and were changed later, but if there is any hope for you at all, it is at the undead hands of those you despise." He gestured toward the pages Weyland held. "I include those … remainders as well as the rest of us."

"I am relieved," Weyland responded. "You do seem to glimpse the gulf that yawns between myself and all of you; and by 'you' I mean both human beings and so-called vampires, since to me you are all the same. No, not quite the same—" His eyes narrowed, and he drew himself up with the air of one who had come to a conclusion. "Let me answer your original question. Then tell me about 'our' strategy, if you can. You ask why I attack vampires, by which you mean your kind. I assure you they are not my first choice, but since all of you have divided up the available ordinary population into herds, or protected allies, or fugitives too wary to tolerate my approach, nothing remains accessible to me but your kind, and I take you when opportunity offers, which is when you sleep. And that is because I am not of your kind, except in hunter's mimicry. I walk in sun or moonlight as I choose.

"Unfortunately the blood in your veins is, if you will pardon me a crude expression, only secondhand. It nourishes poorly. I need to drink more from your kind than from the common run of humans. You are easy prey, and at the moment the only regularly available prey, but believe me, you are not very satisfying food.

"And," he added, with a hard glance in which a flame of restrained rage burned, "because I loathe the whole squabbling lot of you, I am not particularly grieved to see you suffer as a consequence of my requirements."

Saint-Germain kept still for many seconds. "Well," he said quietly, "at least you are candid." He held out his hands for the papers. "I would say be grateful, but you cannot be grateful; I would say be reasonable, but you know no reason; and so I will say be prudent. Surely even you can appreciate prudence. Do not show your contempt to anyone but me, for that alone will condemn you."

"I see," said Weyland acidly, "that you take my point. And I trust that you do not hold yourself so high above your fellows as to imagine that no one else will. What makes you think, little man, that you can help me in any way?" He studied Saint-Germain with chilly speculation. "What makes you want to?"

Saint-Germain hesitated, then rose and bowed. "I doubt I could explain it to you. Were I like you, I would leave you to the wolves."

WHEN THE THIRD DAY of the hearing concluded, both Weyland and Saint-Germain were irritated and tired. They emerged from the Florentine Room on the mezzanine to find a group of Fundamentalists waiting, all of them carrying the tall, inverted black crucifixes that were the mark of their sect. The escort of Watchmen closed ranks in wedge-formation, but the fanatics pressed them hard, struggling to get through and touch him who had become the focus of their ardent attention.

"Free him!" shrieked a woman in blood red robes, "free the Annunciator of the Antichrist!"

"Give him to us, we are his people!" cried another, but this call was drowned out by a bellow from a large man with a shaven head.

"He *is* the Antichrist!" roared this individual, and at once two of his followers fell to struggling with the red-robes. "Free the Antichrist, he has come to lead us!"

"Keep them back, can't you?" Weyland snarled. "They'll be

clipping bits of my ears off for talismans if you let them."

"Hurry up," panted one of the Watchmen, "there's more of them today."

"More every day," Weyland said. "If this is a sample of the public order you hope to create, Saint-Germain, I think I'd be better off dead. So don't worry yourself over the way things are going in that circus in there. I told you you'd be useless."

"In that case, would you prefer I leave?" His voice was even, his expression no more revealing than if he had been discussing the vandalism at the nearest school, but purpose burned in his dark eyes.

Weyland shot him a cold look. "Ask me again in the solitude, such as it is, of my cell."

Saint-Germain turned as Inspector Samson hurried up to him. "Is anything the matter?"

"No." But he was clearly upset. "Just get him to the nearest elevator, and you come with me."

Saint-Germain's brows went up, but he said nothing. Instead he let the nearest Watchman take Weyland's arm and moved behind him.

"All right," said Saint-Germain, deliberately standing so that few of the Fundamentalists could see their hero being hustled into the elevator surrounded by Watchmen. He met Samson's eyes. "What do you want to say to me?"

"I need to discuss something with you," said Samson with an uneasy look around the lobby.

"My suite, perhaps?" Saint-Germain suggested with a faint, sardonic smile.

"Yes, yes," said Samson. "In half an hour? Three o'clock?"

Saint-Germain shrugged. "If it is convenient." He looked toward the elevator in time to see the doors close on Weyland and the Watchmen.

As Saint-Germain came into the holding cell, he stopped, his shadow impinging on the early light. "I've had an offer," he said to Weyland.

"To sell me to those lunatics to be chopped into relics?" Weyland said bitterly.

"Nothing so extreme," said Saint-Germain, though his brow was creased with uncertainty. "No. What we have here is an offer to guarantee that you will be given into the keeping of Inspector Samson. He will be your jailer and he will conduct a series of experiments to determine how it is that you are so different. At least," he went on with a faint look of consternation, "that is what he claims."

Weyland's expression froze and his pale eyes widened.

"Oh, you child," he whispered. "You babe, you *human!* You have no idea what you are telling me, have you? No idea at all. And I have a certainty. First you brought this stupid, futile light of hope, damn you to Hell, I let you bring it. And now you bring the extinction of that light, and you only glimpse what it means, don't you? Go away, leave me alone, I don't want to look at you."

Saint-Germain put a single sheet of paper on the table. "I don't recall telling you I recommend accepting the offer," he said gently.

Slowly Weyland's shoulders loosened and his eyes grew shuttered and thoughtful. "Well, well," he murmured after a moment. "You are not so naive as I assumed. I think I have misjudged you. But don't you misjudge me. I would rather sit here in my damned chains and wait for destruction in full than spend my last days straining after phantom of salvation like some witless fool. I would rather run my head against this wall until the bone cracks and leaks my life out than prance like a goat to disguised slaughter, all decked in garlands of either black roses or electrodes and monitor cables. Do you understand me? Is there the least possibility that you understand a tenth of what I say to you?"

"I think I can manage that," said Saint-Germain. He took up the paper and returned it to his case. "Shall I refuse this out of hand, or would you prefer the door be kept open?"

Weyland smiled a slow, thin smile. "Refuse," he said, "of course. If they want me on their dissecting table, make them take me, fair and square."

ON THE EIGHTH NIGHT, Fundamentalists testified fervently to the miracles they had seen since Weyland's activities had first been noticed in the city, and to the visions they had had of him. They swore they had seen him in solemn conversation with demons or new-raised spirits of the dead, transforming water into blood for hungry worshipers, and preaching his vision—described in voluminous and impassioned detail—of the New Order to come with the arrival of the Antichrist.

Saint-Germain patiently and persistently requested corroborating details, evidence, sometimes bare coherence. Weyland answered tersely the questions put directly to him, most of which required little but a simple no. It was a lurid session concluding when a group of Fundamentalists, those who called themselves Crux Tenebre, took over the hearing room and spent the last hour before dawn singing hymns to Weyland, imploring him to herald the coming of the Antichrist and to select one of them to dispatch him as the sacrifice that would bring about that magnificent event.

At last Weyland rose in the dock and announced, "Unless you want to have to drag me in here tomorrow and try to obtain my cooperation by main force, you will keep these creatures out." He was escorted from the hearing room, his Watchmen guards hanging onto him like puppies.

The chief bailiff posted an order blocking the Crux members from the hearing until the verdict of the Magistrates was announced.

"That means nothing," declared Sister Marie LeMatte who stationed herself at the main entrance to the Magistrates' Center. "We will be here to revere the holy Weyland until he is hailed in Hell as the voice of salvation."

The chief bailiff heard her out, then assigned twice the number of Watchmen to the Cruxers as he had before.

Saint-Germain watched all this with apparent disinterest. "All they're doing is confusing the situation," he said to Samson as they approached the elevator. "They are like children who are enthralled by the latest fad, but dangerous children for all that."

Samson stared after the departing Cruxers with anxious eyes. "What if they break into Weyland's cell? They've said they want to bring him out, to offer him to his flock."

"Oh, yes," said Saint-Germain, his laughter short and irritated. "They would be delighted to venerate him … to pieces. And sell those pieces as holy relics." He was almost through the lobby when he stopped, his attention taken by figures across the street.

"What is it?" Samson asked.

Saint-Germain regarded the distant gathering, then, "Who are they?"

Samson followed his gaze and swore under his breath. "Dammit. We haven't been allowing any of them into the hearings, but they hang around outside every day. They're common men of the city, not undead; rebels and malcontents I think, though I can't prove anything. There's turmoil among our humans over all this. Weyland frightens them, but the really vengeful ones would like to see him free to go on doing what they want to do themselves—kill vampires. They even regard him as some sort of hero, like a lethal but useful god out of ancient myths."

"How do you deal with them?" Saint-Germain did not shift his gaze from the distant humans.

"I just try to keep them clear," Samson said. "I have my hands full with Cybertooths and Cruxers, and with these rebels besides—I don't want riots here." He motioned to some of his Watchmen to disperse the humans.

"No." Saint-Germain raised his hand to halt the half-dozen officers moving toward the revolving glass door. "Leave them alone. Our situation is too volatile already."

Samson stepped in front of him, and nodded to the Watchmen signaling them to carry out his orders. He said to Saint-Germain, "Pardon me, but this is my job."

"And my job—which you requested I do—is to protect Weyland." He saw that the officers were milling about near the door. "Let me have half an hour with them. As part of my job." With that, he moved past Samson and went directly out of the Magistrates' Center toward the shadowy humans.

THEY HAD LENGTHENED Weyland's chains so that he could at least pace his cell. He paced, listening to the silence of the building around him and tasting the panic that periodically choked him. He paced to keep at bay the dark dizziness that still overwhelmed him without warning. He paced between boredom and the terrors of his own imagination and told himself he did it to keep his body strong, his sinews supple.

When the crisp footsteps sounded in the hall, he turned almost eagerly.

"You!" he said. "But it's daylight; the sun has been up for hours."

Saint-Germain, preoccupied and tired looking, let himself into the cell without more answer than "Indeed."

"I see no one here after sunrise but ordinary men," Weyland added tensely. "You're not like these Beaux, exactly, are you?"

"No," was the curt answer. He went to sit in one of the plastic chairs. "I've been outside, among the humans. Do you know that many of them sympathize with you?"

"Oh, them," said Weyland with exasperation. "They drop notes in through the ventilation grill, you'll find some in among the reports you brought me to study. It's all romantic nonsense, of course; or bait to draw me into a pretended escape in the course of which I could conveniently be killed."

"Nonsense or not, they have tried to contact you," Saint-Germain pointed out. "They want something from you."

"Everyone wants something from me," Weyland said. "But this lot is useless, they won't do anything. They're too frightened of all you undead, not to mention their terror of me—imagine, a vampire who hunts whomever he hunts in daylight! There can't be many of them who actually want me set free, outside of their own fantasies of power and revenge."

"Those few will be heard; not that their testimony will alter the final disposition, since vampires will judge you, and most of them think you are worse than a murderer. They want the Magistrates to order your death." His face was pale as he said this, and he looked down at the tabletop, ashamed.

Weyland studied him a moment. He returned to his bed and sat down, sifting a coil of chain between his hands. "Don't you?" he said in a conversational tone. "I half want it myself sometimes. My God, I never thought to hear myself say that! Are you listening? This is a historic moment for me. I am tired of this. I am tired to death of all of this, this place, these hearings, all of them—and you too, Saint-Germain. I am tired of not understanding you. I should have thrown myself into the claws of your saint-hungry friends out there last night. But you would like to prevent that, you want some other outcome that I can't imagine. They want me dead. You don't. Will you tell me why?"

Saint-Germain sat quietly, paying no heed to the sudden attention Weyland riveted on him. "We cannot afford your caprice. Like it or not, we all must come to terms with one another, we must learn what it is to be civilized, to tolerate each other." He turned abruptly, catching Weyland with his compelling gaze. "You, and anyone like you, will be how we determine if we are hunting animals or creatures with … souls."

Weyland leaned his head back against the wall. "I am to be your lesson, then? Your example? Of the hunting animal you hope to transcend, surely. But what gives you the right to build your damned civilization on my back, what gives you any rights regarding me at all?" He laughed and held up his fettered wrists which showed dark bruises where the steel had rubbed his skin. "An academic question, you understand. These give you the right, don't they?"

"No," said Saint-Germain wearily. "If anything, they support your view, I suspect." He was staring at the far side of the room now, but what he saw was far distant from that improvised cell. "Not that humanity offers any model much better than our own. But there have been times when there was compassion, and that is a start."

Weyland leaned forward intently. "How old are you? A hundred years? Six hundred? A thousand? I think I am thousands of years older than anything remotely akin to me on this planet. Don't talk to me about history. I am senior to you, I am your elder."

"You are what I was," said Saint-German, "more than four thousand years ago. But I have changed."

Demon Star sauntered through the lobby, serenely ignoring the stares of those who had just heard her testify before the five Magistrates. She had marked the occasion by painting a bloody heart on her cheeks and silvering the white spikes of her hair. Behind her the rest of her Cybertooths flocked, basking in her reflected glory. Inspector Frederick Samson had waited for this moment. He had listened impatiently to her in the hearing room. He had to speak with her, to gain her support. Since he had so unexpectedly been given the approval of Magistrate Isodora Ruthven in the Weyland matter, he had developed a number of plans, and new information indicated that he had better act quickly on one that included the Cybertooths. He went after Demon Star, not too quickly, but fast enough to intercept her before she and her pack reached the door.

"I have to speak with you, my lady," he said, having decided that 'Miss Demon Star' sounded ridiculous even to his Beaux ears.

Demon Star halted and raked her eyes over Samson. "The inspector. What do you want?" She held out her hand so he had to kiss it or be inexcusably rude; it was the hand that held the riding crop.

"We need to talk," said Samson when he had—reluctantly—kissed her hand. "It's urgent, and it's in both our interests. If you don't speak with me, we may both be disappointed."

She cocked her head, looking more like an alien artifact than ever. "How do you mean, disappointed?" She made a sign to her followers and they drew back, huddled together and surrounded by others who had left the hearing room.

"It might be best to go to my office," he suggested. "Not so many distractions."

"Beaux like you in your elegant rigs, you mean, or those Cruxers?" Her laughter was loud and cutting, making itself heard throughout the lobby.

"I mean everything," Samson said through clenched teeth as he tried to remain polite. "Won't you come with me? It would be best if you do."

Demon Star contemplated the ceiling where the gilded scenes of frolicking gods were faded and watermarked. "I don't have anything to say that I didn't tell the Magistrates, and you don't need to hear any more so-called testimony from anybody else, either. How long are you planning to drag this out, anyway?

"The Renegade was in our territory. He made remainders of some of my pack, he got some of our cattle. That's all there is to it. You turn him over to us. We'll handle him. We've got the right."

Samson grabbed her arm. "*Not here!*" he hissed.

She shrugged and strolled into the elevator ahead of him, carelessly signaling her pack to stay and await her return. In Samson's office she took the one comfortable chair and adopted a pose of exaggerated patience while he moved about the room moving papers and files from one place to another.

Finally he said, "I hear rumors. My Watchmen tell me your gang and the Cruxers are talking together, about this animal Weyland. If this is true—"

"Sure it's true," Demon Star said lazily. "I'm gonna give them some style. Anybody with a pinch of guts could get off on being the leader of a cult, for as long as it was fun, anyhow."

"Don't do it," Samson said, facing her.

"Just like a cop—always telling everybody what kinds of fun they can have and what kinds they can't," she jeered.

"Don't get that rabble together to break in here and take him," Samson said. "You might be able to do it, all together you just might, I give you that; and then—you don't understand what's at risk here."

"Oh no," she drawled, "'course I don't. Nobody like me could ever understand anything so complicated, right? It's stamped all over your superior face, Inspector. You damn Beaux think you understand the whole damn world, which is why you're the ones who should hand out justice to everybody else."

"Listen!" he said. "I'm not talking about justice. I'm talking about walking around in daylight, so you never have to worry about anything like Weyland again, and you never have to go to sleep looking over your shoulder in case some stray human is sneaking up to slice your head off while you're helpless."

"Cut to the suck," she said with sudden steel. "You're up to something. What?"

He hesitated, licking his dry lips and trying to decide how much to tell her. He circled behind his desk and sat down there, fortifying himself against her scorn. "All right. All right. I want to find out what it is in his makeup that allows him the same freedom as human beings. If I can work on him for a while, I can find answers that all of us can benefit from—but not all at once, do you see my meaning?" He leaned confidentially nearer and lowered his voice. "And if you wanted to be present, to be part of the proceedings, to learn for yourself what there is to be discovered in him, that could be arranged. But outside observation would be strictly limited."

"By you," she said, tapping the crop idly against her booted leg. "As the Renegade's keeper, is that what you're hoping for? Crap, Inspector. You Beaux stick together, you've got it all fixed up already. We all know that."

"Then you're wrong," Samson said forcefully, changing his tactics. "Would I talk to you about this if I didn't need your help? Which would you rather have, broken relics to string around your neck for decoration, or the secret of Weyland's strength and sunlight-tolerance?"

"What good would his secrets do for the rest of us?" she challenged.

He saw that he had her, or almost, and he relaxed slightly and glanced out of his window at the new-risen moon. "We have a little time till dawn," he said. "Let me tell you something about being a genius at science in a time when science was starving its young to death."

At least, Weyland thought, pacing, they were not starving him to death. Not yet. What they were doing filled him with despair and baffled rage, and in the daylight hours not spent in sleep to match the normal vampiric schedule now forced on him, he chewed this rage.

That there should be such a thing as a "normal" vampire infuriated him from the start. Now the complexities of a world crowded with competitors had defeated him, and the defeat was bitter. He did not remember his previous lives, but he knew that each had ended in the small defeat of the long sleep. This ending now had the feel of something final, and not at the hands of some impersonal natural force or even a human being stumbling on his lair, but because of these swarms of undead in whose existence he had never even believed.

Only the daylight hours brought relief from the murmurings and howlings of his self-styled worshipers outside the high, barred vent to his cell. They sang and danced up there. They chanted prayers to raise him bodily into their hands, and they told him just how they would convert him into the centerpiece of the new religion, at least until the ritual of his death brought the One True Evil Presence palpably into the world.

He leaned his cheek against the cool cement wall and thought about death. Death at the hands of one mob or another, death under the knife of that eager-eyed inspector, death in some neatly "legal" form that would satisfy the more fastidious Beaux—he sweated and trembled, thinking of it, and somewhere in his thoughts the black surge of dizziness stirred threateningly.

This new occupant of his mind was a lingering effect of that nightmarish moment of attack, when his had been the throat bared, his the wrenching terror as his own blood was drawn.

Perhaps they had contaminated him with some foulness of their own in that frightful moment. Perhaps even if he survived this mad trial, he was no longer fit to survive in their world.

In his thoughts, Death smiled. It had pursued him through lifetimes, and he, in a way, had pursued it.

What was it, after all? These undead didn't know that, not even this cool little man Saint-Germain; which was just as well, since what he did know and deigned to try to communicate was curiously opaque and obscure.

Still, Weyland had come to enjoy their sparring matches, which were at least a diversion from the dreary night hours of the hearings and the empty ones of daylight. And Saint-Germain had a neat, well-cared-for look about him that Weyland approved of, however grudgingly. He knew himself at this point to be a rather shaggy, grimy figure, but found he no longer cared. Let this Saint-Germain keep up the sartorial standards.

Weyland found him puzzling. He was clearly trying to accomplish something that he felt to be of importance, with a minimum of the showy fuss that seemed so dear to these undead.

And here he was again, perhaps for the last time. Even the Magistrates were showing impatience with the process lately. Some sort of summation was in the offing, and then—a decision.

Weyland smoothed his hair back with his hands and composed

himself for what he thought might be his last interview with Saint-Germain.

"They want to end the hearing tonight," he told Weyland as he came into the cell. He was dressed with more elegance than before, though in the same restrained un-Beauish style. Instead of the usual sheaf of papers, he now carried a small leather case embossed with a heraldic eclipse. "The Magistrates sent me word just after sundown."

"So this is my last chance to dazzle them with my virtue and brilliance?" Weyland raised a sarcastic eyebrow. "Or rather with yours, my advocate."

Saint-Germain dismissed his remarks with a shake of his head. "The Magistrates have announced they'll make a decision by sunrise. My summation will be tonight. I thought you'd like to know." He did not take a seat and his dark eyes seemed tired. "Is there anything you want?"

Weyland bit back the retort that sprang to his lips—there was, after all, quite a list of things he wanted—and concentrated on stilling the shaking of his hands. He looked Saint-Germain in the eye.

"Whatever you've been trying to do," he said slowly, "I have seen that your intention was clean and your execution, if I may be allowed the term, competent. Whatever happens, that must merit recognition." He shrugged. "Of course, there is no desirable outcome for me, so it's a good thing you have acted for your own aims all along. Mine were lost from the moment I woke in this Hellish version of the world. I will remember you, while I can."

Saint-Germain left without speaking.

TWO OF THE large adjoining meeting rooms had been opened up to give more space in the Florentine Room to those who wanted to see the climax of the hearing. On one side, Demon Star and her pack gathered with other Cybertooths, all as touchy as cats. Across the room the Crux Tenebre cult sat among the many Fundamentalists, some of them singing, some praying, a few seemingly transfixed by visions. In the wedge between them, Beaux in their finery preened and waited for the final statements to begin. There were no humans present except the Watchmen who circulated through the aisles, determined and jittery.

Inspector Samson followed the five Magistrates toward the

high-fronted desks that had been set up at the end of the room. He managed to exchange a single, speaking glance with Magistrate Ruthven before taking his place beside the bailiff.

Finally, when the crowd had been called to order, after a frenzied plea from the Cruxers and a sullen demand from the Cybertooths, Samson rose to speak. "All during these hearings, it has been my position that we are here to serve justice. Our justice must embrace the good of all the community if it is to have any meaning at all. We have been asked to free Edward Weyland, we have been asked to destroy Edward Weyland, we have even been asked to venerate him. But I have maintained that our cause can best be served if we *understand* Edward Weyland, and learn what it is about him that renders him so unlike the rest of us. I have submitted my proposals to you, Your Honors, and I ask that you consider them before you condemn him to any form of execution for his crimes."

He sat down, flushed with the excitement of the moment and heartened by the faint, approving nod from Magistrate Ruthven. With her help, he had a chance at last to prove his talents and his theories with discoveries that could change the nature and destiny of the entire vampire community.

For the moment, however, the hearing room was filled with whistles and catcalls and prayers in response to his remarks, and it took some little time for the Watchmen to restore quiet.

"Saint-Germain?" said the oldest Magistrate, a tall, cadaverous Beau with eyes like hot coals.

Saint-Germain did not rise at once. When he did, he came directly toward the Magistrates, locking eyes with each of them in turn. "Do you remember what it was like?" he asked, his voice low. "Do you remember how you had to live when we were few and people were many? Do you remember being called a monster and watching those of your blood die for being monsters? Do you remember?" He paused, watching them closely. "Do you remember having to hunt? Do you remember being a killer? Your Honor?" He addressed the oldest Magistrate.

The old man nodded. "I remember."

"Yes." Saint-Germain paused. "We all do. And that is what we are making of Edward Weyland. Everything we dreaded in humans we are now if we treat this vampire as we were treated." For the first time he turned away from the Magistrates and approached Weyland; his dark eyes were intent. "One of those … remainders is of my blood. She was a nurse, and she came to my life in 1857. You ended that for her, more surely than if you had cut her in pieces, and for that I loathe you, and will loathe you for all time."

Weyland, until now a listless observer of the proceedings, started and seemed about to speak. But he sat back again in impassive silence. Saint-Germain moved forward, forcing himself to address the Magistrates; he did not want to see Weyland's face now. "If it were only my need, I would roast him in hot coals. But that is him speaking in me, the beast we are, the thing that makes people call us creatures of death."

He looked around the crowded rooms. "But we do not kill. We instill life. Where death comes, we can banish it. Only those who see death as ultimately binding think us malign, and destroy us because of our life. If we accept the bond of blood, we accept the ties of life as well, and we revere it as no mortal human can. And it is for that reason," he went on, moving back toward Weyland once more, "for our cherished life that I ask you to treat this … this monster as the ghost of what we have been, that you do not condemn him to execution, either at the hands of his rivals—" he nodded toward the Cybertooths—"or his predators; that you free yourselves in freeing him." He swung his arm around, his small hand leveled at the Magistrates in order, binding them together invisibly. Only Magistrate Ruthven resisted his compelling gaze.

"Weyland cannot be forgiven, for what he has done is unforgivable. But we can, in mercy, pardon him. Find him a preserve where he can hunt or sleep, as he wishes. But do not give him up to death." The room had grown very still. "What are we: creatures of death, or of life?"

In the hush that followed, he left the Florentine Room.

THE MOON HAD SET, but the crowd remained. They milled and prowled around the walls of the Magistrates' Center, forming eddies of tense conversation and whorls of excited argument.

In his office Samson looked down at them, chewing his knuckles. If he had lost in the hearing room he had lost all, and his thoughts took him darkly down among the mob where he could lose himself, his office, and his failure if he must.

The basement cell was quiet. Weyland sat on the bed. He had not spoken for some time. At last, stretching his long legs out in front of him, he said, "Your story about the nurse; was it true?"

From his place by the door, Saint-Germain said, "Yes."

Weyland nodded, his dark-hollowed eyes steady on Saint-

Germain. "Ah," he said. "Loyalty. I am familiar with the concept, though I don't see the point of making a fetish of it. But you humans do love to define some higher moral ground for yourselves and then twist yourselves and everyone else into knots trying to take that ground and hold it. I am not like you, I told you that at the start; my aspirations are not so high."

Saint-Germain looked out through the bars of the door. "Is that how it seems to you?" He did not expect an answer.

Weyland looked down at his fetters. "It will feel good to be free of these chains." He added in a distant tone, "How do you think they will decide."

After a moment Saint-Germain said, "I don't know."

A MUSICAL INTERLUDE

In a carrel of the university library tower a student slept. Over him stood Dr. Weyland, respected new member of the faculty, pressed by hunger to feed.

The air was warm despite the laboring of the cooling system. Quiet reigned; summer courses brought few students into the stacks. On his preliminary tour of this tower level, silent in crepe-soled shoes, Weyland had noted the presence of only two: this sleeping youth and a young woman sitting on the floor reading in the geology section.

In nervous haste Weyland moved: he rendered the sleeper unconscious by briefly pressing shut an artery to the brain. Then, delicately tipping the lolling head to fully expose the throat, he leaned close and drank without a sound. When he was done, he patted his lips with his handkerchief and left as silently as he had come.

The youth whose blood he had drunk breathed a gusty, complaining sigh across the page on which his pale cheek rested. He dreamed of being unprepared for a history exam.

In the men's room on the ground floor Weyland washed the scent of his victim from his hands. Damp-palmed, he smoothed back his vigorous iron-gray hair, which in this climate tended to stick up in wiry tufts. He frowned at his reflection, at the tension lines around his mouth and eyes.

In his second week in New Mexico, he was still feeling upset from his recent experiences in the East. Yet now he must behave with calm and self-confidence. He could not afford mistakes.

No odd rumors or needless animosity must attach themselves to him here. All modern cities seemed so large to him that he had miscalculated about this one: Albuquerque was smaller than he had expected. He missed the anonymity of New York. No wonder he couldn't shake this nervousness. Walking back through the somnolent afternoon for a nap in his temporary quarters, the home of an assistant professor, would relax him. Then he could sleep, as his digestion obliged him to, on the meal he had just taken in the library.

As part of the department head's efforts to settle him comfortably in his new surroundings, social arrangements had been made in advance for him. Tonight he was to attend the opera in Santa Fe with some friends of the department head's wife, people who ran an art gallery here in Albuquerque. Weyland hoped the evening would contribute to his image as an austere but approachable scholar. The strain of sociability would be supportable, given the all-important nap.

He walked out into the brilliant summer sunlight.

THE TOURISTS AMBLED through the opera house. From the ridge on which the building lay they could look south toward Santa Fe, east and west toward mountains. Even on hot days breezes cooled the opera hill. The deep, concrete-enclosed spaces of the house were wells of shadow. The house manager, who was guiding the tour, led the visitors through the wings and down an open stair. They emerged onto a sunny concrete deck that backed the entire building—stage area in the middle and flanking work areas—in a north-south sweep.

Raising his voice above hammering sounds and a whine of power tools, the guide said, "Most of the technical work gets done here on the deck level." He pointed out the paint and electrical shops and, just behind and below the stage, the big scenery lift between the two open staircases.

The group drifted onto the shaded southern end of the deck, which became a roofed veranda adjoining the wig and costume shop. They stood like passengers at the rail of a cruise ship, looking westward. Someone asked about the chain-link fence that ran behind the opera house near the base of the hill.

The house manager said, "The fence marks off the property of the opera itself from the land that the founder, John Crosby, had the foresight to buy as a buffer against growth from Santa Fe. Nobody will ever be able to build close enough to give us problems with noise or light, or wreck our acoustical backdrop—that hillside facing us across the arroyo at the bottom of our hill."

The tourists chatted, lingering on the shady veranda; even with a breeze, it was hot out on the exposed deck. Cameras clicked.

Looking down, a man in a safari suit asked disapprovingly, "What's all that trash down there?"

The others moved to look. On the deck they stood perhaps thirty feet above a paved road that ran below the back of the opera house along the west face of the hill. Beneath them the road gave access to a doorway and a garage entry, on either side of which huge piles of lumber and canvas were heaped high against the stucco wall.

"That's discarded sets," the guide said. "We have only so much storage space. Old productions get dumped there until we either cannibalize them for new sets or haul them away."

A woman, looking back the way they had come, said, "This building is really a fantastic labyrinth. How does everyone keep track of where they're supposed to be and what they should be doing during a performance?"

The guide said, "By the music. You remember the stage manager's console in the right wings, with the phones and the mike and the TV monitors? The whole show is run from right there by the numbers in a marked copy of the score. Our stage manager, Renee Spiegel, watches the conductor's beat on the monitor, and according to that she gives everybody their cues. So the music structures everything that happens.

"Now, when we want to shut out the view of the mountains for an indoor scene, say, we use movable back walls ..."

"Dr. Weyland? I'm Jean Gray, from the Walking River Gallery. Albert McGrath, my partner, had to go to Santa Fe earlier today so we'll meet him at the opera. You just sit back and enjoy the scenery while I drive us up there."

He folded his height into the front passenger seat without speaking or offering his hand. What's this, Jean wondered, doesn't the great man believe in hobnobbing with the common folk? Her friend the department head's wife had impressed upon her in no uncertain terms that this was indeed a great man. He fitted the part: a dark, well-tailored jacket and fawn slacks, gray hair, strong face—large, intense eyes brooding down a majestic prow of a nose, a morose set to the mouth and the long, stubborn jaw.

They also said he'd been ill back East; give a guy a break. Jean nosed the car out past striped sawhorses and piled rubble exclaiming cheerfully, "Look at this mess!"

In precise and bitter tones Dr. Weyland replied, "Better to look at it than to listen to it being made. All afternoon I had to endure the bone-shattering thunder of heavy machinery." He added in grudging apology, "Excuse me. I customarily sleep after eating. Today a nap was impossible. I am not entirely myself."

"Would you like a Rolaid? I have some in my purse."

"No, thank you." He turned and put his coat on the back seat.

"I hope you have a scarf or sweater as well as your raincoat. Santa Fe's only sixty miles north of Albuquerque, but it's two thousand feet higher. The opera is open-air, so because of the lighting nothing starts till after sunset, about nine o'clock. Performances run late, and the nights can get chilly."

"I'll manage."

"I keep a blanket in the trunk just in case. At least the sky's nice and clear; we're not likely to be rained out. It's a good night for *Tosca*. You know that marvelous aria in the third act where Cavaradossi sings about how the stars shone above the cottage where he and Tosca used to meet—"

"The opera tonight is *Tosca?*"

"That's right. Do you know it well?"

After a moment he said distantly, "I knew someone in the East who was named after Floria Tosca, the heroine of the story. But I've never seen this opera."

AFTER LAST NIGHT'S PERFORMANCE OF *Gonzago*, a dissonant modern opera on a bloody Renaissance theme, the *Tosca* lighting sequence had to be set up for tonight. Having worked backward through Acts Three and Two, the crew broke for dinner, then began to complete the reversed sequence so that when they finished at eight o'clock the lights and the stage would be set for the start of Act One.

Everyone was pleased to abandon the dreadful *Gonzago*, this season's expression of the Santa Fe Opera's commitment to modern works, in favor of a dependable old warhorse like Puccini's *Tosca*. Headsets at the stage manager's console, in the lighting booth, in the patch room and at the other stations around the house, hummed with brisk instructions, numbers, comments.

Renee Spiegel, the stage manager, pored over her carefully marked score. She hoped people hadn't forgotten too many cues since *Tosca* last week, what with doing three other operas since. She hoped everything would run nice and tight tonight, orderly and by the numbers.

Jeremy Tremain gargled, spat, and stared in the mirror at the inside of his throat. It looked a healthy pink.

Nevertheless he sat down discontentedly to his ritual pre-performance bowl of chicken broth. Tonight he was to sing Angelotti, a part which ended in the first act. By the opera's end the audience would remember the character, but who would recall having heard Tremain sing? He preferred a house that did calls after each act; you could do your part, take your bows, and go home.

The part he coveted was that of the baritone villain, Scarpia. Tremain was beginning to be bored with the roles open to him as a young bass—ponderous priests and monarchs and the fathers of tenor heroes. He had recently acquired a new singing teacher who he hoped could help him enlarge the top of his range, transforming him into a bass baritone capable of parts like Scarpia. He was sure he possessed the dark, libidinous depths the role demanded.

He got up and went in his bathrobe to the mirror again, turning for a three-quarter view. You wanted a blocky look for Scarpia. If only he had more jaw.

Weyland stared balefully out the car window. His library meal weighed in his midsection like wet sand. Being deprived of rest after eating upset his system. Now in addition he'd been cooped up for an hour in this flashy new car with an abominably timid driver. At least she had stopped trying to make conversation.

They overtook the cattle truck behind which they had been dawdling, then settled back to the same maddeningly slow pace. He said irritably, "Why do you slow down again?"

"The police watch this road on Friday nights."

He could hardly demand to take over the driving; he must be patient, he must be courteous. He thought longingly of the swift gray Mercedes he had cherished in the East.

They took a stop-light-ridden bypass around Santa Fe itself and continued north. At length Jean Gray pointed out the opera house, tantalizingly visible beyond a crawling line of cars that snaked ahead of them past miles of construction barriers.

"Isn't there another road to the opera?" Weyland said.

"Just this one; and somehow during opera season it does tend to get torn up." She chattered on about how Santa Feans had a standing joke that their streets were regularly destroyed in summer solely to annoy the tourists.

Weyland stopped listening.

IN THE PARKING LOT young people in jeans and windbreakers waved their flashlights, shouting, "This way, please," to incoming drivers. People had formed a line at the standing-room window. The ushers stood, arms full of thick program books, talking in the sunken patio beyond the ticket gate.

TREMAIN CHECKED IN with the stage manager, who told him that the costume shop had finished mending the shirt for the dummy of Angelotti used in Act Three. That meant that tonight Tremain wouldn't have to strip after his part was over in Act One, give up his costume to the dummy, and then change back again for curtain calls. He took this for a good sign and cheerfully went down to the musicians' area to pick up his mail.

Members of the orchestra lounged down here, talking, playing cards in the practice rooms, getting their instruments from the cage in back and tuning up. Tremain flirted with one of the cellists, teasing her into coming to the party after the show tonight.

In the narrow conductor's office off the musicians' area, Rolf Anders paced. He wished now for just one more run-through with the backstage chorus in Act Two. The assistant conductor, working from a TV monitor, had to keep his backstage players and singers a fraction ahead of Anders and a fraction sharp for their music to sound right out front.

Anders looked forward to shedding his nervousness in the

heat of performance. Some people said that every opera conductor should do *Tosca* each season to discharge his aggressions.

Three ticket-takers stationed themselves beside the slotted stub boxes, and the long iron gate swung wide. The people who had pooled on the steps and round the box office began to stream down into the sunken patio in front of the opera house. First comers sat down on the raised central fountain or the low walls containing foundation plantings of white petunias. From these vantage points they observed the clear but fading light flooding the sky, or watched and discussed the passing pageant.

Here an opera cape from another era, the crushed black velvet setting off an elegant neck; there blue jeans and a down-filled vest. Here a suit of Victorian cut complete with waistcoat, flowered buttonhole and watch chain, the wearer sporting between slim, ringed fingers an even slimmer cane; there a rugby shirt. Here a sport jacket in big orange-and-green checks over green slacks—and there, unbelievably, its double just passing in the opposite direction on a larger man who clearly shopped at the same men's store. Everywhere was the gleam of heavy silver, the sky hardness of turquoise, sparkle of diamond, shimmer of plaited iridescent feathers, glitter of baroquely twisted gold.

A church group of white-haired women, come for the evening in a chartered bus, stood goggling, a bouquet of pastel polyester flowers.

The house manager, in sober evening dress, moved nimbly through the crowd, sizing up the house, keeping track of mood and movement and the good manners of his ushers.

Jean, standing on her toes, spotted McGrath—stumpy, freckled, thinning on top—at the fountain. He had with him young Elmo Archuleta, a painter he was wooing for the gallery.

"That's Albert McGrath; would you mind going over and introducing yourself?" she said to Dr. Weyland. "I have to make a dash for the ladies' room." Jean and McGrath were at odds over her plans to leave the gallery and return to the East. These days she spent as little time as she could around McGrath.

Dr. Weyland grunted disagreeably, tucked his raincoat over his arm, and went to join them.

God save us, thought Jean, from the grouchy great.

"PLEASED TO MEET YOU, PROFESSOR," McGrath said. So this was the hotshot anthropologist the university people were crowing about; handsome, in a sour, arrogant way, and he still had his hair. Some guys got all the luck.

McGrath introduced Elmo, who was scarred with acne and very shy. He explained that Elmo was a hot young local artist. Jean was undoubtedly trying to steer the kid away from the gallery, to retaliate for McGrath's refusal to let her walk out on their partnership. McGrath let slip no chance to praise Elmo, whose work he really liked. He flourished his enthusiasm.

The professor looked with undisguised boredom at Elmo, who was visibly shrinking into himself.

"Nice ride up?" McGrath said.

"An exceedingly slow ride."

Here comes Jean, thank God, McGrath thought. "Hiya, Jean-girl!" She was little and always fighting her weight, trying at thirty-two to keep looking like a kid. And sharp—you'd never guess how sharp from her round, candid face and breathless manner. Smart and devious, that was Easterners for you.

The professor said, "I think the altitude has affected me. I'd like to go in and sit down. No, please, all of you stay and enjoy the parade here. I'll see you later inside. May I have my ticket stub, please?"

He left them.

Jean smiled at Elmo. "Hi, Elmo. Is this your first time at the opera?"

"Sure is," McGrath answered. "I got him a seat down front at the last minute. And speaking of last-minute luck, I've wangled an invitation to a party afterward. Lots of important people will be there." He paused. She was going to let him down, he could see it coming.

"Oh, I wish I'd known earlier," she said. "I have to be back in Albuquerque early tomorrow morning to meet some clients at the gallery."

McGrath smiled past Jean at a couple he knew from someplace. "I'll take Elmo and the professor with me, then. He doesn't seem exactly friendly, this Weyland. Anything wrong?"

"He barely said a word on the way up. All I know is what hear: this is a high-powered academic with a good book behind him; bachelor, tough in class—a workaholic, recently recovered from some kind of breakdown."

McGrath shook his head. "I don't know why they hire these high-strung, snotty Easterners when there's plenty of good local men looking for jobs." Giving Jean no time to respond, he walked away to talk to the couple he knew from someplace.

Jean said, "Is McGrath treating you okay, Elmo?"

"He's like all gallery people. They treat you nice until you sign up with them, and then they bring out the whip." Elmo flushed and looked down at his shiny boot toes; he liked Jean. "I didn't mean you. Are you still trying to get clear of McGrath?"

She sighed. "He won't let me out of the contract. He keeps saying New Mexico needs me. That's what happens when you're dumb enough to make yourself indispensable."

"How come you don't like it out here anymore?"

"I'm not as adaptable as I thought I was," she said ruefully. "The transplant just isn't working."

Elmo studied her brown hair, its soft, dull sheen. She was ten years his senior, which somehow made it easy for him to like her. He hoped she wouldn't go back East. That felt like a bad wish toward her, so he said impulsively, "Why don't you just up and go? You got enough money to fly back to New York."

She shook her head. "I need to go home with at least as much as I brought out here. You can't live in New York on the stub of a plane ticket."

Weyland took his seat. The theater was quiet, the stage set—there was no curtain—was softly illuminated. The house doors had just been opened, and most of the people were still out on the patio.

He definitely did not feel right. The tedious trip had put an edge on his fatigue. And they always wanted to talk; all the way up he had felt the pressure of Jean Gray's desire for conversation distracting him from the restful sweep of the land and sky.

Now, here, the fashionable crowd had reminded him uncomfortably of something—Alan Reese's followers, the spectators at the cell door … All left behind now. He thrust away the thought and leaned back to look a long time through the open roof at the deepening evening. If he could only walk out now into the dark, quiet hills, his keen night vision would aid him to find a hollow where he could lie down and settle his system with a nap—though at best sleep was difficult for him. By nature perpetually on the alert, he was roused by the least disturbance. Still, he could try—he wondered whether anyone would notice if he rose and slipped away.

Too late: another blink of the house lights, and the crowd came drifting down among the stepped rows of seats. Jean Gray sat down next to him, McGrath next to her.

She said to Weyland, "Well, what do you think? It's not a great big opera house like the Met in New York, but it has charm."

He knew he should respond, should make some effort to ingratiate himself. But he could bring himself to offer only a curt syllable of assent, followed by sullen silence.

With Anders standing ready beside her, Renee Spiegel said into the console mike, "Places, everyone, please." The backstage speakers echoed, "Places, everyone, please."

She signaled the final blinking warnings of the house lights and then dispatched Anders to the podium. His image walked onto her TV monitor screen.

There was no foot-shuffling applause from the musicians when Anders entered the pit; he had lost his temper with them too often during rehearsals. The audience applauded him. He bowed. He turned and opened his score.

Spiegel, watching him on the monitor, called the lighting booth: "Warning, Light Cue One …"

Anders breathed deeply and gave the down beat.

"Cue One—"

Out crashed the first of the chords announcing the power of the dreaded Minister of Police, Baron Scarpia.

"Go!" Spiegel said.

The lights came up on an interior portion of the Church of Sant' Andrea della Valle in Rome, the year 1800. Scarpia's chords were transformed into the staggering music of flight. Tremain, as the escaped political prisoner Angelotti, rushed onstage into the church to hide.

In the lighting booth between the two sections of the balcony seating, a technician hit the switch that started the tape player. A cannon shot boomed from the house speakers. The technician grinned to herself, remembering the time her partner, stepping inside to relay a cue invisible from within the booth, had put a foot among the wires and yanked them out. The cannon shots of Act One had been drums that night.

Things could go wrong, things did go wrong, but it was never what you expected.

Floria Tosca on this stage bore no resemblance to the thin, dark woman named Floria whom Weyland had known in New York. This singer probably wasn't even a brunette—her eyes looked blue to him. His uneasy curiosity allayed, Weyland watched inattentively. He was turning over and over in his mind the layout of the university buildings, reviewing the hunting methods he could employ there until less risky opportunities to secure his prey developed.

Something on stage caught his attention. Scarpia was addressing Tosca for the first time, offering her on his own fingertips holy water from the stoup. He lifted his hand slightly as she withdrew hers, so that their contact was prolonged. After a startled glance of distaste at him, Tosca plunged again into jealous anxiety over her lover Cavaradossi's unexpected absence from the church. Scarpia moved downstage behind her, step for step, singing a polite inquiry into the cause of her distress. His tone was caressingly sensual and insinuating over a lively pealing of bells and courtly flourishes in the strings.

Intrigued by Scarpia's calculated maneuvering, Weyland lost interest when Tosca flew into a tantrum. He went back to pondering his new hunting ground.

The Te Deum, the great close of the first act, began. What a spectacle it was, Jean thought admiringly. The small stage seemed enlarged by the pageant in white, black, and scarlet entering at a grave, swaying pace behind Scarpia's back.

Scarpia mused on his own plans, oblivious to all else. He had deduced that Tosca's lover Cavaradossi was aiding the fugitive

Angelotti out of sympathy with the latter's support of Bonaparte. Now Scarpia hoped that Tosca would go to Cavaradossi, and Scarpia's men would follow without her knowledge and take the quarry.

The Police Minister's soliloquy, the lighter bells sounding the theme of his first suave approaches to Tosca, the great B-flat bell tolling, the organ, the choral voices, the measured booming of the cannon, all combined to thrilling effect; and the rich public virtue of the religious procession was set off against Scarpia's private villainy. As his sinuous melody wove around the solid structure of the celebrants' Te Deum, the long crescendo built.

Scarpia's voice seemed to ring effortlessly over the music, first an iron determination to recapture Angelotti; then a glowing outpouring of lust, luxuriant, powerful with assurance that soon Tosca would lie in his own arms—"*Illanguidir,*" the voice glided down then surged upward with erotic strength on the final syllable; "*—d'amor …*"

Waking abruptly to his surroundings, he joined the chorus in full voice, and suddenly the morality of the State, as conveyed by the liturgy, and the personal evil of Scarpia were also united: one the underside of the other, both together the essence of official hypocrisy.

Scarpia knelt. Three times brass and drums shouted the savage ascent of whole tones declaring his implacable ferocity, the lights vanished, the first of the three acts was over.

Jean sat back, sighing deeply. Around her people began to clap, standing, shouting, or turning to talk excitedly to one another.

Applauding, she turned also, but Dr. Weyland had gone.

Weyland walked in the parking lot. People moved among the cars under pools of light from the tall lampposts, talking and laughing, singing snatches of melody. They took from their cars scarves, gloves, blankets, hats. The breeze had an edge now.

Facing the wind, Weyland opened his jacket, unknotted his tie, and undid the top button of his shirt. He felt unpleasantly warm, almost feverish, and very tired. Even if he were to plead illness and retire to the back seat of the car, he knew he was too restless now to sleep.

He turned uneasily back toward the patio, a concourse of loud, volatile humanity. Crowds of people, their feelings and bodies in turbulent motion, always seemed threatening him—unpredictable, irrational, as easily swept to savagery as to tears. And the music had been powerful; even he had felt his hackles stir.

Why? Art should not matter. Yet he responded—first to the ballet, back in New York, and now to this. He was disturbed by a sense of something new in himself, as if recent events had exposed an unexpected weakness.

Best to arrange the possibility of an unobtrusive exit during the next act, in case he should find himself too uncomfortable to sit it out.

In the musicians' area people drifted and talked. Tremain, done performing for the evening but still in costume, stood reading over the shoulder of a flutist who was absorbed in a battered paperback titled *The Revenge of the Androids.*

The conductor sat in his room massaging the back of his neck, trying to regain his calm without going flat. Now that everyone was warmed up, the evening was taking shape as one of those rare occasions when the opera's life, which is larger than life, fills the house, electrifying audience and performers alike and including them all in one magnificent experience. He felt the temptation to give in before the excitement and rush the tempo, which would only throw everyone off and spoil the performance.

Relax. Relax. Anders took deep breaths and yawned at last.

People congregated around the Opera Guild booth, where posters, T-shirts, and other souvenirs were being sold.

"I know Scarpia's an awful monster," said a woman in a tailored wool suit, "but he has such wonderful music, so mean and gorgeous, it makes the old heart go pitapat. I'm always a little bit ashamed of loving Puccini's operas—there's that current of cruelty—but the melodies are so sensuous and so lyrical, your better judgment just melts away."

The younger woman to whom she spoke smiled vaguely at her.

"The second act is a real grabber," continued the wool-suited woman. "First Scarpia tells how he likes caveman tactics better than courting with flowers and music. Then he has the poor tenor, Cavaradossi I mean, tortured until Tosca gives in and tells where

Angelotti's hiding, and they haul Cavaradossi off to prison. And *then* Scarpia says if she wants to save Cavaradossi from execution for treason, she has to come to bed with him. He has this absolutely palpitating, ecstatic music—"

The young man who was her escort drawled, "Rutting music."

The young woman smiled. High again, thought the wool-suited woman disgustedly; where does she think she is, some damn rock concert?

"Come on," the wool-suited woman said. "We have to buy a T-shirt for Brother. A friend of mine is selling for the Guild tonight: that's her—that little lady with the short white hair and bright eyes. See the magenta sari she's wearing? She got that in India; she's been to China too; a great traveler. Hi, Juliet, let me introduce my sister ..."

JEAN TOOK HER INTERMISSION COFFEE BLACK, which was bad-tasting but not fattening. "What a show we're getting tonight—a perfect introduction to opera for you, Elmo."

"I didn't like it," Elmo said unhappily. "I mean, it was like watching an animal in church pretending to be a man."

"You know," Jean said, "I read somewhere that Puccini had a strong primitive streak. He loved hunting, shooting birds and such. Maybe it wouldn't be too far off to see his Scarpia as a sort of throwback to a more bestial, elemental type." Elmo looked lost. Jean shifted gears: "You know the costume Tosca wore, the plumed hat, the dress with rustling skirts, the long cane? It's traditional; the first singer to play the role wore a similar outfit at the opening in Rome, in 1900."

Unexpectedly Dr. Weyland spoke close beside her: "Sarah Bernhardt wore the same in Sardou's play *La Tosca* more than ten years earlier. She carried also, I believe, a bouquet of flowers."

"Really?" Jean said brightly. "Nights when rain blows onto the stage here I bet the Toscas wish they were carrying umbrellas instead of canes or flowers. One night it really poured, and a man sitting in the unroofed section in front of me put up a villainous-looking black umbrella, which isn't allowed because the people behind the umbrella-wielder can't see. He turned out to be John Ehrlichman, of Watergate memory."

"And to be both prepared and unprepared," said Dr. Weyland urbanely. He turned to Elmo. "Young man, I noticed that you have a seat on the aisle down in front. May I change seats with you? No reflection on Miss Gray—she does not snore, scratch or fidget—but I have trouble sitting so still for so long, no matter how fascinating the occasion."

Jean smiled in spite of herself. The man had charm, when he chose to exercise it. She wished he didn't make her feel so silly and so—so *squat*.

Elmo said uncertainly, "I'm in the second row. It's pretty loud up there, and you can't see so well."

"Nevertheless, I would consider the exchange a great favor, I must get up and stretch my legs now and then. An aisle seat on the side would be a mercy for me and those around me."

THE PIT BOYS BROUGHT UP A SNARE DRUM to set in the wings near the stage manager's console. Spiegel herself was momentarily absent, seeing to the administration of oxygen to a chorister from St. Louis. The Santa Fe altitude could be hard on lowlanders.

The assistant technical director circulated, hushing the chattering choristers who milled outside the dressing rooms. Behind the flat that enclosed the smaller, more intimate second-act set depicting Scarpia's office, a minuscule orchestra assembled on folding chairs. They would play music to be heard as if from outside, through an open window of the office. A TV monitor was positioned for the assistant conductor to work from.

In the small prop room a final test was run with the two candlesticks which Tosca must appear to light at the end of Act Two. The candlesticks were battery-powered, their brightening and dimming handled by a technician using a remote-control device adapted from a model airplane kit.

The house manager called in to Spiegel, back at her console, advising her to delay the start of Act Two: the lines outside the ladies' rooms were still long.

ELMO SAT IN HIS NEW SEAT, relieved to be at a greater distance from the stage. Down front, he had felt like a bystander trapped into eavesdropping on somebody's very private business.

Now as Scarpia mused alone on the anticipated success of his plans, Elmo felt safely removed and free to study the scene: the inlaid-wood effect on the stage floor, the carved shutters of the window behind Scarpia's curly-legged dining table, a fat-cushioned sofa placed across from a big writing table all scattered with books and papers.

Suddenly Scarpia's singing turned ferocious—bang, bangety-bang-bang, up and down. Shocked, Elmo stared at the man. Though large of frame, Scarpia was almost daintily resplendent in silk brocade: over knee breeches and lace-trimmed shirt, a vest and full-skirted coat of a delicate pale blue. From this Dresden figure came a brutally voluptuous voice. The words were close enough to Spanish for Elmo to catch their drift. They were about women: What I want I take, use, throw away, and then I go after the next thing I want.

Elmo squirmed in his seat, uncomfortably aware of Jean sitting between himself and McGrath. It seemed indecent for any woman to overhear from a man such a fierce declaration of appetite.

ONE OF SCARPIA'S SPIES brought the news: they had not found the fugitive Angelotti at Cavaradossi's villa, to which Tosca had led them. They had, however, found, arrested, and brought back for questioning Tosca's lover, Cavaradossi. Scarpia began to interrogate Cavaradossi over the cantata performed by the unseen small orchestra and chorus.

Into a pause glided a familiar soprano voice, Tosca's voice leading the chorus. Cavaradossi murmured impulsively that it was *her* voice. A glance passed between the two men: Cavaradossi's back stiffened slightly; Scarpia lowered his powdered head and pressed on with his questions, rejecting any complicity with the prisoner even in admiration for the woman who fascinated them both.

The stage director, watching from the back of the house with the standees, found herself delighted. Such a small bit of new business, and it looked great. Suddenly the triangle of Tosca and the two men flashed alive.

JEAN THOUGHT BACK to the last part of Act One. If that had been a telling embodiment of the two-faced nature of society, here was something quite different. The choral work heard now from offstage was not, like the Te Deum earlier, a pretentious ceremonial of pomp and power. Instead, strings and voices wove a grave, sweet counterpoint against which Scarpia's interrogation, by turns unctuous and savage, gained in ferocity.

He was like a great beast circling his prey while outside was—Art with a capital A in the person of Tosca, Rome's greatest singer, whose voice crested the swell of the music supposedly being performed elsewhere in the building.

Scarpia turned suddenly, irritated at finding that voice so distracting, and slapped the shutters to, cutting off the choral background.

Jean whispered into Elmo's ear, "You're right about him being like an animal."

Behind the set a kneeling apprentice fastened the shutters with tape. There must be no chance they might drift open again or be blown in by a gust of wind.

"Places, judge's party," said the backstage speakers. The hooded torturers and scarlet-robed judge assembled at their entry point in the wings.

Weyland saw Cavaradossi taken out, marched downstairs among the judge and his assistants for the continuation of the interrogation in the torture chamber. Only two remained on stage: Scarpia, composed and watchful, and Tosca, newly arrived in his office and trying to hide her alarm. Scarpia began to question her with elaborate courtesy: Let's speak together like friends; tell me, was Cavaradossi alone when you found him at his villa?

Now the pattern of the hunt stood vividly forth in terms that spoke to Weyland. How often had Weyland himself approached a victim in just such a manner, speaking soothingly, his impatience to feed disguised in social pleasantry … a woman stalked in the quiet of a bookstore or a gallery … a man picked up in a park … Hunting was the central experience of Weyland's life. Here was that experience, from the outside.

Fascinated, he leaned forward to observe the studied ease of the hunter, the pretended calm of the prey …

Tremain strolled on the smoking deck, feeling left out. The fictional Angelotti was supposedly hiding offstage in a well at Cavaradossi's villa. When next seen he would be a suicide, a corpse "played" by a dummy. Tremain himself had nothing to do but cool his heels in costume for two acts until the curtain calls. He would have liked to chat with Franklin, who played the sacristan and was likewise finished after Act One; but Franklin was in one of the practice rooms writing a letter to his sick daughter back in Baltimore.

Tremain went down to the musicians' area and out the passageway to the south side of the building. There were production people standing three deep on the stairs that led up to the little terrace off the south end of the theater. From the terrace you could see fairly well without being noticeable to the seated audience.

He turned away and headed downhill toward the paved road sunk behind the opera house.

To lunging music, Scarpia luridly described for Tosca how in the torture chamber a spiked iron ring was being tightened round her lover's temples to force him to tell where Angelotti was hiding—unless she chose to save Cavaradossi by telling first.

In the trap under the stage where the torture chamber was supposed to be, Cavaradossi watched the conductor on a monitor, crying out on cue and instructing Tosca not to reveal Angelotti's hiding place. Dressers stripped off the singer's shirt and substituted a torn one artfully streaked with stage blood (a mixture of Karo syrup and food coloring whipped up by the assistant technical director). They dabbed "blood" across his forehead and rubbed glycerine onto exposed areas of his skin where it would shine in the stage lights like the sweat of pain.

"Piu forte, piu forte!" roared Scarpia to the unseen torturers, demanding that they increase the pressure. Tosca cried that she couldn't stand her lover being tortured anymore. Her voice made a great octave leap down to dark, agonized chest tones.

In the trap Cavaradossi gave a loud, musical cry.

Weyland had made a mistake, exchanging his seat for one so near to pit and stage. This close, the singers in their costume finery were too large, too intense. Their violent music assaulted his senses.

Under locked doors in his mind crept the remembered odors of heavy perfume, sweat, smoking tallow, dusty draperies, the scent of fresh-mixed ink. He had been in rooms like Scarpia's, had heard the click of heels on beeswaxed floors, the thin metallic chime of clocks with elaborate ceramic faces, the sibilance of satin cuffs brushing past embroidered coat skirts.

More than once in such an office he had stood turning in his hands his tradesman's cap, or rubbing his palms nervously on the slick front of his leather work apron, while he answered official questions. When questions were to be asked, Weyland, always and everywhere a stranger, was asked them. Often from another room would come wordless shrieks, the stink of urine, the wet crack of snapping joints. He had grown adept, even brilliant, at giving good answers.

Another artful scream from the hidden tenor jerked him back into the present. He tensed to rise and slip away—but the music, storming out of the pit, gripped him. Its paroxysms of anguish—deep shudders of the cellos, cries of horns and woodwinds—pierced him and nailed him in his place.

Tosca broke down and revealed Angelotti's hiding place; the blood-smeared Cavaradossi was dragged on stage, reviled her, blasted out a defiance of Scarpia and an allegiance to the Bonapartists that doomed him to execution for treason, was hauled away.

In the fifth row center a man turned off his hearing aid and went to sleep. He didn't like the story, and he'd eaten too much *carne adovada* at the Spanish restaurant. Later, hearing rapturous talk about what a great performance this had been, what a privilege to have witnessed it, he would first say nothing, then agree, and finally come to believe that he too had experienced the magical evening.

Scarpia's voice flowed smoothly again as the orchestra returned to the elegance of the lighter strings. He bade Tosca sit down with him to discuss how to save her lover's life. He took her cloak, his fingers crushing the russet velvet greedily, and draped it over the back of the sofa. Then he poured out wine at his table, offering her a glass in dulcet tones: *"É vin di Spagna ..."*

Thrusting aside the wine, she stared at him with loathing and flung him her question: how much of a bribe did he demand? *"Quanto?"*

And the monster began to tell her, leaning closer, smiling suggestively: he wouldn't sell out his sworn duty to the State for mere money, not to a beautiful woman ... while the orchestra's avid, glowing chords prefigured the full revelation of his lechery.

Elmo swallowed, stared, listened with a dazzled mind. He had forgotten Jean sitting next to him, as she had forgotten him.

THIS IS THE HOUR I have been awaiting! cried Scarpia. The spare, almost conversational structure of the music grew suddenly rich with the throbbing of darker strings and brass as he disclosed the price of Cavaradossi's life. In tones sumptuous with passion he declared his desire: How it inflamed me to see you, agile as a leopard, clinging to your lover! he sang in a voice itself as supple as a leopard's spring. At last he claimed the brazen, eager chords of lust in his own fierce voice.

Resonances from the monster's unleashed appetite swept Weyland, overriding thought, distance, judgment.

THE LADY IN THE SNAKESKIN-PATTERNED DRESS glanced at the professorial type sitting next to her in the aisle seat. Heavens what was wrong with the man? Sweat gleamed on his forehead his jaw bunched with muscle, his eyes glittered above feverishly flushed cheeks. What was that expression her son used—yes this man looked as if he were *freaking out*.

JEAN SAT GROANING SILENTLY at the back of her throat for the tormented woman on the stage, who now rushed to the window—but what use was suicide, when the brute would kill her lover anyway? With the devotion of a romantic spirit, Jean gave herself up to the beautiful agony of the second act.

Tremain strolled in the dark down behind the opera house cigarette in hand, head cocked to the music above him. He drew a hot curl of smoke down his throat: bad for a singer, but you can't be disciplined all the time. Anyway, except for wearing this absurd scraggle of glued-on beard and long gray hair and staying in his ragged costume until the curtain call, he could do as he pleased. Caruso had smoked three packs a day, and it hadn't hurt him. Great appetite was a sign of great talent, Tremain hoped.

From the opera house came a distant, explosive crash. He identified it at once and smiled to himself: Scarpia and Tosca had finally overdone the pursuit scene and toppled the water pitcher from the dinner table. Must be having a wild time up there tonight.

One more smoke and he would go listen close up with the others. He looked out at the sparkling lights of Los Alamos to the west and mouthed Scarpia's words silently to himself.

With ghoulish delight Scarpia gloated, "How you hate me!" He strode toward Tosca, crying in savage triumph, "It is thus that I want you! ... Throes of hatred, throes of love ..."

The breath strained shallowly in Weyland's throat. His hands ached from clenching. Tosca's cries drew from him a faint whining sound: he too had been pursued by merciless enemies, he too had been driven to the extremity of desperation. Tosca fled Scarpia, darting behind the desk from which pens and papers scattered to the floor. The dance of hunting rushed toward a climax. Weyland trembled.

He could see the voracious curl of Scarpia's lips, the predatory stoop of the shoulders under the brocaded coat as he closed in on her ... as she flew to the sofa with Scarpia a step behind her ... as Scarpia lunged for her. To the urgings of the horns, Weyland's mouth twisted in a gape of aggression, his eyes slitted cruelly, small muscles started convulsively beneath his skin, as the prey was flushed into flight again—as Weyland sprang in pursuit, as Weyland roared, Mine!

Startled movement at his side distracted him: the woman sitting there jerked away and stared at him. He stared wildly back, then surged to his feet and fled past an usher who was blind to all but the drama onstage.

Hurdling a low gate between the patio and the dark slope beyond, he plunged down the hillside. The dry rattle of a military drum followed from the opera house. Impressions blurred in his molten mind: rows of pale tents, restless lines of tethered horses, smells of smoke and sewage and metal polish, wet rope, wet leather; and always, somewhere, the tapping of drums and the bark of voices. He heard them now.

Yet he caught no sentry's footfall, no gleam of white crossbelts marking the presence of solitary prey. Where was the camp whose tumult he heard—those lights to the west? Too far, and too bright. Perhaps a night battle? He sought the scent of blood and black powder; he listened for the muffled cries and weeping of a moonlit field in the battle's wake, where a vampire might feed unnoticed and unresisted among the tumbled casualties.

In that year of revolution and royalist repression 1800, Weyland had followed Bonaparte's Grand Army.

Tonight there was no need for the assistant technical director to trot about backstage hushing people as Tosca began her great aria, "Vissi d'Arte." Tonight people were already quiet, listening.

A percussionist who would ring bells for the beginning of the next act came out of the musicians' passage and headed for the already-jammed side terrace. Her attention was trained on the music. Anything that could be heard from outside the opera house she did not notice.

Impelled by unbearable tension, Weyland rounded the corner of the building and padded swiftly along the sunken road that ran behind it.

There was a man up ahead there; a spark in the darkness, an emanation on the night wind of body warmth, sweat, and smoke. Long hair, breeches, loose and ragged sleeves, a gleam of starlight on shoe buckles as the figure turned its back to the breeze—detail sharpened as Weyland closed the distance with silent strides.

A little flame jumped in the man's cupped hands.

Body strung tight on the rich, wild throbbing of his own heart, mind seething, compelled to strike, Weyland slowed for the final rush.

Tremain's concentration on the poignant strains of the "Vissi d'Arte" was interrupted. Turning, he glimpsed a tall form looming, huge pupils of the eyes shrinking rapidly like a cat's before the wavering match flame. Tremain's mouth moved to frame some startled pleasantry, and his mind said, It's only the night that makes this scary.

Hands of iron seized him and slammed him away forever beyond the singing.

The high notes of the "Vissi d'Arte" burned clear and steady, the low notes smoldered with emotion. Anders followed like a lover, breathing with the singer's breathing. Only once she faltered, and Anders's lifted left hand restored her while his right, held low and armed with the baton, translated for the players in the pit.

At the close of her beautiful, vain plaint, the audience exploded. They screamed, they cracked their palms wildly together—briefly. The pace of the drama had caught them up and would brook small delay.

Weyland's mouth was full of blood. He swallowed, pressing the limp form tighter in his arms, burrowing with greedy lips past the disordered neckcloth.

His stomach, irritated by his earlier, incompletely digested meal, rebelled. Retching, he let the body drop and tried to rise, could only stagger to one knee, heaving. He must not leave vomit for dogs to find, for hunters to examine by torchlight. He swallowed regurgitated blood, gagged, his throat seared; knelt panting and shivering in the darkness.

A droning sound passed high above him—his sense of present time and place flooded back. Looking up, he saw the sinking lights of the airplane pass out of sight behind the faintly lit mass of the opera-house wall rising above him.

And before him on the ground lay a man not dead but dying; quick exploration revealed a crepitation of bone shards under the skin of the temple where Weyland's fist had crushed the skull. Apart from one smudge on the throat, there was no blood. He crouched in panic above the dying man. He had struck without need, without hunger. From this man dressed as in an earlier time—costumed, rather, a performer in the opera surely—he had been in no danger.

He was in danger now. This kill must be disguised.

He rose and crossed the road. The hillside dropped steeply toward the brush-choked arroyo below. A man might fall—but not far enough or hard enough to smash his head in. Also, he could see a fence partway down which would break such a fall.

He looked back up at the opera house itself, which crested the hill like a vessel breaking forward from a deep wave. The south side reared up three stories over the roadway into a knife-sharp corner like a ship's prow against the night sky. From its deck a man might drop and crack his skull here below. And where the hillside sloped up to meet the north end of the opera-house deck, one might mount that deck as if stepping aboard from the surface of the sea.

Weyland shouldered his victim, ran along the road, and scrambled up the stony hillside onto the deck. Then he turned and, bending as low as he might with his burden, sprinted down the deck toward the high southern prow.

A WOMAN IN THE BALCONY focused her glasses on Scarpia. Now that he had wrung from Tosca assent to her own rape, he was deceitfully arranging Cavaradossi's supposedly mock execution in exchange. This was worth coming all the way from Buffalo. Scarpia was such a nasty brute, but so virile—better than Telly Savalas.

THE ASSISTANT TECHNICAL DIRECTOR, crossing behind the stage with some cables to be returned to the patch room in the north wings, was too close to the music to hear the faint susurration of movement out on the deck below. He was absorbed in checking for production people who might be lounging on the back stairs, making noise—but tonight there was no one.

Outside the patch room, for an instant he thought he saw someone sitting in the corner with drooping head. It was only the dummy, supposedly the corpse of Angelotti who had killed himself rather than be recaptured. The soldiers would hang up the "body" at the start of the last act, a bit of business special to this production. People needed something to watch during that long, delicate opening.

Every night of *Tosca* the assistant technical director saw the dummy slumped there, and each time for a second he thought it was real.

Weyland flung himself down with his victim on the veranda outside the costume shop. The windows of the shop were yellow with light but largely blocked by set materials stacked outside. He could hear no sound of footsteps or voices on the terrace above the veranda.

He rested his forehead against the low concrete rampart, pressing his sleeve against his mouth to muffle the rasp of his own breathing. His back and arms burned with strain, and a cramp gripped at his gut.

How long before the second act ended? Once again the music was quiet and conversational. Weyland could hear Scarpia gallantly agreeing to write the safe-conduct that Tosca demanded for herself and her lover before she would actually yield her body. A dirgelike melody began. It was not loud; Weyland hoped it would cover whatever noise he made back here.

The dying man was heavy with the quicksilver weight of unconscious people, as if any shift could send all his substance running instantly into one part of his body. Weyland hefted him by the arms against the low parapet. The man groaned, his head rolled on Weyland's shoulder, and one of his hands plucked aimlessly at Weyland's knee.

Looking down past him, Weyland decided: there, between those heaped-up masses of rubbish, where the paving came right to the foot of the wall—a fall, he judged, of some thirty feet. Not a lot, but enough to be plausible.

Now, under the sobbing lamentation of the music, he rolled the man's upper body out along the rampart, bent and heaved the legs up—the man dropped. There came only a dull sound of impact from below.

No shout was raised, but during a performance, uncertain of what had been glimpsed in the dark, no one backstage would call out. They would simply arrive—and if Weyland had not been seen yet, he might be at any moment, for he had been aware of someone moving on the stage level above during his dash along the deck. He had to get off the deck at once. For fear of being seen, he didn't dare run the length of the deck again to reach the low end. And he couldn't risk trying to find his way out through the backstage area in the midst of the performance.

He looked over the rampart once more. Out of the piled-up theater trash below and to his left there thrust, end on, a huge structure made of two thick sheets of plywood joined by two-by-four braces, like the steps of a crooked ladder. Farther down was some sort of platform, warped and buckled, and—stage trees? He could make out sausagelike branches with bristling ends.

If he hung from the rampart at the full stretch of his arms, his rubber shoe soles would reach within perhaps five feet of the braced structure. And if the whole twisted heap didn't collapse under him when he landed on it, he might climb down.

Taking no more time for thought or fear, he lowered himself over the rampart and let go his hold, crouching as he dropped to grab at the pale wooden ribs below. His landing was unexpectedly solid and jarring; whether there was noise or not he couldn't tell, because suddenly the music burst into a thundering crescendo. He began to clamber down the crossed wooden struts.

The whole pile leaned and creaked and shifted obscurely beneath him. He smelled dust. Under the blaring music he was keenly aware of his heart pounding, his gasping breath, and somewhere below the cracking of wood. He caught hold of one of the spiny trees, which dipped drunkenly under his weight, and he let go and slithered down in a rush, fetching up breathless on all fours on the asphalt.

Hurriedly, he examined his victim. The skull was pulped, the man was dead. Weyland looked up: the circumstances would certainly suggest that the unlucky fellow had fallen from the veranda or the balcony above.

Still no sounds of alarm or investigation. The stormy music was dying away into falling tremolo chords under the soprano's furious shouts—Die! Die! Weyland listened to the deep sighs of the strings while his heartbeat slowed and the sweat of fear and effort dried on him. He was as safe as he could make himself. Even if murder were suspected, who would connect this dead performer and an Eastern professor, total strangers to each other?

He turned away without looking at the body again—it no longer concerned him—and walked back up toward the parking area. Just beyond the reach of the parking-lot lights he stooped to brush the dust from his clothing, in the course of which he struck his own knee a painful blow; his hands would not obey him with their customary precision.

The numbers on his watch face jiggled slightly with the tremor in his wrist: 10:40. Surely the second act would end soon and he could return to mingle with the crowd before the final act.

At last he allowed himself the question: what had happened to him? That blow was his oldest way: it paralyzed yet left the prey living, blood still sweet, while he fed. What had made him use that ancient method, when from these refined modern times he had learned appropriately refined ways?

But what elation in that instant of savage release! Thinking of it now he felt his muscles tingle, and his breath came in a sharp hiss of pleasure.

ONSTAGE, SCARPIA LAY DEAD. Tosca had stabbed him with a knife from his dinner table when he turned, safe-conduct in hand, to embrace her at last. To his lust-motif, inverted and muted to a sinister whisper in the strings and flutes, Tosca set a lighted candle down at each of his outflung hands. On a sudden loud chord she dropped a carved crucifix onto his breast, and when the snare drum rattled ominously again, she snatched up her cloak and gloves and ran for her life. The dead man was left alone on the stage for the last stealthy, menacing bars of Act Two.

The lights blinked out, applause crashed like surf. Two stagehands in black ran from the wings to stand in front Scarpia—Marwitz, the baritone—while in his pale costume he rose and slipped down through the trapdoor.

Marwitz hurried away to find Rosemary Ridgeway, his young Tosca. His chest was full of the champagne feeling that meant success. He had been in this business for a long time, and he knew what "perfect" meant: that somehow the inevitable errors had been knit into a progression of actions so rich and right that everything fused into a vivid, indivisible experience never to be forgotten—or duplicated.

He hugged Rosemary hard outside the dressing rooms. "I knew, I knew," he chortled into her disordered hair, "because I was so nervous. I could sing Scarpia in my sleep by now, nervous is good—it means even after so many times something is still alive, waiting to create."

"Were we as good as I thought we were?" she asked breathlessly.

He shook her by the shoulders. "We were terrible, terrible,

what are you saying? Pray to stay so bad!" With the jealous gods of theater thus propitiated, he made to embrace her again, but she stood back, looking into his face with sudden anxiety.

"Oh, Kurt, are you all right? You really fell tonight when I stabbed you—I felt the stage shake."

"I am not so heavy," Marwitz said with offended dignity. Then he grinned. "My foot slipped, yes, but don't worry—you killed me very nicely, very well. They will award you two ears and a tail for it, wait and see."

"I LIKED HOW THE WATER PITCHER was busted and she couldn't wash blood off her hands like she's supposed to," said a woman in gold lamé, "so she just wiped it off on Scarpia's dinner napkin."

Her friend frowned. "They should call it *Scarpia*, not *Tosca*. It's not a love story, it's a hate story about two strong people who take each other out—along with a couple of poor jerks who wander into the crossfire."

A man in a raccoon coat shook his head vehemently. "You feel that way because this fellow played Scarpia too civilized, like an executive. He's supposed to be just a jumped-up hoodlum. Tosca's line about him after the torture was originally 'The dirty cop will pay for this.'"

"What is it now?" inquired the friend.

"'A just God will punish him.'"

"Well, who changed the line?"

"Puccini did."

"Then he must have thought the 'dirty cop' line made Scarpia look too much like a hoodlum: he's meant to be smooth," the friend declared. "Myself, I never knew a hoodlum with legs as nice as this Scarpia's. Isn't it a shame that men quit wearing stockings and britches?"

The woman in gold lamé glanced around disparagingly. "No it isn't, not with the boring hindquarters most guys got. Maybe legs were cuter in days of yore."

MCGRATH HAD RUN into a client. He brought her a drink from the bar. She had taste: the plaster cast on her left arm was painted with a frieze of red-brown Egyptian tomb figures.

"Personally," McGrath said, "I think this opera's a bunch of cheap thrills set to pretty music."

The client, who had bought two bronzes from the gallery this year, reacted critically. "Other people do, too; they honestly feel that *Tosca's* just a vulgar thriller," she observed. "I think what shocks them is seeing a woman kill a man to keep him from raping her. If a man kills somebody over politics or love, that's high drama, but if a woman offs a rapist, that's sordid."

McGrath hated smart-talking women, but he wanted her to buy another bronze; they were abstract pieces, not easy to sell. So he smiled.

He wished he'd stayed with fine silver, turquoise, and Pueblo pottery.

JEAN AND ELMO STROLLED AROUND and around the fountain in the opera-house patio.

"Opera can really shake you up," Elmo ventured, troubled.

Jean nodded fervently. "Especially on a night like this, when the performers are going all out. And a responsive audience throws the excitement right back at them so it keeps on building."

"But why does the bad guy get such great music?"

"Listen, Elmo, do you read science fiction? Tolkien? Fantasy stories?"

"A little."

"Sometimes those stories tell about what they call 'wild magic'—magic powers not subject to books or spells, powers you can't really use because they're not good or bad or anything to do with morality at all; they just *are*, uncontrollable and irresistible. I think this music tonight is like that—deep and strong and nothing to do with right or wrong."

Elmo didn't answer. That kind of talk reminded him of his wife's relatives over near Las Vegas, New Mexico, who sometimes reported great leaping wheels of witch-fire flying about the mountains at night.

SOLDIERS ASSEMBLED IN THE TRAP under the stage. When the third act opened, they would mount onto the platform of the Castel Sant' Angelo, where Cavaradossi was being held for execution. The dummy of the suicide Angelotti was prepared for them to lug onstage and hang from the castle wall according to Scarpia's Act Two orders.

Behind the set of the platform wall, the crew chief oversaw the placement of the landing pad on which the dummy, heaved over the wall with a noose around its neck, would arrive. The pad was two stacks of mattresses roped together side by side, twenty in all to cushion the fall not of the dummy but of Tosca, when she leaped off the battlement in the end.

Weyland came out of the men's room having cleaned up as thoroughly and unobtrusively as possible. At his seat down in front he put on the raincoat he had left folded there. The coat would conceal the split in the shoulder seam of his jacket and any stains or rips he might have missed.

Both terror and exhilaration had left him. He was overcome by lethargy, but he no longer felt ill; his hunting frenzy had burned all that away. A mood of grim pleasure filled him. It was good to know that living among soft people in a soft time had not weakened him; that adapting enough to pass for one of them had not damaged his essential lionlike, night-hunter nature. Even a flagrant misstep need not be fatal, for his ancient cunning and ferocity had not deserted him. He felt restored.

These thoughts passed and sank, leaving him spent and peaceful.

Rosemary Ridgeway took off the brunette wig, rumpled from her scuffle with Scarpia, and set it on its Styrofoam head to be combed out afresh. How absurd to try to become the libretto's dark beauty of whom Cavaradossi had sung so meltingly in the first act: *"Tosca ha l'occhio nero."* Rosemary's eyes were blue, and she couldn't tolerate contact lenses to change them. On the other hand, she didn't quite have the nerve—or the force and reputation—to emulate the great Jeritza who, libretto be damned, had played the role blonde.

Rosemary knew she was young to sing Tosca. Yet tonight her voice had acquired maturity and control, as if all of Marwitz's encouragement and advice had suddenly begun to work at once. If only the miracle would last until the end!

She sat gathering strength for the final act and scratching at her scalp, which already itched in anticipation of the beastly brown wig.

Just before the house lights went down, the woman in snakeskin glanced nervously at the man beside her. She had hoped that he wouldn't return; he'd been so caught up in the second act that he'd scared her. You were supposed to appreciate the opera, not join in.

Now he seemed freed of his earlier agitation, and she saw with surprise that he was really a fine-looking man, with the strong springing profile of an explorer, or an emperor on an ancient coin. Though he did not appear what she would call old, maturity had scored his cheeks and forehead, and he sat as if pressed under a weight of long thought.

He seemed not to notice her covert scrutiny. The curve of his upturned coat collar was like a symbolic shield, signaling a wish to be left alone.

She hesitated. Then it was too late for a conversational gambit; the last act had begun.

A horn called. Slowly, to the lighting-board operator's counts in the booth, the lights grew infinitesimally stronger, simulating the approach of a Roman dawn over the Castel Sant'Angelo.

Usually, once the Angelotti dummy had been flung over the wall and disposed of, the assistant technical director and his stagehand companion would stretch out on the mattresses and doze. The sound of shots—the firing squad executing Cavaradossi—would rouse them for the flying arrival of Tosca leaping to her death.

Tonight these two technicians stayed awake and listened.

Tosca recounted to her condemned lover Cavaradossi the events that had led to her stabbing of Scarpia. At the swift reprise of the murder music, the woman in snakeskin felt the man beside her stir in his seat. But he didn't leap up and bolt this time. A sensitive soul, she thought, observing that he listened with closed eyes as if he wanted nothing to distract him from the music; perhaps a musician himself, a pianist or a violinist? She looked at his fine, long-fingered hands.

Holding Tosca's hands in his, Cavaradossi sang in a caressing tone, 0 sweet, pure hands that have dealt a just, victorious death …

Elmo, appalled, felt tears run down his cheeks. He didn't dare blot them for fear of calling attention to them. The doomed lovers were so sure the execution would be make-believe and then they would escape together. They sang with such tender feeling for each other, so much hope and joy.

How frightening his tears, how strange the pleasure of his tears.

The execution squad fired. Cavaradossi flung himself backward into the air, slapping a little plastic bag of stage blood against his chest. Red drops spattered on musicians in the pit below.

At the crack of the guns the tall man grunted, and the woman in snakeskin saw that his eyes had flicked open. He stared about for a moment, then shut them again.

For God's sake, the wretched philistine had been sleeping!

The opera was over, the singers took their bows. Rosemary, high on triumph, wanted no one to miss out. Fumbling for Marwitz's fingers in the fall of lace at his cuff, she said, "Where's Jerry Tremain? Isn't he going to take his bow?"

Amid a barrage of applause they all walked forward together on the stage, joined hands upraised. There were many curtain calls. Tremain did not come. No one knew where he was.

The ticket gate was jammed with slowly moving people still chattering excitedly or, like Elmo who made his way among them silently with Jean, trying to hang on to memories of the music.

Dr. Weyland was outside already, waiting by the ticket office. He looked sort of rumpled. Elmo spotted a clutch of burrs stuck to the professor's trouser leg and a long scrape across the back of his hand. He heard Jean's quick intake of breath as she noticed too.

"Are you all right?" she asked anxiously. "It looks as if you've hurt yourself."

Dr. Weyland put his injured hand into his pocket. "I walked a little beyond the lights during intermission," he admitted. "I tripped in the dark."

"You should have come and told me," Jean said. "I could have run you back into Santa Fe."

"It's only a scrape."

"Oh, I'm so sorry—I hope this hasn't spoiled your enjoyment of the opera. It was such a wonderful performance tonight." Her dismay made Elmo want to hug her.

Dr. Weyland cleared his throat. "I assure you, I found this opera very impressive."

Elmo caught an undertone of strain in the professor's voice. He was relieved, glad that he himself was not the only man to have been moved by the experience.

Maybe being moved was good; maybe some paintings would come out of it.

WHILE WAITING FOR THE PARKING LOT TO CLEAR they picnicked on fruit and cheese laid out on the trunk of Jean's car.

"This is what opera old-timers do," McGrath said. He passed around cups of wine. "Here's a drink to get us started; I've lined up something special for us—a big party in town. Lots of Santa Fe people and some of the opera singers will be there. Jean, you just follow that blue Porsche over there—that's our ride, Elmo and me—and drop the professor off at the party with us. We'll find him someplace to bunk for tonight and bring him back down to Albuquerque with us tomorrow."

"No, thank you," said Dr. Weyland, turning away the wine in favor of water. "I'm tired. I understand Miss Gray is returning to Albuquerque immediately, and I'd prefer to go with her."

McGrath said heartily, "But people are waiting to meet you! I already told everybody I was bringing a famous Eastern professor with me. We don't want to disappoint folks."

Dr. Weyland drank. "Another time," he said.

"There won't be another time," McGrath insisted. "Not like this party. You don't want to turn your back on old-fashioned Western hospitality."

Dr. Weyland deposited his empty cup in the garbage bag. He said, "Good night, Mr. McGrath," and he got into the passenger seat of the car and shut the door.

"Well, up yours too, fella," said McGrath, throwing his own cup under the car. He wheeled toward the blue Porsche, snapping over his shoulder, "Come on, Elmo, folks are waiting!"

Driving down, Jean found her memory playing over and over the final thunderous chords after Tosca's suicide. They were from Cavaradossi's farewell aria in Act Three, the melody of *"O dolci baci, o languide carezze."* Sweet kisses, languid caresses. Puccini's closing musical comment, perhaps, on the destructiveness of outsized passions.

In fact, Scarpia himself had remarked in Act Two that great love brings great misery. That was just before his paean to the superior joys of selfish appetite. Yet he had been destroyed by his lust for Tosca, surely a passion in itself? How to distinguish appetite from passion? Or did art raise appetite to the level of passion, so that they became indistinguishable?

Had Dr. Weyland been more accessible, she would have loved to discuss this with him on the way home. She wondered whether he was lonely behind his facade.

Moon-flooded countryside flowed past. On either hand the rolling plateau was adrift with blunt constructions that dawn would show as mountains. Weyland did not miss his old car now, his whispering Mercedes. He was tired and glad not to be driving under that immense, glossy sky; better to be free to look out. The scenery was silver with reflected moonlight. The cool wind brought fresh night smells of earth, water, brush, cattle drowsing at the fences.

The woman spoke, breaking his mood. She said hesitantly, "Dr. Weyland, I wonder if you realize you've made an enemy tonight.

McGrath wanted to show you off at that party. He'll take your refusal as a spit in the eye of his beloved Western hospitality."

Weyland shrugged.

"I suppose you can afford to be offhand about it," she said, sounding resentful. "Not all of us can. Elmo will bear the brunt of McGrath's bruised feelings tonight. My turn will come tomorrow when they get back. McGrath can't hurt you, so he'll hit out at anyone within his reach. You haven't made things any easier for me."

His voice crackled with irritation: "Perhaps it hasn't occurred to you, Miss Gray, that I'm not interested in your problems. My own are sufficient."

Marwitz and Rosemary lay curled close, too tired for sex, too happy for sleep. They dozed on and off while shadows of moonlight inched across the flagstones outside the French doors.

She murmured, "When the water pitcher fell I was sure Act Two would end in disaster."

"I would wish many more such disasters for us both," he said. Silence fell. Too soon the season would end and they would go their separate ways.

At length he said, "I wonder what happened to young Tremain. How unlike him, to miss his bow and a party after."

Rosemary yawned and wiggled closer against his warm middle. "Maybe he came later, after we left."

"Which we did indecently early." He nuzzled her ear. "Surely everyone noticed."

Rosemary guffawed. "Anybody who hasn't noticed by now has got to be as stupid as a clam!"

Marwitz sat up. "Come, we have wine left—let's go out and drink in the moonlight."

They wrapped themselves in the bedspread and padded outside, arguing amiably about just how stupid a clam might accurately be said to be.

Weyland got out of the car. He said, "Thank you for bringing me back. I regret my ill temper." He didn't, but neither did he care to make another unnecessary enemy.

The woman smiled a tired smile. "Don't give it a thought," she said. The car with Walking River Gallery stenciled on its side pulled away.

When it was out of sight, Weyland walked. The pavement was lit by the late-risen moon. No dogs were left out at night on this street, so he could stroll in peace. He needed the exercise; his muscles were stiff from exertion followed by long immobility. A walk would help, and then perhaps a hot soak in his host's old-fashioned tub.

Walking eastward on a hill-climbing street, he watched a mountain rise ahead of him like a harshly eroded wall. Its ruggedness pleased him—an angular outline stark against the night and unmuted by vegetation. He could feel the centuries lying thick over this country—perhaps a factor contributing, along with his physical indisposition, to that headlong tumble tonight through his own personal timescape.

The kill itself had been good—a purging of anxiety and weakness. Catharsis, he supposed; wasn't that the intended effect of art?

But the tension leading up to the kill—memory made him shudder. The opera had broken his moorings to the present and launched him into something akin to madness. Human music, human drama, vibrant human voices passionately raised, had impelled him to fly from among his despised victims as they sat listening. He feared and resented that these kine on whom he fed could stir him so deeply, all unaware of what they did; that their art could strike depths in him untouched in them.

Where did it come from, this perilous new pattern of recognizing aspects of himself in the creations of his human livestock? Such mirrorings were obviously unintentional. His basic likeness to humanity was the explanation—a necessary likeness, since without being similar to them he could not hope to hunt them. But was he growing more like them, that their works had begun to reach him and shake him? Had he been somehow irrevocably opened to the power of their art?

He recoiled violently from such possibilities; he wanted nothing more from them than that which he already, relentlessly, required: their blood.

The mountain ahead of him was, he saw, to be envied; it could be wounded by these human cattle, but never perturbed.

The morning tour drifted out onto the concrete deck at the rear of the opera house. The guide pointed west: "On clear nights when we leave the back of the stage open, the lights of Los Alamos . . ."

A heavyset man standing by the rampart glanced down at the road below. He leaned out, not believing what he saw, his breath gathering for a cry.

Elmo made a painting of dreamlike figures from the opera dancing on a sunny hilltop, towered over by a tall shaft of shadow like a wellfull of night. In memory of the young singer who had died the night of *Tosca*, Elmo called the painting *The Angel of Death*.

PEREGRINES

Mary Anne said, "I'm really sorry, Edie, but here it is the end of June and we only have two people signed up for your session."

I thought, *God damn it all to hell; so what else is new?* I said, "Oh."

She sighed sympathetically over the phone. "I don't know what to tell you. We have lots of takers for Bill Ballingham and Susan MacCain's classes, but somehow ... Look, I'm being interviewed tomorrow on local radio about the workshop. I'll take the opportunity to talk you up. But unless there is a last-minute flurry of sign-ups, I'm afraid you're just not on this year."

We chatted a while longer, me feeling my usual urge to scream in protest while simultaneously apologizing for the failure of my name to attract business. There went my autumn respite in Ashland, plus the fifteen hundred dollars the playwriting workshop paid for a two-week teaching stint. I'd even gotten my interstate travel permit from the Homesec office down at Battery Park.

Mary Anne's news was a big disappointment and money out of my pocket; so what else is new? The deal has always been (and that's forty-seven years' worth of always) that people respond well to me, with enthusiasm even, *as long as I'm in the room.* As soon as I'm out of their sight, it's as if I had never been there. Any effect I've had goes up in smoke and I am erased from living memory, so any goodies on offer naturally get handed to someone else.

I started tracking this when I was in my twenties, about the thousandth time that a friend—a *friend*—said to me in a baffled voice, "Edie, I'm really sorry—I don't know why I didn't think of you for this project, you'd have been perfect, but your name just didn't come up." Or, "Gee, how in the world did we forget to call you about going to the shore with us? I *know* we all talked about it." Or my excellent comment, greatly appreciated at the moment of utterance, comes back to me later as a clever quote—attributed to somebody else. My voice, speaking those same deathless words, is simply replaced in the hearers' memories by someone else's voice. Anybody else's, it doesn't seem to matter whose.

Without constantly treading water hard, I would sink without a trace, apart from a few copies of my tarot chapbook, *Master Packs: Personal Vision and Tarot,* and maybe a script of my first play, *Sleight of Heart,* moldering away on some obscure theater bookshelf.

I know, it sounds like whining. It *is* whining, but that doesn't make it untrue, or even an exaggeration. This cloak of invisibility has been a major factor in my life, sometimes *the* major factor. I don't talk about it much for fear of people tagging me as a loser and running like hell, the way folks very sensibly do when they encounter a Jonah. I run myself when I catch the smell of bad luck on someone else. I've got more than enough of my own.

Doesn't all this make you want to read on? I didn't think so. Well, force yourself; it's only a story. It doesn't take long and then you'll forget it anyway.

I threw out the dregs of my tea and rinsed the grinning-cat mug Ted had drunk his coffee from for the nine years of our marriage. Then I clumped downstairs to the street, carrying my writing pad in a worn leather case with my tarot deck. John's bookstore, Second Sight, was ten minutes and a few blocks up along Christopher Street toward Sixth Avenue.

I read tarot cards there every morning and some afternoons as well, at twenty-five dollars a head; as in all bad times, people were looking for reassurance any place they could. A good month of readings would make up for the lost gig in Oregon, as well as giving me material for the column on divination that I was supposed to start writing for the *New York Post* in the fall.

Last time I traded readings at a psychic fair I was once again struck by this about the tarot: no matter how apposite the reading, no matter how deeply it strikes into the heart of your concerns, as soon as you walk away from the reader's table you forget nearly everything she told you. The few outstanding bits that stick are inevitably distorted by your memory; nothing really stays. Reading tarot is perfectly ephemeral work for a perfectly ephemeral person—disappearing readings from a disappearing woman.

John, dark, slender, and upright as a clipper's mast, was humming to himself as he checked the buy-sell and catalog sites on the net with his requests-list at hand. Everything about John was elegant. His face was a long oval of polished teak that always made my fingers tingle with a longing to touch. I couldn't look at him without thinking of those whip-lean African runners who win marathons.

He turned toward me and smiled so that the corners of his eyelids crinkled up into the lineaments of kindness and humor; irresistible. "Edie! Guess what we got a request for this morning? A kid walked in here and asked me for a book by Ernest Hemingway—'The Old Man in the Suit'!"

So we started the morning trading reminders of some of the more outrageously ignorant and silly requests he's had, like "How to Kill a Mockingbird". "The Catchup and the Rye," though, must have been somebody pulling John's leg.

I greeted Gene and Mike, two retired sailors who were already ensconced in the Tibetan Esoterica corner over their perennial chess game. I sat down at my own beat-up but still pretty marquetry table beside the store window and laid out a practice spread. The colorful images sometimes attracted a passerby to come in and even to sit down in the battered tin folding chair across from me for a reading. John said I should find a more comfortable chair for them, like the one I sat in myself. But I didn't want to encourage a querant to park across from me asking repetitious questions for an hour while other potential clients gave up and drifted away.

That morning the demonstration spread I'd dealt startled me. There were more Major Arcana—the cards for concepts too big to be contained in any of the four suits—than should have shown up in a casual layout.

The Fool—inner impulses, positive and negative—and Judgment, which is about the gaining of insight; and Death, which is either about dying *or* about the closing of one significant phase of your life and the opening of another, take your pick (that's the tricky part). The six of Cups: memory, children, nostalgia. And the Magician, which is power through knowledge.

Oh, and The Tower, a castle struck by lightning. That means catastrophe.

So let's see, I thought: *if I obey an impulse (The Fool) and write a different play (death of the play I've been working on), using insight gained through reading cards in John's store (Judgment) and also pandering to the persistent American fixation on youth and childhood (six of Cups), I could at last become successful and in control of my life (The Magician)—and then (The Tower) get hit by a bus.*

Or—

"Customer, Edie," Gene growled, looking up from the chessboard with a knowing glance. He thought card readings were bunk (which of course they often are, except for mine and a few other readers' I've come across).

Bella Salazar came barreling in all smiles and sparkle, demanding to know what the cards had to say about meeting a man on her summer vacation (she rented a place at Montauk with a slew of friends every August). Some other reader had apparently mentioned a tall, dark stranger to her. Like all my clients, she went to the competition over at The Crystal Wolf or even Madame Lela, Advisor, as often as to me. She'd come to me just to hear it all again.

"Bella," I told her over a new layout, "see this ten of Swords next to these Pentacles? Are you considering some kind of business partnership?" I tapped the two of Cups. "Because if you are, you need to be careful. The other person in this business situation—that's the Pentacles—isn't trustworthy."

Bella started talking fast, trying to steer the reading toward her desires instead of what the cards were pointing out. I stuck to my guns, partly on principle and partly because I was really worried about her. And, in one of the darker corners of my heart, I think I wanted to make her to focus on the possibility of her own luck turning sour for a change.

One of the less attractive aspects of sailing your life's journey under a curse is that sometimes you can't help resenting other people's good luck. Actually, there are no *attractive* attributes, unless you count an impetuosity that is often mistaken for courage. It's really recklessness: why worry when you know things will go badly no matter what you do?

Bella had drawn an astrological chart for me years ago, when I sold the house after Ted's death and moved back into the city. She said my assessment of my life experience was dead right. "Saturn," she said, "opposes your natal Sun. So Old Man Saturn—that's authority, limitation, discipline, denial, and frustration—blocks the desires of your heart. Your Sun is the expansive, hopeful impulse of your spirit, the will and energy to succeed. A natal Saturn opposition is a real challenge; it's a shadow. It means always being obscured by others, always checked and obstructed in what you attempt."

For this I'd had to pay her a consultation fee, though it was worth it for the entertainment value alone. She showed me one of her source-books which advised propitiating Saturn by tossing bread to crows or ravens, which are Saturn's birds, or giving charity to an old, sick, Black man on a Saturday night. Honestly, that's what it said, and what's more I couldn't give him anything but something sour or bitter or salty. I could just imagine how well that would go down: "Here's a nice pickle for you, sir, and have a good weekend."

"Just watch out, Bella," I insisted now over the cards. "This spread advises vigilance, not daydreaming about Mister Right on the beach."

She tossed back her long dark hair—Bella liked to affect a gypsy look—and launched a new chapter in her perennial argument with the cards. In the midst of her I-shall-not-be-crucified-on-a-cross-of-cards speech, I noticed a boy standing close to the window glass and looking in at me. I wish I could have seen myself at that moment, doing an absolutely classic double take: I recognized him, from a very vivid dream I'd had over the weekend, a dream forgotten until just now.

I used to write down my dreams. It hadn't seemed worth doing in a long time—sufficient unto the day is you-know-what—but after you journal your dreams for a while your memory stays trained.

I'd dreamed that three dark-skinned people in grubby-looking sheepskin coats had brought me a quiet boy, about ten or so, and asked me to hide him for a while from his enemies. They showed me a miniature building, a sort of ginger-bread-trimmed Parthenon brightly painted in scarlet, white and gold, set inside a deep wooden box. The box was steadily filling with red liquid, as if the model temple were drowning in blood.

So, in the dream, I knew it was serious. This little boy had a mystical destiny *and* bitter enemies determined to keep him from it. He was something like a young but very important Tibetan lama with the Chinese after him, or at least that was pattern in which my dreaming mind had cast the story.

With some misgivings, I'd agreed to help. The dream people had told me the boy's name, but I couldn't pronounce it.

Looking at this real kid outside John's store window, I felt very uneasy.

He was a short, square-built child of about eight or ten with thick, dusty looking black hair trimmed off below the ears. Brown-skinned and solemn-faced, he had an Asian curve to his eyelids; he would have looked perfect in one of those Peruvian wool hats with the ear flaps, too. He wore a yellow T-shirt, grubby jeans, and sandals made of tire-rubber with thick plastic cross-straps.

He looked at me and I looked back.

Bella came clanging to her conclusion like a runaway trolley hitting the end of the line: "Two of Cups means a love affair, you've told me so yourself!"

"Yes," I said, looking at the cards again. "Sometimes it does, but not in this layout. Here it's a business partnership—those Pentacles. Bella, listen to me: it looks like a bad idea."

"This *reading* was a bad idea." She slapped a twenty down on the table so hard that two cards sailed off onto the floor. Then she flounced out.

Ah, the glory and influence of the mighty seer! As I stooped down to retrieve the stray cards, someone tapped on the frame of the open street door.

The boy stood there with another, taller kid, this one a rawboned adolescent with a nervous smile pasted on his sharp-planed face. He too was dark-skinned and black-haired, but they didn't look related; their builds were too different.

The tall one stepped hesitantly into the store and softly addressed not John but me. "Please, Missis—to working? Strong, cheap working."

I would have said no, but John at once stepped from behind the register to greet them. Listening to whatever hard luck story the tall one told him, John began nodding and murmuring sympathetically. I knew he'd be feeding them lunch, at least.

John, second son of an African diplomat and a Swiss biochem heiress, had spent his youth bumming around the world in search of enlightenment, as he would tell you nostalgically at the drop of a hat. He said he'd met a few holy men who really were holy, so he'd come home a firm believer in generosity toward strangers lest you find that you'd been entertaining angels unawares.

This meant that I would occasionally find he'd let in a street person to sleep in the stock room on a wet night. Sometimes they stole books, or our supply of instant coffee. One gouty old creature of indeterminate sex left a tip behind in the morning.

Now he set these two kids to work on the sidewalk outside the store with a wide push broom and a plastic trash bag. And sure enough, John sent out for pizza for all of us (could I read the man or not?), which left the store reeking of cheese and tomato sauce for hours afterward. That was John, a grownup who somehow retained a kind of youthful generosity, sweet and hopeful.

When Mike and Gene left late that afternoon, the two strangers were working on the tall oak counter that John had salvaged from a failed haberdashery on Seventh. They rubbed the hulking thing down lovingly with stinky furniture oil, which the dry old wood drank up greedily. They were obviously dragging the job out; I wanted them to wind it up and take off. They made me nervous.

Even in the comparative anonymity of lower Manhattan it wasn't smart to take in strangers, particularly dark-complected strangers who spoke broken English. People have been known to report their friends and neighbors to Homesec for less, ever since the Statue of Liberty bombing.

And then there was my dream, which I couldn't quite shake off, and which had metaphorically, at least, suggested danger. Who were these two, anyway? I kept expecting them to wrap themselves in colorful blankets, whip out a nose flute and guitar, and start tootling a version of "El Condor".

At last they were done, reluctantly surrendering the rags John had found for them to work with. While he was paying off the older one for their day's work and I was stuffing my cards back into their carved case, I glanced out the front window and saw the younger boy do something impossible.

He was squatting on the curb, and as I looked he reached down with both hands and stood up again, holding something at about his chest height with both hands, face bent close over it.

I knew what it had to be. For two weeks I'd been stepping over a flattened bird corpse in that gutter, bone and feathers ironed thin by the tires of cars pulling in and out. It was too black for a pigeon, probably a starling or a grackle; I'd been careful not to look closely enough to find out.

The boy hunched over this grisly remnant for a moment, and then suddenly he threw his arms high with his stubby fingers spread. The tattered, misshapen thing arced up, dropped, spread its wings, and flew away toward West Fourth Street.

The older boy gave John a final heartfelt thank you, collected the younger kid, and walked off down the street with him in the soft spring evening.

I didn't mean to bring any of this up with Alec over dinner that night; it wasn't political enough for him. My cousin was a graduate student in journalism who wrote for what remained of the *Village Voice*. He was full, as usual, of outrageous news—a breech in the Israeli Wall, the bombing of some embassy in Australia, and another gray whale die-off in the Pacific. It wasn't easy to catch his attention with anything less than an atrocity, with pictures.

I did manage to get him to look at the freshest draft of my new play, several pages of which acquired yellow curry spots in the process. It was about a couple of orphans of the First Southwest Water War.

Alec said, "I don't know, it just seems a little—cluttered, you know? Like you're trying to cover too much ground at once, but ground you're not really involved in, personally. Which you aren't, Edie, you've never been west of Pennsylvania. Your first one was better."

He meant *Sleight of Heart*, which had been extravagantly praised in its opening production. It had even won a contest, giving me the forlorn hope that I might actually write successfully for the stage. In fact *Sleight* was currently scheduled for a new production in a little upstairs theater in Chelsea in October. This was nice, but hardly thrilling. *Sleight* is your typical American playwright's first play, basically "How My Family Fucked Me Up". No politics, lots of psychology and bad interpersonal behavior; very unthreatening to the closed mind or the public peace.

"I've done my 'first play'," I said. "I just came to it late. I need to move on."

"Well, you're trying, I'll give you that," he said, dipping up runny mango chutney on a shrimp cracker. "Maybe you should switch to something set right here; a play about the next SARS mutation, for instance."

"SARS is your bailiwick," I said. "You cover the damned thing every time a new version blows into town."

"Yeah," he said, "but there's no *news* in it any more. Which means it's ready to be turned into art, right?"

I didn't want to get into an argument about it; I changed the subject.

"Two kids came looking for work at the store today, too old to be urchins, too young to be bums. Hispanics, I think."

"That's old news too," he said, "unless you know how they got across the shiver-river." He meant the stun-barrier along the US-Mexican border, on which he had done a story that had gotten him a month of detention by Homesec. They never said that was who they were, but everybody knew. Alec said afterward that spending a few weeks with his head in a black bag had sharpened his political eyesight mightily.

His languid, know-it-all attitude (much worse since his return from jail) annoyed me. Just to needle him I said casually, "I saw the younger one bring a dead bird back to life today."

Alec laughed with his mouth full. "Come on, Edie!" he crowed. "You know better than that, you of all people!"

Me, of all people: my mother's family had owned a theatrical supply business with a specialty in magicians' paraphernalia, and my dad had been a gambler and small-time card sharp; all eons away now, as illusory as a magic trick itself, but very educational in a basic and persistent way.

"So," I said, "where were the wires, the springs, the misdirect, the switch? Where was the *audience*? This kid, 'Hollith' or something like that his name is, he pulled off a miracle right there on the sidewalk and nobody paid any attention!"

"You were there."

"I don't believe in miracles." I scowled down at my chicken curry; they'd been out their special lamb dish, just for me. "But when I went and looked, the bird was gone."

"Then the kid took it," Alec said with a shrug.

"Don't be ridiculous! What for? Jesus, Alec, you could smell that thing from inside the store!"

"So what did he say when you asked him about it?"

"I didn't get to ask," I admitted. "The older one hustled him away right afterward. Serchio; he's the sharp one of the pair."

Alec dabbed at a drip of chutney on his shirt with his napkin. "Some cultures use animal parts as charms. This boy had his back to you, right? Somebody on a bike or blades must have zipped by in front of him, and you caught the motion over the kid's shoulder and thought the bird was moving."

"Don't strain yourself trying to be inventive," I retorted. "I know what I saw."

He flushed and looked away. Alec had been struggling to write a novel for years, in brave defiance of the slow death of print fiction (except for the established brand-authors, of course, or the ghosts writing interminably in their names). It wasn't nice of me to jab him like that. Ted used to tell me, "If you don't watch it, Edie, you're going to turn into a mean, bitter old woman." He was a smart man.

"Sorry, Alec," I said.

He left me the bill; fair enough.

On the way home I remembered another scrap of my dream: the visitors had told me, very delicately for fear of pushing me and my good intentions too far, that the fugitive boy came from a society that was pretty primitive, by our standards. They said he might act in ways upsetting to me (although normal in his own country), particularly regarding the treatment of animals.

Living animals or dead ones, they hadn't specified.

Next morning the boys were back, this time working a noisy, dented machine that John had rented to shampoo the ancient carpeting throughout the store. They did a very thorough job, unloading and moving bookshelves to get at places that hadn't seen the light of day since the first postponement of elections.

At midmorning they turned off the machine (thank God) and relaxed for a bit. Hollith wandered over to me. He gave me an inquiring glance and picked up my tarot deck. I winced, remembering the dead bird in those small brown hands; but I was curious, too, about how he would react to the images.

He studied the card on the bottom, then set the deck carefully down on the table again and stood waiting.

I am not sentimental about children. Ted and I had managed two miscarriages, nothing more (it's not just that good things don't come my way but that I'll get *promised* something good—and then Saturn cancels delivery). Since my sister Janet's son was killed in a high school shooting, I've tried to ignore children altogether. Dylan's death is what led to my taking the early retirement package that got me out of the classroom. I'm not made of stone.

So I would have ignored this boy, but he looked me calmly in the eye and said, "Please you teaching cards, Missis. I to learn."

So much for my assumption that Serchio spoke for both of them. Hollith had a low voice, slightly hoarse. Maybe he was asthmatic. Up close, there was a tang of tobacco smoke about him.

I picked up the deck and dealt the bottom card. "That's The Magician. It's a good card. It means having all the skill and power you need for the challenges that come to you."

The boy studied the image. "Mishishan," he said.

When he'd gone back to work, John, reshelving books close by, said, "I think he likes you, Edie."

The envious undertone in his voice was very unlike him. His expression softened as he looked after Hollith, who squatted, bent nearly double, to help Serchio make an adjustment to the carpet-cleaning machine.

John added, "I searched for years, and now that I'm done traveling, the people I was looking for come to me."

I wanted to hug him, but we weren't on a hugging footing with each other. So I began to worry instead.

THE NEXT DAY John was downtown attending to the endless official paperwork it took to keep any business free of harassment by Homesec. Ingrid, his current girlfriend, minded the store. I don't think she even noticed when I took advantage of John's absence to approach the older boy.

"Come on, Serchio," I said briskly, "I'll buy you guys lunch."

"Yes, for me," he said. "Thank."

"What about him?" I tilted my head toward the younger boy.

Serchio shook his head. "Not eat today," he said.

"What?" I said.

"Special day," he said, and shut his mouth, watching me. Something ethnic or religious, probably; *let it alone*, I thought.

We left Hollith napping on the old green corduroy couch, with a copy of *Stella Luna*, from the kid-book section, tucked under his cheek like a pillow.

Serchio followed me obediently over to the T-Square Cafe. I chose seats at a low coffee table in the back, as far as we could get from the audio speakers.

"Serchio," I said, "is that your real name?"

"Good name," he said hopefully, "no?"

"Do you have papers, you and Hollith? Do you have a Green Card, a legal right to be here?"

"Hol-*luth*," he corrected. He riffled through a beat up issue of *Self* magazine someone had left on the smeared tabletop.

"Look," I said, "John is a good man. I will not see him get into trouble for taking you two in. Where do you come from, Serchio?"

"Nildai," he said promptly. "Aldai, Rundai."

"Where is that, India? South America?"

"Also Kanikatal," he said, looking up from the magazine. "Many place."

"Hollith—Hol*luth* isn't your kid brother, is he?" God knows stray kids get nabbed by predators all the time, and it wouldn't have surprised me much in this case. There was something secretive and cold about Serchio.

He closed the magazine and looked at me. His eyes weren't dark, as I had thought, but a tawny hazel.

In a confidential tone he said, "I guard to Holluth."

A plump girl with iridescent feather inserts where her eyebrows used to be served us coffee and cake. When she'd gone, Serchio added softly: "Holluth to be high man, his country. Some bad ones hunt; hunt him. I guard."

My dream, goddamn it; I saw the brightly painted model of the temple, drowning in blood.

"Is it something about religion?" I said warily. Good grief, what if they were Muslims?

Unconcerned, Serchio licked white lemon icing off his fingers. "Many danger to traveler, yes?" he observed blandly. "Many land, many danger, far to home. Holluth just only boy. Later, changing; become—strong, so strong soul. Spirit leader. Now, just kid. I guard. Him." He grinned, proud of having negotiated all that and come up with the right pronoun too. "Also, learning. Holluth to study here."

"But you can't just hang around John's store," I hissed. "You're *illegals*, I know you are!"

Serchio reached forward and tapped my wrist delicately with the bent knuckle of his forefinger.

"Not to stay long," he murmured. "Go away soon. No worry."

"What about—look, I saw him *do* something. I thought he made something dead came back to life. A dead bird, and they don't come any deader. Don't shake your head, I saw him. What *was* that?"

He took a breath, his face smooth with cunning. I was a teacher once, and I know that look.

"Don't think up a story!" I said sharply. "Just tell me."

"Trick." He twitched one shoulder in something not even a shrug.

"What do you mean, what kind of trick?"

"Little trick. No worry."

I folded my arms. "Damn it. That's not good enough. Explain."

He fixed me with a measuring stare. Then he said, "Watch Holluth close. Then *you* esplain. Good gift, you hand," and he touched the back of my hand again. "You eye." A flick of his fingers toward my eyes made me flinch. "Holluth watch you; you watch Holluth. Both to learn."

He reached for the remaining piece of cake on my plate: "Take back for him, later? Small boy, like sweet."

And he padded out into the spring haze.

Well, of course, a trick. But *what* trick?

WHEN SOMEONE (like John, say) offers me support, a platform of friendship or trust to work from, it generally collapses, sooner or later: Saturn's influence. Then I feel guilty for having seduced them into being injured, along with me, by my bad stars. It doesn't make for easy friendships.

But sometimes the slow-moving train wreck that is my life falls behind a bit. Then I can pretend, for a while, that things run along as normally for me as they do for other people.

Like during that summer.

John's bookstore was in a good location. He'd had the space air-conditioned, too, and so far enough people were getting their cards read to make my hours there worth it. Between readings, I could work on the new play.

John didn't care about a steady clientele; he had a trust fund. Second Sight was his pastime and his passion, not his livelihood. He owned the whole building and lived very literally above the store, on the two upper floors.

As for me, I didn't give much of a damn about books any more but I did give a damn about tall John Balem with his lean, greyhound limbs; John who had the wide, warm eyes of a Mediterranean tomb painting, John whom I loved.

He did not love me. He was ten years my junior and unlikely to fall for a retired middle-school teacher with a sweet tooth and hair that had never quite recovered from my first bout of SARS (or maybe from the treatment that had saved me). Besides, if he were ever to fall in love with me, you could practically guarantee that the store would catch fire or some prick from Homesec would shut him down just for the hell of it. With a Saturn Affliction (another charming term the astrologers use), love tends to be a lot more trouble than it's worth.

Ask my first husband, whom I hadn't the heart to try to hold onto once he realized what was blocking his tenure at Columbia:

my Saturn shadow, of course. Not to mention how it ruined poor Ted, who never would have started smuggling cheap drugs in from Canada if not for his slow decline as a textbook rep. The shadow had gotten him too.

According to Bella, Saturn was supposed to start working *for* me (and, presumably, mine) in the latter part of my life; which was now. Maybe the old bastard couldn't keep me in mind long enough to remember to flip the switch from "stop" to "go," per the usual human schedule, at mid-life.

Did I really believe any of that stuff? Of course not.

And absolutely. My life proved it to me every day. Between my upbringing and my weird little talent with the cards, I suppose you could call me a skeptic, which is not the same as an unbeliever. There's a ton of bunkum out there, and a handful of people who can handle spiritual tools with talent that goes beyond mere manipulation. It's mostly not real, but that doesn't mean it never is.

And believe me, there *is* such a thing as bad luck.

"But Edie," John had said, commiserating about my canceled workshop, "it's not as if you're one of these poor wannabes, writing your heart out year after year and never getting a production!"

In fact, the sale of *Sleight of Heart* to the movies, plus Ted's insurance money and my teacher's pension, allowed me to scrape by in Manhattan while I worked on my new play. The movie was never released, but Alec had invested the money for me, and not badly either. Mustn't grumble, as my English grandma used to say; meaning, take your lumps in silence since nothing you say can divert the inexorable rain of lumps. She didn't say the silence had to be happy.

I can't deny it; I was not generally a jolly person. Check out Francisco Goya's "black paintings," in particular the nightmare image titled *Saturn Eating his Children*. The gnawed torso that the mad old monster clutches in his fists isn't smiling.

I wasn't even writing, really, just reworking the same few scenes over and over, because what was the point? *Sleight of Heart* had filled a theater in Seattle pretty well, right up until a more prestigious play by a radical European intellectual had been brought in to follow it. Since then, new stagings had been few and far between. None of my subsequent scripts did even that well. *Portia Faces Death* had never even had a staged reading.

I was angry a lot of the time, on a low, background simmer, which I considered a cut above the norm I saw around me (depressed, all of the time). But I slept well, maybe because my anger wore me out.

John, sweet John, slept badly. He had insomnia, and I liked to think that it was because of an unacknowledged yen for me, nagging at his drowsy mind. No harm in imagining.

That Wednesday night, he was just too excited to sleep, too full of plans. I met him for coffee at a tatty old Starbucks that stayed open late. To my consternation, he told me that he had decided to invite the foreign boys to camp in the basement of his building. They had nowhere to sleep, he said, and were living behind a dumpster in back of a closed-up midtown hotel. The city shelters were out of the question, of course. Homesec regularly checked there for illegals, fugitives, and suspects of all kinds.

"Don't do that, John," I said, glaring after our waitperson. I'd been brought the wrong order—a decaf cappuccino instead of an espresso with cream. For some reason the Saturn influence is particularly virulent in restaurant situations (plausible explanations could often be found, as in, "We just don't know what happened to your dinner order, Ma'am—we found it in the fried-noodle basket"). The sheer *pettiness* of it grated.

"Look," I said, "you don't know these guys. What if they're drug runners or worse? What if they steal from you?"

"Edie," he said earnestly, "I don't want you to worry, all right? I had a long talk with Serchio this afternoon. Believe me, those boys are harmless." He smiled, with a nostalgic distance in his gaze. "I want to return the many kindnesses shown to me when I was a spoiled kid bopping around the world with too much money in my jeans and not enough sense in my head. These two remind me so much of tribal people I met then, people living a simpler life, a more numinous life."

Numinous. Sometimes I despaired of my fine John, cushioned by his family wealth against the rougher edges of ordinary life in our faltering wreck of a nation. Yet I could hardly refrain from grabbing his slender, generous hand and kissing it right there in public view.

"All right, what language do they speak to each other?" I said, attacking instead. "It might be some form of Arabic."

He looked alarmed. "No, no; one of the Andean dialects, more likely."

"How about learning English, though?" I persisted. "Holluth, at least, should be in school."

"I know. You let me talk to Serchio about that. Traditional people tend to take advice better from a man."

I let that by without comment. It was merely the truth.

My espresso came at last, without the cream I'd asked for. I know when I'm licked; I slugged it down, black and bitter, from the small white cup. "I think you should give them a little extra money, say thanks, and send them on their way."

"Edie," he explained patiently, "they need help. Somebody's after them. Serchio told me—things are shifting, where they come from. It's too dangerous there, that's why they're on the road like this. They were persecuted at home. In Holluth's tribal group, community rituals that used to be open to all have been replaced by individual treatments, for pay. Only the rich get help now. A caste of priests are taking over and telling people what they can and can't do. Holluth is supposed to bring back the virtues of the old ways, egalitarian ways, respectful ways; if he survives to go home."

"That's Serchio's story. If you ask me, he's full of crap."

John turned his cup in his long, thin fingers. Then he leaned nearer, his head very close to mine so that I could smell the bite of his aftershave. "Someone was waiting for them in the alley tonight, after closing. Edie, I saw—"

"A performance," I interrupted, "whatever you saw, it was some kind of an act put on for your benefit. They've picked up on how receptive you are, John. They're playing to your susceptibilities."

"No, no, I was watching, I would have seen if there was some kind of setup." I felt this conversation spiraling outward, beyond control.

"Watching?" I said.

"Holluth hasn't eaten for the past two days; that tipped me off. It's what people do when they're preparing to encounter spirit-beings."

I couldn't help it, I snorted with derision.

"Just listen," he said. "They were smoking in the alley by the store. The phone rang and I looked away for a minute to answer it, and when I hung up I heard a scuffling sound outside. I opened the door a crack and looked—I was worried that maybe La Migra had them out there. But it was just Holluth, jumping around and trying to kick away something tangled around his feet. For a minute I thought it was the two boys fighting; except how could this little kid have knocked Serchio down on the ground?

"Then Holluth shouted in their language, and something came whipping down between the walls of the alley. I couldn't see exactly, but it grabbed the attacker off the boy and shot back upward, carrying the—the thing away with it."

I stared, my heart stamping hard. "A *thing* came down from the sky and hauled away another *thing*? John—"

He shook his head. "A hawk; it was a hawk, maybe an eagle, even. Edie—the creature it dragged away—I heard it smacking against the alley walls as it was carried up, still struggling. It was a snake, a big, writhing snake."

He sat staring and blinking with amazement at what his mind's eye was seeing.

"I thought you couldn't see that well in the dark," I said, disbelieving. But believing, too. And if something like that *were* real, naturally it would happen before John's eyes, not mine. Sometimes it wasn't John I wanted, not really, but rather to *be* John, seeing with his dark, kind eyes before which true mysteries would display themselves, feeling with his warm heart, thinking with his eager and accepting mind that never aged.

"I couldn't see," he whispered. He closed his eyes. "But I did, Edie. Not just with my eyes. For the first time, truly, not just with my eyes."

"And where was Serchio while this magical ascension was occurring?" I inquired tartly.

He shook his head again, mute.

"It was a flashback." I tried for a softer tone. "A visit from the ghost of the rain forest, John. One of your ayahuasca trips from the old days came back to haunt you, that's all. Those two remind you of those times, you said so yourself."

He sighed. "Sometimes you are so right, Edie. But not this time."

My cream came, much too late. I glared at it and said, "Magic Realism is so passé."

John smiled sadly. "I'm not wise myself, or gifted. I just sell books and mystical paraphernalia, so I give someone like you, someone with a real psychic talent, a place to use it. I'm shackled to the physical, myself, but I recognize spiritual power in others."

"Tarot is just a game," I said. This was a lie; sometimes it is, sometimes it isn't. "I don't know how to explain it, but that doesn't mean I can be played for a sucker by a couple of con artists."

He looked at me with such pained concern that I wanted to slap him awake. "Edie. The cards really speak to you. Why do you think your clients come back for more?" He stopped, and then went on in a lower tone, "Besides, you saw. I watched you watching Holluth reanimate that dead bird. And tonight I saw him fight off some kind of a demon, with the aid of—" He gestured upward. "Spirit help." His eyes glittered.

"Illusion," I snapped. "He's a kid, traveling with an older, smarter operator. Holluth, the wizard-boy, doesn't know to flush the damn toilet if you don't remind him. And Serchio is a con artist if ever I've ever seen one, and believe me, I've seen plenty."

John stared past me at the rain-drizzled window, his whole body taut with longing. "So have I. These guys aren't like that. They're real. I want to learn from them."

He wanted to keep them with him, he meant. He wanted to tame them.

I WENT LOOKING for Serchio early, before the store opened the next day. He and Holluth were standing in the side alley, smoking sweet-spiced bidis and waiting for John to come downstairs and unlock the door for them.

"Morning, Missis," Serchio said, politely putting out his smoke. Holluth tucked his own quenched fag over his ear. He looked pretty perky, demon serpents and magical hawks notwithstanding.

"Serchio," I said, "John is going to ask you and Holluth to bed down here in the store basement at night. I want you to say no. Tell him you already have a place."

"But don't having," Serchio said, smiling. "John is kind."

"Well, I'm not," I said. "And I know it if you don't: if anybody asks questions about you two, John will be screwed."

"John is kind," Serchio repeated, "and raining tonight."

I hooked my thumb at Holluth. "Serchio, you sleep somewhere besides this store or so help me, I'll call Children's Services on you myself."

I must have sounded convincing. Holluth pulled his hand out of the slash pocket of his yellow plastic windbreaker and pointed at me. He held a gray feather, the rounded tip aimed at my chest, and he uttered an indescribable sound. I felt the air ripple heavily, like a wake of ocean water pouring invisibly in my direction, a sensation that made the hair stand up on my scalp. The vibration rolled past on either side if me, and something thumped and clattered loudly behind my back.

Serchio grabbed the boy's shoulder, barking a command. Holluth ignored him, frowning down at the feather in his hand the way a movie gunman glares at his pistol when it has jammed. He twisted out of Serchio's grip and turned his back on both of us.

"Jesus," I breathed. I felt cold.

Slowly, I turned my head to look back over my shoulder. The old delivery van parked in front of the Korean grocery across the street had dropped its driver-side door onto the tarmac. I thought, with a thrill, of the title of a book John had lent me once about a magical murder in Australia: *A Bone is Pointed.*

Holluth had pointed a feather at me, expecting it to do something. Which it had, apparently.

"Bad guys chase last night," Serchio said calmly to me, making no effort to deny what had just happened. "Little bit nerves now. Say sorry, Holluth." He repeated more loudly, "Holluth, say sorry."

"Sorry, Missis," Holluth said in his husky voice, and began kicking at the base of the alley wall with the toe of his sneaker.

The latch to the side door clicked and John let us all in. As soon as we stepped inside, I told him that Serchio and Holluth would be sleeping on the roof of my four-story walkup.

I had a sort of greenhouse up there, over an abandoned apartment with nobody in it to complain about leakage. I had rigged a sizable waterproof tarpaulin over my small store of tools and supplies. The boys were not likely to be seen if they were careful, and there were other roofs nearby to run over and rusty fire escapes to rattle down if they did have to make a run for it, which was better than being cornered in John's basement.

I wasn't going to let them spend any more time with him than I could help. They weren't good for him. He was too experienced to be chasing New Age rainbows like some teenaged airhead.

Of course he protested my fait accompli. Serchio stood nodding and smiling while we argued, as if he didn't understand any of it, just wanted to please. But he stood a little behind me, holding Holluth's hand in his, demonstrating his choice.

I'd never known John to be a fighter. He advanced by persisting, his voice only getting softer, more persuasive. When he still couldn't move forward, he bent around the obstacle to reach what he wanted.

"All right, then," he said at last, "but, Serchio, I want you and Holluth to keep coming to the store daytimes. I still have work for you, paid work. You can't expect Edie to carry the costs of your food, and you'll need cash for other expenses."

On the spot, I think, he came up with the additional work he had in mind: he wanted them to shift all the cartons and shelving in the stockroom so that they could patch and paint the walls and ceiling and refinish the floor in there. If he couldn't have them all to himself, he at least wanted them under his eye during store hours.

The stockroom, where nobody went but us.

I thought about it later—why I was so dead set against John's view of the visitors. I'd been so whipsawed about this kind of thing—learning to see through tricks and traps as a kid, and then finding my own small talent that was *not* a trick. Yet all the spells and mumbo jumbo of Bella Salazar and people like her hadn't been able to stop the fundies from turning the country into the biggest banana republic in the Western hemisphere. So what did "magic" boil down to?

Now here was this little kid and his keeper, and the boy's ability was gigantic, life-and-death, and so far as I could see, untroubled by any ripples of doubt. Maybe I was just envious; Ted would have said so, and he would have laughed and made horrible puns until I laughed too.

But Ted was gone and John, with his sentimental yearning for the "numinous," was there instead, entranced by these kids, who could turn out to be dangerous in several different ways. I meant to protect him, even if it meant taking them home with me instead of seeing them move into John's basement.

Getting up the stairs at home kept me in reasonable shape, though I cursed and swore the whole way (going down, you could hear my knee-joints grinding from out in the street). Serchio and Holluth trotted home ahead of me that evening, lugging my bags of supplies, taking the stairs like two gazelles.

The old brownstone tenement had been empty for two years except for me, up top, and Mrs. Minetta who lived in back on the ground floor. She was very deaf and nearly blind. Together and without ever speaking of it, we were waiting for the next round of luxury-tower construction to stamp our decrepit block out of existence. The most recent building boom had been choked to a halt by yet another war-driven economic crunch. We were safe in our squalor for the time being.

I didn't let the boys into my apartment but showed them up onto the rooftop, with its sun-bubbled tar and guano-streaked parapets. They had blankets to sleep in and a covered plastic bucket for a toilet which they would have to empty down in the basement where the super had once lived. They seemed to find this arrangement entirely satisfactory, being clearly used to much rougher conditions.

Like in my dream, except there had only been one foreigner entrusted to me. Though frankly I didn't think of Serchio as in my charge, so "entrusted" didn't exactly apply. But I had them diverted, at least part of the time, from John's store.

ALEC CAME BY Second Sight next morning.

"Hey," he said, "look what I found on one of those vendor's tables on Fourteenth Street." He handed me a beat-up copy of my book, *Master Packs*, to put on John's used bookshelves. I was glad to see it there again; someone had shoplifted the previous copy, which was flattery of a kind. Some card readers have told me that they swear by my book, although it went out of print three months after publication. Used copies go fast.

"Nice present," I said, stretching up to give him a peck on the cheek. "I can use a little pick-me-up. I got a phone call this morning; the revival of *Sleight* is off. Bad code violations in the theater; they've been closed down indefinitely."

He grimaced in sympathy. "The whole city's falling apart, isn't it? Look, let me take you to lunch, cuz."

He was peering past me at the two boys in the stockroom while we talked out in front. They'd brought a pizza for their own lunch, and today Holluth was digging in with gusto. Apparently no hawks or snakes were due in that night.

Over vegetarian sandwiches at Patel's Alec said, "They are interesting, your boys—unusually calm and self-contained. Did you see? They had a radio in there but they weren't listening to it."

"John thinks they're some kind of specially authentic primitives," I growled. My mood was, as you might expect, pretty foul. "Witch doctors; medicine men. He's regressed to his mental state in his twenties—gullible and starry-eyed. He's let them bewitch him, Alec."

"I've got a couple of ideas about them, some research I can do." Alec patted my hand. "Don't be jealous, Edie."

Alec's an arrogant bastard sometimes, but he's never been stupid.

THEY CAMPED ON my roof all that summer. At least they escaped the bugs up there; a rare visit from the exterminator occurred while I was out, and Mrs. Minetta of course forgot to send him up to my apartment.

I had never had tomatoes like the ones grown on my roof that year, such succulent green beans, such sweetly perfumed squash. If I could have expanded the dirt boxes to cover the whole roof, I'd have made a fortune at the Farmers' Market in Union Square. Holluth had an astoundingly green thumb. Serchio displayed an unexpected gift for numbers, so John started teaching him bookkeeping at the store. He told people that Serchio was an exchange student from India studying small business techniques, and that Holluth was his visiting kid brother.

On days that Holluth stayed home I would call him down to my apartment and try to teach him to read, using books borrowed from the store. In the privacy of my little yellow kitchen he would lean quite unselfconsciously against my side and study the illustrations intently. The small-boy scent of him was much like the remembered scent of my nephew, but overlain with smoke and pizza smells.

Holluth had more old scars on his solid little body than Dylan had ever had, confirming a rougher, earthier, and more routinely dangerous background. Most visibly, a thin weal of raised flesh divided the black hair just over Holluth's right ear. I didn't ask about it, or about the faded blue tattoos on his thin arms.

Curiously, I found that his attempt to put a hex on me with that feather warmed me toward him. A person who is distressed when his black magic malfunctions is basically serious, and I respected that. I certainly liked his impetuous act of aggressive self-defense better than Serchio's duplicity, and I appreciated how, without missing a beat, the smaller boy had switched from wanting me to teach him the tarot to seeing me as expendable when I made a threat. That was the kind of reflexes you needed to keep you up and running in this world.

We'd had a muffling distance between us, like any teacher and pupil, mediated always by the watchful, controlling presence of Serchio. From that point on Holluth and I interacted more naturally, on a basis of guarded, mutual respect. Coming from a different culture he wasn't easy to read, but I thought our little contretemps had reset both of us to a live connection.

As a student, he was a challenge. I kept trying; I liked unpacking and applying some of my old skills, and I did have some encouragement. Once I found him lying in the shade of the roof awning chanting to himself snatches of a text we had gone over recently—"Twelve liddel girrs in two straight line." So he memorized what I read to him, though I don't think he ever connected print on paper with spoken words. He was satisfied to sing the story after me, mimicking my voice without a trace of mockery.

At one point I thought he might be retarded. But he looked at me with those dark, sober eyes, and I remembered how American Indian children were called stupid when they were only retreating from a competitive style of education that was completely alien to them.

I tried changing the orphans in my Water Wars play into two Hispanic boys. It didn't help.

Remarkably, there was no trouble. After the first week, I stopped listening for van doors slamming in the street and cops banging up the stairs, like on the night Homesec had taken a family of Algerians from the third floor. Serchio and his younger charge were apparently good at keeping their profiles low, despite the fact that some nights I heard what sounded like dancing up there on the roof, quick steps in a regular rhythm. Then there would be quiet punctuated by whistling sounds, like some kind of signals.

I ignored it all and minded my own business. Serchio's knuckle tapping my wrist, his fingers flicking at my face, had wakened caution in me. And what I really cared about was insulating John from them.

Sometimes I would wait till I knew they'd gone out and go upstairs for a peek. I never found anything but their meager belongings stowed under the tarp in an old wooden crate. I often didn't hear them come back upstairs during the night, but there they would be after sunrise, pouring hot tea from their red plastic thermos bottle. They loved lapsang souchong. I indulged them in this one expensive taste. It was a small thing, an easy thing and safe, like tossing meat scraps to captive leopards.

John never really forgave me for stealing them out from under his nose. Whenever I came to the store he asked about them, their lives on my rooftop, their habits and routines pursued out of his sight. I was noncommittal and tried to avoid his reproachful looks.

He had long conversations with Serchio at lunchtime or at the end of the business day, while I selected books with Holluth (*Ferdand de Boll*) or went over card spreads with him. I thought Serchio had more sense than to tell John anything important, like why the birds didn't strip my roof garden plants that summer, as usual.

The falcon kept them away.

One predawn in July I was roused by a staccato piping sound drifting down past my bedroom window. I shrugged on my bathrobe and huffed up the stairs.

Holluth stood silhouetted against the pale sky, bare feet planted apart on the parapet; Serchio wasn't around. As I watched, the boy made the whistling call again with his hands cupped around his mouth. For a minute nothing happened. Then a bird flew up from below the parapet and settled, fluttering, in his outstretched palm.

It was a small bird, indistinct in that early light, very black; I thought I knew exactly what bird it was. I'd have believed myself still asleep and dreaming except for how the cool summer dawn softened the air, damp with the breath of the Hudson River. And my feet were cold.

Holluth raised both hands over his head, the bird quiet in the cage of his fingers. He threw back his head and sent a high, harsh call up into the sky.

Almost at once, something dark and compact plummeted down at incredible speed, banking at the last minute but still striking hard enough to knock Holluth's raised hands aside. I flinched back into the shelter of the doorway housing. Wings dug loudly into the air, *whup*, *whup*, and the hawk surged upward again with the little bird twitching in its talons. I saw dark dappling on the hawk's under parts, and then it swooped away toward a clutch of tall condos and office buildings to the north.

Holluth turned to look at me then, while he licked at a thin line of blood that ran down from his palm along his forearm.

I scurried back downstairs, shivering.

Peregrines have nested for years in the upper ledges of Manhattan skyscrapers; I may have seen them myself from time to time without knowing it. They're migratory up and down the east coast, building their springtime nests in the most inaccessible heights of human constructions now that the forests are gone and the cliffs are covered with high rise condos.

I don't think anyone has ever seen a wild hawk take prey offered in the naked hands of a human being. It was almost as good a trick as John's huge serpent being carried away into the sky. I didn't understand it, and I didn't know how to think about what I had seen, so I pushed it to the back of my mind and said nothing about it, particularly to John.

That was the day that the cooler, wetter weather arrived.

DURING QUIET HOURS at the bookstore Holluth sat across from me in the querant's chair, his chin braced on his square small hands, studying the cards. He didn't learn the meanings particularly fast, but his attention span was remarkable for a child and once he learned he did not forget. Sometimes he'd pick out a card and hold it against the side of his head, with his eyes closed. I asked him why.

He looked at me as if it were a trick question. "To learn song."

"What song?" I said. "Can you sing it for me."

"My song for me, Missis," he whispered, dropping his gaze. "Other song for you."

I mentioned this, lightly, to John, doling out what I had that he wanted, to draw the light of his attention. He gave me that sorrowful look that meant I was treating casually something precious that he wished had been offered to him instead of to me.

"Spirit beings train a young shaman by teaching him songs of power," he said. "Those cards tell you the future. He wants them to tell him things too."

Good luck, laddie, I thought; so far as I could tell, whatever it is that makes a person more than just a fake with the cards, Holluth didn't have it. What I think about the tarot is that it's a way of disconnecting the rational mind so that you can reach out with your naked intuition and pick up some of the thought patterns of your querant; if you're any good, that is. Holluth was clearly coming to it from another direction, stolid as an engineering student.

Reader or not, though, Holluth's presence had a strong effect on my own card reading business. Lots of people came in, often just to get out of the rain (it had turned into quite a wet summer), and then requested readings. Some clients asked Holluth to sit in, which Bella explained to me one morning.

In consolation for the business deal that had, as I had foretold, gone wrong, I gave in and did a three-card spread for her on a particular question. It was about the Montauk vacation again, now only a week away.

"I want the little boy here for this," she said, craning her neck to look around for Holluth. "Where is he?"

He was out buying shoes with Serchio, or so they'd said; who knew? More likely sneaking in to see a movie, I told her. John said Holluth loved movies.

Bella sighed. "I'd rather wait 'til he's here, Edie."

"Why?" It took something major to divert her when she was hot on the trail of a better future than the one she saw coming for herself.

She pooched her lips, holding out (sometimes when you predict bad things and they happen, you catch a little of the blame just as if you had caused the black events instead of just getting a sniff of them in the wind).

I shuffled the deck; Bella primed to talk was Bella talking, sooner or later.

Sure enough, after about twenty seconds she flopped forward with her elbows on the table and said in an urgent whisper, "The guy you did a reading for last week—Richie, from the magazine store on Greenwich? He's been sick for almost a year, something he was exposed to in the Army, he thinks. He's not sick now, not since you read the cards for him while that kid watched. He says the boy has healing powers."

I hooted. This was over the edge, even for Bella.

"No, really, Edie." She glanced around to make sure no one could overhear. "Richie only came for that reading because of what happened to Luanne after you read for her with the kid looking over your shoulder."

"Who's Luanne?"

"Nature's Foods, the weekend clerk. She's had a lump in her breast for months, scaring the life out of her. She just saw the doctor again, and the lump is gone." Bella hitched closer, pleading. "I have a spot on my lung, Edie. Sometimes it's hard to breathe. Another SARS outbreak could kill me. When will Holluth be here again?"

Well, I couldn't keep that to myself. I told John about it as we closed up that evening. "Can you believe it?" I scoffed. "Next thing you know they'll be lighting shrine candles outside the store. I *told* you those boys would be a problem!"

John let me rant on. He got a far-off look, though, and out in the alley, holding the bin open for me to dump in some store trash, he said at last, "The boys won't let anything bad happen to us on their account, Edie. Don't head home yet, come back inside for a minute; I need to explain something."

He pulled the shade, sat me down at my card table, and brought me a can of soda from the half-fridge in back. "Let's lay our cards on the table, here." A quick smile, shy and complicit at the same time, and then gravity again. "Serchio has finally admitted to me that Holluth is a shaman. He can heal because the Peregrine falcon is his ally."

"Shamans are crooks who pretend to dig tumors out of people with their fingers. For pay, of course. You know better than this, John."

He ignored this and went on, speaking with an annoying calmness. "The true shaman gets his call sometime in childhood or adolescence. He attracts power animals that take him on spirit journeys to other worlds and teach him to master different kinds of power; a wolf, a whale—a hawk."

"So what about Serchio?" I said, trying to break the spell (*but I saw that dead bird fly, and I saw the falcon strike*). "Is he a shaman too?"

"He's the shaman's helper, the one who tends the fire and beats the drum."

"Serchio? That guy wouldn't stand around beating a drum for anybody."

John smiled serenely. I could have kicked him. "What do you think, then? What is Holluth?"

"Dangerous, that's what he is; they both are." Sexy, I thought, surprising myself with the thought, about Serchio. He was, too, in a slinky, rawboned way. I didn't like the thought and wished I could unthink it.

John sighed. "I shouldn't have said anything. You get so upset about these kids! What is it, were you brought up too Christian to tolerate a few small pagan miracles?"

"I was brought by people who sold professional fakers their stage setups. My Dad played a lot of poker. He only won when he cheated, which was a lot of the time. You're naive, John, in ways that I'm not." *But the boy pointed that feather, the boy gave the hawk a sacrifice …*

Folding his arms across his chest, John replied, "You won't have to put up with them much longer. Serchio says their enemies are closing in, so they can't stay. They'll be gone soon."

Serchio had told me weeks ago that they'd be moving on. Confirmation now brought no relief. I read in John's face that when they did finally leave, he meant to go with them.

Alec invited himself over. He said he had some news, but strung me along all through spaghetti and salad. We talked about a Carol Churchill revival we had both seen, a wild, almost choral piece that struck home as a conversation among the newly dead. I had thrown my own new play away afterward, and then had to fish the crumpled pages out of the trash again. Not that I told Alec that.

Leaving the dirty dishes on the table, I went down to sit on the stoop with him in the mild, dewy night. He reached over lazily and poked my knee. "Hey, guess what? I've solved it. I know what pattern your magic boy fits."

I tucked an old sports section of the Sunday *Times* between my behind and the wet stone step and muttered gloomily, "He's a baby medicine man, according to John."

"Oh, it's more than that," Alec said. He sounded very pleased with himself. "I was thinking about the woman you mentioned, the one with the vanishing lump, and I asked myself: who cures the lame and the halt and, in this case, the lumpy? For that matter, who raises the dead, even if it's only a dead bird? Actually, revivifying a dead bird is a perfectly appropriate miracle for a Messiah-in-training from some remote tribe of hunter-gatherers."

I snorted. "Oh, stop it, Alec."

"He even has his first disciple—Serchio. His second too, if John is as smitten as you think." He chortled. "John the Baptist, maybe?"

"You're crazy," I said. But I was thinking, *The dead bird flew away, and came back to be offered up to the Peregrine.*

"Also you say he has enemies, which is par for this particular course even if his aren't priests or kings but mysterious pursuers who can turn into flying snakes. Sounds more like magical rivals who want to shut the kid up."

"Oh, baloney, Alec! He can barely speak English, he's not saying anything."

"Not yet." Alec raised an admonitory finger. "Serchio is trying to make sure the kid grows up enough to be listened to when he does talk, back where people are primed to hear what he has to say. The two of them are only hiding out here till their local prophecies start coming true. Then, the triumphant return, amazement, revelation!"

"Sure," I scoffed. "Holluth will amaze a bunch of savages by showing them how to tie a napkin around their hawk's neck before feeding it a live bird."

"Lots of people from hunter-gatherer tribes converted really fast to Christianity, you know." Alec loved an argument. "And all the ayahuasqueros in South America claim to be Christian; they include prayers to Jesus in their ceremonies. I'm just saying, there doesn't have to be a conflict between a Judeo-Christian religion and a hunting society with a leaning toward shamanism. There are good ways and bad ways to do any spiritual practice; according to the anthropologists, sorcerers and witches are shamans gone bad so why couldn't they have an exalted type of shaman at the opposite end of the spectrum? Anyway, who says you can't have a Messiah unless you've got cities and some priest-ridden religion all written out in a book?"

I said, "Alec, Holluth picks his *nose*. Are you telling me that little Jesus picked his *nose?"*

He laughed. "What do you think? There are Gospels that Jesus raised hell as a little boy, changing the neighbors' kids into bushes and rocks and things for teasing him. That's why those particular Gospels got axed. The early Church fathers couldn't stand the idea of their Messiah bullying his little playmates."

"Holluth is no Jesus Christ!" I protested.

"Well, no, not exactly." Alec gazed up thoughtfully at the dim night sky. "He couldn't return as actual *Jesus*. There's controversy over what Jesus looked like. A lot of folks wouldn't go for a little brown kid built like a dump truck."

"So Holluth is the Second Coming of Somebody Else?"

"I'm just saying he seems to be following in some very famous footsteps, however crudely."

"Crudely! He pointed a goddamned feather at me, Alec, with destructive intentions. He's a savage little primitive."

"So?" he retorted. "Who says there weren't other Messiahs before Jesus, rougher models cut to suit Paleolithic societies? People like Jesus could have turned up among the cavemen, teaching that they should share the hunting grounds and flint mines instead of killing each other over them. We wouldn't know, because nobody could write yet."

"You don't really believe that."

He yawned largely, like a sleepy lion. "I'm no more religious than you are, Edie. But if there's really a new Messiah due—and candidates have been popping up all over the world for decades now—well, the kid could fit the pattern."

I stood up. "Journalism is making you crazy, you need another line of work. In any case our *visitation* by little Jesus of the Raptors is almost over. John says they're leaving soon, on the run from bad guys like that snake-thing John says he saw."

Alec laced his fingers behind his head and leaned back on the upper steps, eyes closed. "The flight into Egypt," he murmured. "Except for the snake part."

"Whatever you've been using today, Alec," I said, "you're not sleeping it off here. Thanks for the theory. Now go home. I want to get some sleep myself."

But, for a change, I didn't, not right away. I couldn't stop thinking about that hawk.

A HIGH, COLD CRY woke me very early. I pulled on a robe and hustled myself up the stairs, still half asleep. The boys were gone. So were their blankets, and their beloved red plastic thermos. The old crate they'd stored their things in was placed neatly under the tarp, with nothing in it now but my gardening tools.

Oh no, I thought. *They've run out on us.*

But above the Hudson I saw a hawk circling. Its call came down to me again, sharp and hectoring, and I thought, *If you're still hanging around, maybe they're still here too.* I went back down to dress and walked fast over to the bookstore. The streets were full of the peculiar moist tenderness of the city's air at dawn. I didn't see another soul.

At Second Sight the blind was still down, but the side door was unlocked. As I let myself in, Serchio reached past me and shut the door again, quickly but quietly. All the lights were on inside. I saw blood crusted across his wrist, like claw marks that had just scabbed over. His shirt was stained and he smelled hot and unwashed.

Holluth crouched at the foot of the tall wooden counter with his arms over his head, making little sounds. I pushed past Serchio and squatted down to give the little boy a gingerly hug. Holluth rolled into my arms and sobbed on my shoulder with his thin arms tight around my neck, which left me leaning clumsily into his warm weight to keep from falling over backward.

"Holluth, what—?"

Serchio said in a weary tone, "He still cries for his mother when something goes wrong."

I glared up at him, my arms around the weeping boy, my knees pinging like tight-drawn rubber bands. "What happened to your accent, Serchio? You goddamned fraud, I knew it!"

He shrugged. "I have a gift for languages; otherwise what good would I be to Holluth on his journey? John keeps first aid things here somewhere, doesn't he?"

He did, and I used them on Holluth who had a cut on his cheek and some other scrapes; as far as I was concerned, Serchio could look after himself. The boy didn't say anything while I doctored him, keeping silent except for some subdued snuffling and coughing. I didn't ask him any questions. By the time I finished being artful with the Band-Aids to make them cover all his scratches, he had fallen into a doze. I lugged him over to the sofa where he curled up at once, asleep or passed out.

In the stockroom Serchio was sitting on a stack of book cartons, eating a bagel and a chunk of old cheese from the fridge. I perched on the third step of the paint-crusted stepladder, facing him.

"Talk," I said, "or I'll have the cops here in five minutes, and no pointed feathers are going to stop me, either."

He tossed back water from a paper cup. "Holluth met the witches and drove them away. They marked us both this time, but still we won. I was right to bring him here. He's grown stronger."

"He's all scratched up. I thought you were guarding him."

He crumpled the damp paper cup in his fingers and studied its twisted shape. "His people believe that each soul plans its life before being born. They believe he chose to be what he is now, and also what he will become. Sometimes helping him means standing back and letting events draw out his strengths."

I wiped my hands on my shirt. "Tough love, right? You fake!" But fake *what*, exactly? It was driving me crazy.

"Try not be angry with us," he said. I could see his focus change, snap! just like that, from Holluth and his accomplishments to me and what Serchio thought he could wheedle out of me. "Let him sleep there until John comes. We'll leave for good before noon."

"Taking what with you?" I saw that they had a backpack and an ancient L.L. Bean duffle, one end reinforced with gray duct tape, stacked against the counter's end. *Blankets*, I thought, *spare clothes*. "What do you want from John?"

"What he gives us. Money for work, to buy food."

"Why him?" I demanded. "Why this bookstore?"

Serchio's lips curled in a grin. "You. Holluth saw you through the window. He came here to find power. You showed him power in your cards."

Tarot's just a trick, I thought automatically, the comforting lie again. "This isn't the land of the spirits," I said coldly. "There are no magic animals here to help the kid out."

"But there are; and not only animals."

He shot me an odd, secretive glance, and this opened the dusty air between us somehow so that for a split second I saw a deep red shine in his hair; also a flash, a glimpse, of a sharp, velvety muzzle, a narrow pink tongue licking cheese crumbs off dark lips.

"*Fox!*" I gasped. Coyote, trickster, here in John's store? "Liar!" I said, with a breathless laugh: gotcha! "Holluth already has his power animal, the hawk."

"A great shaman finds many helpers." Again the keen stare, interrogative this time; assessing. "Are you one?"

"No."

No? How could I say so, how could I be sure? Everything was changed. He was Fox, and Holluth was a boy-shaman; I felt something at my core bend, crack, and accept it. Chilly sweat broke out on my face. "Why should I help you take Holluth away? People here say he can cure them."

"Holluth didn't come here to stay. He came to find power to take home to his own people."

"We're people too," I protested. "How about using whatever he's found here to help the people who *live* here?"

Serchio looked at me with sympathy now, maybe; hard to tell, with those tawny eyes. "It is true," he said, "you do have lots of witches, educated and rich and rotten in the heart. But, Edie—for Holluth's own people it's worse. All they know is spells and curses and fear of the night and of each other, a dark, hard, frightening world. They haven't had their *first* coming yet."

I thought, *God damn it, Alec was right.*

He tossed the crumpled cup lightly, overhand, into the waste basket in the corner. "It was foretold, a long time since: Holluth will bring changes. He'll come home transformed by his spirit journey, and also transform the people around him. People are waiting for that day."

Furiously, I blinked back hot and sudden tears. "We're waiting too!"

He seemed nonplussed for the first time. "Not for Holluth. Didn't your cards tell you? You have new messengers too, already born and growing."

"Sure, sure, everybody's been expecting Jesus for generations, and a lot of good it's done them." I slapped my thighs in frustration. "Look around you, look at us! You've been here long enough to see that what a mess we're in. It just gets worse and nobody turns up to fix any of it!"

Stretching out his long legs in their tight jeans, Serchio shook his head. "Oh, Edie; you think someone like Holluth comes and *fixes* things? Is that what happened after your Christ showed himself? The person cures, teaches, points a better way to the people near him. By the time the rest of your world learns about it he's dead, usually in some ugly way. Then the lies start, and the wars over what that person really said or didn't say."

Two thousand years and more of human history, thrown in my face by a fox-man; what could I say to this summary of the life and times of Christ, Buddha, Ghandi, who knew how many others who never made it even as far as they had? Poor Holluth, curled up on the couch: the boy from my dream, the Expected One, the Magic Boy—but not *our* Magic Boy. Somebody else's.

I let out a breath, defeated. "What do you need?"

"You'll know."

"How?"

He smiled slyly. "We'll tell you."

I frowned at him. "You'll draw attention to yourself, moving. You could stay on my roof a while longer." That, at least, was a risk I was familiar with.

He shook his head. "Holluth needs his education. We have people to see out in your deserts and forests."

"Deserts, yes," I said. "Forests? What planet do you think you're on?"

His silence was sudden and absolute, and it said, *not our own.*

Some greener place, then, still in the grip of ancient demons of land, sea, and sky. *Your world.* Words he had spoken moments before came back to me, ringing hard, like a steel bell. It hadn't been mistaken English, and he'd been speaking literally.

"Oh shit," I groaned. I yanked at my own hair with both hands to wake myself up and get out of this insane conversation. "Shit, shit, shit!"

Serchio came over and put his paw—hand, paw, my vision shifted maddeningly—on my arm. It rested there, warm and light. "Just let us stay for now," he said. "No police. John is bringing his car from where he keeps it, in some uptown garage. He said he would drive us."

Everything became very clear: the quiet, mote-dancing air of the bookstore, the lingering bite of the furniture oil they had rubbed into the tall wooden counter, Holluth's snuffly child-snores. My thoughts followed each other as calmly and simply as sentences in one of the children's books Holluth loved so much: these two would take John away with them. John would leave me behind with no more than a backward glance, however kind that one glance might be. He would get what he'd been wanting for years, ever since he'd put down roots in this building: to leave, cut loose, to close his store and follow a holy man.

"Serchio," I said, "there's something I want, too. I want a cure."

Crouching, he looked at me, puzzled. "You're not sick."

"No," I said. "Not in my body. In my life. There's this, this shadow over my whole life, Serchio, like a curse—"

He said, "The raven, yes. It covers you."

I gawked, mouth open. Then I whispered, "You can see it?"

He nodded, watching me curiously.

I breathed deeply. "Holluth has to get rid of it. I want him to point his damned feather, or do whatever it takes to open my Saturn cage and *let me out*."

"But there is no cage," he said. "You chose the shadow, as Holluth chose all this."

My throat closed, choking my voice into an angry hiss. "Chose, my ass! What are you talking about? Bella showed me on my chart, it's the stars, not me! And you owe me, Serchio, you both owe me!"

He took my hand in both of his. "Edie," he said anxiously, "don't you understand? The shadow belongs to you, it's part of you."

My throat hurt with the effort not to yell, but I didn't pull away. As long as he held my hand like that there was a chance that he would stop this horrible nonsense and do as I asked, now, before the two of them left for good. I leaned closer toward him, vibrating with anger and need.

"Holluth cured a woman," I said, "a stranger who did nothing for him, he cured her of *breast cancer!* What about me? How much would it take, just to roll this boulder off my life? I hid you, I protected you!"

As I said this, I understood why Serchio had agreed to hide out on my roof instead of in John's basement. He'd wanted the shield of my Saturn shroud over himself and Holluth. What hid me from the sunlight of my heart's desire also hid me *from* spite and persecution—while I slowly suffocated in the dark.

I sat appalled and silent. Serchio bent nearer, patting my hand. He gave off a shocking amount of heat, or maybe I was just turning to cold stone where I sat.

"Ah, no, Edie," he coaxed, his head so close to mine that his coarse hair brushed my temple, "it's impossible. Even if Holluth could do what you ask, Old Shadow Man would tear your heart out with his talons as he left."

"You're afraid," I spat. "You're afraid my damned curse would attach itself to you instead—or to Holluth, your precious Holluth!"

Now he let me go, straightened up, and stood back from me. "That could happen," he said gravely. "You know more about these things than you realize. Think, and you'll see that it's wrong for Holluth to try to drive away the darkness that you've chosen to give shape to your light."

I got up and walked dully out of the stockroom to go sit at my tarot table, watching the street outside brighten. A red pulse shook in my head with each beat of my heart. If I'd seen a way to turn the two of them in to Homesec without getting John arrested too—and me with him—I would have taken it.

YEARS LATER—a matter of ten minutes, perhaps—John ducked in siwftly at the side door, carrying a bulging plastic shopping bag which he set down on the counter. His face looked gray, and his voice came strained and breathless. "I don't think I can drive you boys. I know I said I would do it, but you have to understand—everything's changed."

Serchio slumped against the front door, his forearm across his eyes. Holluth sat up on the old couch, looking fearfully at John.

I watched all of them from the center of exhausted anger, unable to care at all, while my voice said mechanically, "What's happened, John, what's wrong?"

He crossed to the window with his long, loose stride and stood to the side, carefully easing the edges of two blind-slats apart so he could look outside without being seen. "They'll be watching us," he said lowly. "I'm sure of it; the street, the whole block. Richie told me, over at Nature's Gifts. I stopped there for some snacks to take in the car, and he said the Homesec came and took away the Koreans across the street last night. That's why their store is closed this morning. You can see that their front door's been sealed, over there."

He turned back to all of us, his eyes glaring wide. "Four this morning, right across the street there; I was awake upstairs, reading, but I never heard a thing. There's some new uproar with Korea, it's in the papers, so they're rounding people up again. They'll have left watchers, in case they missed anybody. So it's impossible now: three men of color piling into a car with luggage—they'll see us, they'll stop us."

Nobody spoke for a minute. Then Serchio said softly, "You are rich, John. Would they really trouble you?"

John laughed angrily, the first trace of spirit he had shown since he'd come in. "Yes, I'm rich compared to most people. But I'm not white. It can make a hell of a difference, Serchio, as I'm sure you know yourself just from your time here."

Serchio said softly, insistently. "We can't stay any longer. We must go."

John said helplessly, "Then go, Serchio." He gestured limply at the white plastic sack, lumpy with bags of chips and cans of soda from Richie's store. "Take that, it's for you. I'm sorry."

"Help us," Serchio said. "You said you would help us."

My anger vanished. I sat frozen with dread that he would change John's mind, even use magic on him somehow to make John do as he had promised. I couldn't think of anything to say to prevent it. I watched John, wavering, open his mouth to speak, shake his lowered head, and rub both hands across his close-cropped scalp so that I heard the whisper of his hair against his palms.

He turned suddenly to Holluth. "Can you do something, Holluth? A spell, a protection? Something to give us an edge?"

Holluth glanced anxiously at Serchio. "Try," he husked. "Must be trust."

Serchio nodded, his eyes intent on John. "Trust," he echoed. "You've seen things before, John. You know things can be done."

Sweat gleamed on John's forehead. "Sometimes, yes. But the shirts the shamans said were made bulletproof at the Ghost Dance turned out to be ordinary shirts, against ordinary bullets."

"Cards," I croaked, spinning the deck through my hands, searching desperately for the cards I needed, cards I could palm, rig somehow—The Tower, where was The Tower? I held the cards so that I could see them, just, with my peripheral vision even though my gaze was fixed on John. "I'll do a reading for you. Then you'll know how it will come out if you go with them."

John stared at me for a moment—I didn't dare look at Serchio—and then he sat down across from me, reaching for the deck. I kept out only two cards, one palmed and one pinned under my elbow where my wide sleeve masked it. John shuffled the rest, quickly and thoroughly.

As I was about to take the deck back from him, Holluth was

suddenly there, reaching between us. He said hoarsely, "Let me listen cards, Missis. Practice."

And John handed the boy my tarot deck.

I couldn't just grab it back. I sat there, not breathing, while Holluth fanned out my dog-eared cards and presented them so John could pick a Significator, a card to stand for himself as querant. John licked his lips and chose true: The Hermit, the card of the spiritual seeker, which Holluth laid down carefully, squarely in the middle of the inlaid tabletop.

"Past," he said, dealing a card off the top, face down, and setting it to the left of The Hermit. "Future." One to the right. "Later;" another card to the right; "Finish." A third card again to the right. A simple timeline layout, four cards in a horizontal row, I noted as I frantically fought to clear my mind so that I could invent a threatening interpretation no matter what cards Holluth turned up.

I needn't have worried.

The "past" card, turned over by Holluth's stubby fingers, was The Magician; but the image was changed. The figure of the robed alchemist had a feature that I had never seen in any deck. On his shoulder perched a falcon, head turned so that one fierce yellow eye looked out at the beholder. The grimy card, worn at the corners, looked as if it had been in my deck for years.

"Future" was the six of Swords, reversed, followed by The Tower. Holluth's "finish" was blank, a pale smear inside the delicate line meant to frame an image.

There are no blank cards in the tarot deck.

John's breathing was faint and rapid as his gaze flickered from card to card and back again, and again to the empty one in the last place.

Holluth squared up the rest of the deck into a neat rectangle with both hands (the outsized cards were still hard for him to handle). He put it down and waited in silence. So the reading itself was up to me. It was no test; the meaning could hardly have been plainer.

I cleared my throat. "The Magician in this placement means that Holluth's visit is now in the past, or passing, as he travels onward. Here, centrally, are you, John—the spiritual pilgrim. Next, six of Swords reversed; you may travel if you wish, but the journey is ill-omened. Then, The Tower: it all goes to Hell. Catastrophe; ruin. The final outcome—something, I'm not sure what it means."

But I did I know what it meant. I made myself say it. "Erasure. The end."

"The end," John whispered. He grated the tin chair back, not rising though, as if his long legs had no strength. He sat slackly, a man with all is strings cut. Then he put his face in his hands and wept.

Serchio pushed away from the door frame and headed for the stockroom, nudging Holluth on ahead of him. At the door, he glanced over his shoulder at me. Oh, those topaz eyes, knowing eyes! His yellow stare carried a challenge: *We gave you the cards you needed to keep John safe; now you give us what we need. That's how it works.*

I left the palmed cards on the table with the others (how had my deck acquired two Tower cards and that damned blank?) and followed them. Holluth shut the door quietly behind us.

"I can't drive you," I said immediately. "I only drive automatic. John's car is stick shift."

Serchio stood casually, hpshot and graceful, among the stacked cartons of books packed up for return. "John is right, a car is too noticeable now," he observed. "We'll go another way."

"What other way?" I said.

"A shaman's way," Serchio said.

Holluth touched my elbow discreetly. "Please, Missis," he said. "You to hide us. No, not house again—hide in you shadow." He spread his arms outward from his sides, like the wings of a bird. "Tell raven, come cover us down his wings. Then, enemy don't to see."

My mind translated sluggishly and I almost laughed. He thought my Saturn shadow was mine to command.

"I can't," I said, "it isn't like that, Holluth. I don't know how."

His sudden, sweet grin made me blink. "He with you always," he said cheerfully. "Just you walk along, I sing him to help us."

Looking down at his bright, round face, I surrendered. I breathed out my anger, my fear, and my well-aged resentment on one long breath. "Yes, all right. Let's try it." My voice came out faint and squeaky, but I meant it.

Holluth dug paper and tobacco out of his jeans pocket and began to roll a smoke, singing softly in his own language. We each took a puff, and then Holluth sang some more, blowing smoke into the four corners of the room. I don't remember the rest clearly, just the taste of the sweetened tobacco, the light, rapid drumming of Serchio's palms on his thighs, and that high, slightly stuffy-nosed child-voice calling and chanting as my vision cooled and dimmed.

At seven a.m. we left for the Port Authority bus terminal, shielded by the curse that had blighted my life for as long as I could remember. Looking back at John from the street doorway, I felt my heart twist hard. He sat staring blindly at the icons on his computer screen while Gene and Mike, who had shown up while we were in the back and, oblivious as always, had settled down over their chess game in the Eastern Esoterica corner.

Enveloped in a dimness like the moving shadow of a cloud, we paused outside on the sunny sidewalk. The sharp call of the falcon dropped straight down on us from the top of the sky beyond the buildings, piercing through the veil that sheltered us.

We walked up Eighth Avenue, me in the middle with one of them on either side, holding my hands and swinging them. Holluth sang softly and chirped and occasionally skipped along beside me, looking very young. This gave his work of sorcery an appearance of childish play, like any young boy lost in the magic of his own imagination as he walked uptown with his family.

The shadow traveled with us, large enough to embrace all three of us in the darkness under its outstretched wings. Where its soft edge slid silently over the pavement, pedestrians just stepped aside with barely a glance at us. Most of them had their faces buried in newspapers, reading about the new Korean crisis.

I squinted upward once, and what I thought I saw was the peregrine falcon, gliding high above us where a raven should have flown: one bird casting another's shadow.

The shadow went with us into the terminal, or at least the dimming of my sight did. None of the Homesec cops on duty turned our way, and there were a lot of Homesec cops (the crisis, of course). Well, we were nothing much to look at, I imagine: two boys with battered baggage and a middle aged woman in jeans and a sweater with a dazzled expression (I probably looked zonked out on dope). The cops' flat, impersonal glances fled over us like water over stone, catching on nothing, deflected by my darkness.

We bought tickets, magazines, and gum, and went to wait at one of the gates. I watched Holluth, who slumped down in a pink plastic seat three chairs over, absorbed in one of the picture books he had chosen from the store shelves. A bus was already waiting to carry the two of them as far as Raleigh-Durham, the first leg of their journey south. From time to time a passenger climbed in and settled down to await departure.

Serchio, sitting beside me, touched my wrist for the last time. "Thank you, Edie. I didn't tell you, but if we hadn't left there our enemies would have come into John's store after us, and believe me, they're worse than your police. But now we have disappeared." Up close his breath was rank, but I didn't rub his light kiss off my cheek. "Abracadabra!" he said.

"But why Brazil?" I said.

"There are people to visit in the Amazon Basin." Serchio arched his back and yawned. "Holluth still has a lot to learn about plant helpers."

Drugs that make you throw up and have good or bad trips, he meant. John had told me about his own experiences as a young man. You could die, he'd said, or go permanently mad.

"You could get peyote here," I said. "Good strong plant-stuff. I can get you a name." Alec would know someone. "Don't go, Serchio. We need so much help right here."

Serchio cocked his head to the side, listening. "That's our boarding announcement. Thank you for the tickets." He bent to collect their luggage.

Holluth put *Hank the Cow Dog* back into his canvas book bag and came over to politely shake my hand. I told him to hold his bag open and I tucked my tarot deck inside it, next to *Where the Wild Things Are.* Then he stumped up the steps after Serchio and not long after the bus roared and shook and backed away, swinging into the lane leading down out of the terminal.

I guess a person on a spirit journey doesn't hug the power-people who consent to help him on his way. Some of them must be a lot more prickly than I am. Maybe they carry bigger shadows around.

"INCREDIBLE," ALEC SAID. "Just like that? You put them on a *bus?"*

"That's right," I said.

"I don't understand why you're leaving town too." Alec nudged my suitcase dubiously with his foot, as if he thought I might have an anaconda in there. "You know how dangerous it is to travel. My parents will come down on me like a ton of bricks for just letting you go like this. Where are you going? *Why* are you going?"

My things were packed up and stored in John's basement, my bank account was emptied. The travel permit that should have taken me to Ashland is on its way to Mexico in Serchio's pocket. Bella says I'm crazy, that Homesec will catch me. I don't know how to explain that my shadow hides me. Out of sight, out of mind, does have its uses, it seems.

She arrived at my door yesterday, out of breath and damp

from climbing my stairs, fierce with curiosity. "Is John taking you on some New Age pilgrimage or something?"

I said, "Not John, no."

Bella gave me a wounded look. "I don't get it. Where are you going, then?"

"Out of New York, for starters."

She sighed and folded me in a pillowy hug. "I'll miss you, Edie," she said. She will, too, for a day or so.

And I'll miss her, but the one I'll miss the most is John. I miss him already. He has a nervous tremor in his hands now and he won't look me in the eye. The magic he'd yearned for all these years was much kinder and warmer than what actually came to him at the bookstore; when that wild magic called, he shrank back.

I saw that happen, I saw him age into a different man, older and afraid. He can't forgive me for having seen that.

I don't even know how to tell him how sorry I am.

The Fool; Judgment; the six of Cups; the Magician; The Tower; and Death. The practice spread that day last spring was mine. The Magician, with no magical falcon in attendance, was me. I was the Fool, too, acting on impulse over a child, the six of Cups.

Death? Well, my life has certainly changed course. This evening, I'll head uptown on Fifth and catch one of the express buses that take commuters out of Manhattan, and then I'll take a train further. No one will give me a second glance, a middle-aged woman reading a paperback on the local.

I have the small, gray feather that Holluth pressed into my palm when he shook my hand before boarding the southbound bus. This morning, I stood on my roof and tossed that feather up in the air. It drifted down and settled pointing north. So north I'll go, as long as my money and my health hold out.

It may be that I'll come upon someone, somewhere, who'll be glad to share the shelter and the shield of my Saturn affliction.

LISTENING TO BRAHMS

ENTRY 1: THEY HAD ALREADY WOKEN UP Chandler and Ross. They did me third. I was supposed to be up first so I could check the data on the rest of our crew during their cold sleep, but how would a bunch of aliens know that?

Our ship is full of creatures with peculiar eyes and wrinkled skin covered with tiny scales, a lot like lizards walking around on their hind legs. Their skins are grayish or greenish or even bluish sometimes. They have naked-looking faces—no hair—with features that seem polished smooth. The first ones I met had wigs on, and they wore evening clothes and watered-silk sashes with medals. I was too numb-brained to laugh, and now I don't feel like it.

They all switched to jumpsuits once the formalities were over. I keep waiting for them to unzip their jumpsuits and then their lizard suits and climb out, regular human beings. I keep waiting for the joke to be over.

They speak English, some with accents, some not. They have breathy voices and talk very softly to us. That may be because of what they have to say. They say Earth burned itself up, which is why we never got our wake-up signal and were still in the freezer when they found us. Chandler believes them. Ross doesn't. I won't know what the others think until they're unfrozen.

I sit looking through the view plate at Earth, such as it is. I know what the lizards say is true, but I don't think I really believe it. I think mostly that I'm dead or having a terrible dream.

ENTRY 2: Steinbrunner killed himself (despite their best efforts to prevent anything like that, the lizards say). Sue Anne Beamish, fifth to be thawed, won't talk to anybody. She grits her teeth all the time. I can hear them grinding whenever she's around. It's very annoying.

The lead lizard's name is Captain Midnight. He says he knows it's not the most appropriate name for a space-flight commander, but he likes the sound of it.

It seems that on their home planet the lizards have been fielding our various Earth transmissions, both radio and TV, and they borrow freely from what they've found there. They are given native names at birth, but if they feel like it later they take Earth-type names instead. Those on Captain Midnight's ship all have Earth-type names. Luckily the names are pretty memorable, because I can't tell one alien from another except by the name badges they wear on their jumpsuits.

I look at them sometimes and I wonder if I'm crazy. Can't afford to be, not if I've got to deal on a daily basis with things that look as if they walked out of a Walt Disney cartoon feature.

They revive us one by one and try to make sure nobody else cuts their wrists like Steinbrunner. He cut the way that can't be fixed.

I look out the viewplate at what's left of the earth and let the talk slide over me. We can't raise anything from down there. I can't raise anything inside me either. I can only look and look and let the talk slide over me. Could I be dead after all? I feel dead.

ENTRY 3: Captain Midnight says now that we're all up he would be honored beyond expression if we would consent to come back to Kondra with him and his crew in their ship. *Kondra* is their name for their world. Chu says she's worked out where and what it is in our terms, and she keeps trying to show me on the star charts. I don't look; I don't care. I came up here to do studies on cryogenic nutrition in space, not to look at star charts.

It doesn't matter what I came up here to do. Earth is a moon with a moon now. "Nutrition" doesn't mean anything, not in connection with anything human. There's nothing to nourish. There's just this airless rock, like all the other airless rocks rolling around in space.

I took the data the machines recorded about us while we slept and I junked it. Chu says I did a lot of damage to some of our equipment in the process. I didn't set out to do that, but it felt good, or something like good, to go on from wiping out information to smashing metal. I've assured everybody that I won't break out like that again. It doesn't accomplish anything, and I felt foolish afterward. I'm not sure they believe me. I'm not sure I believe my own promise.

Morris and Myers say they won't go with the Kondrai. They say they want to stay here in our vessel just in case something happens down there or in case some other space mission survived and shows up looking for whatever's left, which is probably only us.

Captain Midnight says they can rig a beacon system on our craft to attract anybody who does come around and let them know where we've gone. I can tell the lizards are not going to let Morris and Myers stay here and die.

They say, the Kondrai do, that they didn't actually come here for us. After several generations of receiving and enjoying Earth's transmissions, Kondran authorities decided to borrow a ship from a neighboring world and send Earth an embassy from Kondra, a mission of goodwill.

First contact at last, and there's nobody here but the seven of us. Tough on the Kondrai. They expected to find a whole worldful of us, glued to our screens and speakers. Tough shit all around.

I have dreams so terrible there are no words.

Entry 4: There's nothing for us to do on the Kondran ship, which is soft and leathery inside its alloy shell. I have long talks with Walter Drake, who is head of mission. Walter Drake is female, I think. Walter Duck.

If I can make a joke, does that mean I'm crazy?

It took me a while to figure out what was wrong with the name. Then I said, "Look, it's Sir Walter *Raleigh* or Sir *Francis* Drake."

She said, "But we don't always just copy. I have chosen to commemorate two great voyagers."

I said, "And they were both males."

She said, "That's why I dropped the *Sir*."

Afterward I can't believe these conversations. I resent the end of the world; my world, coming on as a bad joke with Edgar Rice Burroughs aliens.

Myers and Morris play chess with each other all day and won't talk to anybody. Most of us don't like to talk to each other right now. We can't look in each other's eyes, for some reason. There's an excuse in the case of not looking the lizards in the eyes. They have this nictitating membrane. It's unsettling to look at that.

All the lizards speak English and at least one other Earth

language. Walter Drake says there are several native languages on Kondra, but they aren't spoken in the population centers anymore. Kondran culture, in its several major branches, is very old. It was once greater and more complex than our own, she says, but then it got simple again and the population began to drop. The whole species was, in effect, beginning to close down.

When our signals were first picked up, something else began to happen: a growing trend toward population increase and a young generation fascinated by Earth culture. The older Kondrai, who had gone back to living like their ancestors in the desert, didn't object. They said fine, let the youngsters do as they choose as long as they let the oldsters do likewise.

I had to walk away when Walter Drake told me about this. It started me thinking about my own people I left back on Earth, all dead now. I won't put their names down. I was crying. Now I've stopped, and I don't want to start again. It makes my eyes hurt.

Walter Drake brought me some tapes of music that they've recorded from our broadcasts. The Kondrai collect our signals, everything they can, through something they call the Retrieval Project. They reconstruct the broadcasts and record them and store the recordings in a huge library for study. Our classical music has a great following there.

I've been listening to some Bach partitas. My mother played the piano. She sometimes played Bach.

Entry 5: Sibelius, Symphony No. 2 in D, Op. 43. Tchaikovsky, Variations on a Rococo Theme, Op. 33. Rachmaninoff, Symphonic Dances, Op. 45. Mozart, Clarinet Quintet in A major, K581. Sibelius, Symphony No. 2 in D, Op. 43. Sibelius, Symphony No. 2 in D, Op. 43.

Entry 6: Chandler is alive, Ross is alive, Beamish is alive, Chu is alive, Morris is alive, Myers is alive, and I am alive. But that doesn't count. I mean I can't count it. Up. To mean anything. *Why* are we alive?

Entry 7: Myers swallowed a chess piece. The lizards operated on him somehow and saved his life.

Entry 8: Woke up from a dream wondering if maybe we did die in our ship and my "waking life" in the Kondran ship is really just some kind of after-death hallucination. Suppose I died, suppose we all actually died at the same moment Earth died? It wouldn't make any difference. Earth's people are all dead and someplace else or nowhere, but we are *here*. We are separate.

They're in contact with their home planet all the time. Chu is fascinated by their communications technology, which is wild, she says. Skips over time or folds up space—I don't know, I'm just a nutrition expert. Apparently on Kondra now they are making up their own human-style names instead of lifting them ready-made. (Walter Drake was a pioneer in this, I might point out.) Captain Midnight has changed his name. He is henceforth to be known as Vernon Zeno Ellerman.

Bruckner and Mahler symphonies, over and over, fill a lot of time. Walter Drake says she is going to get me some fresh music, though I haven't asked for any.

ENTRY 9: Beamish came and had a talk with me. She looked fierce.

"Listen, Flynn," she said, "we're not going to give up."

"Give up what?" I said.

"Don't be so obtuse," she said between her teeth. "The human race isn't ended as long as even a handful of us are still alive and kicking."

I am alive, though I don't know why (I now honestly do not recall the exact nature of the experiments I was onboard our craft to conduct). I'm not sure I'm kicking, and I told her so.

She grinned and patted my knee. "Don't worry about it, Flynn. I don't mean you should take up where you left off with Lily Chu." That happened back in training. I didn't even remember it until Beamish said this. "Nobody's capable right now, which is just as well. Besides, the women in this group are not going to be anybody's goddamn brood mares, science-fiction traditions to the contrary."

"Oh," I said. I think.

She went on to say that the Kondrai have or can borrow the technology to develop children for us in vitro. All we have to do is furnish the raw materials.

I said fine. I had developed another terrible headache. I've been having headaches lately.

After she left I tried some music. Walter Drake got me *Boris Godunov*, but I can't listen to it. I can't listen to anything with people's voices. I don't know how to tell this to Walter Drake. Don't want to tell her. It's none of her business anyhow.

Entry 10: Chu and Morris are sleeping together. So much for Beamish's theory that nobody is capable. With Myers not up to playing chess yet, I guess Morris had to find something to do.

Chu said to me, "I'm sorry, Michael."

I felt this little, far-off sputtering like anger somewhere deep down, and then it went out. "That's okay," I said. And it is.

Chandler has been spending all his time in the communications cell of the ship with another lizard, one with a French name that I can't remember. Chandler tells us he's learning a lot about Kondran life. I tune him out when he talks like this. I never go to the communications cell. The whole thing gives me a headache. Everything gives me a headache except music.

Entry 11: I was sure it would be like landing in some kind of imitation world, a hodgepodge of phony bits and pieces copied from Earth. That's why I wouldn't go out for two K-days after we landed.

Everybody was very understanding. Walter Drake stayed on board with me.

"We have fixed up a nice hotel where you can all be together," she told me, "like the honored guests that you are."

I finally got off and went with the others when she gave me the music recordings to take with me. She got me a playback machine. I left the Mozart clarinet quintet behind, and she found it and brought it after me. But I won't listen to it. The clarinet sound was made by somebody's living breath, somebody who's dead now, like all of them. I can't stand to hear that sound.

The hotel was in a suburb of a city, which looked a little like LA, though not as much as I had expected. Later sometime I should try to describe the city. There's a hilly part, something like San Francisco, by the sea. We asked to go over there instead. They found us a sort of rooming house of painted wood with a basement. Morris and Chu have taken the top floor, though I don't think they sleep together anymore.

Ross has the apartment next door to me. She's got her own problems. She threw up when she first set foot on Kondra. She throws up almost every day, says she can't help it.

There are invitations for us to go meet the locals and participate in this and that, but the lizards do not push. They are so damned considerate and respectful. I don't go anywhere. I stay in my room and listen to music. Handel helps me sleep.

ENTRY 12: Four and a half K-years have passed. I stopped doing this log because Chandler showed me his. He was keeping a detailed record of what was happening to us, what had happened, what he thought was going to happen. Then Beamish circulated her version, and Dr. Birgit Nilson, the lizard in charge of our mental health, started encouraging us all to contribute what we could to a "living history" project.

I was embarrassed to show anybody my comments. I am not a writer or an artist like Myers has turned out to be. (His pictures are in huge demand here, and he has a whole flock of Kondran students.) If Chandler and Beamish were writing everything down, why should I waste my time doing the same thing?

Living history of what, for whom?

Also I didn't like what Chandler wrote about me and Walter Drake. Yes, I slept with her. One of us would have tried it, sooner or later, with one lizard or another. I just happened to be the one who did. I had better reasons than any of the others. Walter Drake had been very kind to me.

I was capable all right (still am). But the thought of going to bed with Lily or Sue Anne made my skin creep, though I couldn't have said why. On the Kondran ship I used to jerk off and look at the stuff in my hand and wonder what the hell it was doing there: Didn't my body know that my world is gone, my race, my species?

Sex with Walter Drake is different from sex with a woman. That's part of what I like about it. And another thing. Walter Drake doesn't cry in her sleep.

Walter and I did all right. For a couple of years I went traveling alone, at the government's expense—like everything we do here—all over Kondra. Walter was waiting when I got back. So we went to live together away from the rooming house. The time passed like a story or a dream. Not much sticks in my head now from that period. We listened to a lot of music together. Nothing with flutes or clarinet, though. String music, percussion, piano music, horns only if they're blended with other sounds—that's what I like. Lots of light stuff, Dukas and Vivaldi and Milhaud.

Anyway, that period is over. After all this time Chu and Morris have committed suicide together. They used a huge old pistol one of them must have smuggled all this way. Morris, probably. He always had a macho hang-up.

Beamish goes around saying, "Why? Why?" At first I thought this was the stupidest question I'd ever heard. I was seriously worried that maybe these years on Kondran food and water had addled her mind through some kind of allergic reaction.

Then she said, "We're so close, Flynn. Why couldn't they have waited? I wouldn't have let them down."

I keep forgetting about her in vitro project. It's going well, she says. She works very hard with a whole team of Kondrai under Dr. Boleslav Singh, preparing a cultural surround for the babies she's developing. She comes in exhausted from long discussions with Dr. Boleslav Singh and Dr. Birgit Nilson and others about the balance of Earth information and Kondran information to be given to the human babies. Beamish wants to make little visitors out of the babies. She says it's providential that we were found by the Kondrai—a race that has neatly caught and preserved everything transmitted by us about our own culture and our past. So now all that stuff is just waiting to be used, she says, to bridge the gap in our race's history.

"The gap," that's what she calls it.

She has a long-range plan of getting a ship for the in vitros to use when they grow up and want to go find a planet they can turn into another Earth. This seems crazy to me. But she is entitled. We all are.

I've moved back into the rooming house. I feel it's my duty, now that we're so few. Walter has come with me.

Entry 13: Mozart's piano concertos, especially Alfred Brendel's renditions, all afternoon. I have carried out my mission after all—to answer the question: What does a frozen Earthman eat for breakfast? The answer is music. For lunch? Music. Dinner? Music. This frozen Earthman stays alive on music.

Entry 14: A year and a half together in the rooming house, and Walter Drake and I have split up. Maybe it has nothing to do with being in the rooming house with the other humans. Divorce is becoming very common among young Kondrai. So is something like hair. They used to wear wigs. Now they have developed a means of growing featherlike down on their heads and in their armpits, etc.

When Walter came in with a fine dusting of pale fuzz on her pate, I told her to pack up and get out. She says she understands, she's not bitter.

She doesn't understand one goddamned thing.

Entry 15: Beamish's babies, which I never went to see, have died of an infection that whipped through the whole lot of them in three days. The Kondran medical team taking care of them caught it, too, though none of them died. A few are blind from it, perhaps permanently.

Myers took pictures of the little corpses. He is making paintings from his photos. Did I put in here that swallowing a chess piece did not kill Myers? Maybe it should have, but it seems nothing can kill Myers. He is as tough as rawhide. But he doesn't play chess, not since Morris killed himself. There are Kondrai who play very well, but Myers refuses their invitations. You can say that for him at least.

He just takes photographs and paints.

I'm not really too sorry about the babies. I don't know which would be worse, seeing them grow up as a little clutch of homeless aliens among the lizards or seeing them adapt and become pseudo-Kondrai. I don't like to think about explaining to them how the world they really belong to blew itself to hell. (Lily Chu is the one who went over the signals the Kondrai salvaged about that and sorted out the sequence of events. That was right before she killed herself.) We slept through the end of our world. Bad enough to do it, worse to have to talk about it. I never talk about it now, not even with the Kondrai.

With Dr. Birgit Nilson I discuss food, of course, and health. I find these boring and absurd subjects, though I cooperate out of politeness. I also don't want to get stuck on health problems, like Chandler, who has gone through one hypochondriacal frenzy after another in the past few years.

Beamish says she will try again. Nothing will stop her. She confided to Ross that she thinks the Kondrai deliberately let the babies die, maybe even infected them on purpose. "They don't want us to revive our race," she said to Ross. "They're trying to take our place. Why should they encourage the return of the real thing?"

Ross told me Beamish wants her to help arrange some kind of escape from Kondra, God knows to where. Ross is worried about Beamish. "What," she says, "if she goes off the deep end and knifes some innocent lizard medico? They might lock us all up permanently."

Ross does not want to be locked up. She plays the cello all the time, which used to be a hobby of hers. The lizards were only too pleased to furnish her an instrument. A damn good one, too, she says. What's more, she now has three Kondrai studying with her.

I don't care what she does. I walk around watching the Kondrai behave like us.

I have terrible dreams, still.

Symphonic music doesn't do it for me anymore, not even Sibelius. I can't hear enough of the music itself; there are too many voices. I listen to chamber pieces. There you can hear each sound, everything that happens between each sound and each other sound near it.

They gave me a free pass to the Library of the Retrieval Project. I spend a lot of time there, listening.

ENTRY 16: Fourteen K-years later. Beamish eventually did get three viable Earth-style children out of her last lot. Two of them drowned in a freak accident at the beach a week ago. The third one, a girl named Melissa, ran away. They haven't been able to find her.

Our tissue contributions no longer respond, though Beamish keeps trying. She calls the Kondrai "Snakefaces" behind their backs.

Her hair is gray. So is mine.

Kondran news is all about the growing tensions between Kondra and the neighbor world it does most of its trading with. I don't know how that used to work in economic terms, except that borrowing and swapping figured pretty largely. Apparently it's all begun to break down. I never saw any of the inhabitants of that world, called Chadondal, except in pictures and Kondran TV news reports. Now I guess I never will. I don't care.

Something funny happened with the flu that killed all of Beamish's first babies. It seems to have mutated into something that afflicts the Kondrai the way cancer used to afflict human beings. This disease doesn't respond to the cure human researchers developed once they figured out that our cancer was actually a set of symptoms of an underlying disease. Kondran cancer is something all their own.

They are welcome to it.

ENTRY 17: I went up into the sandhills to have a look at a few of the Old Kondrai, the ones who never did buy into imitating Earth ways. Most of them don't talk English (they don't even talk much Kondran to each other), but they don't seem to mind if you hang around and watch them a while.

They live alone or else in very small settlements on a primitive level, pared down to basics. Your individual Old Kondran will have a small, roundish stone house or even a burrow or cave and will go fetch water every day and cook on a little cell-powered stove or a wood fire. They usually don't even have TV. They walk around looking at things or sit and meditate or dig in their flower gardens or carve things out of the local wood. Once in a while they'll get together for a dance or a sort of mass bask in the sun or to put on plays and skits and so on. These performances can go on for days. They have a sort of swap economy, which is honored elsewhere when they travel. You sometimes see these pilgrims in the city streets, just wandering around. They never stay long.

Some of the younger Kondrai have begun harking back to this sort of life, trying to create the same conditions in the cities, which is ridiculous. These youngsters act as if it's something absolutely basic they have to try to hang on to in the face of an invasion of alien ways. Earth ways.

This is obviously a backlash against the effects of the Retrieval Project. I keep an eye on developments. It's all fascinating and actually creepy. To me the backlash is uncannily reminiscent of those fundamentalist-nationalist movements—Christian American or Middle-Eastern Muslim or whatever—that made life such hell for so many people toward the end of our planet's life. But if you point this resemblance out, the anti-Retrieval Kondrai get furious because, after all, anything Earth-like is what they're reacting against.

I sometimes bring this up in conversation just to get a rise out of them.

If I'm talking to Kondrai who are part of the backlash, they insist that they're just trying to turn back to old, native ways. They don't recognize this passion itself as something that humans, not Kondrai, were prone to. From what I can gather and observe, fervor, either reactionary or progressive, is alien to native Kondran culture as it was before they started retrieving our signals. Their life was very quiet and individualized and pretty dull, as a matter of fact.

Sometimes I wish we'd found it like that instead of the way it had already become by the time we got here. Of course the Old Kondrai never would have sent us an embassy in the first place.

I talk to Dr. Birgit Nilson about all this a lot. We aren't exactly friends, but we communicate pretty well for a man and a lizard.

She says they have simply used human culture to revitalize themselves.

I think about the Old Kondrai I saw poking around, growing the kind of flowers that attract the flying grazers they eat, or just sitting. I like that better. If they were a dying culture, they should have just gone ahead and died.

Entry 18: Ross has roped Chandler into her music making. Turns out he played the violin as a kid. They practice a lot in the rooming house. Sometimes Ross plays the piano. She's better on the cello. I sit on my porch, looking at the bay, and I listen.

Ross says the Kondrai as a group are fascinated by performance. Certainly they perform being human better and better all the time. They think of Earth's twentieth century as the Golden Age of Human Performance. How would they know? It's all secondhand here, everything.

I've been asked to join a nutritional-study team heading for Kondra-South, where some trouble spots are developing. I have declined. I don't care if they starve or why they starve. I had enough of looking at images of starvation on Earth, where we did it on a terrific scale. What a performance that was!

Also I don't want to leave here because then I wouldn't get to hear Ross and Chandler play. They do sonatas and duets and they experiment, not always very successfully, with adapting music written for other instruments. It's very interesting. Now that Ross is playing the piano as well as the cello, their repertoire has been greatly expanded.

They aren't nearly as good as the great musical performers of the Golden Age, of course. But I listen to them anyway whenever I can. There's something about live music. You get a hunger for it.

Entry 19: Myers has gone on a world tour. He is so famous as an artist that he has rivals, and there are rival schools led by artists he himself has trained. He spends all his time with the snakes now, the ones masquerading as artists and critics and aesthetes. He hardly ever stops at the rooming house or comes by here to visit.

Sue Anne Beamish and I have set up house together across the bay from the rooming house. She's needed somebody around her ever since they found the desiccated corpse of little Melissa in the rubbish dump and worked out what had been done to her.

The Kondran authorities say they think some of the Kondrachalikipon (as the anti-Retrieval-backlash members call themselves now, meaning "return to Kondran essence") were responsible. The idea is that these Kondracha meant what they did as a symbolic rejection of everything the Retrieval Project has retrieved and a warning that Kondra will not be turned into an imitation Earth without a fight.

When Dr. Birgit Nilson and I talked about this, I pointed out that the Kondracha, if it was them, didn't get it right. They should have dumped the kid's body on the Center House steps and then called a press conference. Next time they'll do it better, though, being such devoted students of our ways.

"I know" she said. "What is becoming of us?"

Us meant "us Kondrai," of course, not her and me. She likes to think that we Earth guests have a special wisdom that comes from our loss and from a mystical blood connection with the culture that the Kondrai are absorbing. As if I spend my time thinking about that kind of thing. Dr. Birgit Nilson is a romantic.

I don't talk to Sue Anne about Melissa's death. I don't feel it enough, and she would know that. So many died before, what's one more kid's death now? A kid who could never have been human anyway because a human being is born on Earth and raised in a human society, like Sue Anne and me.

"We should have blown their ship up and us with it," she says, "on the way here."

She won't come with me to the rooming house to listen to Ross and Chandler play. They give informal concert evenings now. I go, even though the audience is 98 percent lizard, because by now I know every recording of chamber music in the Retrieval Library down to the last scrape of somebody's chair during a live recital. The recordings are too faithful. I can just about tolerate the breath intake you hear sometimes when the first violinist cues a phrase.

It's different with Ross and Chandler. Their live music makes the live sounds all right.

Concerts are given by Kondran "artists" all the time, but I won't go to those.

For one thing, I know perfectly well that we don't hear sounds, we human beings, not sounds from outside. Our inner ear vibrates to the sound from outside, and we hear the sound that our own ear creates inside the head in response to that vibration. Now, how can the Kondran ear be exactly the same as ours? No matter how closely they've learned to mimic the sounds that our musicians produced, Kondran ears can't be hearing what human ears do when human music is played. A Kondran concert of human music is a farce.

Poor Myers. He missed the chance to take pictures of Melissa's dead body so he could make paintings of it later.

ENTRY 20: They are saying that the reason there's so much crime and violence now on Kondra isn't because of the population explosion at all. Some snake who calls himself Swami Nanda has worked out how the demographic growth is only a sign of the underlying situation.

According to him Kondra made an "astral agreement" to take in not only us living human survivors but the souls of all the dead of Earth. Earth souls on the astral plane, seeing that there were soon going to be no more human bodies on Earth to get born into, sent out a call for new bodies and a new world to inhabit. The Kondran souls on the astral plane, having pretty much finished their work on the material world of Kondra, agreed to let human souls take over the physical plant here, as it were. Now the younger generation is all Earth souls reborn as Kondrai on this planet, and they're re-creating conditions familiar to them from Earth.

I have sent this "Swami" four furious letters. He answered the last one very politely and at great length, explaining it all very clearly with the words he has stolen for his stolen metaphysical concepts.

Oh, yes: Another dozen K-years have passed. I might as well just say years. Kondran years are only a few days off our own, and Chandler has stopped keeping his Earth-time calendar since he's gotten so deep into music.

Chandler is now doing some composing, Ross tells me.

Ross rebukes me when I call the Kondrai snakes, talking to me as gently and reasonably as the Kondrai themselves always talk to us. That makes me sick, which is pretty funny when I recall how she used to vomit every day when we first came here. So she can stop telling me how to talk and warning me that it's no good to be a recluse. No good for what? And what would be better?

Nobody ever taught me to play any instrument. My parents said I had no talent, and they were right. I'm a listener, so I listen. I'm doing my job. I wouldn't go to the rooming house and talk to Ross at all except for the music. They are getting really good. It's amazing. Once in a while I spend a week at the Retrieval Library listening to the really great performances that are recorded there, to make sure my taste hasn't become degraded.

It hasn't. My two crewmates are converting themselves, by some miracle of dedication, into fine performers.

Last night I had to walk out in the middle of a Beethoven sonata to be alone.

Entry 21: Sue Anne had a stroke last week. She is paralyzed down her left side. I am staying with her almost constantly because I know she can't stand having the snakes around her anymore.

She blames me, I know, for having cooperated with them. We all spent hours and hours with their researchers, filling out their information about our dead planet. How could we have refused? In the face of their courtesy and considering how worried we all were about forgetting Earth ourselves, how could we? Besides, we really had nothing else to do.

She blames me anyhow, but I don't mind.

A wave of self-immolation is going on among young Kondrai. They find themselves an audience and set themselves afire, and the watching Kondrai generally stand there as if hypnotized by the flames and do nothing.

Dr. Birgit Nilson told me, "Your entire population died out; many of them burnt up in an instant. This created much karma, and those who are responsible must be allowed to pay."

"You're a Nandist, then," I said. "Swami Nanda and his reincarnation crap."

"I see no other explanation," she said.

"It all makes sense to you?" I said.

"Yes." She stroked her cheek with her orange-polished talons. "It's a loan: We have lent our beautiful material world and our species' bodies in exchange for your energetic souls and your rich, passionate culture."

They are the crazy ones, not us.

Entry 22: Some wild-eyed young snake with his top feathers dyed blue took a shot at the swami this morning with an old-fashioned thorn gun.

They caught him. We watched on the news. The would-be assassin sneers at the camera like a real Earth punk. Sue Anne glares back and snorts derisively.

Entry 23: Dreamed of my mother at her piano, but her hands were Kondran hands. The fingers were too long, and the nails were set like claws, and her skin was covered in minute, grayish scales.

I think she was playing Chopin.

Entry 24: Sometimes I wish I were a writer, to do all this justice. I might have some function as a survivor.

Look at Sue Anne: Except for some terrible luck, she would have created out of us a new posterity.

Myers is doing prints these days, but not on Earth themes

anymore, though the Kondrai beg him to concentrate on what's native to him. He says his memory of Earth is no longer trustworthy, and besides, images of Kondra are native to the eyes of reborn Earth souls now. He accepts Nandism openly and goes around doing Kondran landscapes and portraits and so on. Well, nobody will have to miss any of that in my account, then. They can always look at Myers's pictures.

Walter Drake died last winter of Kondran cancer. I went to the funeral. For the first time I wore makeup.

Myers, the arrogant son of a bitch, condescended to share a secret with me. He used this face paint, plus a close haircut or a feathered cap, to go out incognito among the snakes so he can observe them undisturbed. Age has smoothed his features and made him thin, like most Kondrai, and he's been getting away with it for years. Well, good for him. Look at what *they're* trying to get away with along those lines!

Being disguised has its advantages. I hadn't realized the pressure of being stared at all the time in public until I moved around without it.

They said, "Ashes to ashes and dust to dust," and I got dizzy and had to sit down on a bench.

Entry 25: Four more years. My heart still checks out, Dr. Birgit Nilson tells me. I put on makeup and hang out in the bars, watching TV with the Kondrai, but not too often. Sometimes they make me so damn nervous, even after so long here. I forget what they are and what I am. I forget myself. I get scared that I'm turning senile.

When I get home Sue Anne gives me this cynical look, and my perspective is restored. I play copy-tapes of Dvorák for her. Also Schubert. She likes the French, though. I find them superficial.

To hear Brahms and Beethoven and Mozart, I go to the rooming house. I go whenever Ross and Chandler play. While the music sounds the constant crying inside me gets so big and so painful and beautiful that I can't contain it. So it moves outside me for a while, and I feel rested and changed. This is only an illusion, but wonderful.

Entry 26: Poor Myers got caught in a religious riot on the other side of the world. He was beaten to death by a Kondracha mob. I guess his makeup job was careless. Dr. Birgit Nilson, much aged and using a cane, came to make a personal apology, which I accepted for old times' sake.

"We caught two of them," she said. "The ringleaders of the Kondracha group that killed your poor Mr. Myers."

"Kondrachalations," I said. Couldn't help myself.

Dr. Birgit looked at me. "Forgive me," she said. "I shouldn't have come."

When I told Sue Anne about this, she slapped my face. She hasn't much strength even in her good arm these days. But I resented being hit and asked her why she did it.

"Because you were smiling, Michael."

"You can't cry all the time," I said.

"No," she said. "I wish we could."

Dr. Birgit Nilson says that Kondrai are now composing music in classical, popular, and "primitive" styles, all modeled on Earth music. I have not heard any of this new music. I do not want to.

ENTRY 27: At least Sue Anne didn't live to see this: They are now grafting lobes onto their ugly ear holes.

No, that's not the real news. The real news is about KondraSouth, where a splinter group of Kondracha extremists set up a sort of purist, Ur-Kondran state some years ago. They use only their version of Old Kondran farming methods, which is apparently not an accurate version. Their topsoil has been rapidly washing away in the summer floods.

Now they are killing newborns down there to have fewer mouths to feed. The pretext is that these newborns look like humans and are part of the great taint that everything Earthish represents to the pure. The official Kondrachalikipon line is that they are feeding themselves just fine, thank you. The truth seems to be mass starvation and infanticide.

After Sue Anne died, I moved back into the rooming house. I have a whole floor to myself and scarcely ever go out. I watch Kondran TV a lot, which is how I keep track of their politics and so on. I keep looking for false notes that would reveal to any intelligent observer the hollowness of their performance of humanity. There isn't much except for my gut reaction. The Kondran claim to have preserved human culture by making it their own would be very convincing to anyone who didn't know better.

Even their game shows look familiar. Young Kondrai go mad for music videos and deafening concerts by their own groups like the Bear Minimum and Dead Boring. I stare and stare at the screen, looking for slipups. I am not sure that I would recognize one now if I saw one.

I hate the lizards. I miss her. I hate them.

ENTRY 28: Ross and Chandler have done the unthinkable. At last night's musicale they sprang one hell of a surprise.

They have trained two young Kondrai to a degree that satisfies them (particularly Gillokan Chukchonturanfis, who plays both violin and viola).

Now the four of them are planning to go out and perform in public together as the Retrieval String Quartet.

The Lost Earth String Quartet I could stomach, maybe. Or the Ghost String Quartet, or the Remnant String Quartet. But then, of course, how could Kondran musicians be in it?

I walked out in protest.

Ross says I am being unreasonable and cutting off my nose to spite my face, since as a quartet they have so much more music they can play.

To hell with Ross. The traitress. Chandler, too.

ENTRY 29: I cut my hair and put on my makeup and managed to get myself one ticket, not as Michael Flynn the Earthman but as a nameless Kondran. The debut concert of the Retrieval String Quartet is the event of the year in the city: a symbol of the passing of the torch of human culture, they say. An outrage, the Kondracha scream. I keep my thoughts to myself and lay my plans.

Lizards are pouring into the city for the event. Two bombings have already occurred, credit for them claimed by the Kondrachalikipon, of course.

As long as the scaly bastards don't blow me up before I do my job.

The gun is in my pocket, Morris's gun that I took after he and Chu killed themselves. I was a good shot once. My seat is close to the stage and on the aisle, leaving my right hand free. I have had too much bitterness in my life. I will not be mocked and betrayed in the one place where I find some comfort.

ENTRY 30: Now I know who I wrote all this for. Dear Dr. Herbert Akonditichilka: You do not know me. Until a little while ago I didn't know you either. I am the man who sat next to you in Carnegie Hall last night. Your Kondran version of Carnegie Hall, that is: constructed from TV pictures; all sparkling in crystal and cream and red velvet—handsomer than the real place was, but in my judgment slightly inferior acoustically.

You didn't notice me, Doctor, because of my makeup. I noticed you. All evening I noticed everything, starting with the police and the Kondracha demonstration outside the hall. But you I noticed in particular. You managed to wreck my concentration during the last piece of fine music I expected to hear in my life.

It was the Haydn String Quartet Number One in G, Opus 77. I sat trying to hear the effect of having two Kondrai among the players, but your damned fidgeting distracted me. *Just my luck*, I thought. *A Kondran who came for a historic event, though he has no feeling for classical Earth music at all.* All through the Haydn you sat locked tight except for these tiny, spasmodic movements of your head, arms, and hands. It was a great relief to me when the music ended and you joined the crashing applause. I was so busy glaring at you that I missed seeing the musicians leave the stage.

I watched you all through the interval. I needed something to fix my attention on while I waited. The second piece was to be one of my favorites, the Brahms String Quartet Number Two in A minor, Opus 51. I had chosen the opening of that quartet as my signal. I meant to see to it that the Brahms would never be played by the traitors Ross and Chandler and the two snakes they had trained. In fact, no one was ever going to hear Ross and Chandler play anything again.

What would happen to me afterward I didn't know or care (though it crossed my mind in a farcical moment that I might be rescued as a hero by the Kondracha).

I wondered if you would be a problem—an effective interference, once the first note of the Brahms piece sounded and I began to make my move. I thought not.

You were small and thin, Dr. Akonditichilka, neatly dressed in your fake blazer with the fake gold buttons; a thick thatch of white top feathers; a round face, for a lizard; and glasses that made your eyes enormous. I wondered if you had ruined your eyesight studying facsimile texts taken from Earth transmissions. I could see by the grayed-off skin color that you were elderly, like so many in this audience, though probably not as old as I am.

You fell into conversation with the Kondran on your left. I realized from what I could overhear that the two of you had met for the first time earlier that same day. She was now exploring the contact. "Oh," she said, "you're a doctor?"

"Retired," you said.

"You must meet Mischa Two Hawks," she said, "my escort tonight. He's a retired doctor, too."

The seat to her left was empty. Retired doctor Mischa Two Hawks may have withdrawn to the men's room or gone out in the lobby for a smoke.

You must understand; my mind made automatic translations as fast as the thought finished: Imitation retired, imitation doctor Mischa S. (for Stolen names) Two Hawks was in the imitation men's room or smoking an imitation cigarette.

His companion, an imitation woman in a green, imitation wool dress, wore a white wig with a blue-rinse tint. God, how Beamish used to rage over the tendency of Kondran females to choose the most traditional women's styles as models! Beamish would have been proud of my work tonight, I thought.

Green Wool Dress, whose name I had not caught, said to you, "The lady with you this afternoon at the gallery—is she your wife? And where is she tonight?"

You shook your head, and your glasses flashed. It pleases me that the nictitating membrane prevents you snakes from wearing contact lenses.

"We used to go to every concert in the city together," you said. "We both love good music, and there is no replacement for hearing it live. But she's been losing her hearing. She doesn't go anymore; it's too painful for her."

"What a pity," Green Wool Dress said. "To miss such a great event! Wasn't the first violinist wonderful just now? And, so young, too. It was amazing to hear him."

Damned right it was. Chandler had literally played second fiddle to his own student, Chukchonturanfis. For that alone I could have killed my old crewmate.

I shut my eyes and thought about the gun in my pocket. It was a heavy goddamned thing. I thought about the danger of getting it caught in the cloth as I pulled it out, of missing my aim, of my elderly self being jumped by you two elderly aliens before I could complete my job. I thought of Chandler and Ross, no spring chickens themselves anymore, soon to die and leave me alone among you. The whole thing was a sort of doddering comedy.

Another Kondran, heavyset for a lizard and bald, worked his way along the row of seats. He hovered next to Green Wool Dress, clearly wanting to sit down. She wouldn't let him until she had made introductions. This was, of course, retired doctor Mischa Two Hawks.

"Alkonditichilka," you said with a little bow. "Herbert." And the two of you shook hands across Green Wool Dress. All three of you settled back to chat.

Suddenly I heard your voices as music. You, Doctor, were the first violin, with your clear, light tenor. Dr. Two Hawks's lower register made a reasonable cello. Green Wool Dress, who scarcely spoke, was second violin, of course, noodling busily along among her own thoughts. And I was the viola, hidden and dark.

If this didn't stop I knew I would use the gun right now, on you and then on myself. I listened to the words you were saying instead of your voices. I grabbed onto the words to keep control.

"A beautiful piece, the Haydn," you were saying. "I have played it. Oh, not like these musicians, of course. But I used to belong to an amateur chamber group." (How like you thieving snakes, to mimic our own medical doctors' affinity for music-making as a hobby!) You went on to explain how it was that you no longer played. Some slow, crippling Kondran bone disease. Of course—your lizard claws were never meant to handle a bow and strings. What was your instrument? I missed that. You said you had not played for six or seven years now. No wonder you had twitched all through the Haydn, remembering.

Some snake in a velvet suit pushed past, managing to step on both my feet. We traded insincere apologies, and he went on to trample past you and your companions. They were all hurrying back in now. My moment was coming. The row was fully occupied, so I sat down and pretended to skim the program notes for the next piece.

On you went, in the clear, distantly regretful tone. I couldn't stop hearing. "It's been a terrible season for me," you said. "My only grandchild died last month. He was fifteen."

Your voice was not music. It was just a voice, taking a tone I remembered from when I and my crewmates first began to be able to say to each other, "Well, it's all gone, blown up—mankind and womankind and whalekind and everykind smashed to smithereens while we were sleeping." It's how you sound instead of screaming. You have no more acute screaming left in your throat, but you can't stop talking about what is making you scream, because the screaming of your spirit is going on and on.

My eyes locked on the page in front of me. Had you really spoken this way, to two strangers, at a concert? The other two were making sounds of shock and sympathy.

"Cancer," you said, though of course you meant not our kind of cancer but Kondran cancer, and of course even if you were screaming inside it wasn't the same as the spirit of a human being screaming that way.

You leaned forward in your seat to talk across Green Wool Dress to Dr. Two Hawks. "It was terrible," you said. "It started in his right leg. None of the therapy even slowed it down. They did three operations."

I sneaked a look at you to see what kind of expression you wore on your imitation human face while you recited your afflictions. But you were leaning outward to address your fellow doctor, and the back of your narrow lizard shoulders was turned toward me.

Between you two, Green Wool Dress sat with a blank social smile, completely withdrawn into herself. I tried to follow what you were saying, but you got into technical terms, one doctor to another.

The musicians were tuning up their instruments backstage. The gun felt like a battleship in my pocket. Under the dimming lights I could make out the face of Dr. Two Hawks, sympathetic and earnest. Amazing, I thought, how they've learned to produce the effect of expressions like our own with their alien musculature and their alien skin.

"But it's better now than it was at first," Dr. Two Hawks protested (I thought of Beamish's babies and the death of Walter Drake). "I can remember when there was nothing to do but cut and cut, and even then—there was a young patient I remember, we removed the entire hip—oh, we were desperate. Dreadful things were done. It's better now."

All around, oblivious, members of the audience settled expectantly into their seats, whispering to each other, rustling program pages. Apparently I was your only involuntary eavesdropper, and soon that ordeal would be over.

The audience quieted, and here they came: Ross first, then Chandler (the Kondran players didn't matter). Ross first: You wouldn't see the blood on her red dress. No one would understand exactly what was happening, and that would give me time to get Chandler, too. I needed my concentration. My moment was almost here.

On you went, inexorably, in your quiet, melancholy tone: "As a last resort they castrated him. He lost most of his skin at the end, and he was too weak to sip fluids through a tube. I think now it was all a mistake. We should never have fought so hard. We should have let him die at the start."

"But we can't just give up!" cried Dr. Two Hawks over the applause for the returning musicians. "We must *do something*!"

And you sighed, Dr. Akonditichilka. "Aaah," you said softly, a long curve of sounded breath in the silence before the players began. You leaned there an instant longer, looking across at him.

Then you said gently (and how clearly your voice still sounds in my mind)—each word a steep, sweet fall in pitch from the one before—"Let's listen to Brahms."

And you sat back slowly in your seat as the first notes rippled into the hall.

After a little I managed to uncramp my fingers from around the gun and take my empty hand out of my pocket. We sat there together in the dimness, our eyes stinging with tears past shedding, and we listened.

THE STAGESTRUCK VAMPIRE

"Why don't you do it yourself?" my husband asked me, some time in 1984. I had just had another inquiry from somebody I'd never heard of and who had no credits of her own to back her up, offering to make a stage script out of my novella about a modern vampire, *Unicorn Tapestry*—no charge to me, of course, and a split of "the profits" to each of us when the play got produced.

If nothing else this was a nice change from, "I have a great idea for a story, so you write it and we'll split the money"; but it still felt insulting. But was it insulting *enough?*

Enough to provoke me into doing the job myself, that is. I certainly would not have been my first choice to do a stage adaptation. I grew up in New York City avoiding theater, because it always felt so—well, so *stagey*. There they all were, pretending to try Jacob Wirtz for atrocities committed at Andersonville Prison while he was in charge of the place—while I (and all of us in the audience) couldn't help but hear the cop car and ambulance and fire truck sirens whooping up and down outside on Broadway. The actors' sweaty sincerity and overbearing voices (it's not easy to outshout a siren) were merely embarrassing.

I was spoiled, see. I was a reader, sometimes of six or seven books at a time, armloads of them dragged home from the public library every week since my early teens. So I was accustomed to the theater of my own mind, where concentration was absolute (just ask my mother!) and not even sirens could penetrate. Compared to that, of course mere flesh and blood players on a physically limited stage seemed forced and artificial. When Steve and I had moved to Albuquerque in 1969, the comparative poverty and amateurish nature of local theater efforts (much improved since, I am glad to say) had put me off the stage more firmly than ever.

On the other hand, he had persuaded me to go to the Santa Fe Opera with him since it was so close at hand—an hour and a half in the car—and his first, oh-so-canny choice, *La Boheme*, had swept me off my feet. So in some respects I was a bit more interested in the whole idea of live bodies on a stage than I had ever been before.

And I kept getting these enthusiastic notes and calls from people who thought *Unicorn Tapestry* had great stage-potential. It had already won me a Nebula from the Science Fiction Writers of America for best novella of 1980, and it was widely anthologized because of that, which meant people looking for stage material tended to stumble across it in collections of shorter SF and fantasy.

If for no other reason than to have a quick and easy way of turning their inquiries off ("I've already written a script, thank you, goodbye"), I finally decided to give it a try myself.

Actually, a couple of movie options had been taken on the story of my vampire, and I had occasionally considered trying to make a film script of *Unicorn Tapestry*. But I'd heard the horror stories that go with the much bigger big bucks of screenwriting (for having to deal with Hollywood, mainly) and tales of how excruciatingly difficult it is to actually sell a script for TV or movies as a beginner. Stage money, such as it is, is much less and much longer in coming, but you do not have to be an established name in the industry to get your script read, let alone keep it intact as you wrote it *and* maybe have major input into your premier production.

And plays are still made out of words, while screen stories are made primarily of images, the fewer words the better. I am a words-writer by trade and by talent, not an image-arranger.

Nor do you need an agent to market a play (a good thing, since you can't get one without a previous production under your belt already, the old catch twenty-two). Regional and local theaters are always looking for scripts. All you need is lots of postage and patience.

Moreover, it's not so rare for a play, if it succeeds, to become a film.

The stage script that came out of my jump into the field of playwriting in 1984, a sixty-five page piece titled *Vampire Dreams*, was in fact performed at the Magic Theatre in San Francisco in March, 1990. You can see that it was a longish road. Not that I *knew* it was going to take that long. If I had, well . . . I'd have done it anyway.

To begin with, although I knew I was a complete ignoramus about theater I was emboldened by the fact that I wasn't trying to originate a script de novo. This was "only" a matter of adapting a piece of my own in which lots of people more experienced in theater than I was saw exciting dramatic potential. Actually, I saw that potential myself.

The novella is about a thousands-years-old vampire who goes into therapy after a "breakdown" to save his job as a college professor, and the complex and evolving relationship that develops between him and his female therapist. There's lots of dialog, the revelations of which provide the kind of "action" that live stage does so well. Although the novella is the backbone of an entire novel about the vampire character, I thought I saw a way to adapt the ending of the book to work for a play made from the central chapter.

So, how do you turn a story into a play? I hadn't a clue, so I read up on tips for beginners.

I learned that nonprofit theaters (which is where the unknown playwright gets to test and refine her script before tackling more commercial venues) are perennially strapped for cash. Even well-established theaters that run playwriting contests (another excellent entry point for the tyro) struggle to keep costs down. This means that one way of making your script more attractive is to keep cast numbers low and make your set requirements minimal.

Perfect: my story's set was a psychiatrist's office.

But my heroine, Floria, interacts in the story with a number of people, by way of establishing the reality and weight of her life independent of her struggle with her weird client. I needed to get rid of the people as on-scene actors, but still present her relationships with them to an audience.

For starters, I pulled the therapist's rocky relationship with her daughter out of the action and turned it into several conflict-ridden conversations over the telephone from Floria's office, with the audience party to only the mom's side: scratch one actor. Then I conflated the therapist's cellist boyfriend and the dean of the vampire's college into one character, put him on the phone too, and reduced the office receptionist to the unheard end of conversations held with an office intercom.

Let's hear it for technology. If you've ever wondered why there are so many phones, tape-machines, computers, and other techno-gimmicks in modern plays, now you know: they can cut down on the number of actors to be cast, rehearsed, costumed, and, most importantly of all, paid.

I kept Floria's colleague, Lucille, so she would have someone knowledgeable to react to reports of what was going on with this crazy client; and I kept Kenny, another client that Floria is desperate to get rid of, for contrast—he's a whiny, self-absorbed kid, immature and aggressive, and his interference precipitates the climax of the action.

So, how long a script could I get away with? How much room did I have to fit my story into?

My reading indicated that two-act plays or long one-acts have, for the most part, replaced the three- and even four-acters of previous times. Remember Shakespeare? Ibsen? Those turgid, wordy nineteenth-century stage plays that were the basis of most of the operas of the time?

Those were set up to be an evening's entertainment, and I mean a whole evening; the audience was made up of people who didn't have the option of just flipping a switch at home and watching *The Sopranos* and then *Six Feet Under.* When the high-rolling theater patrons went to the theater it was an outing, what with dressing to the nines, getting the horses harnessed up, and driving over. Once they got there, they damn well wanted their money's worth and they got it.

Nowadays, a running time of one and a quarter hours, plus a fifteen minute intermission, is considered full-length. I recently saw a much-cut version of George Bernard Shaw's *Man and Superman* featuring the fastest words-per-second delivery in human history. This was the actors' attempt to squeeze as much of the still-voluminous text as they could into the reduced attention spans of modern audiences.

This is why it's easier to make a script of a story than of a novel—you have much less to cram in—unless you have Sir Andrew Lloyd Webber eager to write you a score for the thing.

I picked up these basic hints and tips in a couple of weeks of reading, said that's enough of that, and began to write my play. I deliberately ignored the books on the actual craft of playwriting until long after the fact.

People who teach "creative writing" tend to teach patterns telling what a writer "may" and "may not" do in a story or a novel (I teach creative writing sometimes, and I always hear stories from my students about other teachers, usually college instructors, who do this). I suspected that people who teach playwriting might do something similar, and I didn't need advice on how to tease a dramatic story from my characters: I *had* a story, and I (and all those people who had contacted me wanting free rights to turn it into a play) thought it was pretty dramatic as it was.

I can see with hindsight that if I had read any of the hundreds of books explaining how to "craft" the "well-made" play, I wouldn't have dared to try half the things I did in my script—like having lots of small scenes, and writing a play that *wasn't* about my goddamned family. Some of these worked, some didn't, but at least I didn't rule anything out at the start.

So, having cavalierly turned my back on further "guidance" (such as a playwriting class or workshop), how to actually begin?

In the most obvious way: I copied out my story's dialog directly, and lo, it fell naturally into scenes. Most modern fiction is written in scenes anyway, as opposed to long lectures, stream of consciousness musings, and description, as found in older novels; this is the meaning of the very good writing advice, "Show, don't tell."

Only I had *forty-five* scenes, and even without a class or a manual I could tell that this was too many.

I began to cut, conflate, and otherwise bully this string of conversations and events into a less formidable number, and wound up with the basic thirty that I thought I could count on to carry the action, mood, and meaning of the piece pretty well.

Even thirty was risky; the definition of the "well-made play" emphasizes a continuous flow of action and the illusion of things happening in real time (classically, within the hours of one single day). Many theater pundits jealously defend this concept from the quick scene shifts and elastic timeline that typifies their rivals, television and, to some extent, film. (In fact some theaters rejected my completed script solely because the multi-scene format reminded them of TV, as they explained to me at irritable length in their rejection letters).

However: if you actually examine a number of current plays, I guarantee that in a very large proportion of them you will find a more or less tightly constructed string of small scenes with blackouts or other intervals in between, often accompanied by music—to the enrichment of the theatrical experience, in my opinion. Theater, a living art after all, has adapted to the demands of screen-accustomed audiences, who want more motion, more scope, more speed, and more variety in what they see than the stodgy old "well-made play" had to offer (except in the hands of absolute masters, of course, but those are few and far between and I sure never saw myself in that role).

So, scenes—some short, some long, all confrontations of characters dealing with each other over the central problem—the predatory monster in therapy, and what they all said and did.

But what to do about the internal ruminations of my heroine, Floria the therapist? In the printed story these are central to demonstrating her character and her reaction to her very odd client and her own off-the-rails life. In movies, you strip all that away and try to replace the interior monolog of your point of view character with tricks of music, lighting, and images that you hope will carry the message.

Here, what I couldn't externalize in dialog with Lucille the colleague (whose part thus became much stronger) I tried stuffing into monologues spoken by my heroine directly to the audience (what used to be called "asides" in Shakespeare). Heck, it worked in *Amadeus*, it worked in *Equus*.

But I am not Peter Shaeffer, and it didn't work in my play. The monologs came out clunky and pretentious, and I gave them the chop. Eventually, some of this material Floria wound up dictating into her tape recorder as case notes; but a good deal of it turned out to be unnecessary, once I had an actress in the part. She could "act out" the internal thoughts and emotions without words.

For descriptions of the action, I put in stage directions. Little did I know: the first thing that actors do with a script is to cross out all the stage directions. They must develop their own stage business at their own rhythm, deriving it from the words as they speak them and in accordance with their director's interpretation of the play.

Published scripts commonly include elaborate set descriptions and stage directions, and this had misled me: in fact, these are descriptions of how things were done at the premier production, to help a reader re-create that production in their mind's eye. Far from being a blueprint for all subsequent productions, they are directions that any confident director will quickly cast aside in the search for his own unified vision of the work as *he* intends to present it (especially if the playwright is dead; a few playwrights are known for insisting on a particular staging and blocking, but this is rare—probably because experienced playwrights feel that freezing the physical elements can also freeze the creative energy of subsequent productions).

At last, my script was done! Well, it was presentable, anyway;

a playscript, unlike a novel, can be edited from start to finish in an afternoon, so the temptation to never really be done—to keep tinkering and polishing—is huge.

It ran about seventy pages, double-spaced, and looked very spare to me. I even had a title: *Body Work*. It had taken me only a few months of tinkering with my abstract of the original story to achieve all this—a piece of cake! It sure beat spending a couple of years on a book. Why hadn't I tried writing a play before?

I read my script out loud onto a tape—who knew better than I how those lines should be spoken?—and, listening, caught a number of lines that had been fine on paper but that sounded awkward, silly, or pretentious when spoken. This convinced me that the advice to get your script read out loud by others as soon as possible was sound.

Steve and I rounded up some people from his law office and had a reading, sitting in chairs in our living room. It was perfectly ghastly—well, they were all lawyers—but everybody seemed to enjoy the experience tremendously. And more bad-sounding lines rang in my ears, to be cut or revised drastically.

Now it was time to take my revised script to a local theater group. Every city of any size has at least one; there are a fluctuating number here in Albuquerque, from four to eight or so, and this is by no means a major cultural hub. Most college or university theater departments welcome the chance to work with local playwrights too, although often they are dominated by the narrow views of the American Realist school, which means they love a play about how your family fucked you up but despise one about a vampire, say.

But I found a group of local actors who regularly worked together under the auspices of someone from the university with a broader viewpoint than this, and they agreed that while *Body Work* was not ready for production it was ready for a pre-production process known as a directed reading.

That is, actors walk around a rehearsal space, using chairs and boxes to represent elements of a set, and carrying scripts from which they read their lines while they mime action that they have developed with the director. Bare bones as it was, this was a thrill—imagine, my words, my very words, spoken as if they mattered, by other people! I think I was hooked right there.

A small audience of local theater people sat in as an audience, and afterward there was a discussion. I learned from all this, in a rather public and humiliating way, much more about where the script was slack, foolish, unintelligible, or vastly susceptible to completely wrong-headed interpretation, although more from the performance itself and the audience's comments than from the participating actors. Actors, being human, mostly suggest changes which benefit their own particular roles rather than the play as a whole.

Learning in public like that makes a powerful impression. I couldn't kid myself: my ideal creation for the stage was in fact a terrible play, with glints of potential.

So I went home and revised. And revised. Between bouts of fiction writing, I would pull out the script and revise some more, switching scenes around, moving dialog from one scene or even one character to another, checking back with the original story for anything wonderful that I had either missed or included and then cut.

Meanwhile, I went to lots of local productions, and on visits to New York I would see plays six nights running to make up for all the years I had avoided theater.

I loved it; something had changed—my youthful skepticism once overwhelmed by Puccini's music in Santa Fe, all my disdainful distance from the vivid meta-life on the stage vanished. Suddenly I was gripped by the power of the sheer physicality of actors on a stage, the impact of which comes, I think, from their immediate vulnerability. There they are, right in front of you, literally making a spectacle of themselves and depending on the playwright's lines and the director's vision and the mutual support of the whole cast and crew to keep them from looking totally ridiculous.

One effect of this experience was to make me cut even more lines. Instead of using words to try to constrain and steer the actors in the direction I demanded that they go, I made more and more white space on the page, trying to leave as much room as possible for them and their own creativity. Now I was eager to have my beginner's effort enhanced by the skills of these people.

And having seen the play up and moving once, however sparely, I longed to see it up again. Clearly the object was not, for a tyro anyway, to make a perfect script and have it staged, but to jump in with the imperfect work and learn from the first production how to make it better; in other words, to take some risks of my own.

In New York I bought the latest copy of the *TCG Theatre Directory* at a theatrical bookshop and marked it up. I began sending out my script.

I had a list of theaters culled from newspaper and magazine articles and reviews, from friends, relatives, and professional theater people I knew or was coming to know, but spamming overloaded theater staff with inappropriate work is not appreciated. Some theaters do only classics, or only musicals, or mostly comedy, or only plays for children or plays written about their locales, and so on. I supplemented the *Directory* listings by reading reference works in the public library, in the 720.2 range, for more information about the history and emphasis of each theater before I ventured into the next, as it were, stage.

Body Work went out to about thirty theaters in the course of 1985-86. Each script, Xeroxed and spiral bound, cost me about $6.50 to produce, and despite the inclusion of SASE's they often didn't come back to me. Postage, then, was $2.40 each, first class, with a cover letter and SASE with return postage enclosed. Multiple submission is standard, but expensive.

Multiple rejection followed as the night the day.

I got lots of encouragement ("very interesting, sensitively written," and "please do let us see your next play"); some insults ("We are not interested in a vampire play", and a command to resubmit the script in three page increments to be edited by a self-styled expert who would thus teach me how to write); some stupidity (a complaint that instead of a clever "explanation" the vampire does indeed turn out to be a vampire); some form letters, some returned-unreads ("We are not reading unsolicited", "We are undergoing restructuring right now") some vast and endless silences—and no takers.

Reply time, when there were replies, varied from six weeks to—well, in one case a year and a half. The standard was about three months, and the answer was NO.

It was drawer-time for my play. I had books to write, and anyway I was an author and not—obviously—a playwright.

Now, work in a drawer—any kind of work—butters no parsnips, and the impulse to keep taking it out and working on it again is strong, and healthy. Some successful plays have sat home being revised by their authors for ten years or more before they were good enough to attract that success. But I was discouraged, and the drawer it was.

Then, in 1987 off we went again: two young men in New York contacted me asking to write a script from my story for production off-off-off Broadway.

They were not happy to hear that a script already existed, nor that my lawyer husband insisted that for copyright reasons there must not be two scripts for the same play, theirs and mine. I sent them my script. They didn't like it (I think they already had their own script completed, having written it first and then come to me for permission, and they were damned if they were going to give up their own script). We said goodbye.

Two months later, they called again to tell me that they now had an opportunity to contribute a short version—about an hour long—of their play to a festival celebrating the 25th anniversary of the Cafe La Mama in New York. Seven playlets were to be performed under the overarching title *The Seven Deadly Sins*, and these guys already had a shorter version of their unauthorized script accepted, calling it *Lust and the Unicorn*.

I cringed at the title, I ground my teeth over the submission of an unauthorized script without permission; but any play taken from the story would necessarily include the same dialog as my script did (in fact they had assured me that they had added no original lines at all), and I was itching to hear those lines in a real production.

I asked my lawyer—my husband Steve—for advice.

After some hard-nosed negotiation on the phone, the New York guys unhappily agreed to a compromise. They would not use my script, but they would have to bill their version as "based on the full-length play *Body Work* by S. Charnas." I wasn't happy either, but I also agreed.

Well, New York! La Mama, a famous hangout of poets and musicians and Greenwich Village creatives! How could I resist?

In the event the playing time got cut down to about forty minutes, which didn't bother me; what was being cut was, after all, their version, not mine.

I flew to New York to see the show; I was amazed, stunned, galvanized.

We sat in this tiny, bare performance space and watched a pared-down version of my story played out in a compressed period of time, with bits of mysterious, modernist music added at the scene breaks. Old friends, a musician and his wife, attended the same night that I did. Afterward Charlie turned to me and said, in tones of pleased surprise, "That was *good!*" Which had obviously not been their expectation.

The story was what was good, the basic framework, and the dialog from the story; and the production was powerful, even though my middle-aged vampire was played by a twenty-six year old dancer.

No; because of it. What he lacked in years he made up for in physical authority and sheer erotic expressiveness. We had, I was told, numbers of repeat customers in the audiences over the next week, most of them female. They were coming back to see this kid again.

The guy playing Kenny, Floria's other client, played him as slightly retarded; I heard audience members discussing whether the actor really was retarded or not, and he was invited to an audition for another show. My Floria got no such invitation, but, as she lamented afterwards in a nearby diner where the cast repaired for a late meal, a woman with dark hair and a normal instead of a pneumatic figure didn't get offers the way the male actors did.

Me, I was dazzled. The lines were still my lines, and they worked. I went home and revised my script until I was sure I had incorporated the best of what I'd learned in New York.

Then a new theater contact read the changed version for me and said, "But you stop the story just when it gets most interesting—what happens *after* these two make love?"

Some strong, conflict-sparked material came out of the struggle between my vampire and his therapist in the new, post-coital scene, and that sent ripples of change rolling backward through the whole script. Newly optimistic about the play's prospects, in 1988 I sent it out again, now titled *Vampire Dreams*, to a dozen regional theaters. I tried not to hit the same ones I had submitted it to before.

Nonetheless, it came limping home again, copy by copy.

Except that in January of 1989 I got a phone call from someone at the Magic Theatre in San Francisco. They wanted my play for a two-week run as the leadoff work of their "Springfest" of three brand new plays—in March of 1990, which seemed awfully soon.

Everyone at the Magic was efficient, if you could catch their attention—most staff people do an amazing amount of work under a mind-boggling degree of pressure. Theaters run on such narrow economic margins, and competition for involvement by the stage-struck is so keen, that dead wood gets pruned very quickly (unless sheltered by protection of some kind). Theater people often have towering egos, but I found that they had towering skills to go with them.

Events moved with the speed of light. By February I had a contract in hand, a short and simple document setting the performance schedule (nine performances starting on or about March 21), mutual guarantees (script originality, the usual publishing-type warranties and indemnities, a 6% royalty for me on ticket sales and a nice credit in the billing), rights for the theater to extend the contracted run or to remount the play any time during the next five years, and travel expenses.

The producer (in this case the administration of the Magic) promised to pay my way out, economy, during rehearsals; to put me up; and to pay my expenses while in San Francisco up to one hundred twenty five dollars a week for up to four weeks.

Having no agent for this kind of contract, I consulted my theatrical contacts. They said, "Make sure you know how much revision of the script they expect to get out of you; and if they ask for a percentage of all future royalties from the play, say no—they shouldn't get that for just nine performances." The Magic did indeed ask for this (as theaters routinely do), and I did say no. They also asked for a cut of any future media rights, and again I said no, backed up by the fact that media rights to the original book were under option in Hollywood at the time.

Actually, having a good reason didn't matter, since the Magic only asked for a slice of media income *after* our basic contract was signed; their situation is so constantly in flux that there are bound to be slip-ups like this.

Example of flux: an actor in another play in performance at the Magic called in on the day I appeared at the theater to introduce myself: he was out, down with appendicitis. Since the Magic had no money to pay understudies, the director was asking around the office to see if he could find a staff person to take over the part of the downed actor for that evening's performance!

The question of revisions was interesting: it had never occurred to me that a certain amount of rewriting might be *expected.* I couldn't get an answer about how much was expected, though, since the director of my play was unreachable. He was head of the theater department at U.C. Santa Cruz where he had classes to teach as well, and he was also flying regularly to Los Angeles and other places auditioning actors for U.C.S.C.'s summer theater festival. To work on my play, he would be commuting almost daily for five or six weeks to and from San Francisco.

This frenetic activity is not, I discovered, unusual; to make enough income to live decently directors often work on several projects at once, jetting around like orchestral conductors and opera singers.

In fact, I hadn't realized that the Magic's yearly Springfest was set up as a workshop situation where the playwright, neophyte or veteran, was *supposed* to revise the play. As one of my own purposes was to learn as much as I could about making my script better, this suited me perfectly.

I had just entered my fifties and had plenty of energy. I knew that my personal work pattern flourished on sudden, intense, and highly demanding bursts of energy, which sounded ideal for this situation (the corollary is that I easily get bored with projects when they slow down or settle into a grind, and when I'm bored I'm useless).

I took the precaution of sending to the Magic Xeroxed copies of the original novella, *Unicorn Tapestry*, for the director and cast, so that they could start out with a clearer idea of what I had thought I was doing in the script.

I was as high as a kite. The whole thing was better than the first time I got a book accepted, because this play business just went on and on—scheduling my visit for rehearsals, trying to find and talk with my director, fielding calls from the artistic director of the Magic about the details—a lovely, exhilarating furor altogether, with a payoff only a few weeks away!

In the middle of February, off I went to San Francisco for the start of rehearsals.

"HOW SEXY DO you see this play?" The question had been raised with me over the phone back in January, by John Lion, Artistic Director of the Magic.

I'd covered my startlement (one reason for having the play produced was to find out how sexy it would play on stage, wasn't it?) with perfectly true but weasly platitudes about the spectrum of possibilities that I saw, ranging from obliquely sexy to Very Sexy Indeed.

"Good," he'd growled, and I'd figured that somehow I had passed a test.

Some weeks later, driving me in from the San Francisco airport, Eugenie Chan gave me the background to John's question. Eugenie was the Literary Manager (a much nicer term, I thought, than the more usual "dramaturg," which sounds like someone throwing up in a particularly flamboyant manner), and she was kind enough to give me a heads up.

John Lion had a distinguished theater career (including receiving the Margo Jones Award and working regularly with the likes of Sam Shepard and Michael McClure, among many other well-known playwrights). He had founded the Magic Theatre in the sixties, when in each of its successive venues the audience could generally count on seeing nude actors onstage. It had remained a very sixties kind of outfit, and, under Lion's leadership, very proud of its iconoclastic bumptiousness.

Over a quarter-century later, the theater was experiencing hard times. A more business-oriented manager, Harvey Seifter, had been hired by the Board to come to the rescue. Now, at the end of a transitional period of double leadership, John Lion was in the process of moving on, retiring, or being booted out, depending on your point of view.

Harvey, currently billed as Managing Director, was shortly to take John's place as Artistic Director. They didn't see eye-to-eye, which was only to be expected given that Harvey was supposed to change the theater's direction to draw in new audiences and income so as to keep the whole outfit afloat. My play was John Lion's last choice for the Magic—and, apparently, it was meant as a spit in the eye of the new, more classically-oriented management.

So John saw *Vampire Dreams* as very sexy indeed. Harvey probably saw it as a final hangover from the old days and a damned nuisance, to be gotten over with so that he could get on with his own plans. And I was right in the middle.

But I can't say that I gave much of a damn; I was too excited, as I got my tour of the tiny suite of theater offices in the Magic's two-stage space at the Fort Mason complex. I was much more interested in meeting my director, Michael Edwards, the person who would be shepherding my play, my script, into reality.

The first thing he said to me over lunch was that he had chosen my play from three scripts offered to him by the Magic because he loved the language in it. The second thing was, "I like the story this play comes from much better than the playscript. Could you bring the script more in line with the story?"

The cast, I found, agreed, lamenting the lost "poetry" of many story scenes I had left out of the script in order to make room for new material at the post-coital end. Poetry? What the hell? I have a tin ear for poetry, how could they think that anything I wrote was poetic? But of course they weren't seeing the words on the page but hearing them, as delivered by themselves, and to them it sounded like poetry.

With flattery like that, how was I to object?

So my first job was to rewrite the play, reintegrating a lot of the material I had jettisoned to make room for the denouement that had won John Lion's approval in the first place. Welcome to the infinitely adjustable world of theater.

Speaking of which, my actors were not at all the people I had pictured in my mind's eye.

My tall, craggy-faced vampire was to be played by a wiry guy of five foot six with a Van Dyke beard and an incipient bald spot in the middle of his curly dark hair. Floria, the therapist, was five foot eight and had stopped smoking not long before, incurring the usual weight gain, about which she was clearly uncomfortable.

The disparity in their sizes—vampire and victim, predator and prey, small guy and large woman—simply hadn't registered with my director. He also directed operas at the New York Metropolitan and was accustomed to big heroines and little heroes.

But the actors felt the disparity (they ended up making jokes about it during rehearsals), and so did I (I am fairly tall myself, so this is an area in which I've had some piquant experience of my own). And from the word go the actors knew every reservation I felt about each one of them; experts in body language, they read me like a picture book.

At the first rehearsal we all sat around a table in the vestibule of the Magic's larger performance space (not in use that night) and the actors read through the script out loud, tasting and testing the lines. I was appalled, immediately hearing problems that had somehow survived all my revisions. Dismay kept my mouth shut as more work, work under pressure that must meet the requirements of professionals who knew much more than I did, loomed.

Having gone through it fairly rapidly once, they began again with the first scene, slowly this time, with much discussion, finding the points where the tone, subject, or tension changed ("beat changes" in Michael's terms), and—oh, horror!—being asked by the director to justify every damned line.

"Now, Earll, why do you say that here?" he'd say, and Earll Kingston, my Weyland-to-be, would concentrate fiercely until he found and articulated a motivation that worked for him as an actor—while I, who *knew* the "correct" motivation because I had bloody well put it in there, sat mum. Or else I *didn't* know, not in a way I could explain, having blithely charged ahead without worrying about the motivation. A line of dialog on a page of story text, supported by all the other verbiage around it, just isn't as crucial as that same line in a script, standing there nearly naked and required to do much more of the work of carrying the story.

It was, in its way, awful—having each line tugged and worried like a loose thread until it was drawn tight to the fabric of the whole piece again; and wonderful, because to my amazement, these people could do it. They thought about it and talked about it until every line in my script made sense, which was more than I had ever done with those lines. I could even hear, with cringing clarity, where the tone was too much the same for too long ("He's still testing her here, is that right, Earll?").

The director confided during an early conference with me that he was not entirely happy with the cast members, in terms of their suitability to these particular parts. However, due to the last minute rush in the selection of the play by the Magic, these were the best he had seen at auditions.

Oh, and one other thing.

In October, 1989, San Francisco had endured a big, fat, scare-the-hell-out-of-everybody earthquake, the one that pancaked a couple of freeways. Every show scheduled for the fall in San Francisco ended up opening in early spring instead, most of them just before or just after the opening of the Magic's Springfest. The pool of available actors was already depleted when Michael got there, after *Vampire Dreams* was belatedly accepted as John Lion's final pick.

Michael, misgivings or no misgivings, was wonderful with his cast. He was endlessly patient, coaxing and cajoling, reassuring and encouraging, earning their trust and reliance with his vigorous but unflappable support.

I only wished that I had more time to sit down and talk with him about the play and the rehearsals. Most nights he drove back to Santa Cruz in order to teach his classes there the next morning. Of course, it's quite possible that he was just as pleased *not* to have long discussions with his playwright about what he was making of the play under her very eyes . . .

My own schedule shaped up very quickly: I would go to the theater at mid-morning (a bus ride down from my digs in Pacific Heights and a short walk along the Marina) and work on revisions left over from the night before, usually forgetting both lunch and dinner—this was the only visit I ever made to San Francisco during which I lost weight. My on-going task was to get new pages printed and Xeroxed in time for that evening's rehearsal.

Since most of the actors had regular daytime jobs so they could eat between shows, rehearsals ran from 7:30 in the evening to 11:30 most nights. They would arrive munching take-out dinners, and rehearsals would run until the stage manager called a halt (union rules—these were Equity actors). Then somebody would give me a lift back up the hill so I could tiptoe upstairs and fall into bed around midnight.

I was housed with one of the theater's Board members in a handsome old home on Pacific Heights. My hosts were gracious, my room was fine, it was perfect—except that the Board member's house was in the process of having its outside repainted. I was regularly awakened early in the morning by painters on a scaffold outside my windows, starting the work day with a discussion, say, of a tarot reading one of them had had the night before at a party.

But somehow my brain had to keep working, crisp and clear and in high gear all the way through. It had to. There were a *lot* of changes.

Remember those Xeroxed copies of the original story I had sent on ahead? Well, everybody had been very good and had read them. I had paraphrased and toned down much of the story's dialog for the stage, thinking it would sound too melodramatic. But everybody—cast, director, stage manager, all—insisted that the original dialog in the story was much better than the doctored dialog in the script. Let's hear it read in the original, they insisted, and we all turned to the climactic scene of the story.

Earll Kingston and Sandy Kelly Hoffman read the lines right from the book, and to my amazement they sounded wonderful.

So much for the wisdom of the mind's ear. Until you hear it spoken by professional actors who know how to make the best of a line, you haven't really heard it.

And that's how I came to spend those mornings (and some evenings, during the rehearsals themselves) in a virtual tornado of rewrites, working from several older versions of the script—which were closer to the original story—which I asked my husband to Fed-Ex to me in San Francisco. This meant putting in lots of high-pressure hours at a monstrous and ancient IBM computer with an archaic text program called Displaywrite that I had never seen before. There was no manual—the machine had been donated to the theater minus any instructions (not that a manual would have helped, of course).

I had used the machines in the word processing center at Steve's law office for years to write fiction on (working with the much smaller night shift, so that there was always a machine free), but I had never encountered this particular set up before. The result was countless episodes of accidentally erased or lost work which had to be redone on the spot, often more than once, in a fury of frustration. Then, when I had finally typed the whole script in, the printer died; I had to learn to use the office Apple instead, starting all over again with another unfamiliar word processing program and keyboard arrangement.

I usually got to use the Apple after the office staff had gone home, which meant that there was no one knowledgeable around to help me out when my fifteen minutes of basic instruction failed me. More lost time, as I spent hours retyping vanished parts of Act One while much of it was still being rewritten; and Act Two still hadn't been touched.

So much for nailing down in advance the amount of revision I was responsible for. I was the writer: I wrote, and I rewrote, gradually getting the best of the writing tools at my disposal.

At each rehearsal, even at the beginning when everybody was still sitting around the table going over and over lines, things happened to the text; changes came in a never-ending cascade, each one a response to a previous change or to a new challenge, each one necessary. A speech about the American cultural romance with Death had to be cut—"Overwritten," Michael said, and he was right. A scene in which the vampire presents the therapist with a symbolic image on a poster from the Cloisters went. For the back rows of the audience to be able to actually see the art, Earll would have had to stagger onstage carrying something the size of a billboard.

They told me we needed a scene that was in neither the story nor the play, a scene that I had in fact deliberately avoided writing but had had Floria describe in her notes. It had become painfully clear that unless Weyland gave her physical proof that he really was a vampire, the audience was bound to think that she was just a fool being manipulated by a clever psychotic into sharing his delusion. This would make her not a heroine but a pathetic twit not worth spending an evening with.

You drop hints in print—the reader's imagination fills in the blanks and vanquishes doubt through the willing suspension of disbelief on which all fiction depends. On stage, with real, physical people moving around and talking, if you want people to believe one of those real people is a vampire you are going to have to damn well prove it, or at least give the illusion of proving it.

He should show her his fangs, they said; or, in this case, the sting under his tongue.

Oh no, oh NO, I said. It will look like a scene in a dentist's office. People will laugh. I can't write it.

Michael asked the actors to improvise the necessary scene; Richard Bloom, the Stage Manager, taped it for me. I never did refer to the tape, just wrote from what I remembered—they were that good. They were hesitant, soft-voiced, slow, feeling their way along, but words came, and they were good words. I polished them up a bit and the scene went in.

In the middle of the second week we started blocking scenes. We cleared the table and chairs out of the way (except for what was needed to take the place of stage furniture), and the actors began going through physical motions that might go with the words and the silences in the script. The list of props ("Let's have some flowers in a vase right there that she can fuss with when she crosses left") got longer, which made the Stage Manager shake his head unhappily because of our tight budget.

I wrote and rewrote. By the end of the second week, I was beginning to come under pressure to complete the final form of the script soon so that it could be blocked all the way through, and so the crew could know what changes we needed to the set and could start lining up the lighting cues and sound cues for the whole performance. You do a lot with lights (and with darkness) in a show with a strong fantasy element.

"Sound cues" meant cues for all the business with phones and tape recorders, plus music in the blackouts between scenes. Perhaps sparked by Michael's opera experience and the references to Puccini's *Tosca* in the text, the idea of music between scenes came naturally and early. A sound man, Rodney, was due to deliver a tape he'd made using themes from *Tosca* any day now—later, as it happened, since he was doing the work gratis and on top of his regular job with a sound company across the Bay.

Michael heard the tape, didn't like it, and sent Rodney back to do something different and better—which, against all odds and at the risk of losing his real job over it, he did, and in time to have his work incorporated into the show during the first technical rehearsal a mere two days before opening. And it was good stuff, too, modern-sounding but also melodically easy on the ear, and very evocative.

Once we got onto the actual stage—in the smaller theater at the Magic, entirely appropriate to an intimate piece like *Dreams*—I began to see just what I had let myself and everybody else in for with my play's structure of thirty-odd scenes, with my vampire and therapist duo in most of them.

There was no time for costume changes at all for the two leads except during the intermission, so they wore essentially the same clothes for each whole act (comprising weeks of fictional time), like characters in a comic book. Rolled up sleeves or a draped scarf became our visual indicators of passing time.

Actors who had just exited but were due to enter the next scene from the other side of the stage had to race around behind the set and get themselves into position for the next entrance, all during a short blackout. This meant putting bits of fluorescent tape all over the floor so they would know where to put their feet and avoid breaking their necks in the dark. Moreover, because our set also had to serve (dressed and colored differently but not basically restructured) for two more plays following mine, we ended up with only the forward portion of a rather small stage as an active playing area, squeezing the actors' physical scope and making their quick exits and entrances even more hazardous.

And there was an absolutely necessary waste basket Stage Left that got the hell kicked out of it in passing by just about everybody.

This is not to mention the physical wear and tear on the actors. The two leads are middle-aged people and so were the actors playing them. Being onstage in almost all of the swift parade of scenes, and getting on and off between one and another of them, proved a demanding workout. Sandy said it was a damned good thing she had stopped smoking.

By the start of third week, with the Stage Manager looming menacingly at me every time a new change was proposed (while my director blithely declared that we could keep making changes right up to and beyond opening night), I saw that there were practical limits to the number of further changes we could make.

Actors' preparation for nine performances is just as demanding as for nine hundred performances. They are understandably reluctant to keep learning new lines (lots of extra work) and new versions of old lines (an invitation to disastrous omissions and mistakes) for such a short run. Moreover, with the best will in the world they sometimes simply *can't* make more changes.

Earll kept saying "Well, I refuse" where I had written, and wished to hear, "Well, I decline," which has a different sound, meaning, and weight. After a number of efforts at correction, I let it go. If you try to force changes, actors can forget the line altogether in performance out of sheer confusion. This is called "drying", and it is not a pretty sight; you do not want it in your performances.

Besides, our Weyland (who had started out rather tentatively) was going from strength to strength, and I didn't want to create hitches that might interrupt that progress. In fact, an actress from the next play on came to a rehearsal with her nine-year-old son and left after Act One; he wanted to go, she told me later, *because he was scared of our vampire* (and what's more he had nightmares afterward).

On the other hand, our leading lady had started off on a high (there are not that many good parts for middle-aged actresses) but was becoming less and less happy with her part. She reported that her husband, running lines with her at home, opined that Floria was on the defensive too much of the time, being manipulated, harangued, and verbally beaten up on by everybody else.

I had to admit that it was true that the Devil had, as usual, all the best lines. This was a serious problem.

Playing Floria had to be fun for Sandy, not just a tough slog upstream, so I made changes to brighten and strengthen Floria. The effect on the play was brilliant, if I say so myself.

I realized that I hadn't allowed, originally, for a problem I should have expected, in a play about a vampire. Some actors have said, famously, that they won't go onstage with a child or a dog, because no matter what you do the audience's attention will not be on you but on the more unusual presence with which you are sharing the spotlight. An actor onstage with a legendary monster—or, it transpired, even just another actor portraying a legendary monster—is in that same boat: all eyes would to be on the monster even if the monster had no lines at all.

Because of this, I had unknowingly underwritten Floria. In print, the story is told from her point of view, which automatically gives her the necessary weight. For the stage version, I had to give Sandy a lot more to work with. Once I did this the whole play became much better balanced and its tension became more taut and effective as well.

Meanwhile, bit by bit I saw the actors finding things to do and ways to work with my lines that astonished me: so much variety of action to be had out of a desk, a sofa, a window-frame, a file cabinet, a Mister Coffee machine, and that damned waste basket! The props people had a fit over Michael's inspiration that Kenny's long speech in Act Two should be given from a phone in a street booth, but by god they found us one.

The continuous adrenaline rush of involvement in such high-powered group creativity was glorious. It also engendered a degree of cocksureness that led me eventually to make the one mistake I had been most strongly warned against: I took my leading man aside and essentially directed him myself, about the delivery of a crucial line. None of us, including Earll, were happy with it as it was. "Why don't you try it like this," I said, adopting what I thought was Michael's style of direction.

Earll nodded, tried it, and got scolded by Michael for being too melodramatic. Earll, quite rightly, complained to Michael about being criticized for something that hadn't been his idea in the first place. Michael came and gently lectured me in a tone that made it quite clear that if I tried anything like that again, I was probably going to be sent home at once; and that made perfect sense to me. I was more than chastened, I was mortified.

If the playwright tells the actors how to speak his lines, their spontaneity is cramped and their insecurity increases. They know that the author has an ideal look and sound in mind for every line and moment of the play. Having that ideal spelled out to them, and knowing that they can never live up it regardless of what they do, has a deadly effect on their own creativity.

So I was told, kindly under the circumstances, that in future I must shut up and relay my desires to the actors through the director and *only* through him. This was not as easy as it sounds, since Michael was so often absent (Richard, the Stage Manager, was already handling much of the rehearsal time in his place) and so he was concentrated and under pressure when present. But from then on, I managed it.

Suddenly my three weeks were up. It was time for me to go home and attend to other business.

Mind you, Act Two, in its revised form, had yet to be fully blocked and was only going to get half the amount of rehearsal that the first act had gotten. All that rewriting and reblocking had cost us precious time: opening night was just two weeks away.

I had to go—other business put on hold at home required my attention, and besides, I had felt the production changing, drawing together, closing itself in around the actors and the director in a way that moved me further and further away from the core of what they were doing. I wasn't quite comfortable hanging around now, with no rewriting left to do. I felt that they were all blanking my presence out in a way that was necessary to what they were doing.

My creative input was finished. I needed to back away, signaling my trust in their talents and getting out of their way.

I spent an hour in a funny little import store on Lombard Street, a place lined with bins full of foreign trinkets, where I bought a handful of odd but pretty little objects—a glass egg, a tiny carved Ho Tei figure, small and inexpensive things—and I gave one of these to each of the actors before I left. For good luck, I said. To remind you of my gratitude, and my faith in you.

Then I went home. Not that I got much done in the two weeks that followed. Cut off from something so vital and crucial that was continuing on without me, I think I even got a little paranoid. Nobody called me, nobody told me anything. *What were they doing to my play?*

When I returned, two days before opening, I learned the worst: Michael and the cast had cut some lines and reversed the order of two scenes in Act Two!

"Wait 'til you see what they're doing with it," Michael said, reading the dismay on my face. "You'll like it."

I waited; I saw; I loved it, and I told them so.

The technical rehearsal, a run-through of everything except the actors themselves, was a revelation. The tech designers and the Stage Manager sat in the middle of the orchestra seats at portable control boards with headphones on, and ran through all the cues, speaking softly through microphones to the operators in the booth high at the rear of the theater. They had calm, capable voices and conveyed the atmosphere of a jumbo jet cockpit. When they were done, they had to go backwards through the cues, resetting everything for the forward run at the dress rehearsal. I rejoiced to see that the Magic crew had done a spectacular job of transforming the stage into a plane of fantastic reality that I had always assumed could only exist in the mind of a reader with a printed text.

That night, the dress rehearsal augured well for a good opening night, after a day off for everybody to rest and gather their energy for a huge effort.

We needed to be *better* than good.

Thanks to the October earthquake postponing everything to early spring, we were to open in competition with, among six or seven other notable shows, Tom Stoppard's new play *Hapgood*, a Shirley MacLaine extravaganza, Paul McCartney performing in Berkeley, and Milan Kundera's *Jacques and his Master*, right across the hall from us in Magic's own larger performance space.

I have a lot of friends in San Francisco, from the people at the Other Change of Hobbit bookstore which specializes in science fiction and fantasy, to SF convention goers and colleagues I'd known for over twenty years in the business, to family (my stepson and his wife and kids live in San Francisco).

Everybody, bless them, came to opening night.

Which almost didn't happen.

Earlier that evening, the actors were sitting on the edge of the stage listening to some last-minute comments by Michael, and in a typical actor's loosening up exercise Earll flung out his arms and flopped backward onto the stage. There was a hollow clunk, and he sat up again holding his head, bleeding freely from a laceration in his scalp.

Floria's desk had been moved during the rehearsal of another Springfest play that afternoon, and had been replaced too far forward; one corner had been where it shouldn't have been, and had laid the crown of Earll's head open.

And, just as for *Jacques and his Master*, we had no understudies.

Everyone was absolutely galvanized, in the coolest possible manner. In no time at all we had piled into somebody's car and driven Earll to the emergency room of a nearby hospital. The nurse on duty—a theater fan, thank god—heard our story and took pity on us. She slipped us in ahead of a sparse early-evening crop of unfortunates, patched him up, and returned him to us positively bouncing with adrenalin.

So our vampire did his first performance with a line of butterfly bandages holding his scalp together.

The performance went very fast and was a bit stiff, but nobody collided with anyone else or fell off the stage or dropped more than a phrase or two. The waste basket (for which we had obtained a permit from the Fire Department so that Weyland could drop some burning papers into it in the last scene) was not kicked into the wings. Earll said, "Well, I refuse!" instead of "Well, I decline," as usual. We ran about an hour and a half, with a fifteen minute intermission.

People didn't clap after the first act curtain—but they did at the end, with enthusiasm. This allowed my heart to disengage from my glottis before I was swamped with excited approval by a pack of gratifyingly delighted friends.

Harvey Seifter, with whom I had had some acrimonious clashes over getting enough work time at the Apple during the Magic's office hours, congratulated me with real, if rather surprised warmth.

John Lion said, "Well, you did it, kid." I guess that even without anybody tearing anybody else's, or their own, clothes off on stage *Vampire Dreams* was still "sexy enough".

Michael Edwards said congratulations and goodbye. The director's job is done as soon as the show opens. It was now up to the Stage Manager to keep performances up to scratch, posting daily notes in the single dressing room that everyone used, to call the cast's attention to dropped lines, missed cues, muffed action and other errors in the previous night's work.

Advice to fledgling playwrights: *make friends fast with your stage manager.*

The party after opening night was, as befits a small nonprofit theater, just a bunch of us hanging out 'til very late at a nearby joint where the actors replenished themselves with pizza and stuffed potato skins. We didn't wait up for next day's newspapers; everyone had jobs to go to, and we doubted that there would be any reviews for such a short run.

That week or a few days into the next, every damned paper in town plus the *Sacramento Bee* reviewed us: four loved us, one hated us, and everybody grumbled about the ending—except one critic who praised the second act as pure genius. No wonder theater people are insecure.

Luckily for us, it was apparently impossible to write a review of this show, even a pan, that wasn't fun to read (lots of bad puns) and informative enough to intrigue many readers. Subscription tickets had moved weakly, but walk-in sales increased as the run continued, despite a nearly total lack of advertising (that budget again).

After the first Friday performance, I got up on the stage with the cast and we fielded questions from the audience about the show; this is standard for new plays in workshop-type situations. Thank God for all my experience with convention panels, lectures, and meet-the-author sessions in libraries and schools! It was a breeze, yielding among other unexpected things a list of alternatives to the "needle" under Weyland's tongue that he shows to Floria to prove the truth of his nature—everything from "sting" to "leech."

The actors really settled into the show by the beginning of the second week. The lines I had written, including the new and revised ones, tended to be long and complex, which is a problem for American actors. Most of them are geared to the "Pass-the-salt-mother-never-loved-me-fuck-you" dialog of the school of American Realism. Not surprisingly, at first a lot of my words got lost.

When they all stopped gabbling their lines at top speed in order to get through them without forgetting anything or losing the audience's attention, the play began to relax and breathe. It lengthened naturally to a richer and more ample hour and forty minutes. This allowed the audience to relax too, and not only to breathe but to laugh, increasingly often and (usually) in the right places. I began to realize that I had written not only a drama but a comedy. Spotting this from the outset gave audiences the confidence in the tone of what was going on that led the applause we had been missing after the first act.

There is no thrill I know of to rival that of hearing a hall full of strangers laugh out loud, together, at something you have written. It means you have provided them with a shared moment of delight and release. This feels like the prerogative of a god.

My five-foot-six vampire, having found dry humor as the touchstone of his performance (instead of trying to become some tall, svelte Frank Langella clone) and encouraged by audience response, grew positively frisky, energizing every scene he was in—and he was in most of them.

Audiences began to take sides. One night they applauded Weyland on a particularly snappy exit line (maybe they were just wishing they'd had the gall to say that to *their* therapists). We spotted familiar faces: some people came to see the play a second time, and they brought their friends.

I attended every performance, sitting well back so that I could see the audience as well as the stage, and I made notes of my own (I could already see that a few changes here and there would leave more time for a laugh at this line, or tighten the tension of that one).

The audience members were sophisticated enough to appreciate the jokes, and incredibly quiet the rest of the time. Far from being put off by complex language and lines that, once they went by, were *gone* rather than being hammered home by repetition, people quickly caught on and listened harder so as not to miss anything. If I'd had classes that attentive back when I was teaching, I'd never have been able to tear myself away from the classroom.

Far from rejecting the portrayal of a "real" vampire on stage (bald spot and all), these people were clearly grateful for an excuse to suspend their disbelief and wallow in fantasy, and they were willing to pay good money for the privilege. I think American theater tends to lurch from the pillar of "Pass-the-Salt" to the post of fat-headed but rousing imports like *Phantom* or *Les Miz*, meanwhile declining non-musical, homegrown stage playfulness and fantasy because it's not the grimy realism that they think audiences want. And then they wonder why audiences are shrinking.

Our audiences grew.

I don't think I've ever been so happy for such an extended period in my life.

For one thing, you never get tired of hearing your own words spoken by talented actors (except the words you wish you hadn't written, of course). Each time it really is different: new facets of your story are revealed to you as well as to the audience (and, often, to the actors themselves). Each performance is like the projection into reality of the shadow play that goes on in an individual reader's mind when she reads your printed story; and it's a different reader every night, or the same one on different nights who brings a different mindset to every performance.

At the same time, I could see that it was the lighting, the music, the actors' movement through space and interplay on the stage that enchanted the audience, much more than the words. A script is just a script, but a play is what is built from the script by the entire theater crew, and this construction is completed by each night's audience in its own way. The group nature of the achievement just about stopped my heart every time I witnessed it.

Unfortunately, the real world does not stand aside for mere joy.

In the real world, it was clear to me and some others I spoke to that Harvey Seifter was not particularly happy with the competition that *Dreams* was building, slowly but surely, for his own prized production running concurrently on the larger Magic stage. This was a mannered, hyper-intellectual exercise gilded by having been written by a European intellectual: Milan Kundera's *Jacques and his Master*. Harvey had brought it to the Magic himself, had directed it, and took great pride in it.

I saw it one night. The house was by no means sold out, and I thought the play stilted and boring as hell, but my judgment was not exactly impartial.

Harvey decided to extend the run of *Jacques* so that there was no place to put the next scheduled Springfest play—except in our space, the smaller stage. This meant that our run could not be extended beyond the scheduled ninth and final show—although *Vampire Dreams* was *making money* and was playing, that last weekend, to nearly full houses strictly on word of mouth.

As we closed, the actors said ruefully, "We're really ready to open now." I went to a quiet cast party at the home of the actress playing Lucille, and we toasted our aborted success and the joy we had gotten out of it nonetheless.

I went home—and began working on new script revisions, incorporating the lessons I had learned from the performances I'd seen. The final version was accepted for publication, some years later, by Broadway Play Productions, Inc. (copies can be ordered through their internet site).

Meantime, I burbled on to all who would listen about how wonderful it had been to work with the cast, director, and crew at the Magic. Another, more experienced, playwright responded enviously, "You had an unusually positive experience."

She was probably right. The show has had two productions since, one a pleasure, one an agonizing train wreck (but that's another story). A theatrical agent I spoke to once said, "Getting a play produced is a hundred times more difficult than getting a book published, you know."

I know; and getting it successfully, happily, rewardingly produced is even more so. I was insanely lucky.

But I sure did not get rich. Royalties from the Magic run were due me by contract within five days of closing. Months later I managed to obtain a statement—they owed me $384, if I read the columns aright—but times were tough, and what with one thing and another they never have paid me—a not-unheard-of outcome with regional theaters, I've heard since, and one of a number of reasons for the existence of the Dramatists Guild, to which I now belong.

I inquired about this several times, and then gave up. I remember, during those frantic revision sessions at one or another of the Magic's computers, being asked not to double-space script pages because the theater needed to save on paper costs. Theater makes no one rich, and besides, if I drop in at the Magic on a visit to San Francisco they say, "When will we see a new play from you?" and "Tell us when you'll be in town next time, and we'll get you get you comped to whatever shows you'd like to see."

I am, of course, writing another play right now. My father is in it.

I have a horrible feeling that I may be writing my version of "Pass the Salt."

THEY'RE RIGHT, ART IS LONG

In the winter of 1972–3 I set about completely rewriting my first book, a science fiction novel. Written in what one editor had called a "private code" (a common problem with first novels), it was unreadable by anyone but its author, as I'd discovered by sending it off to Joan Kahn at Harper.

Sadly, she found the book impenetrable. I objected that this was not a definitive reaction as she was editor of the Harper's mystery line (she was the only editor I knew, having met her when she came to New Mexico to visit Tony Hillerman, so on the off chance I'd sent my precious book to her). She explained, rather gently under the circumstances, that she had had a sci-fi enthusiast on her staff read it to check her assessment. He'd also found it unreadable.

So, was my authorial career over before it was begun? I faced this yawning chasm of possibility in tears of frustration and self-doubt.

In this book (titled at that time *The Boyhouse Book*) I had let my imagination run wild, depicting a future in which our technological present had been pretty well obliterated by a global disaster. This had left me free, given a pretty crude technological base for my poor handful of survivors, to invent an elaborate future religion—and invent, and invent, and invent. I'd ended up with a baroque ideology complete with mystifying terminology (well, isn't religion a mystery?), drug-induced hallucinations, and plenty underlying assumptions that I had never explained, since for one thing they made perfect sense in my mind, and for another explanations would have taken up the entire book (I did say "elaborate," didn't I?).

In desperation, I let my husband persuade me to give him the manuscript to read on the plane home from New York. He started writing queries in the margins as he read; within five pages I saw that my glorious religious construction simply suffocated my story from page one.

Now, my husband was not a science fiction reader any more than Joan Kahn was; but he has a keen eye for clarity. As a lawyer, he spends a lot of his working time rewriting other lawyers' documents so that they are actually readable and coherent. His judgment on my precious book was therefore to be taken seriously; I found it crushing, however constructively intended.

It was also a good kick in the head: I realized that for the entire first chapter of my novel (which was as much as I let him wade through), what the reader saw was not my characters, my colorful and ingenious setting, or the kernel of the exciting and shocking ideas that I was so pleased with, but a bunch of invented words and terms that acted as a repeated, sharp braking action on the narrative flow. I had meant these inventions to be intriguing indicators that we sure weren't in Kansas any more, Toto. The unfolding context was supposed to clarify meanings for the reader as she went along.

Instead, my neologism-ridden narrative was a ride in a stick shift car driven by someone who's never driven anything but an automatic transmission: one sharp stop after another, as the reader encountered yet another locution that made perfect sense to the characters (and to the author) but was gibberish to anyone else (i.e., "code").

I went home brooding on the injustice of the world, the sad lot of The Artist, and, underneath all that, the possible fatal inadequacy of my own creative impulse. When I was done brooding, I returned to work.

The first step was to reduce, if not dismantle, the drug-based religion in my book, that elaborate and scintillating structure that I had thought was the supporting framework of the whole story, the satirical heart of my wry take on "the future."

I think now that my great construction had in fact been just doodling in the margins, which I had mistaken for the text itself. Not that there's anything wrong with playfulness in art (Paul Klee, Alexander Calder, and even Picasso in some moods come to mind). But this was play of a particularly sterile kind, designed to endrun or even leapfrog the challenge of writing a strong story around passionate, vivid characters.

I was horrified when my beautiful design fell away. What remained was the classic and all-too-familiar tale of a young hero adventuring through a blighted futuristic landscape in search of his powerful but aloof father, along with a couple of male companions-in-adventure. It wasn't nearly as daring and original as I had thought.

Except maybe for the underlying satirical impulse.

The story itself had started out as one long scathing attack (as I saw it), set off by my loathing of the Nixon Administration. The trigger had been an article in an issue of *Harper's Magazine* about a nuclear strike drill in the capitol.

Apparently while the city poked along in total ignorance, the government bigwigs had been rounded up to be whisked off to a secret, underground city near D.C. where they could carry on governing, surviving in ingeniously designed safety while the rest of us fried. There was no time to run home and collect their wives (people in high office didn't have domestic partners or husbands at this time; they were—ostensibly—red-blooded heterosexual men, and they had wives); but the V.I.P.'s would of course be accompanied by their secretarial staff. I envisioned all those youthful aides and the like, certainly better breeding stock than the older women married to Senators, Cabinet members, and Generals.

No, the article didn't point this out; but it wasn't hard to read between the lines.

The point of the story was that the only political luminary to object to leaving his wife to burn was Chief Justice William O. Douglas. He said he wasn't going into the hidey-hole without her, and that was that.

Whatever else he had been in his life and was at that stage, to my mind this guy was a Hero of Humanity by virtue of daring to take such a position and hold it.

Inspired by a fury of contempt over the behavior of the others, not to mention the plan itself, I had set my story in the world that the other guys, the ones who did run away to hide from the consequences of their own failures and stupidities, would find after the radiation died down and they had to come out and deal with what was left. In other words, I brought their chickens home to roost, gleefully and with a bravura vengefulness.

The major method I'd chosen was to arrange matters in such a way that the descendants of those cowardly bunglers would have to live by the inverse of the Conservative values of the Nixon gang and their supporters.

First of all, religion ruled the remnant society I had depicted but it was a religion based on systematized hallucinations caused by strong mind-altering drugs that were absolutely central to the organization of my society's culture and economy. Secondly, that economy was entirely planned from the top, and rigidly controlled via both natural and artificial scarcities, as in some socialist and communist countries of the time.

Thirdly, rather than the "family values" touted by the Republicans, I had my people living with no family structures at all, the older men pitted against the younger ones and controlling their lives through manipulation of imaginary merit points on which food allocations were based. As for women, there were no wives or daughters or sisters or mothers, only female slaves. Children were raised in institutions very much like orphanages.

Since the men in "the Refuge" (my version of the D.C. hideout) had averted the insanity of unbearable guilt by blaming the descendant women living there with them for everything that had gone wrong, women were so debased that men couldn't possibly form their primary erotic attachments to them, any more than they would marry pigs or draft horses. So, most deliciously of all, the men were by cultural upbringing and expectation, and regardless of personal inclination, homosexual in their love relationships.

I rejoiced in imagining Spiro Agnew in this situation, or any of the rest of them: smug middle-American Babbitts, stodge-brains, and bumbling crooks, welcome to my torture chamber, designed especially with you in mind!

(This is the writer's revenge. In this culture artists have no real weight politically, but we can write our feelings about the powers-that-be and get them published and out into stores for people to read (so far anyway)).

This last inversion of "things the way they ought to be," however, also meant that my poor female characters were reduced to near invisibility; it's tough to write an adventure story about people who haven't got the autonomy to go on an adventure. Oh, there were women on the scene—right there in the first chapter, entering a night-time setting as a work-crew under the supervision of brutal overseers. These coarse, dull, female laborers, many of them barely verbal, were the underside of the men's macho survival culture. To underline this fact I had chosen one from among them—Alldera—who becomes attached to the party of major (i.e., male) characters as "The Girl."

You know The Girl. She used to decorate the covers of pulp

SF magazines, twined in the arms of an alien and screaming prettily while her male rescuer brandished a ray gun in the foreground. She was usually, in the story within, the brilliant scientist's daughter, or else the "Queen" of an anthill-like female-dominated society who must be taught the delights of kissing and of submission by an intrepid male visitor from space.

But you probably know her best from the movies: she's the lone resistance fighter picked up by the patrol of soldiers, the nun accompanying the men delivering guns to the bandits, the spoiled heiress in the lifeboat packed with sailors. She's the helpless, hysterical fool in high heels and lipstick who gets added to the expedition because she can't be left by herself, wandering around witlessly in danger; or because she has some leverage that allows her to force the men to "take her along". She's the one female who stands for (and, invariably, lies down as) the half of humanity that is otherwise absent from the foreground and sometimes from the rest of the scene altogether.

Wherever she occurs, her real function in the story is to be rescued, allowing the good guys to demonstrate their machismo; and to be fought over by the male cast so that The Hero gets to demonstrate his extra-*extra* machismo plus that little soft spot that is supposedly all it takes to make him truly human.

I remember thinking, *There has got to be a prominent woman character someplace in my book, or not just my readers but my friends are going to think I'm weird.* So I added Alldera in, during a visit the adventuring men make to the prison where girls are beaten into "fems" (the term for the female slaves in the men's country of the Holdfast).

A revision of my story was clearly required, making three major men and one grudgingly admitted woman as the foreground cast. That seemed reasonable. It was an adventure story, after all, and girls just slow down the action.

Except for The Girl, of course; but there she was, wasn't she?

Only it hadn't been working out right; in fact it was working out alarmingly wrongly, more so than ever now that I was trying to bring out the satirical impulse of the story by pushing the most deliberately outrageous elements even further.

I had good, sound, tried-and-true literary models for my trio of tough guys: the cynical old warrior (hard but with a heart of gold, and ultimately expendable); the bitter young man seeking a confrontation with his father; and the cheery lad who's a completely untrustworthy rogue. In fact, I had lifted the latter two from the pages of one of my favorite books as a young reader—Prince Michael, the Duke of Strelsau, and Count Rupert of Hentzau, the chief bad guys from Anthony Hope's action classic, *The Prisoner of Zenda*. I'd had these two on my mind for years, certain that I had a story of my own to tell about them but unable to find the right setting—until now.

The changes I rang on the relations among all three major male characters surprised and delighted me, particularly when my two leading men turned out to have a longstanding tragic passion for each other. The resultant high voltage interface brightened everything up amazingly (and taught me something about the dynamics of buddy movies along the way).

The Girl, though, stumped me.

I couldn't find a good physical model for her, not in the movies, not in books, not in the faces in the magazines in the dentist's waiting room. These images weren't even as varied as they are now. The women all had, more or less, the same face: blush-pink cheeks, dark lipstick, huge eyelashes, the nose "fixed" to a pert standard, the whole set in a big smile or a sultry stare—the female masks, comic, tragic, and utterly false and illusory.

My only option was to make Alldera's physicality up myself. In desperation, I adapted the physical frame and aspect of a friend from my school days, a sturdy girl who was not thought "pretty."

Only, what was she like inside? Panic!

The Girl, generally speaking, isn't "like" anything: she's a pawn in a plot about the doings of the important people, the men. Well, that wouldn't work here: how could my men fight over her when they were fixated on each other? Besides, she's rather plain and there are plenty of much prettier sex toys among her fellow fems. Why would they rescue her from danger, since she's merely a plain-looking female servant? As a member of a despised class of not-really-persons, she couldn't even be the haughty minx called to heel by hard times and male superiority.

Exasperated, I called on my own feelings: the rebellious, angry ones that had drawn perfect strangers in the street to stop me when I was a kid and ask me why I was walking around scowling instead of smiling the way "a pretty little girl" should.

This helped.

Unmoderated by any of my own necessary adaptations to my actual society, Alldera began to demonstrate an intriguing toughness. I discovered that she had a secret quest of her own that motivated her joining the men's party as, basically, their packmule.

Thus she became much more important to the plot, i.e. the men's story.

Revisions went well; now I had all my bases covered, even The Girl base.

Meanwhile, something else was going on.

During that winter of 1972-73 I read some germinal feminist books, like Shulamith Firestone's *The Dialectics of Sex* (Bantam, 1971) and *Sisterhood Is Powerful*, edited by Robin Morgan (Vintage, 1970). Bells went off all over the place as I began to "get it." I started seeing that I was a feminist.

As such, I participated regularly in discussion group meetings with other women ("consciousness raising sessions") in which we talked with increasing honesty about our experiences with gender issues, each of us slowly and with dawning joy realizing that she was not just imagining things—nasty things, sad things, about being a mere woman in a masculinist society.

Repeatedly I recognized that other women knew what I knew and felt what I felt, so it wasn't just me being over-sensitive, or not having "a sense of humor."

Sexism was really out there. Suppression, repression, exploitation, contempt and the cruelty exercised by men against women were really out there, not figments of my lurid imagination. So were various twisted forms of female resistance and subversion, as well as the ploy of identifying with the overseer so as to avoid the punishment of the slaves.

We began to point these things out to each other, call them by their names, and talk about how to try to change them.

And then one night, as I was eagerly describing my book to the group and proudly pointing out its feminist elements, I realized that I couldn't tell them about my main characters: of the whole damned bunch of them (and with the supporting cast, there were a dozen or more), only one was female; and while each of the three male adventurers who held center stage throughout told a whole section of the tale from his point of view, I never took the reader inside Alldera's head.

Talk about mortification! Talk about the road to Damascus! I was stunned.

Satirical cleverness and all, I had fallen head first into The Girl trap of stereotypical tokenism.

So I gulped, shut my big mouth, and went home to read my manuscript again. Now I saw that in fact the fourth section of the book, leading up to the climax and resolution of the men's quest, belonged to Alldera. Through her section, I could tell the story of the Holdfast's women—something that no real feminist author would ever skate over as carelessly as I had.

This insight did not make me happy. I was sure that the actual writing of Alldera's section would be an awful grind, a chore to be finished as quickly as possible so that I could get back to the real meat of the book: the men's story.

Imagine my surprise when the writing of her section took off like a rocket, revelation after revelation yanking me breathlessly along while the whole book shifted balance, meaning, and shape as a result. Everything changed, violently, shockingly, and without letup 'til the end.

Alldera's viewpoint forced me to see the humanity and individuality of other fems, the secrets at the heart of femmish social structure, and the blind, arrogant ignorance of even the cleverest of my men. Through Alldera the real story, the story I had buried—with its sharp edges and its harsh contrasts and its acrid tastes and smells and pains—came surging to light. Her insights, her emotions, her desires drew the whole book taut around what had been its secret core all along, and it was not a gleeful slap at the Nixon gang at all—that was just an impulse, an idea to get me moving (a lot of the work of writing fiction is first overcoming fear and inertia).

The core was the fact that while everything else in my future world had changed into its opposite, two elements of current social reality had persisted, exaggerated to gigantic, tyrannical proportions that threatened the extinction of my remnant human race. Both were about gender.

One was the domination of an entire society, including the lives of young men and boys, by selfish, powerful, calculating old men: patriarchy, plain, raw, and narrow. The other was the subjugation of women to a level lower even than that of the youngest boys, to the level of the vanished animals whose places were now filled by the deliberately debased "fems."

The scales fell from my eyes: *here* was my story—not in what I had so blithely changed at all, but in the fierce persistence of what had remained the same.

Seeing through Alldera's eyes, I wrote the best of the stories that had lain dormant inside my clumsy, unfocused, superficial book. I wrote about the crude destructiveness of the sexism that I knew—the sexism that had led those "civil defense" planners in DC to hide a government of old men underground with a lot of young subordinates—but that sexism dragged out of the shadows, made harshly explicit, and driven as far as I could think to drive it.

Once you see you can't unsee again. Once I found the true core of the story, the work took off with a blast of sustained energy that was impossible to resist or restrain.

Mind you, *Walk* as published is a dark, harsh tale, much more so than any of its previous incarnations. Although the book got a lot of attention among readers at the time, many women have since told me that they couldn't get through it because it was too cruel. Some readers have asked how on earth I could write that book without going into a terminal depression myself. They look doubtful when I tell them that writing it, at last in its true form, was one long continuous high that had me floating above my real life for months.

I try to explain by pointing out that the story is as much about stubborn, brave, creative people—men and women—finding their way to others whom they can truly love *despite* the horrible, soul-twisting oppression of their culture, as it is about that tortuous and murderous culture itself.

I certainly felt that way, in the writing. I'm not sure that I was skillful enough at the time to make it clear enough, emphatic enough, for my more timid, angry, or sensitive readers to feel it too.

Inevitably and effortlessly, the last few pages of *Walk to the End of the World* grew to belong not to Eykar Bek, the rebel prince in search of his father, nor to Servan D Layo, the beautiful rogue, but to Alldera the femmish slave—The Girl, but what a girl! Moreover, the story was not over, now that it had become her story. Whatever was to happen next—and it was clear to me that lots more was pressing to happen—would be up to her.

This time, the spark came directly from the feminist ferment in the culture around me which, in the late seventies, mounted many challenges to accepted wisdom of all kinds from feminist writers and scholars. The rebellion was powered by a refusal to take cultural assumptions at face value any more. Female artists, composers, writers, inventors, athletes, soldiers, and high achievers of all kinds whose deeds, and in many cases whose identities, had been dropped out of history (and out of curricula to make room for additional male names) were rediscovered, resurrected and celebrated by women scholars.

As part of this broad effort came a good deal of imaginative recreation of history (imaginative, in the absence of lost data), going right back to humanity's ancient past.

Along with such ideas as the conquest of female-centered, agrarian religions by martial, patriarchal ones and the possible origin of human beings as a shoreline-dwelling, semi-aquatic species, a number of women scholars proposed that the Amazons of Greek myth and legend had in fact been a real, wholly female, warrior culture in pre-Roman Europe. Personally, I thought it was wishful thinking, and nothing that has been brought to light since has changed my opinion. Besides, if there really was an ancient Amazon culture, all it provides is yet another story of a significant enterprise of women reduced to a sidebar alongside the adventures of the great male heroes of myth. Who needs another story of betrayal, failure, and obliteration?

But. What about the idea of an Amazon society *in the future?* Why not, I thought, out there on the cutting edge of time where women warriors could show their stuff unconstrained by "real" history?

Such a society would be a perfect foil for the ultra-masculinist culture of the Holdfast. I even had the perfect location hinted at in my first book: across the western mountains, in the very direction Alldera was last seen taking! Now, here was a project in which to try out my own feminist ideas and ideals, to think it all out on the page with a galloping great thought experiment.

This time, at least, I had a pretty clear idea of what the book would be about before I began it: the background would be a nomadic plains culture of women only, reproducing in some way that didn't require men. The foreground would be the struggle of Alldera and her slave kind to learn from—and recoil against—warrior women who had always been free, finding what freedom could be for such crippled fugitives.

For *Walk* I had done research into the making of primitive plastics and explosives, the farming of seaweed, and other crude technologies designed for my barbarized future. For *Motherlines* I must have read every book in the University library on nomadic cultures, from Blackfoot Indians to Mongol horse people to Laplanders with their reindeer to the shepherds of Europe and the cattle-herders of Africa. I took notes on increasingly grubby index cards: how do nomadic herders dress, what kinds of shelters do they use, how do their social units arise and relate to each other, how do they trade and marry and make war, what do they believe in, what are their songs and their languages like? How do the herd animals' needs and cycles determine the calendars of the people's lives? How does it all connect with the ecology and climate of grassland plains?

At last, using this welter of detail, I set about constructing my own plains tribes.

I found a model of cloning to justify this monogendered branch of the future. Then I made Alldera pregnant (by one of the men she'd traveled with in the previous book) so that once delivered, she would have an indissoluble bond—a kinship bond through a child born among Amazons—to link her to the Riding Women; I saw great possibilities of conflict there.

Then there were other escaped fems and the mini-society they had established for themselves on the free side of the mountains.

I was ready to go.

Well, not really; I hit a huge bump in the road with the first few scenes I wrote.

The men I brought across the mountains—for conflict, for adventure!—kept turning to cardboard. Their scenes just dropped dead on the page. Worse still, everything they touched there curled up and died as well.

The problem was, they did not belong; so attention spent on them seemed wasted and beside the point, a delay and a distraction.

Pretty soon I had to face it: I couldn't jam the free women's society in all its unfolding glory, and the escaped slave fems, *and* my raging Holdfast men into the same book. It would have made too many layers of complexity to handle as a writer, let alone as a reader. The intrusion of men into the Riding Women's lands would change the Grassland tribal society drastically, even while I was trying to explore what it was in and of itself. A culture at war is not the same culture that it was before the war started.

No wonder the male characters were going dead on me: the characters were seizing up under all that friction.

But that meant—that meant I would have to write a book *entirely about women!*

Horror. Or, more accurately, terror.

As a girl and a reader, I had always avoided books "for girls," let alone books only *about* females, and I was sure that everybody else did the same. The only such book I had made it through was Pearl Buck's *Pavilion of Women*, which was all about the wives of a particular Chinese man—who was in the book, however peripherally. It had been pretty good, come to think of it, but I wasn't interested in writing a pretty good book for a handful of doughty readers.

There was also the question (in 1975 or so) of who would publish a science fiction novel about women and only women. SF had long been considered, both within and outside the field, as juvenile literature for immature males, and editors tended to choose books (and, sometimes, authors) with this market in mind. The feminist publishing houses that had sprung up in the sixties didn't handle SF for the most part, or had little experience in marketing it.

Besides, just in practical terms, how the hell could I write a book full of women—free warriors, escaped slaves, two whole societies of women!—and keep everybody straight in my own mind, let alone the reader's, just as physical individuals? The blonde. The brunette. The one from the romance novels: raven black hair (or honey blonde), sapphire blue eyes, a tip-tilted nose, and a wide, generous mouth. Or maybe a pink rosebud mouth (yuck). Oh, and the fiery redhead with the blazing green eyes.

Not to mention the problem of psychological differentiation: I wasn't dealing with Alldera and a few female spearcarriers here, I was contemplating entire societies of—women!

As a culture we had gotten beyond the narrow triumvirate of virgin, mother, and whore (well, some of us had). There were quite subtly shaded female characters to be found in western fiction, lots of them—Lizzie Bennett, Dorothea Brooke, Lily Briscoe, Edith Wharton's women and the like—but they had all been shaped by fairly sophisticated male-dominated societies. My express purpose was to explore what women might be like *without* that domination, living the robust lives of horse-herding nomads. Characters like the better-defined and developed women of Western literature were pretty well useless to me.

I had already decided that the Riding Women were clones of a group of original female survivors of the same cataclysm that had created the Holdfast; thus, no men were required, not even captive ones. I was struggling to come up with a true range of physical types for my tribal clones when, one summer day on the 96th Street crosstown bus, a young woman sat facing me just back of the driver's seat, and something in her posture—some weary, composed grace—caught my eye.

She had straw-blond hair gathered at the nape of her neck, a slim, tanned body, and the oval face of a Modigliani portrait. She wore a simple moss green summer frock; and in her I suddenly saw one of my Riding Women in potentiality.

I began looking about me at real women, strangers—but they had real faces, real bodies, with real, individual voices and gestures and strides. The woman on the bus eventually became Sheel Torrinor, Alldera's coldest enemy among the free women of the plains. Other real women became the rest of Alldera's ad hoc Grassland family. Once I had their images in my mind's eye, the Riding Women's characters formed up clearly through their actions on the page, each one trailed by her "Motherline" of cloned relatives.

My world of women flowered. They weren't all beautiful, or brilliant, or brave, but they were all free. Their world grew varied, full, and fiercely competitive as well as cooperative, political as well as emotional. The tribes of the Motherlines showed themselves to be riven with dangerous blood-feuds (among many other areas of conflict), as the women raided each other's camps for horses, like the warriors of the North American plains tribes. My tribeswomen met seasonally for racing and gambling and wrestling, the way the horse people of the steppes still do.

They became so fascinating that I had to pull back a bit. I'd been writing my version of the artist George Catlin's book about traveling with plains Indians for months and years, or T.E. Lawrence's *Seven Pillars of Wisdom*, about living with wandering Bedouins in Arabia. It was hard to rein in that exploratory impulse. With no men around to tell the women what they could or couldn't do or be, the women of the Motherlines simply expanded their natures and capacities to fill all the niches of behavior on the human spectrum. I wanted to keep traveling with them, recording this extraordinary blossoming of humanity.

But the freedom of the Riding Women was only part of Alldera's story. The story of any kind of freedom also includes the story of the unfreedom against which it defines itself.

In this case, that meant the small group of runaway fems living on the edge of the Riding Women's country, among whom Alldera not only spends time but achieves a hard-won but unlikely position of leadership. I also needed these people, the Free Fems of the Tea Camp, to help demonstrate to readers new to the story (or to remind those who had read *Walk* years before) just what sort of crushing bondage Alldera had escaped from back home.

This was where I encountered the curse of series-books (two does make a series, and I already saw that there was going to be a third—thesis, antithesis, synthesis). I mean the summary of the earlier story, so that the characters continuing into the second book have a known past grounding their words and actions and attitudes. It was difficult. Research was important again, too. I did a good deal of reading about historic slave revolts and the lives of escaped or freed slaves.

I completed this part of Alldera's story in 1976.

My editor, Judy Lynn del Rey at Ballantine, *hated* it. She wrote me a scathing letter of rejection (I think her husband, Lester, wrote the letter and Judy Lynn signed it, since the sentiments expressed were famously Lester's): "This book is unpublishable!" she wrote. She said that I would have to tear it all down, introduce men in order to generate a "real" plot (which meant conflict), and get rid of "the horse-fucking," for God's sake, that had no place in stories meant for adolescent boys!

Oh, yes; the cloning part. The Riding Women mated with their horses, that is, used ritualized and controlled sexual contact with specially prepared colts whose sperm could spark the woman's ovum into reproduction.

A pretty far-fetched idea, certainly, but not more so than some of the projections of genetics that I'd been reading about; and SF with a social rather than scientific focus is allowed to be a whole lot more far-fetched than that. Just not *this* far-fetched, according to Judy Lynn and Lester, who clearly wanted not another book but *Walk* all over again.

They didn't mind that most of the women were, of necessity if not out of personal orientation, lesbian, any more than they had minded my homosexual men in *Walk*. A fair amount of sexually explicit and inventive SF was published by this time, and anyway, male readers were thought to enjoy the idea of women having sex with each other. But those horses!

I have to admit, I knew when I did it that this was more than daring. It was shocking. That's not why I'd done it, although I certainly got a little frisson of delicious satisfaction from the shock factor. But basically I had deliberately chosen this idea as a way of capturing from men, for a moment, the titillating fantasy of women being screwed by beasts, to try to find out what else there was in it besides masculine prurience and misogyny.

I'd read about the woman-and-pony shows men went to see in Tijuana, and the historians' libel of Catherine the Great of Russia involving the same lip-smacking condemnation (that'll teach a woman to be political, successful, and bold! Take *that!*).

And I'd been a horse-mad teenager myself. I knew there really was something special between women and horses, and it wasn't just (if at all) the Freudian notion of poor, dickless females trying to grab a penis for themselves wherever they could, either.

My Amazons of the future, forced by my fiction's strictures to use this method of reproduction, found for me the meaning it might have for a very different culture: a sacred ritual of bonding, women to the earth via one of the earth's most beautiful and vital creatures, and women to each other through the shared danger of what could, under adverse conditions, be a deadly dangerous act. The mating became the central spiritual act of the Riding Women's culture. I couldn't "take it out," as Judy Lynn demanded. And I wasn't about to give up all that invigorating travel with the Riding Women to add, metaphorically speaking, car chases to entertain the boys.

So I met my editor at a convention and told her that I wouldn't change the book. She told me she wouldn't publish it.

Neither, for an entire year, would anyone else. One editor at a prominent publishing house told me she loved the book but couldn't publish it because she believed her authors' readership was still mainly boys, and boys would not read a book that was all about women. "If only this book were written about all *men*," she said, "I'd publish it in a minute!"

A year later my agent found an editor who agreed to take a chance on the book, for a properly modest advance. David Hartwell, then at Berkley Putnam, published *Motherlines* in hardcover in 1978.

Walk HAD BROUGHT ME notoriety, within the small compass of SF/F, along with speaking gigs at colleges and on panels at conventions, as part of the upsurge of feminist writers flooding into the field and bringing lots of female readers with them (or maybe just bringing lots of closet fans of the female persuasion out into the open). Through that first book I had found an agent, and connected with the growing group of feminist writers and fans. I had fallen into an instant creative context, which was amazing.

It had also brought me criticism, mostly from male readers and critics, who thought I was "male-bashing"; and from gay men who missed the point. The Holdfast is specifically constructed as a perverted homosexual society *created by straight men*, not by gay men. I've heard myself described as a gay-hater because the

Holdfast society is so ghastly, just as I intended it to be—but because of deeply patriarchal distortions, not flaws inherent in homosexuality itself.

And then there was the shock of being told, when speaking of the condition of the enslaved fems as a fantasy of sexism pushed to its furthest extreme, that in fact it was merely reality for many modern women, particularly (although by no means exclusively) those who are not white or middle class.

I learned; I flourished. I got to talk to people I admired, like Ursula K. LeGuin and Joanna Russ.

Motherlines brought other lessons, about the misconceptions that grow from the SF reader's encounter with the truly unexpected and the "outrageous." I was excoriated for writing a separatist Utopia, since that "meant" that I must favor women deserting men and forming their own societies. This, despite the fact that to me, the Grasslands society is much too rough and brutal (not to mention short on the arts) to be a Utopia; nor was it intended to be one. Then there was the lack of spaceships, battles, and wizards—and there were those *horses*.

My stepdaughter said, "Couldn't they have used a *stick*, or something?"

Some women strongly objected to my tossing the Riding Women's kids out on their own in the Childpack to sink or swim as a harsh means of weeding out non-viable mutations from the clone-lines. No mother could do that, they said. I've never been a biological mother so I can't say for sure, but I considered this a legitimate part of the thought experiment (I also put that whole mother/child thing on the back burner to return to later).

Motherlines didn't sell as well as *Walk* had (but *Walk*, as a finalist for the John W. Campbell Award for best first SF novel in paperback, had gained more immediate prominence). I minded, but not a whole lot; I was too busy girding up my loins for the third and final book, the synthesis of the masculinist and feminist societies I had created.

I realized that I was facing the other big problem of the book series: managing all those characters from the first two books, plus some new ones in book three, as well as two entire societies (four, of you count the Free Fems in the Grasslands and the secret world of the Holdfast fems as cultures in themselves). How in the world was I going to keep all that straight?

I decided to make an outline, for the first time in my writing life.

Thus I discovered exactly what kind of a fiction writer I am.

One approach to writing a large, complex book is that of the engineer: the author who draws a blueprint and does all the research, and then writes the various structural elements in some comfortable order to fill in the outline she has created, leading neatly to the predestined conclusion. It's something like raising a bridge, or a skyscraper, from detailed plans. This is the preferred method for many authors of fat thrillers and huge fantasy novels; I had seen it embodied when I visited Marge Piercy, poet and novelist, who was writing about the social and political protest scene of the sixties. Her workroom was crisscrossed by taut strings on which moveable index cards were suspended, full of notes and easily moved about, creating a 3-D model of the story she was working on, or maybe a string-and-paper computer.

As for me, I bought a big ring binder with red plastic covers, divided its pages into sections ("people," "settings," "big scenes," "timelines" etc.), and worked up an outline for the third volume of the series. I even wrote some opening scenes, all set after a victorious invasion of the Holdfast by the Free Fems and their Grassland allies.

Once again, everything fell dead on the page, lusterless and still.

My problem was that I was bored. I knew how the story came out, so what was the point of endlessly manipulating things to bring them to that outcome? I just couldn't make myself do it.

Because, it turns out, I was the *other* kind of writer: the organic gardener kind, who finds a seed, plants it, waters and tends and grows it, and finally prunes the mature plant into the most pleasing and coherent form possible for it. These are the folks who invent as they go along, beginning with some questions about an idea and letting the characters work their way in their own styles to an ending that satisfies.

After months of beating my head against the wall of my own lack of interest, I gave up, put away my outline, and did my level best to forget it.

And I did, more or less, as other writing projects found their way into my thoughts and diverted all that stalled creative energy into unexpected channels: a set of stories about a vampire that knit together into a novel; a mainstream novel about a middle-aged woman artist; four Young Adult fantasy novels set in New York City; another vampire novel, on the romance model; a number of shorter stories; and a play that's been staged professionally (though not as often as I'd like).

Like most authors of imaginative literature, I think, I remained an avid reader both within my field and outside it, spurred to keep current by the demands of teaching, by the writing of reviews and essays for various projects, and by the need not to make an ignorant fool of myself at the half a dozen or so conventions that I attend every year. So other living writers' ideas continued to percolate in my head, setting off ideas that got turned into stories, which is how a body of literature is built up: by a process of call and response, a continual conversation among writers and readers, critics and academics, booksellers and publishers.

But because of the particular political climate that I started out in, more of my work has always connected with other feminist work than non-feminist work; more extended conversations and friendships and working relationships have been with feminists (of both sexes) than not; and all of my work has been, inevitably, touched and informed to some extent by a feminist awareness.

So my vampire, for example, in *The Vampire Tapestry*, has been academically deconstructed as female because he struggles to survive under social and psychological strictures that a woman can recognize and empathize with (I hadn't thought it through this far, myself; I only knew that somehow when the story ended, it was about a vampire brought to bay not by a posse of stalwarts led by a patriarch but by a mixed crew of women, kids, and very unmacho guys—a kind of anti-Dracula, in fact).

The heroine of my YA series, Valentine, gets her magic from her grandmother and uses it, among other things, to rescue her mom from the evil courtship of a sorcerer disguised as Val's school counselor. The werewolf in "Boobs" is an adolescent girl who finds strength, joy, and vengeance in her powerful wolf form (and damned well gets away with it, too). Christine, the soprano stolen by the Phantom of the Opera, has all the clever toughness and the steady mind that any artist needs to develop if she is to survive in her chosen field.

Not that I've deliberately clung to obvious feminist themes or "messages"; don't get me wrong. I'm a great believer in Western Union and, now, the fax machine for messages, and I insist on my freedom to write about anything I please, in any way I please, and with any slant that I please, just like any other writer. But it's true that there is something in my internal vision that wasn't there back when I blithely began writing a story entirely about male protagonists going about their masculine business. That "something" slightly (or massively, in some cases) alters the scope of what I *choose* to write, and what knowledgeable readers probably expect to find in my work.

Part of my "voice" as a writer is that I am always aware, at some level, that half of the world is female (there are lots of authors who are hardly ever aware of this; think about it). So my fictional worlds tend to actively incorporate that truth, or else some worked-out and expressed reasons why it is *not* true on spaceship X or among the giant lemurs of planet Plik.

This also meant that I never felt that by putting volume three on hold I was somehow failing my material and my readers. I was still a woman writing from a feminist awareness and leading a lively collegial life with a growing phalanx of progressive-minded writers in my field. Our conversations, at conventions, via the letter circulating groups called Appas, and most recently on email lists set up as spaces for this kind of talk, kept me involved in the continual unfolding of the active and opinionated female presence in SF/F and horror while I wrote other stories, other books, a stage play, the libretto for a musical—I guess what academics and critics could call an "oeuvre," a body of work.

Most of that work is still in print, although sometimes not easy to find; some of it is in this book, easily accessible again.

I was busy and happy, and when fans and colleagues asked me where the promised third volume was, I used to reply that I'd done my part of the work and now maybe it was somebody else's job to write the next part of that story. Or I'd say that I couldn't write volume three because I could no more *solve* the problems of sexism in a book than we were solving them in our society, since I was only a member of our society and not a visionary genius.

This left me, as you may notice, an out, in case the third book never did materialize.

It very nearly didn't.

By the time I did feel ready to tackle volume three again, things had changed mightily. On the plus side, I'd pretty much forgotten that damned outline. On the other hand, women entering SF now as authors were standing up at conventions and beginning their remarks with, "I'm not a *feminist*" as you might say, "I'm not a *cannibal*"; and asserting that this meant they could write about whatever they chose, not being bound to write about women, or about men and women in any particular way, by boring old feminist convictions.

What they really meant, I think, was that they didn't want the label "feminist" to pigeonhole their work and limit its appeal to editors and buyers. And they meant, I believe, that they were afraid of charges of not being feminist enough, or correctly feminist, from women more radical (or less radical) than themselves. So some took advantage of these public occasions to simply opt out of the whole issue—as if that were possible.

These were the Reagan years. The backlash was here. It's been here ever since.

It disheartened me, to tell the truth. I wondered again if any publisher would want to publish a book about extreme sexism in a barbaric future in these reactionary days; and if they did, would anyone read it? Would anyone be able to find it? A number of feminist publishers were in trouble generally, or had no interest in SF. The shrinking number of feminist bookstores had core readerships of lesbians, and most lesbians at that time didn't read SF. SF meant spaceships and monsters to them (as to most general readers) and they had too many real problems to deal with, without the benefit of ray guns.

Then I began to realize that I was also having trouble with this third book in the series *because I was trying to cheat.* I wanted to write the resolution without going through the fire of outright gender war.

In fact, the completion of the story needed not one book but two: a war novel, and a resolution after the war.

I did not even want to write a war novel, most particularly this war novel. SF is always about the present, not "the future" (which is unknowable). My fictional war would have to be rooted in real anger over conditions in the real world—the low-level, simmering anger that all exploited people carry around with them but continually suppress and minimize in order to be able to live sane lives in an insane world. Frankly, I wasn't sure I could live with that anger boiling around on the surface of my awareness for however long it took to write that book. Worse, I couldn't imagine readers willing to plunge with me into the cauldron of rage and retribution that the resulting story must surely be.

What kicked me out of my cowardly paralysis was a vision from left field, not of warfare but of welcome. I daydreamed about a skinny madman, victim of the ongoing dissolution of the Holdfast under the weight of its own inner conflicts, meeting the small army of invading Free Fems with a paean of welcome while they stared at him in wary disgust and disbelief ...

And I was off. I had already done a lot of preparatory reading (slave revolts and revolutions, tribal warfare, guerrilla campaigns, horse-archer cavalry, Rommel in the desert, strategy and tactics in a dozen small wars through history and around the world). Now I just flew along, the gateway to the actual work opened for me by poor crazy Setteo—seer, psychotic, and nobody's idea of a warrior.

The challenges of this book were largely the ones I had expected. Again, of course, I needed to somehow lay out a comprehensible summary of the previous two books' worth of events and relationships. A very problematic character, a pet-fem named Daya, volunteered for the job; she was a gifted storyteller herself (it was one of her entertainment skills as a pet, a sort of geisha). For her own sly purposes Daya began the process of mythologizing my heroine's adventures, which gave me the keystone of Alldera's own conflict—her struggle against being made larger than life in the eyes of others, elevated above what she felt herself capable of doing well.

Then there was the difficulty in handling the extremes of wartime atrocity to which the Free Fems' anger drove them. I tried to be both minimal and selective with these incidents ("show, don't tell" is an indispensable rule, after all). At the same time, I had to make sure that readers—especially those coming into the series at this point for the first time—understood the source: the brutality to which the fems had been subjected in the Holdfast. Nor could I soft-pedal the savageries that the men inflicted in return when they could, not if the war was to be realistic and convincing (nothing sets men off like effectively rebellious women, especially in a completely masculinist culture). Presenting the necessary violence of a particularly bitter little war was an ongoing balancing act.

The real reward of the book, though, the real meat of the story was finding out what the fems (and a handful of Riding Women who joined them) actually would *do* with the power they won over the former masters. This took me to places I had not foreseen, as did the emergence of a beast cult and several factions among the defeated men. Nothing worked out to be simple, nothing was as obvious as the premise of the book might suggest. I loved it.

The Furies (Tor, 1992) was, not unexpectedly, a modest seller. But I hadn't expected it to sell so badly for my English (feminist) publisher that they had to refuse the final book. In fact there were no foreign sales, no awards, no great notice taken outside of that ghetto-within-a-ghetto, feminist SF. Most writers are pretty vulnerable to such setbacks, particularly when the work has been unusually arduous and problematic.

So, what with one thing and another, it took a long time for me to find the spark to ignite the final book.

In fact, inspiration came not from Alldera herself nor from her masters or antagonists, but from her daughter Sorrel, born and raised free in the Grasslands. *She* brought the fresh eye that the saga needed. Arriving in the new, fem-ruled Holdfast as a young woman with a chip on her shoulder (like any child of a great heroine, particularly a heroine who had left her child behind), she offered a lively, appealing way into the new culture as it grappled with basic problems, such as how to raise the children born since the conquest, in particular the boys.

I began to read about experimental communities and theories of psychology and social justice.

This book, once begun, was a joy to write and it went quickly.

It closed a circle (both in my own life as writer and in the lives of the characters themselves) that had been opened a quarter century before with *Walk*, and closed it with an ironic symmetry that pleased me very much. As Eykar Bek had once set out to confront his father in *Walk to the End of the World*, here was Sorrel Holdfaster setting out to confront her neglectful mother, Alldera, in the New Holdfast. Where men had been the masters at the outset now women were, but women who struggled mightily to create a better life than a mere reversal of oppression could provide.

Even Eykar's old lover and nemesis, Servan d Layo, cropped up as a threat—and a promise—in the final book. Helpful rogue that he was, he brought with him a whole new group of people, survivors from a hitherto unknown settlement that starting writing about itself when I was a little way along. This provided the opportunity to right the huge wrong that began *Walk*—the apparent extinction not only of animals but of people of color. Although the Riding Women were of all skin shades, the fems and the men were, through the insane racism of the original founders, white.

Now hitherto unknown black people came down from the north, bringing some of their goats with them; goats are tough, like people. They helped me put back together the beginnings of a world worth living in again, at long last.

By the end, the story had become about how history is made and how heroes are transmuted into gods, willy-nilly; as Alldera and Eykar Bek both ironically acknowledge in the final chapter.

With the publication of *The Conqueror's Child* in 1999, the epic at last came to an end. That this book won a Tiptree Award is an achievement which I cherish (particularly since *Child* never even showed up in the Nebula or Hugo nominations so far as I know). A year later all four books were in print as trade paper editions from Tor, and they are in print still.

So what have we here, when all's done (if not yet said)?

A futuristic, feminist epic busting with ideas I'm proud of and people I love, but too damned big to find its way readily into the classroom? Yep. Alas, it's not one neat, classically fine book, like *The Left Hand of Darkness*, say, or a tidy collection of sparkling short stories that can be assigned for a month-long unit of the fall term.

It's not even a traditional SF/F trilogy, for Pete's sake. It's four wildly ambitious, gritty, passionate novels on a subject that the majority of readers still wishes would just go away. Certainly these are books that I recommend with discretion, taking into account what I know of the reader I'm dealing with. There are still lots of people—and not only adolescent boys—who aren't anywhere near ready to read books with "bestiality" in them, or a fierce gender war, or challenges to long held values and traditions.

All of which left me with the question: what to write next?

Which I suppose means that the Holdfast books are not a "life work," only substantial work done in the course of a writing life (I did wonder about this, believe me). Where do you go from a quarter-century saga of love and war, a cast of thousands (well, maybe a hundred if you count only the characters with speaking parts), and an insistence on engaging all our gender problems head-on and to the death?

I turned, with a big sigh of relief as well as some small regret, to something completely different: a venture into non-fiction.

This was a memoir about my estranged dad, who came to spend his final years living next door to my husband and me here in New Mexico. *My Father's Ghost* was a breeze to write (I had lots of notes and journal entries to work with, to prod my memory), a deeply restful departure from everything I'd ever done, and funny besides. It wasn't my first nonfiction—*Strange Seas* was that, an electronic book chronicling a search into metaphysical matters—and I doubt it will be my last. After making up whole futures, societies, ideologies, and individual lifetimes by the score, writing about stuff that already *is* (and only needs to be articulated) is a guaranteed piece of cake.

Now this collection offers the chance to pull together some of my shorter work, the happy diversions and unexpected forays into fresh territory that helped sustain me during the rougher parts of what feels to me like a fairly strenuous authorial journey. Here's a good place to pause and catch my breath while I figure out my next move.

Part of my problem as a writer in a time that rewards endless series and cookie-cutter fiction (what Ursula LeGuin has called, wonderfully, "extruded book product") is that I'm easily bored. I like change, I hate to repeat myself, and I'm still too impatient and too ambitious to churn out a standard one-per-year item just like my last one, as my first editor wanted me to do way back at the beginning of all this.

You know what? I think I'll reread the Holdfast Chronicles through again, now, before a new writing project takes hold.

I want to look again now at what I did then. I want to see what I would do differently today, and maybe think of some new and intriguing way to do it or something related to it or something completely opposite, or—

Watch this space.